Vincent depended on his boyfriend, James, to stand up for him—until a violent hate crime results in James's murder.

Weeks after his funeral, James reappears, perfectly healthy but changed in ways that neither of them can quite understand. Now, Vincent must uncover what truly happened on the night they were attacked.

In the face of an apathetic police force and a growing number of missing gay men, Vincent and James work to identify the criminals who attacked them.

With James scarred from what happened to him in the weeks between his death and rediscovery, Vincent must learn to stand up for himself and face his real monsters or lose James—and himself.

BLOOD & DIRT

COREY NILES

A NineStar Press Publication

www.ninestarpress.com

Blood & Dirt

First Edition, August 2022

ISBN: 978-1-64890-517-9

Also available in eBook, ISBN: 978-1-64890-516-2

CONTENT WARNING:
This book contains sexual content, which may only be suitable for mature readers. Depictions of homophobia, death of a prominent character, deceased family member, guns, murder, and antisemitism.

For my mother, Amber, my first editor and biggest supporter

CHAPTER ONE

PANTHER HOLLOW

DEAD MAN WALKING. Vincent waited for the elevator in Posvar Hall. Four years was coming down to a single meeting. If the trajectory of his day so far had been any indication of how it would go, he was fucked.

The elevator door opened with a *ding*. Empty. His chest pounded and hands shook, but he forced himself to step inside and press the button for the third floor. The stainless-steel door closed him in, and he stared at his blurred reflection in the metal. Another *ding* rang out as he was dragged past the second floor and again when the door opened on the third. They sounded like the beating drums of a funeral march, and he did his best to ignore them.

Just outside the elevator, a woman spoke with an older man about some foreign conflict. They were both dressed in business casual attire. History professors, which didn't come as much of a surprise in the history department.

"Excuse us," the woman said, and only then did Vincent realize he was standing in the elevator doorway.

"Sorry." He slipped past them, his cheeks blazing. The hallway was empty and silent beyond a little chatter leaking from the office doors that lined the walls. Professor Cowart's office was down the hall on the right. Vincent had figured that out the last time he'd attempted to visit him, but he wasn't going to turn back again. He was going to face him and explain the situation.

Each step made his heart beat faster and hands shake with more fervor. Sweat crawled down his back, and he knew it had little to do with the winter coat he wore or the backpack slung over his shoulders. So much was riding on this meeting. If today was going so badly, then maybe that was a warning sign from some higher power to turn around and come back another day.

Shit.

He stopped, and before he chickened out, he called James. "I don't think I can do this."

"What's going on? What did he say?" Concern dripped from James's words like butter on movie theater popcorn.

"Didn't get there yet."

"I thought you got off work at four?"

"We got slammed right before my shift ended. Didn't get out of there until a quarter after. Then, someone stopped me to ask about Damien Wright. He's the guy I had that thing with freshman year, and apparently, no one has heard from him for like a week. He's in Myths with me. So, I—"

"Okay, that's a lot, and we can talk about it later, but just breathe for a hot second because you sound like an old man in an anti-smoking ad."

He might've laughed at that, under better circumstances. He sucked air into his starved lungs, filling his nostrils with the stench of his own sweat. He hadn't smoked since he started dating James, but a cigarette sounded pretty good right about now.

"Babe, something is always going to happen. You can't keep putting it off."

Vincent exhaled. "I know. I'm just...I don't know."

"Today isn't going as planned, but he has office hours until five, right? So technically, you aren't late."

"Right."

Someone called out to James, and he said something Vincent couldn't quite make out in response before he got back on the phone. "Sorry. Look, I gotta get back to the lab to help clean up for the day. Just don't leave until you come to an understanding. Most of undergrad is proving that you care enough to work for it."

With that, he was gone. Vincent took another breath and let his boyfriend's words wash over him. James was right. He couldn't keep putting off the meeting, but James's ideal outcome was a little harder to swallow.

James spoke from the perspective of a student who'd graduated with honors and breezed through his first year of med school at the University of Pittsburgh. Meanwhile, Vincent had barely survived his first three years of undergrad. To make matters worse, he'd only started caring about Professor Cowart's Myths, Legends, and Folktales class after he got back the rough draft of his final and realized he risked failing out during his last semester.

While he seriously doubted the meeting would end as favorably as James assured him, that didn't mean it would be as disastrous as he presumed. He repeated James's words to himself, screamed them in his mind over every second thought that sprung to life until he reached his destination. By that point, he almost believed them.

The office door was shut. A small wooden plaque was fixed to the opaque glass with "Dr. Charles Cowart" printed on it, and a poster was taped to the door below it:

I've always preferred mythology to history. History is truth that becomes an illusion. Mythology is an illusion that becomes reality. —Jean Cocteau

White text on a galaxy background. Laminated. Vincent wasn't surprised to see the poster. He'd heard Professor Cowart babble on about the quote at least a hundred times in class. Beyond the plaque and poster, he could make out the faint silhouette of someone at a desk through the opaque glass. He brought his ear to the door. Silence broken up by the occasional clacking of a keyboard.

Just don't leave until you come to an understanding.

Vincent knocked on the door.

The silhouette rose and walked over to him. The door swung open. Professor Cowart stood in the doorway. He was dressed in a beige suit with a crimson tie. His salt-and-pepper hair was shaped into a tight Afro that seemed at odds with the unkempt soul patch jutting from his chin.

"Hello." He said it as a statement, but his furrowed eyebrows made it a question.

"Hi, Professor Cowart. I was wondering—"

"Dr. Cowart." He motioned his head toward the plaque.

Vincent wiped the sweat from his forehead and pushed back his hair to keep it from sticking to his damp flesh. "Sorry. Dr. Cowart. I was wondering if I could speak with you."

"And you are?"

"Oh, I'm, ah, Vincent Vicar. I'm in your Myths class." He offered his hand, but Dr. Cowart walked back into his office.

"Take a seat. I'll be with you momentarily."

The office was colored yellow in the afternoon light pouring through the three floor-to-ceiling windows opposite the door. Dr. Cowart took a seat at his desk and resumed typing something on his laptop. Vincent set his backpack on the ground. He sat down in one of the two wooden chairs in front of the desk. The musky smell of tobacco and old books filled the room. The warm light and the smell had a dizzying effect. He felt like he was in a preheating oven.

He took off his jacket and laid it on his lap. Thankfully, he hadn't sweated through his T-shirt. His phone buzzed in his pocket. James knew he was busy, so it was probably some telemarketer. He ignored it. He didn't want to give Dr. Cowart any more reason to dislike him. Trying to sit quietly, Vincent waited for his professor to finish whatever he was doing.

Dr. Cowart typed in no apparent rush.

Vincent focused his attention on the bookshelf behind Dr. Cowart to keep his mind from spiraling down a rabbit hole of what-ifs. Worrying about having to retake the class in the fall as opposed to graduating in a little under two months would only make him a bigger ball of stress. On the stuffed bookshelves were small copper figurines of various characters and creatures from stories they'd studied in class. Vincent could make out a wolf stalking a young, hooded girl just behind Dr. Cowart's head. There was also a Grecian warrior wielding a taut bow, whose name he should know at this point in the semester. The hero's cape was molded to look as if it were blowing in the wind. Like the warrior could come alive at any second and land an arrow between his eyes.

Dr. Cowart shut his laptop. "Without telling me something I shouldn't know, you wouldn't happen to be aware of any reason why Damien Wright has missed my last two classes?"

"No, I'm not."

"Hmmm. It's difficult to keep track of all of you in such a large class, but some students, like Damien, make themselves known."

"Oh?" was all Vincent could think to say. He wasn't sure

if the comment was directed at him or Damien. While missing a week's worth of classes didn't seem like something overachieving Damien would do, Vincent hadn't known him all that well, and he had bigger problems to deal with at that moment.

"You're a senior, correct?"

"Yeah. I mean, yes, I am."

"Not a history major, though, are you?" He rubbed his soul patch thoughtfully like some wise old sage.

"No. I'm general studies." He waited for a lecture concerning the pitfalls of such a degree when just another semester or two could enable him to obtain a more specific and substantial degree.

"Hmmm," Dr. Cowart said, as if that decided something. "Anyway, what was it you wanted?"

"I was wondering if I could talk to you about the grade I received on the rough draft of my final." He took his paper out of his backpack. Dr. Cowart made them print out their essays and submit them in person so that he could write out his feedback, which, in Vincent's case, was little more than a red "D" written on the top of the page with the phrase "off topic" written below it. "I just wasn't sure how my paper was off topic."

Dr. Cowart took the paper and leafed through it. "What was the assignment?"

"To look at a story we discussed in class."

"And for what purpose?"

"To research the historical context and analyze it to

understand its legacy." That was all the assignment guidelines had said.

Dr. Cowart glanced up at him, his eyes narrowing. "And what did you do?"

Vincent wasn't sure what Dr. Cowart was getting at, but he had a sinking feeling he was walking into a trap. "I traced Grimm's *Hansel and Gretel* to the 1635 story, *Nennillo and Nennella*, and then I examined how it was rooted in oral stories dating back to the Great Famine of 1315-1317."

"That's right." He set the paper down on his desk. "And why did you examine this context?"

Vincent resisted the urge to point to his thesis statement on the first page. "I guess to indicate how this absurd story was inspired by real history, which resonated with readers."

"I wanted you to examine the historical context. However, as I discussed in class, realism is of little concern to me beyond understanding why these stories continue to affect those who read them centuries later. Correct me if I'm wrong, but I seriously doubt that modern readers are captivated by how the story captures accounts from the Great Famine of 1315-1317. I want to know why this tale has survived the test of time."

Vincent couldn't remember whether he had attended the class where Dr. Cowart explained the assignment. If he had, he must not have been paying attention. He wished that archer on the shelf would put him out of his misery, but when Dr. Cowart continued to stare at him, he realized his question wasn't rhetorical. "I don't know."

"Which is why you earned such a low grade on this assignment." Dr. Cowart slid the paper back to him. His lips tightened like he was fending off a smirk.

Vincent swallowed in an attempt to push down the anger bubbling up inside him. "Because of this grade, I risk failing the class."

"I don't believe this grade would have been so devastating if you had a higher grade going into the assignment. That being said, I assign the draft of your final at midterms to ensure there is plenty of time for revisions. I suggest you use the next two months wisely."

Vincent wanted to interject. Flip his desk. Do whatever he had to do for Dr. Cowart to understand that it was virtually impossible for him to pass the class unless he got a perfect grade on every assignment, including the final draft. Tell him he was already drowning in loans he couldn't pay off and he couldn't afford to be there another semester. Explain that it was tough working two jobs and keeping up with all his course work. Demand a new grade.

But he didn't.

Unlike James, he didn't have the drive and hard work to back up his words. As much as Dr. Cowart wasn't softening the blow, Vincent had gotten himself into this situation, and he would have to try, and undoubtedly fail, to get himself out of it.

He collected his things and stood up. "Thanks for taking the time to meet with me."

"Of course." Dr. Cowart opened his laptop. Vincent was at the door when Dr. Cowart added, "History isn't about observation. You have to dig into it and see what's between the dirt and worms."

Vincent wondered what great historian had said that quote and whether Dr. Cowart had it printed, laminated, and hanging somewhere in his office. As soon as he got into the hall, his phone vibrated. Below a missed call from an unknown number that surely belonged to a telemarketer was a text from James, asking how it was going. Vincent called him.

"So, what happened?"

The eagerness in his voice made Vincent feel sick. "Can we go for a jog?"

"What? It's cold out, it's supposed to like rain or slush tonight, and it'll be dark in another hour or so. What happened?"

"Sun's still out. It's not that cold. The rain isn't supposed to hit us until later. We have time. Please?" Vincent needed to get away from campus and pump his arms and legs until he forgot about everything except filling his lungs with air.

"Was it that bad?"

Vincent didn't think he could explain just how poorly it'd gone without crying in the hall. "I'll explain everything later. Can you bring my sweats and meet me at Schenley Park? We can park on Overlook Drive."

"If you insist, cutie."

"Thanks."

"Just hurry. It'll be dark soon."

VINCENT COULD TELL James was pissed from the second he parked his sputtering and kicking 1995 Ford Escort behind him. James leaned against the trunk of his car, back straight and arms crossed like a parent who'd caught his child sneaking into the house after curfew. His blond hair was askew from presumably running his hands through it in frustration, and his heart-shaped lips were pursed. More adorable than threatening, but Vincent kept the thought to himself.

Vincent got out of his car and hurried over to him.

"Twenty minutes for one mile?" James asked.

"Sorry. I got stuck behind this fucking fender bender in front of Phipps, and I couldn't get around him."

James's expression remained unchanged. "Why didn't you answer any of my calls?"

"Phone died, and I lost my cigarette lighter adapter, remember?"

"You're a hot mess."

"Love you too!"

James pulled him into a hug. "You're lucky you're cute."

Vincent nuzzled into his chest for a moment before remembering what had brought them there. Pulling away, he asked, "Did you bring my clothes?"

"Back seat, but I think it might be too late for a jog tonight."

While bursts of pink and orange shot through the trees, the night sky was starting to form. "We still have time. A mile and a half in and a mile and a half back out. We'll be done long before six."

"How about we forget about the run and just go home and open a bottle of wine and talk about what happened? I want details."

His skin was crawling, and wine would do little to stop that. The entrance of the trail was just across the street, promising fresh air and a little distance from the university. He needed a good run. Otherwise, he'd be restless all night. "Please?"

James raised one of his pale eyebrows. "Okay, but let's make it quick."

Vincent kissed him and got in the car to change.

James walked around to the window facing the road to prevent passersby from seeing him. "What exactly did he tell you?"

Vincent pretended not to hear him. He didn't know how to tell James, who'd talked him down from the ledge all night and again right before the meeting, that he'd completely folded. He kicked off his khakis and pulled on his sweatpants. They were an older pair from freshman year that fit a little tight. His faded Pitt hoodie was also snug. Where had James found these old things? He normally jogged in gym shorts and a sweatshirt. He also preferred to jog with his pocketknife, but he wasn't exactly in a position to complain.

"Did you hear me?" James asked when he got out of the car.

"No. Did you say something?"

"How'd it go? With Dr. Cowart?"

Vincent looked toward the start of the trail. "It'll be dark soon."

James sighed. "Let's go, then."

They jogged across the street and down the trail. At the fork separating Panther Hollow into the upper and lower trails, Vincent took them right, down the lower trails, which were a little less treacherous. He immediately felt better. Like he was back in Butler, his hometown, jogging through the woods near his house. The distant sound of cars zooming past on the surrounding streets was the only discernible difference.

He moved quickly down the winding dirt path and used the speed to propel himself forward across a stone bridge at the bottom. His breath rang in his ears as he blew small plumes of smoke in the cold spring air. For a moment, he forgot about everything. He wasn't worrying about his class or how James would inevitably pity him for being incapable of getting anything right. He was just running.

"Hold on." James slowed to a stop. He rested his hands on his knees and cocked his head to one side. "Did you hear that?"

Vincent hadn't been paying much attention. "Hear what?"

James shushed him. His red face was screwed up in concentration.

A rustling of leaves in the distance followed by a snapping twig made the hairs on the back of his neck stand on end. He surveyed the woods around them, but he didn't see anything out of the ordinary.

James laughed. "Just fucking with you. I needed a second to catch my breath."

"Asshole." Vincent pushed him. "I think I heard something."

"Yeah, me trying to catch my breath."

"No, I'm serious."

"I mean, take your time, but we better get going soon if you plan to get in three miles."

Vincent didn't know why he was acting so paranoid in a public park. Anything from another jogger to a deer could have broken that twig, and the more time they spent discussing it, the less time he could run. Vincent started again, but he kept an ear out this time. He couldn't shake the sinking feeling that they were being watched.

There wasn't much he could hear over the sound of their shoes crunching on frosted ground and James's heavy breaths. James forced in air harder and harder until he requested that they walk for a little while. They were over a mile in, and Panther Hollow Bridge loomed overhead through the bare trees. By that point, Vincent was ready for a break himself.

"I don't know—how you—do this every day," James said between breaths.

Vincent didn't know how James ate whatever he wanted, only worked out occasionally, and still weighed fifteen pounds less than him despite being nearly a foot taller. "Your body eventually adjusts to the torture."

They continued in silence. The conversation Vincent was avoiding gave weight to the crisp air. He searched their surroundings for another topic of discussion. The sun was starting to set, and the swirled sherbet sky brought the dead woods to life. "It's beautiful out."

James kicked a rock on the path. "So, I'm assuming Professor Cowart didn't change your grade?"

Vincent swallowed. He couldn't think of any way around that one. "No, he didn't."

"Want to talk about it?"

"Not really." Vincent looked down at the trail to avoid making eye contact.

James stepped in front of him, placed a cold hand under his chin, and lifted his head until they were face-to-face. There it was, written all over his sad eyes and frowning lips. Pity. He kissed Vincent. "I'm sure we can figure something out."

Vincent pulled away. He wished James would yell at him or tell him how disappointed he felt. Anything other than pity. "We should get going. Right after we pass through this tunnel, we'll end up at the visitors' center. We can turn around and jog back from there."

"Wait. Did you hear that?" James cocked his head to one side again, but he wasn't nearly as convincing.

"You don't honestly think I'm stupid enough to fall for—"

James covered Vincent's mouth. This time he heard it. Someone was making kissing noises and laughing. The sound echoed in the empty woods in a way that made it impossible to pinpoint where it was coming from. Heart pounding in his ears, Vincent pivoted, searching the trees for a source, but in the setting sun, there were too many shadows to make out anything for sure. The person could be standing a foot from them, and he'd be none the wiser.

He tore his gaze from the trees to look at James. His eyes were wide with fear, and his body was tense. A sprinter waiting for the shot of a starting gun. The second they made eye contact, James let out a nervous laugh. "Probably just some kids messing around. We should get going. You said there's a visitors' center up ahead?"

The voice didn't sound childlike to Vincent. It sounded deep and rough.

"Yeah. Leads out to the sidewalk. We can walk around to the cars." Up where there were streetlights, busy roads, and other people.

They hurried down the path. More of a fast walk than a jog. Vincent didn't like the idea of running now. He didn't want whoever had mocked them to think they were scared, and it wasn't like they were being chased. It was just some kids messing around like James had said.

The sun had disappeared below the horizon when they reached the tunnel formed by one of the massive stone arches that supported Panther Hollow Bridge. There was still enough light to make out their surroundings, but not for long. The stone walls of the tunnel shrouded the path in darkness, convincing Vincent that a long walk back to their cars through the woods would be a much safer option.

He turned to James, who seemed to have come to a similar conclusion. "So, you still want to get in those three miles?"

"Absolutely," James said. They started back the way they'd come.

They hadn't taken more than a few steps in that direction when a man yelled, "Where you goin'?"

A scream escaped Vincent's throat. Just ahead of them, a stocky man stepped out from behind a tree, crushing dead leaves and frosted earth under his heavy step. A smile stretched across his face, and in one hand, he held a crowbar.

CHAPTER TWO

SUNDOWN

WHATEVER AIR WAS left in Vincent's lungs evacuated. The man had a tool that could rip a nail from solid wood or pry open a locked door. He'd followed them, and his taunting left little question as to what he planned to do with the weapon.

Vincent reached into his pocket for his knife. He'd never used it, but at least he could try to intimidate the man with it. All his trembling fingers found were his keys, which, against a crowbar, were even more useless than the four-inch blade that sat on his dresser back at their apartment.

James was a few inches taller than the man, but the

stranger was big enough to beat both of them to a bloody pulp with his bare hands. Equipped with a crowbar, he was deadly. Images of purple eyes swollen shut and broken limbs contorted in unnatural angles flashed in Vincent's mind. He looked around in the hope of finding something in the woods they could use to defend themselves.

There was nothing. Only the ever-darkening sky and hum of the city that was less than a mile away but might as well be on a separate planet for as much good as it'd do them.

Vincent had made a mistake dragging James into the woods at dusk.

James stepped in front of him. Voice wavering, he said, "We don't want any trouble."

Vincent couldn't make out the man's face well in the darkness, but he could see that his white smile had disappeared. "No shit. Dirty fucking sodomite."

"What the fuck did you call me?" James took a step toward him.

Everything was going from bad to worse, and it was happening too fast for Vincent to process it. All he knew for sure was the last thing they should do was get closer to the man.

"James, please." Vincent grabbed his hand and tried to pull him back, but he didn't have enough strength in his shaking hands to move him.

"I called you a dirty fucking sodomite!" The man closed the distance between him and James to a matter of feet.

James stared down at the crowbar, and something in his disposition changed. He seemed to realize, over his fog of anger, just how dire their situation had become. He backed away, pulling Vincent along with him.

The man didn't move from his spot. He just looked at them, and as they went further down the path, his white smile returned. The amused look on his face made Vincent's blood run cold. If the man wanted to beat them up, why wasn't he chasing after them? Was this some sort of sick prank?

It didn't feel like a prank. Everything about this felt wrong. Vincent looked to James, who appeared to be thinking the same thing. "I say we run. He's far enough away that he won't catch us easily."

Vincent didn't like the idea of turning his back on the man, but James was right. Their best bet was to run for it. They might have a chance if they could make it through the tunnel and up the cobblestone road. "Okay."

"Now." James let go of his hand, and they booked it down the path.

Vincent pumped his arms and moved his legs as fast as they would go, taking in as much cold air as his lungs would allow. They hurried into the tunnel. The sound of their shoes hitting the dirt reverberated off the massive stone walls, making it impossible to hear whether the man was following them.

He shot a glance over his shoulder as they went. The man was nowhere in sight. He was so relieved he almost wanted to laugh. They were going to make it out of this night unscathed.

Just before they reached the mouth of the tunnel, two figures stepped onto the path.

Vincent and James slowed to a stop.

"Please, help us!" Vincent said between heavy breaths. He started to walk over to them, but James grabbed his hand and pulled him back.

"Wait," James said in a low voice.

The two figures didn't say a word. They weren't asking what was wrong or running away from them. It was almost as if they were expecting them. That's when it hit him. He turned around. The stocky man stood at the other end of the tunnel. He hadn't intended to kill them—at least not on the path. He'd been herding them, and Vincent and James had followed along like unwitting lambs to the slaughter.

"What do we have here?" One of the two figures stepped forward. He was tall—at least six feet—and had a lean, muscular build. As he got closer, Vincent could see that his head was shaved, revealing some combination of numbers tattooed above his right ear.

They backed away from him.

"They were swapping AIDS in the middle of the trail for everyone to see," the stocky man said.

Vincent jumped at the sound of his rough voice and whipped his head around to find that the man was nearing them.

"Ugh," let out the third man in disgust. Vincent wasn't sure if he could even call him a man. He looked like he was sixteen at most. Just a kid. His blond hair was so fair it almost looked white. He was taller than the stocky man, but he had the same lean, muscular physique as the tall man he followed.

James pulled Vincent sideways against the wall of the tunnel. The men drew closer. They were surrounded and outnumbered, and there was no way they could fight them off or run away. They were at the mercy of these monsters.

Tears clouded Vincent's vision. "Please."

"Please," the tall man mimicked. He snorted and spat in Vincent's face. "Pathetic faggot."

The warm sludge dripped down his cheek.

James lunged forward, pushing the man back. "Don't you fucking touch him!"

"Looks like we got a brave fag on our hands." The tall man straightened up. He reached into his back pocket, pulled out a pistol, and aimed it at James.

Vincent froze at the sight of it. Looked like a semiautomatic, but he couldn't be sure in this lighting.

Just one pull of the trigger and James would be dead.

James raised his hands in the air and backed up to the wall beside Vincent. "I didn't mean that. I'm sorry."

"Not so brave now, are you, faggot?" The man cocked the pistol and pushed the barrel into James's forehead with such force that his head cracked against the wall.

"Please, don't!" Vincent begged between sobs. This couldn't be happening. They couldn't just kill them.

But the terrifying truth was, of course, that they could

do whatever they wanted. They had the weapons. They had the power, and Vincent and James were helpless.

The kid sprinted to the tall man's side. "Shit, someone's coming."

With the pistol still pressed to James's skull, the tall man motioned for the stocky one to take care of it. He rested the crowbar on his shoulder and walked toward the opening of the tunnel.

The voices of a man and woman talking and laughing as they made their way down the cobblestone road traveled into the tunnel. They sounded just as oblivious and content as Vincent and James had been only a few minutes ago. Vincent considered screaming to warn them, but it was only a thought. The tall man still held the pistol to James's head. He couldn't imagine the consequences of disobedience at this point.

A finger rubbed over his knuckle, and he nearly let out a scream in shock before he realized James was trying to get his attention. The tall man was busy watching the opening of the tunnel. He turned his head ever so slightly so he could see James out of the corner of his eye.

James was mouthing something.

Vincent checked on the tall man, whose focus hadn't wavered. He turned a little more in James's direction.

When the time is right, run, he mouthed.

Vincent gave a curt nod. With the tall man and the kid focused on the opening of the tunnel and the stocky man walking toward it, their odds of escaping were getting better by the second. But they'd have to act soon before the stocky man chased off their distraction. Vincent knew that staying meant certain death at the hands of these fuckers, but the very thought of going against the orders of a man who had a gun to James's head further cemented him to the wall.

The man and woman rounded the corner with their arms interlocked. Their faces were illuminated by the phone in her hands. She spoke about something on her screen, which had captivated them. They would've walked right into the stocky man if he hadn't said something.

"Tunnel's closed!"

"Whoa, whoa, whoa." The man put an arm across the woman's chest. "Take it easy."

"Turn around." The stocky man moved the crowbar from his shoulder to his side like a batter preparing for a pitch.

The woman screamed and dropped her phone. Small bursts of light shot through the tunnel before it hit the ground. It landed face up, illuminating the terrificd looks on the pair's pale faces. She pointed into the tunnel. "He has a gun!"

The man shushed her.

"Jesus fucking Christ," the tall man said. "Do I have to do everything? Boy, take this."

The kid hesitated.

"That wasn't a question."

The kid rushed over and took the gun. Now was the time. They'd have no better chance to escape than with the kid. James squeczed his hand. Vincent wasn't sure if it was his cue to run or if it was merely a reminder that their moment was coming. Vincent didn't squeeze back. The gun was still pointed at James's head, and the kid seemed tense—like he'd shoot at the first sign of movement.

It was too risky.

The tall man stopped at the edge of the tunnel. "Are you retarded or something? My friend here told you the tunnel is closed."

James squeezed his hand once more, and Vincent tried to ignore it.

"Sorry," the man said. He picked up the woman's phone. "We didn't know."

"But—" the woman started.

"But what?" The tall man grew more impatient by the second.

"Nothing." The man dragged the woman back from the tunnel. They were leaving.

James let go of his hand. Vincent tried to grab it to keep him from doing something that could get himself killed, but it was too late.

James dove at the kid and—

Bang.

The sound of the gunshot was magnified tenfold as it echoed off the tunnel walls. Vincent shut his eyes as soon as it went off. Something warm and thick splattered across his face, and he screamed, sliding down the wall to the ground.

He shot him.

Vincent couldn't see James like that. He'd rather wait until they shot him, too, so that he'd never have to see what that bullet did to James's head. He probably would've if he hadn't heard some sort of struggle on the ground in front of him.

He opened his eyes. Blood poured from the side of James's head where the bullet must have grazed him, but he was alive. James was on top of the kid, trying to pull the pistol from his death grip as blood spilled onto the young man's face and stained his light hair red.

Before Vincent had a chance to get to his feet, the stocky man had reached them and brought the crowbar down on James's back. James cried out in pain. Vincent pushed himself to his feet and ran at the man, but something hit him in the side of the head before he reached him, and the next thing he knew, he was on the ground, staring up at the tall man. A ringing sound filled his right ear, and he couldn't seem to focus his vision on the man.

He could still hear the muffled sound of the crowbar striking James and his subsequent cries of pain. The stocky man was going to kill him. Vincent tried to stand up, but he'd only made it to his hands and knees when something smashed into his side. The sound of a snapping twig was followed by a rush of pain flooding his chest. He doubled over and wrapped his arms around his head in an attempt to protect it from the next blow. "Please stop!"

Thud.

Thud.

Thud.

The crowbar continued to hit James, but something was missing. There were no cries of pain or pleas to stop. James was silent.

No.

James had just passed out from the pain. That was all. Vincent needed to get the man to stop before it was too late. He couldn't sit up, much less stand, so he crawled in the direction of the sound. Something slammed down on the middle of his back, and he fell to the dirt. Pain rippled through his body.

"Dirty fucking faggot."

There was a weight on the back of his head then that pushed his face into the dirt. He couldn't breathe, and he didn't have the strength to stop whoever was doing it. He was going to die.

"You like eating shit, don't you, faggot?"

The weight twisted, and what Vincent realized was a rubber shoe ripped the hair from his scalp as the man squashed Vincent's head into the earth like he was stamping out a cigarette butt. "Well, eat up. It's your last fucking supper."

Then a hand grabbed him by his hair, and he was on his knees. His face burned and head throbbed, but he hardly noticed because what had been taken away from him had returned. Air. Cold, damp air. He sucked it in, ignoring the way it worsened the stabbing sensation in his chest.

He blinked open his eyes to focus them on James's bloody body. "Please stop! Please just let him go."

The tall man laughed. "You're not in a bargaining position. Boy, come here!" The kid mustn't have listened
because the man added, "Get your pansy ass over here or
you can join the fags in hell!"

There were quick steps in the dirt behind him. He tried
to focus his vision on James. He could have sworn he saw
his back rise and fall. He kept watching to ensure it wasn't
just his eyes. There it was again. He was still breathing.
Thank God. James was alive.

"Get the other one up," the tall man said. "Don't want
him to miss the show."

The stocky man grabbed his crowbar with both hands,
slid it under James's chin, and pulled him to his knees.
James gagged, his eyes shooting open. Tears ran down his
bloody, swollen face, but something about him seemed resigned to what was happening.

He looked at Vincent and mouthed, *I love you.*

"Wait." Vincent squirmed. They couldn't just lie down
and die. He had to do something. "We have money! I have
money. I can give you all of it. It's in our cars. We can take
you there. Just stop this."

"Enough," the tall man bellowed. "We don't have all
day."

The kid came into view. He carried the pistol out in
front of him. The gun shook so much that it could hit any of
them if he pulled the trigger too soon. He walked up to
James.

The stocky man stepped to the side of him, still holding
the crowbar under his throat. "This time, don't miss."

The kid cocked the gun.

"No!" Vincent thrashed his head back and forth. Hair ripped from his scalp. He didn't care. Nothing mattered except stopping the kid from pulling that trigger. "You don't want to do this. You can still walk away. We won't tell anyone what happened. Please!"

The tall man kneed him in the back and wrapped his arm around his neck in a headlock so tight Vincent could barely breathe, much less speak. The kid pointed the gun at James's chest.

The kid turned his head away.

Vincent squeezed his eyes shut.

"No," the tall man said.

Vincent reopened them. The kid looked just as shocked.

"Boy, I want you to watch him die."

Vincent tried to move, but the tall man tightened his hold, crushing Vincent's windpipe.

The kid looked down at James and pulled the trigger.

Vincent shut his eyes, and the shot rang through the tunnel. Vincent stopped moving. He hung in the tall man's arm by his neck, tears rolling down his face. The tall man let go of him, and he fell to the ground that was soaked in warm liquid. He didn't open his eyes. He couldn't see James that way. He waited for the kid to shoot him. He was ready to die.

The tall man grabbed him by his hair. "Want to see what the boy did? Huh?"

He'd have to pry open his eyes if he wanted Vincent to see James.

The tall man dropped him again, and Vincent landed on his back. "Fucking pussy."

"We gotta hurry," the stocky man said. "I hear sirens."

"Almost done," the tall man said.

Vincent could hear the sirens too. They were faint. Several blocks away, if not more. He didn't care now. They were too late. He didn't want to be saved. The end of the pistol pressed into his forehead, and he took a breath of relief.

"Don't you get weak, boy," said the tall man. "You should be proud. You are cleansing the world of this undesirable filth."

"Yes, sir."

He waited for him to cock the gun, but it didn't come.

"Fuck. It's jammed!"

The sirens were getting louder. Couldn't be more than a couple of blocks away.

"Just do it already," Vincent choked. He didn't want to feel this pain or know that James was dead. He just wanted it all to be over. He welcomed the dreamless sleep that death would bring.

"What did you say?" The tall man's foul-smelling breath hit his face.

Vincent forced his eyes open and stared directly into the tall man's eyes. "Do it."

The man drew away, and something hard hit him in his side. "Shut the fuck up!"

Vincent screamed in pain, but he kept his eyes open.

"Do. It."

"Give me that." Then the tall man was back in eyesight. He swung the blood-soaked crowbar over his head and brought it down on Vincent like he was splitting a log. The crowbar grew larger and larger in Vincent's vision as it traveled through the air to meet his skull.

And then, there was nothing.

CHAPTER THREE

ADRIFT

CONSCIOUSNESS CAME IN waves.

He was falling, body twisting and tumbling through a blur of dead foliage and bare trees, and before he reached the bottom, he was pulled out to a sea of unconsciousness.

He came to on his back. Freezing cold rain hit his face like little pinpricks. The trees towering over him changed from brown to red in the flashing lights. They reminded him of when his mother bundled him up as child and drove through some of the ritzier neighborhoods in Butler so that they could gawk at the Christmas lights in December.

"A free light show," she'd told him.

He heard her words now, whispered in his ear. Even the sirens couldn't drown it out.

He reached for the lights, and that's when the pain hit him. Everything hurt. Arms. Legs. His chest felt like it was on fire, and his head throbbed. He rubbed his forehead where the pain was the sharpest to find a massive protruding bump.

He'd been beaten.

He was at the bottom of a slope just off the trail.

Those lights were emergency services.

James.

If he had survived the attack, then maybe James had made it too. James was stronger, and not all gunshot wounds were fatal. James just needed medical attention before he lost too much blood. Vincent rolled onto his stomach. The moment he tried to push himself up from the wet earth, he was gone again.

Distant voices called out in the darkness, drawing him back to shore. He couldn't understand what they were saying. He wanted to cry for help, but every time he tried to fill his lungs with enough air to scream, a sharp pain in his chest forced it back out.

He'd have to find James and get him back to the trail on his own. The thought of him lying alone somewhere in the woods was the only thing pushing Vincent to move in spite of the pain. He dug his fingers into the mud and crawled forward, doing his best to focus his vision through the rain.

In the flashing lights from above, he spotted a dark

mound behind a thick stump a few feet ahead of him. It looked like a pile of dirt—except for the pair of muddy white sneakers jutting out from it.

He moved as fast as his broken body would let him, fighting off waves of nausea and exhaustion. The closer he got to it, the more the iron smell of blood filled the freezing air. Around the stump, James lay on his back. His body was covered in a mixture of gore and dirt that made it impossible to tell what condition he was in.

Vincent shook his arm. "James, wake up. Oh God. Wake up."

James didn't move.

Vincent pressed his ear to his muddy chest and tried to ignore the hammering rain and roaring sirens. There, under the chaotic symphony filling his ears, he heard it.

Ba bum.

Ba bum.

His heartbeat was faint, but he was still alive.

Vincent sat up and pulled James onto his lap. The pain from the motion was so sharp it only hit him after he was cradling James in his arms—terrible and searing, as if someone had jammed a red-hot iron poker through his ribs. He opened his mouth to scream, but nothing came out. The world darkened around its edges.

No.

He couldn't pass out now.

James needed him.

He breathed through the pain and concentrated.

Something warm spilled over his legs. He touched it and brought it up to the light. Blood dripped from his hand. James's blood. It thinned in the rain. He needed to stop the bleeding fast, but there was nothing around him except trees and fucking mud.

Mud.

He grabbed a fistful of it and smeared it over James's back. He couldn't tell exactly where the bullet had entered and exited his body, so he packed mud all over his back and chest.

Tears burned his cheeks as he worked. "You have to make it. Because I can't do this without you. You hear me?"

He could feel his mind slipping. He shoved his hand into the dirt to try to keep himself upright and kissed James on the forehead, praying beyond anything else, even his own survival, that James would make it through this. "I need you."

The undertow returned and swept him back out to sea.

The next time he stirred, the ground was moving under him. He blinked in an attempt to slow it down, but it wasn't moving on its own. He was being carried over someone's shoulder up the hill. The sirens were growing louder, and there was a trail of footprints in the mud behind them.

"James?"

"I have you," he said.

The arm wrapped around his waist squeezed him a little tighter.

Vincent clung to his words as he drifted away again.

I have you.

WHEN VINCENT CAME to, he was in bed. His alarm was going off, and despite the layers of blankets on top of him, he was freezing. He buried his face in his pillow. He just needed a few more minutes of shut-eye before he faced the day.

"Time to wake up." James pulled him close and planted a wet kiss on the back of his neck.

"Never." Vincent tucked his nose under James's arm to warm it, but his arm was soaked.

"What the—" Vincent pulled away. He assumed it was sweat until he opened his eyes. Blood-tinged mud encased James's arm. Worms tunneled in and out of his flesh, leaving little black holes in their wake.

"Don't worry, I have you." James tightened his hold on him.

Vincent screamed and tried to pry himself free, but it was no use. James was too strong. He was crushing him in his arms. Just when Vincent was sure that his body would break under the pressure, the mud covering James gave way, and Vincent sank inside him. Mud filled his mouth as he was buried alive.

I have you.

Vincent woke with a start. White lights blinded him, and pain crashed over him like a tidal wave, leaving him disoriented and gasping for air. He didn't know where he was or what was happening, but the pain was so great that everything beyond ending his torment was an afterthought. He blinked away the black dots clouding his vision to find himself alone in a hospital room.

Machines hummed in his ears. Tubes shot air up his nose. Something was clamped to one of his fingers, and an IV was in his other arm. Nothing seemed to be there to relieve his pain. He hoped not. If this was the tip of the iceberg, he welcomed death. He felt like he'd been pulverized in a garbage disposal, and his head pounded with such force he had trouble focusing his vision on anything for very long.

A remote was wrapped around his guardrail near his right hand. He'd been in enough hospitals with his mother to know that the red button with a white cross in its center was the call button. He pressed it with as much force as he could muster—as if the action would somehow make the nurse come faster.

While the minute hand on the clock above the door only ticked once by the time the nurse reached his bedside, it felt like an hour had passed. She was out of breath. "You're awake?"

"Everything hurts," he rasped. He hadn't realized just how dry his mouth was until he spoke.

"I'll have the doctor call something in for your pain. In the meantime, let me get you some water."

She soon returned holding a plastic mug with a straw sticking out of it. She brought it to his lips. "Here we are."

Vincent took a sip. The water burned all the way down, but his mouth and throat immediately felt better. He wished the rest of his body could be fixed so easily. "Thank you."

"No problem." She set the mug on the overbed table. "I'll be back as soon as I can. Just hang in there."

The mug grew hazy. He shut his eyes in the hope of stopping the stomach acid from crawling up his throat. He soon found that taking shallow breaths prevented the pain in his chest from mounting. The rest of his body wasn't as manageable. He kept waiting for the pain to plateau or his body to grow numb to it, but every time he was convinced he could handle it, a new wave of injuries was brought to his attention. Each served as a reminder of what those monsters did to them. Every swing. Every hit. His body was a photo album of the horror they had survived.

He couldn't imagine how much pain James must be in somewhere else in the hospital. James had taken the brunt of their attack, and even though he'd carried Vincent to safety, he'd been shot. What Vincent felt was probably a drop in a bucket compared to what James was going through.

When the nurse returned with three capped syringes—two full of clear liquid and one off-white—he asked, "You wouldn't happen to know how James Beaumont is doing?"

Confusion wrinkled her forehead. "Who?"

"James Beaumont. He came in with me. We were—attacked."

"I'm honestly not sure, honey. I wasn't here when you came in. This will make you a lot more comfortable." She hooked up one of the clear syringes to something on his IV and emptied it. She then did the same with the off-white syringe before finishing with the other clear one.

The pain dulled almost instantly, like all the sharp edges had been buffed away. He didn't have time to savor the relief for long. The nurse had questions. Vincent answered them to the best of his ability. His name was Vincent Vicar. He was in a hospital somewhere in Pittsburgh. The date was a little foggier. He believed they'd been attacked on the twentieth or the twenty-first, so it was probably around the twenty-second of February.

"You're at UPMC Presbyterian, but it's actually the twenty-seventh of February."

"What?" He didn't think he was that off on the dates.

"You've been unresponsive for the past six days."

"Six days?" Vincent said—more to better process the words himself than anything. He had been out for close to a week.

"I know this is a lot to take in." She glanced at the door. "But it looks like you have some visitors if you're up for it? They've probably been here more than me in the past week."

"Yeah, I'm up for it." Vincent followed her gaze, but his visitors were standing off to the side in the hall so he couldn't see them from his position. Knowing James, he'd already recovered enough to be discharged while Vincent was out, but he didn't know who else would be with him.

"If you need anything, please don't hesitate to call for me. I'll be just down the hall." She headed out of the door and said something to the people in the hall that he didn't catch.

"Thank God you're up!" Sam rushed into the room. He

should have known she'd be his other visitor. While she was the same age as Vincent, she'd been best friends with James since middle school, and he seriously doubted she'd left James's side since the attack.

As she got closer, his suspicions were confirmed. She was dressed in a wrinkled hockey jersey belonging to her boyfriend, Tyler, her long blonde hair was matted and greasy, and she had dark-purple bags under her bloodshot eyes. "We were so worried about you."

Vincent looked to the hallway for James. What he found was the bloated stomach and red, puffy face of his father. "Henry?"

Was the pain medicine having a greater effect than he thought? He hadn't spoken to Henry in almost four years. Henry didn't even know where he lived, so Vincent wasn't sure how the hell his father knew he was in the hospital.

"Son," Henry said, like the word would somehow cement their nonexistent bond. He waddled to the end of his bed. He must have read the confusion written all over Vincent's face because he looked down at the linoleum floor, revealing a small bald spot that had formed on the top of his head, and explained, "I'm still your emergency contact."

Vincent didn't have time to deal with him now. He looked around Henry into the hall, but no one seemed to be waiting to come in the room. He turned his attention back to Sam, who'd sat down in one of the two seats beside his bed. "Where's James?"

"We can talk later," she said, waving her hand in an overly flippant manner. "More importantly, how are you feeling? Are you comfortable?"

She hadn't answered his question.

"I'm fine. How's James?"

She pressed her hand into the side of his pillow, avoiding his gaze. "I can stop by your apartment tonight if you want some things. I'll grab you another pillow. There's hardly anything to this one."

"The pillow's fine."

Sam continued to test its firmness. "Honestly, it's not a problem. I mean, this is as thin as a pancake and I—"

"Sam, forget about the damn pillow." He didn't realize he'd yelled until she jumped back, her glassy eyes fixed on the floor.

What had gone unsaid settled in the room like humid air, making it hard for Vincent to breathe. "How bad is he?"

Tears streamed down her face. "Don't worry about that now."

"Is he still in the hospital? Sam. Please. Look at me."

He regretted asking her to do it the second he looked into her eyes. They told him everything he feared. The worst possible outcome.

She wrapped her arms around him and buried her face into the pillow next to his head. "I'm so sorry."

Tears blurred the room. He turned to Henry, hoping his face would somehow contradict Sam's reaction, but his averted gaze only confirmed it.

"No." He must be having another nightmare. Soon he'd

wake up, and James would be sitting in one of the chairs beside his bed. James wouldn't be unscathed, but they would get through this together.

All Vincent needed to do was wake up.

Wake up.

"He just didn't make it." Her body shook as she sobbed.

Sam hadn't been in the woods with them. She hadn't heard James's heartbeat or seen him carry Vincent up the hill. She had no idea what she was talking about. "No, he made it. So just stop. Stop lying!"

Sam recoiled.

"Now, Vinny." Henry held his hands up like a crossing guard stopping oncoming traffic.

"No, she's lying!" His breath deepened, and the stabbing sensation in his chest returned, but that was the least of his concerns. Sam was lying to him, and Henry was such a pathetic asshole he was actually going along with it.

Vincent didn't know why she was doing this. He knew she'd never liked him and saw him as more of a stray cat who James had been kind enough to take in than someone who actually deserved her best friend, but this was low, even for her.

"Enough!" Henry hit the plastic footboard.

The bed shook, sending tremors of pain through Vincent's body that snapped him out of his rage. They were looking at him like he was crazy. He rubbed the tears from his burning face. "I'm sorry, Sam. Please just let me see him. I need to see him."

"You've been out for almost a week," Sam said. "I tried to get his parents to postpone the funeral, but they wouldn't wait. And I didn't know when you were going to wake up. If you were going to wake up."

Vincent wouldn't listen to this any longer. He threw off his blankets to find his legs covered in cuts and bruises. He couldn't breathe. He needed to get out of this room and find James and make sure he was okay.

Sam got out of her chair and backed away from the bed. The chair screeched against the linoleum as she stumbled over it. "You need to calm down."

Vincent ignored her. He pulled the clamp off his finger and the oxygen tubing from his nose. One of the machines beside him went off like a siren. He tore the IV from his arm, ripping tape and spraying blood on the white sheets. As he sat up, pain shot through his torso.

Sam ran out in the hall. "I need a nurse."

Vincent gritted his teeth and searched for a button or lever on the side of the bed to lower the guardrails.

"Stop!" Henry grabbed him by his wrists and pushed him against the bed. He reeked of smoke and whiskey. The smell only made Vincent more nauseated and angry.

"Let me go!" The more Vincent struggled to break free from Henry's grasp, the more the blood poured from his arm, gushing even further with each thud of his racing heart.

"I'm sorry about your friend, but you need to calm down!"

"Get the fuck off of me!" Vincent threw himself back.

Whether it was the slick blood covering his arm or the force of his movement, he broke away from Henry and crashed into the bed so hard it knocked the wind out of him. He coughed for air as pain radiated through his chest. The room turned into a mess of unfocused shapes that made him feel sick to his stomach.

"Fuck." Henry's figure backed away from the bed.

Vincent was done with both of them. He didn't need their lies. He would find James on his own. If he squinted his eyes, he could make out the guardrail to his right. Streaks of blood tracked his path on the white plastic. He found a button on the outside. He pressed it and pushed the guard-rail down.

He was working up the courage to swing his legs over the side of the bed when Henry put his hands on his shoulders to keep him down. "When your mother died, I didn't want to believe it either, but it happened, and freaking out like this isn't going to change the fact that he's gone."

"But he isn't dead."

All his strength had left him, but he continued to writhe against the red blur standing over him. Other voices filled the room. Talk of blood pressure and swelling. Pleas to re-lax.

He kept fighting.

James couldn't be dead.

Something sharp pricked his leg, and he could do little more than stare at the blurry figures standing over him before he drifted back to a sea of unconsciousness.

CHAPTER FOUR

QUESTIONS AND ANSWERS

VINCENT PULLED ON his arm restraints. They weren't going to magically unravel, but he could hope. His doctor had explained that it was to ensure his safety. Apparently, on top of two broken ribs, he had a traumatic brain injury that was causing too much pressure on his brain, which required a slew of medications, monitoring, and rest. If he proved he could remain calm today, then he'd get the restraints off tomorrow.

The doctor had visited him early in the morning. Since then, he'd stared into the hall, wondering where Sam and Henry had gone and if they were coming back after his outburst the night before. He felt truly insane for accusing Sam of lying, but what she'd told him didn't make any sense. How could someone with the strength to carry Vincent all the way up to the trail just pass away when emergency services were already waiting for them?

He didn't know what to think. Every time he tried to go over what had happened that night, flashes of the attack riddled his mind—James's defeated face, the men's chilling laughter, the crowbar coming down on him—and all he wanted to do was lock himself in the bathroom. He probably would have if the restraints weren't pinning him to the bed, leaving him at the mercy of anyone who walked into his room.

He attempted to empty his mind and enjoy the momentary relief his medication cocktail offered. The drugs didn't erase the pain, but they made it far more bearable. If he didn't move or take deep breaths, he almost forgot about it from time to time. Then, he coughed or tried to adjust himself, and it flooded back to him.

Sometime after lunch—time seemed to ebb and flow in a strange way with all of his medications—Sam walked in carrying a tote bag over one shoulder and a large Dunkin' Donuts cup in each hand. "Good afternoon."

"You're back?" He didn't even know where to begin to apologize.

"Just went to pick up some of your things," she said, motioning to her bag. "You can't scare me away that easy."

"And Henry?"

"Made him go home and shower. He'll be back soon. I

see you're still in restraints."

He twisted his arms like he was a QVC host displaying a pair of dazzling bracelets. "Deservingly so. Look, about last night…"

"Forget about it."

"I just—"

"You don't have to apologize to me. I've known for a week, and I still can hardly believe he's gone." She cleared her throat. "So, the one with cream and sugar or the one with just cream?"

"What?"

She held out the cups in front of him.

He hadn't had a drop of coffee since before the attack. "Just cream, you amazing saint."

"Good choice. I already started drinking the one with cream and sugar." She set his coffee on the overbed table before she seemed to remember that he was restrained. "I'll get you a straw."

Vincent was sipping his coffee when there was a knock at the open door. A Black woman, dressed in brown slacks and a yellow blazer, stood in the doorway. She was bald and held a manila folder at her side. "Vincent Vicar?"

"Yes?"

"Hi, my name is Adelaide. I'm with social services. Is now a good time to talk?"

He looked to Sam, who shrugged. He didn't see why not. "Sure."

Adelaide walked over to Sam. "And who might this be?"

"A friend, but I might step out to make a call while you two talk." She got up and headed for the door.

"You are more than welcome to stay," Adelaide said.

"That's okay. Nice to meet you." Sam turned to Vincent. "I'll be back soon."

Vincent couldn't tell if he was grateful that she'd left. "What's this about?"

"I'm here to see how you're doing and let you know about our services. Can I take a seat?"

"Of course." He went to wave to the chairs, but his restraints stopped him.

She sat down with a huff. "Thank you. I took the stairs. Don't recommend them. Anyway, how are you feeling today? Are you comfortable?"

"Sure."

She opened the folder in her lap and flipped through a few papers. "I heard you had a rough night."

"Yeah, you could say that." He could feel his cheeks growing red. She probably thought he was insane, and he wasn't too sure he could argue against that.

"Would you like to talk about it?"

"Not particularly." He stared down at his restraints. Even though they were padded, he had messed with them enough that his skin was red around the edges of the straps.

"It can be a lot to go through what you went through. Sometimes, people need time to process everything, and that is totally normal and fine. I just want to let you know that if you change your mind, I'm here."

"Thanks." He wasn't sure if it was her warm eyes or her calming voice, but something about her made him feel like she meant every word that left her lips. The only problem was there wasn't anything to process. He had too many unanswered questions to even begin to consider what had happened to James, and he didn't even know who he could talk to about them without getting upgraded from restraints to a padded cell.

"Now, the police would like to talk to you about what happened, but we can, of course, put a hold on that until you are ready to talk to them. Also..."

Whatever she said next was lost on him.

The police.

He didn't know why he hadn't thought about it sooner. Emergency services had been in the woods with them that night. Maybe they knew something about what had happened that everyone else had missed. Even if they couldn't answer his questions, he'd rest a lot easier knowing the police were looking for the fuckers who did this to them.

"I want to talk to the police as soon as possible," he said, perhaps a bit too forcefully from the way Adelaide sat back in her chair at his words.

"Are you sure? I don't want to—"

"I'm sure."

VINCENT WAS ALONE when Detectives Ralbovsky and
Tillman came to question him that afternoon. Sam and
Henry had offered to stay, but he assured them he would be
fine. He didn't think he could ask about James with them in
the room. The detectives weren't at his bedside long before
he started to regret that decision.

"We know you've been through a lot, but we want to ask
you a few questions, so we can bring those responsible to
justice." Ralbovsky spoke in such a hollow and rehearsed
manner that Vincent wondered how many times he'd said
those words. Looking at the white hair around his temples
and the strained buttons on his shirt, he'd bet Ralbovsky had
repeated that sentence more times than he could count.

"The more you can tell us, the more we can help." Tillman couldn't be more different than her partner. Fitted suit.
Tight ponytail. Muscular build. She looked like she belonged
in an hour-long police procedural. Her hands were tightly
folded together on the black binder in her lap.

Ralbovsky pulled a notepad from his back pocket and
flipped to a fresh page. "So, why don't we start with when
you got to the park?"

Vincent went to scoot up in bed before his ribs made
him think better of it. "Around a quarter after five."

"And do you usually jog in Schenley Park?"

"Yeah."

They continued like this. Question and answer. Vincent
didn't know when or how to go about asking his own questions, and as their conversation drew closer to the attack, he
thought less and less about them. He was too busy trying to

describe what had happened that night.

He'd worked so hard to cast away those memories they were out of reach when he returned to them. The events played back in his mind in distorted flashes. A man, cloaked in shadows, jumping onto the trail. The sound of a crowbar hitting flesh. The dark mixture of blood and dirt. He worked to process them into a coherent series of events, but there were holes in his memory. Film stock with missing frames.

Ralbovsky flipped back through his notebook. "Let me get this straight. These men started harassing you, and then your boyfriend went after one of them, and the guy pulls a gun?"

He'd clearly misunderstood Vincent. He was making it sound like James had been the aggressor. "They threatened us. Harassed us. Called us faggots. The guy had a crowbar."

"The stocky guy?"

"Yeah." Vincent spotted a stray thread on the blanket that was folded down to his waist. He twirled it around his finger. There was still dirt under his fingernails.

"Do you remember anything else about what he looked like?" Tillman asked.

He waded through the disjointed memories again, reliving each moment he came across like it had just happened. He knew he was as safe as he could be in a hospital room with two detectives beside him, but he couldn't stop his hands from shaking and heart from racing. He continued to wrap the thread around his finger. "Nothing more than what I already told you. It was dark out, and everything happened so fast."

The sound of pages being turned filled the room before Ralbovsky said, "And you're sure about the tattoo on the taller guy?"

"Yeah, numbers on the side of his head. Couldn't make out what they were."

Silence.

Ralbovsky looked unconvinced. "You're positive about this?"

He wasn't sure why it was so hard to believe. "I am."

"The reason I ask is because the young couple who came across you two. The ones who called the police. They gave us similar descriptions, but they didn't remember seeing the tattoo."

"Maybe they didn't get a good look at him."

"Like you said. It was dark out."

The skin bulging through the thread on his finger had turned red.

"We just want to make sure we have everything straight." Tillman shot a dirty look at her partner. "What were you and James wearing?"

Vincent resisted the urge to ask what that had to do with anything. "Just some sweats."

"Any Pitt merchandise?"

"What?"

"Any hats or shirts with the school's logo?"

"I think I had on a Pitt hoodie. Why?"

"There have been gang initiations in the past that

involve jumping local college students. From what you described of the young attacker, I wonder if that might be one of the reasons why they singled you out as targets."

What little of his finger wasn't wrapped in thread had turned purple. The three men seemed to have one very specific reason for attacking them, and as fragmented as his memories were, that much was obvious. "They never mentioned anything about Pitt."

His expression must have given some indication of his thoughts on her theory because Tillman quickly added, "I don't mean to imply that we know why they did this. We are just trying to consider the whole picture."

From the mocking kissing sounds to the endless string of slurs, why these assholes had attacked them didn't seem like that big of a mystery. He tried to breathe through his anger and remind himself the detectives were on his side, but this felt more like an interrogation than an interview.

"I understand how hard this is for you. We just have a few more questions." Ralbovsky spoke in the same practiced manner as he had before. An automated detective.

"Now, you said that James carried you up the hill after he was shot," Tillman said like he hadn't just explained it to them a few minutes ago.

"I put mud on the wound to try to stop the bleeding, and the next thing I knew, he was carrying me up the hill." Vincent didn't know what else they wanted.

Tillman exchanged a look with Ralbovsky. "And you're sure about this."

His finger had turned an eggplant purple around the

thread. He twisted it once more, and it broke, unraveling on the bed. "Why would I tell you if I wasn't?"

Ralbovsky shut his notepad. "Well, for starters, your boyfriend wasn't found on the trail."

There it was. The answer to a question he'd forgotten to ask. The gaps in his memory. "I mean, I was kind of out of it by that point. I don't know where they found us."

"Which is why I thought everything might not be lining up." Tillman seemed to be talking more to her partner than Vincent.

They were keeping something from him. "What are you talking about?"

Tillman started to say something, but Ralbovsky spoke over her. "He wasn't covered in mud, and from what we could tell, he hadn't been moved after he fell. You, on the other hand, were found on the trail."

That didn't make any sense. He remembered doing it. Felt the cold earth. Heard his heartbeat. Who else could have carried him up the hill? "That can't be right."

Ralbovsky ignored whatever Tillman was trying to communicate in her darted glances. "Well, as you said, you were out of it by that point."

Vincent tossed the thread to the ground. "Maybe he fell after he got me to the trail, and the rain washed away the dirt. I mean, does that really matter?"

Unlike the rest of this conversation, there was a clear answer to his question. Of course, it mattered. They were treating him like a criminal; like he was hiding something when he was just trying to figure out what the fuck had happened that night.

He waited for them to say something that would show him he was being irrational and they were on his side, but Ralbovsky's only response was "Maybe."

Vincent wanted to be mad, but the crushing realization that even they were against him took all the fight out of him. He answered their remaining questions and flipped through the binder of headshots they had compiled based on the descriptions the couple had given them. A sea of white faces that made him even less certain about the few characteristics he thought he'd remembered about their attackers.

Tillman took back the binder when he finished. "There are plenty more where that came from. We can pull some more based on the descriptions you gave us."

"Do you remember anything else about their faces?" Ralbovsky said. "Like did one of them have a big nose or small ears or a unibrow or anything that might help us narrow down the search?"

Vincent searched the linoleum for the stray thread. It had disappeared somewhere in the comparatively vast white floor. "No."

"Look, you don't have to worry about anyone coming after you. We can—"

"I don't remember."

"Sometimes, when people experience trauma, things can get a little fuzzy for a while. But if anything comes back to you, don't hesitate to contact us." Tillman set a card on the overbed table. "One of us will answer your call at this number, day or night."

As soon as they were gone, Vincent expected tears to come, but he didn't feel anything. He'd left that discussion with more questions than answers, and while he kept waiting for his memories with James in the woods to unravel and reveal themselves to be part of a nightmare, they felt real. He remembered them with far more clarity than virtually anything else that had happened that night, which was only more troubling.

CHAPTER FIVE

BEHIND THE CURTAIN

VINCENT HAD WANTED some time alone to think since the attack, and now he had it, he wished for a distraction. Sam and Henry wouldn't be back until the following morning, and after a dinner consisting of baked chicken, steamed rice, and green beans that he did little more than push around his plate, he had the whole night ahead of him to mull over his discussion with the detectives.

Not that there was much to it. Nothing was adding up, and he'd reached a point where he didn't think there was anyone else left who could answer his questions. The idea made it hard to breathe—to think he'd never know what had really happened in those woods. That James would just disappear from his life. There and gone in a blink of an eye.

It wasn't long before he called for his nurse to hand him the remote for the mounted TV beside the door. He flipped through the channels, searching for anything to pull his focus. Every show seemed so grossly detached from his reality it only made him feel worse. Plastic women screaming at each other in lavish mansions. Eager people answering trivia questions for more money than they probably made in a year. Hour-long dramas and half-hour comedies where order is restored and a lesson is learned in the confines of an episode.

All that was left was the local news, and the possibility that he might run across a story covering their attack compelled him to turn it off. The ensuing silence was even more unbearable. He looked around his room for something else to occupy his time. Sam's bag was on the chair closest to him. He couldn't reach it, but she had already shown him what was inside. A set of clothes to change into after he got his restraints off. A few schoolbooks in case he wanted to catch up on classes. His laptop. They all seemed to belong to someone from a separate life.

Vincent lay there, trying to breathe and think about a happy memory and all the other shit James used to tell him when he talked him down from panic attacks. Nothing worked. All his questions tugged at his mind like a child on a parent's pant leg. He tried to get in a comfortable position to fall asleep, but between his ribs and the restraints, it was a fruitless effort. He was too restless to sleep anyway.

A distraction wasn't enough. He needed something stronger. Something to bring him as close as he could get to oblivion without dying. A couple of blunts or a bottle of vodka would do the trick, but they weren't exactly easy to obtain when shackled to a hospital bed. It didn't mean, however, that the hospital didn't have its own perks.

He called for the nurse, and when she showed up, he explained, "I'm in a lot of pain, and I can't get comfortable."

He resisted the urge to actively wince, which was probably a wise choice because his night nurse, an older, no-nonsense woman, didn't look convinced. "On a scale of one to ten, how would you rate your pain?"

He stopped himself from going right to ten. Or nine. "Eight."

Her expression didn't change. "Okay, I'll have your doctor order something in for your pain."

The nurse returned half an hour later. Three syringes like before. When she finished, he asked her to draw the curtains around his bed; then he was floating again. The volume of his mind had been turned down to a faint whisper. The relief was so intoxicating that going to sleep seemed like an utter waste.

He looked around him at the pea-green curtains and the halo of light pouring in from the gap between the bottom of the curtains and the floor. How beautiful—the way it glowed. He could almost feel the warmth radiating off it as if it were sunlight. Even when he shut his eyes to rest them, he pictured it in his mind.

THE WARMTH HAD dwindled when he woke up. He yawned and went to check the time, but the clock on the wall was obscured by the curtain around his bed. The light leaking under the bottom of the curtain was little help. The hall lights remained on day and night. He searched the gap between the curtain and floor for the warmth he'd found there when he'd been pumped full of pain medicine.

What he found was a piece missing from the ring of light at the bottom of his bed. Something blocked out the light from the hall. He blinked away the fog of sleep and focused his eyes. There was a pair of boots caked in mud. The sight was so strange he just stared at them for a moment before they moved, and their significance registered.

Someone was standing at the bottom of his bed.

Someone with muddy boots who wasn't making himself known.

Oh God.

Their attackers.

One of them had found him. Tracked him down to finish the job the group had started in Panther Hollow. The boots moved around the bed toward him. Flakes of dirt littered the white linoleum in their wake. The curtain moved, hands searching for an opening.

He had to run. Jump out the other side of the bed and get help, his pain be damned. He went to sit up in bed, but the restraints pulled him back down. Fuck. His wrists were still cuffed to the guardrails on either side of his bed. He was trapped, his life in the hands of someone who'd already tried to kill him, and this time, he was alone and truly defenseless.

His heart beat so fast he was sure it'd explode at any second. He squirmed, trying to slip out of his restraints in spite of the knowledge that they wouldn't break. He had to do something to prevent his inevitable demise. The curtain jumped as the intruder hunted for the opening. Tears filled his eyes. Vincent jerked his arms back as hard as he could in the hope of snapping the restraints, but all it did was make the guardrails shake and clatter against the bed.

The fabric went still, and the boots stopped in their tracks. Vincent froze. The intruder's heavy breaths filled the silence. What was he waiting for? Did he think Vincent was asleep or something? If so, Vincent wasn't sure why that mattered. Awake or asleep, he was helpless, and the intruder could kill him long before someone could get to his room to help him.

Vincent sank back in the bed. Maybe it was for the best. To end his torment. If James was really gone, he wouldn't survive this anyway. His death would be the more humane thing to do. Like putting down a suffering family pet.

The only problem was that whoever was on the other side of the curtain wasn't compelled by humanitarian intentions. His death wouldn't be a quick or painless end, especially after he'd had the audacity to survive their first attack. The intruder would make him suffer. Torture him until he could only hope for the relief of death.

No.

He needed to do something and do it quickly. The man resumed his search, pushing into the fabric in a more hurried, frantic manner. He'd find the opening any second. Running wasn't an option. Neither was fighting. Vincent could scream for help, but that could make the intruder end his life long before anyone reached him. After all, it took less than a second to pull a trigger.

An idea hit him then. The call button. He could press it, and his nurse could be on her way before the intruder realized he was calling for help. The last time he had seen it, the remote was wrapped around his guardrail, but now it was nowhere to be found. Gone. Just fucking gone. He must have knocked it off the bed in his sleep.

The curtain grazed against his arm, and he stifled a scream. Only then, mouth clamped shut, did the pieces fall into place. Drawing attention to himself might make the intruder kill him faster, but the intruder didn't want to make a scene. Why else would he search so quietly for the opening and stop when he thought he'd woken Vincent?

They weren't in a secluded park at night. They were in a hospital full of patients, workers, and security guards around the clock. A gunshot would draw attention. The intruder probably planned on killing him in his sleep and sneaking away before anyone noticed he was dead.

But Vincent wasn't going out quietly.

He took in a deep breath and squeezed the plastic railings to fight the pain that erupted in his chest from filling his lungs with air. And then he screamed—a broken, guttural scream that filled the room. Hands pushed through the curtain, searching for his neck to strangle him. He wildly thrashed his body and continued to scream despite the pain and fear and hands demanding his stillness and silence.

The next thing he knew, the curtains were ripped back with a metallic screech and light flooded his bed. Someone was screaming at him. A feminine voice. Vincent stopped fighting and focused on the figure who stood over him. Not one of his attackers, but his nurse. "You have to calm down and tell me what's wrong if you want me to help you!"

"He—was—trying—to kill me," he said between breaths.

Her wrinkled face didn't fill with shock or horror. It softened. "You must have had a nightmare."

"No, this was real. I swear." He searched the room to no avail.

"Talk to me. What do you think happened?" If her raised eyebrow wasn't enough to ensure him she didn't believe a word he said, the way she phrased her question confirmed it.

He probably sounded insane, but he didn't care. He hadn't imagined or dreamed it. This was real. He was positive. His intruder must have run from the room before his nurse got there. "He was trying to kill me."

"Who was trying to kill you?" She spoke in such an exasperated manner Vincent might as well have told her the sky was falling.

Doubt stabbed at him, but he scoured the room for any evidence of the attack. The intruder couldn't have escaped without a trace. He spotted a trail of dirt running from his bed to the hall, and despite the knowledge that his attackers had found him and intended to kill him, he took solace in this confirmation of his sanity.

He pointed to the dirt. "Whoever left that."

VINCENT WAS SO used to being questioned and dismissed that, even staring right at the proof of his intruder's presence, he was surprised they believed him. His nurse remained by his side until security arrived. He must not have hidden the pain that riddled his body too well because she asked if he needed anything for it. He did, but he told her he was fine. If he'd been out of it when the intruder arrived, then he'd be dead. He had to keep his wits about him.

After he talked to the security guards, the police were called, and within another hour, Ralbovsky—eyes puffy, hair askew, shirt untucked—and Tillman—looking as clean and professional at four in the morning as she had the previous afternoon—were at his bedside.

Ralbovsky didn't take notes. His hands were wrapped around a thermos. "So, the guy just slowly walked around your bed?"

"Like I said, I think he must have assumed I was asleep. As soon as I screamed, he tried to strangle me." Vincent made an effort to keep his voice level, even after Ralbovsky refocused his attention on his coffee midway through his answer. He should have known clear proof would do little to convince that idiot of anything he said.

Tillman took the reins. "How do you know he was a man? Did he say anything?"

"He was breathing heavily. And they were all male. In the park." This wasn't exactly rocket science.

Ralbovsky tipped the thermos back, and coffee ran down his chin and onto his shirt. "Ah, shit."

He went to the bathroom and didn't shut the door in his rush. He pulled a handful of paper towels from the dispenser, ran them under the tap, and scrubbed his shirt, swearing under his breath.

"Anyway," Tillman said, "what makes you think it was one of them?"

The more questions she asked, the more Vincent wondered if she and Ralbovsky were a perfect match for each other. "I don't know anyone else who wants to kill me."

"But you didn't see or hear anything in particular that made you think it was one of them?"

"The boots," Vincent said, a little louder to ensure that Ralbovsky heard him as he walked back over to his chair. "The trail was muddy that night."

Ralbovsky plopped down beside Tillman. "Did the boots look the same as one of theirs?"

"I don't know, but they were covered in dried dirt." The shit was all over his room, and his nurse, the security guard, and the detectives had trudged through it. He expected a forensic team to try to lift a shoe print or something off it, but apparently, this didn't warrant such care.

"It's been jumping between rain and snow the last few days. Everything is a little muddy by this point."

"And the attack happened a week ago," Tillman said. Vincent's expression must have somehow conveyed his sentiment of "so what?" because she added, "The mud on their shoes has probably been cleaned or fallen off by this point."

Ralbovsky got to his feet. "Think about it. In the

meantime, we are going to go talk to some workers and check the security footage, and we'll be back to talk to you soon."

Tillman said something else to him before they left, but Vincent wasn't listening. *The security cameras.* They would have caught the intruder coming into his room. How could the detectives dismiss what was so clearly an attack after they saw the footage of it happening? They'd probably come back with their tails between their legs, cursing that they didn't get someone to examine the dirt before everyone, themselves included, ruined the evidence.

They returned far sooner than he expected. Within half an hour, the pair sat beside his bed, Ralbovsky clutching a few sheets of paper. Tillman explained that the person who they believed came into his room nearly knocked over a phlebotomist and her cart down the hall when he fled.

"She didn't get a good look at him, but she said he seemed disoriented and confused," Tillman said.

Vincent supposed anyone who ran into someone would seem disoriented, but he kept that to himself. "What about the security cameras?"

Ralbovsky flipped through the pages in his hand. "With her description, we believe we have footage of the guy entering and exiting the hospital. But he doesn't fit any of the descriptions of your attackers."

Before Vincent had the chance to ask for the photos, Ralbovsky laid them down across his lap. The blurry black-and-white photos showed a man with a hoodie on that made his face impossible to see at the angle of the camera. He was too thin to be the stocky man, too short to be the tall man, and too solid to be the kid. They were right; he didn't fit the descriptions of any of the assholes who'd landed him in the hospital.

That didn't mean, however, that they didn't have another friend who shared their views on gay men. Maybe they hired him to finish the job, knowing that, whether they succeeded or not, they risked being identified.

Looking at the photograph, Vincent couldn't shake the feeling that the figure looked familiar. Like he knew those broad shoulders, those toned arms, those long legs. It was only a feeling, and one he knew would make him sound insane if he vocalized it, but it colored the events of the night in a far more sinister light.

"Given your description of the events as well as those of the workers who came across him, we think it may have been a troubled or unstable individual who you were unlucky enough to come across," Tillman said.

Ralbovsky collected the photographs. "Maybe a former patient or someone who was looking for a loved one."

Vincent couldn't believe they had somehow managed to explain this one away. "Doesn't that seem like an awfully large coincidence?"

"Just as a precaution, we will have a security guard outside your room to ensure that you don't get any more unwanted visitors," Tillman said. "Feel free to call us if anything else comes up or if you remember more from that night."

They got up and left with a few halfhearted comments

about getting sleep and feeling better. They walked right through the dirt on the floor on their way out, crushing any remaining hope of getting some useful evidence out of it.

Even with the security guard sitting in a chair just outside his room, Vincent was awake for the rest of the night. What little faith he had in the detectives had broken apart into useless pieces like the dirt on the ground that a custodian swept away in the morning. Someone was after him. Someone who was probably connected to the fuckers who had attacked them but also somehow looked familiar. Whoever the intruder was, the night had made one thing crystal clear in Vincent's mind.

He was on his own.

CHAPTER SIX

NOTHING

THE AUTOMATIC GLASS doors opened. The nursing assistant, who'd insisted that he ride down to the lobby in a wheelchair, pushed him outside. A cold wind whipped him in the face. Vincent blinked away the tears blurring his vision and searched for Sam's car. She knew he was getting discharged this morning at nine. They had already discussed it at length the night before, but he didn't see her rusted white Beetle anywhere.

Not that he could be certain in the madness surrounding him. Cars sped by on the street in front of him. People walked past him on the sidewalk. Patients and employees funneled in and out of the entrance. He dug his fingers into the arms of the wheelchair and tried to focus. Tried not to think about how easy it would be for his attackers to finish the job if they were somewhere on the street.

For the past week, he only had to keep an eye on a single door to ensure his safety, and he had plenty of company to help him keep watch—nurses, a psychiatrist, a police sketch artist who created three of the most generic portraits of their attackers, Henry after he finished up at the factory for the day, and Sam between classes. Now, he was a sitting duck for anyone who wanted him dead. To make matters worse, the nursing assistant was more focused on her phone, which kept buzzing in her pocket, than a potential threat.

The nursing assistant wheeled him off to the side of the entrance. "Do you see your ride?"

"No." But he saw a man walking down the sidewalk toward them. The man wore a black beanie with a matching pair of headphones. He didn't fit the build of the man on the security footage, but he looked right at Vincent. His eyes were hollow. No pity or annoyance. A glassy stare that Vincent had only seen in photos of psychopaths like Charles Manson and Jeffrey Dahmer.

Vincent might have made a run for it if his legs didn't feel so weak or an outburst wasn't sure to get him put right back in the hospital. His body tensed as the man drew near, in anticipation of a blade or a bullet, knowing full well that nothing he could do would prevent the man from killing him. But the man continued past him, an old Metallica song blaring in his ears. Vincent waited for him to turn around and attack, but he continued down the street.

Just a guy. Vincent needed to relax. Then again, he could be a lookout. To make sure it was Vincent before a car pulled up to the entrance and riddled his body with bullets. Sam needed to hurry the fuck up. When he last spotted a clock on the wall in the lobby, it was ten after nine, so she should've already been waiting for him outside.

"Do you want to, like, call them?" the nursing assistant asked.

Vincent would have loved to call Sam, but his phone was still in his car, and, as far as he knew, the police had his keys. Sam had a spare for his apartment, and he had another key for his car in his dresser, so it wasn't a huge loss, but it meant that he couldn't get hold of her now. Even if he used a hospital phone, he hadn't memorized anyone's phone numbers since he got a cell phone with a contact list.

"She'll be here," he said, almost as much to reassure himself as the nursing assistant.

Minutes passed. Another man walked by him. A truck with a group of men in it slowed near the entrance before picking up speed again. Sweat dripped from his forehead despite the chilly morning air. He couldn't stop himself from seeing every person on the street as a potential threat; from thinking that at any moment, he would be murdered at the hands of the motherfuckers who left him in this broken body.

Beep!

The car horn was so loud and close that he screamed. He followed the sound to find Sam's Beetle parked on the curb to the left of the entrance. Her eager smile fell at the sight of him—he must not have masked his fear as well as he thought.

The nursing assistant knelt beside him. "You okay?"

"Yeah. That's my ride. Thanks." He tried to laugh to show her how silly it was for him to scream, but it sounded more like a strained cough that reminded him his ribs were far from healed.

The nursing assistant wheeled him over to the car. Sam reached across the center console and opened the passenger's side door. "I can help if you need it."

"I'm fine." His legs felt like rubber, but the prospect of getting off this damn street was enough motivation to force himself to step into the car with the nursing assistant's guidance.

After she set his bag at his feet, she said, "Watch your fingers," and slammed the door shut. She had her phone in her hands within seconds, to answer whoever had texted her.

Sam let off the brake, and they rolled down the street. He glanced at the entrance as if to say goodbye to his time at UPMC. Just within the doors, he spotted him. The man wore the same hoodie and jeans as he had in the security cameras. Only now his face was clear. No wonder his body looked so familiar. He wasn't an acquaintance of their attackers or a random, disoriented man.

He was James.

VINCENT COULDN'T BELIEVE his eyes. "Sam. Wait. Do

you see that?"

She slammed on the brakes. "See what?"

He turned to her. Trying to steady his voice, he said, "In the lobby."

He waited for her face to light up with the realization that James was alive, but her eyes narrowed in confusion. "The nurse?"

Vincent looked back at the entrance. Other than the nursing assistant dragging the wheelchair back inside, it was empty. He looked around them in case James had hurried outside, but he didn't see him anywhere.

His stomach dropped.

He could have sworn he saw him.

Not a trick of the light or a blurred image in passing.

James.

"What's wrong?" Sam placed a hand on his shoulder.

The words were on the tip of his tongue. But he would sound insane if he vocalized them. He shook her hand off. "Nothing."

"Doesn't sound like nothing."

Vincent stared at the empty entrance. It had to be nothing. Because why would James sneak around his bed the way the intruder had that night? Why wouldn't he make himself known? It didn't add up. "Honestly, it's nothing."

He must have been mistaken. Seen what he wanted to see. That, of course, raised the question of what he saw in the first place. Had he truly gone insane and imagined

James, or had he seen someone else? Someone who the security cameras had caught last week and had planned to finish the job before Sam showed up. Someone who Vincent had mistakenly identified as James.

Whatever had happened, he wanted to get far away from UPMC. An SUV had stopped behind them, and its tinted windows gave no hint to who was inside. "We better get going."

Sam pulled over to the side of the road. "Just talk to me."

He focused on the SUV in the side mirror. It didn't go around her. His heart pounded in his chest. Someone could open a door and pull out a gun and end both of their lives. "We can talk later. Let's just go."

"What are you thinking about?"

Vincent was ready to scream. "The only thing I am thinking about is how I was sitting outside for twenty minutes—during which time anyone could have attacked or killed me or done anything they wanted to me. You were supposed to be there at nine, and you weren't. So, can we please just fucking go?"

Sam recoiled and started down the road. Only after the SUV turned off on another street could Vincent breathe again and realize tears were running down Sam's face. "Shit. I didn't—"

"No, you're right. I told you I would be there, and I wasn't." She wiped the tears from her face. "I've just been so overwhelmed with everything lately. I was up all last night studying for this test, and I slept right through my alarm.

And it's just a lot to deal with, you know?"

"I know," Vincent snapped. Something about the way she said it—like she was trying to make him understand what a terrible loss she'd experienced and what a chore it was to deal with him—filled him with rage. He knew what Sam was going through far better than she realized. James might have been her best friend, but he was Vincent's everything.

"I know you do. I wasn't trying to say you didn't." She took a breath. "It's just... Well, I lost him too."

Vincent stared out the window at the gray February morning. He should apologize. She'd gone above and beyond for him this week. Before the attack, they had barely talked if James wasn't there to mediate the conversation. Now, she spent nearly every waking hour that wasn't consumed by schoolwork helping him out. And how did he repay her for all she'd sacrificed for him?

Therein lay the problem. He couldn't repay her. She wasn't a family member or close friend who he could lean on with the mutual understanding that he would be there in a second to return the favor. She was James's best friend, and she was only there out of some sense of duty to him. What made it all worse was that Vincent accepted it because he needed it, and he had no one else.

IN SILENCE, THEY drove the rest of the way to the duplex they shared. The old Victorian house had probably been built by some well-to-do family when the steel industry was booming. At some point, the first and second floors had been separated into two apartments, and now it served as an example of what happened to beautiful things when people neglected them. Vincent and James had the top apartment, and Sam and Tyler shared the bottom. Vincent would've moved into a shack so long as he was with James but, staring at the place after he'd been away from it for so long, it was a depressing sight to behold.

Sam parked in front of the house behind Tyler's, or, more accurately, his father's, white Mustang. She offered to help Vincent up the front porch steps, but he told her he could manage. He needed to start doing things for himself.

When he finally reached the front door, Sam unlocked the door and held it open for him. "Do you want to hang out for a bit?"

"That's okay. I might just lay down. I'm exhausted." It wasn't a complete lie. The morning had drained what little energy he had. More than anything, he just wanted to be alone for a little while.

"Let me just grab your key, then." Her apartment door was inside to the right. Sam went about unlocking it. "I don't know why Tyler feels the need to turn every possible lock on this damn door."

Straight ahead was another set of stairs leading up to his and James's apartment. There seemed to be more stairs than he remembered. He started counting them until Sam got the door unlocked.

"I'm home," she called into the apartment. She searched through the key rack just within the door. "I know it's in here somewhere. I just used it the other day to get your stuff."

Tyler hurried over to them from the kitchen, the bun of hair on top of his head bouncing from the movement. He was dressed in a shirt and jeans that both looked intentionally distressed. In one hand, he held a paper plate over his head, which prevented Vincent from seeing what was on it. "Who wants tacos?"

Sam glanced back at him. "What?"

"It's Taco Tuesday, my lady." He kissed her on the cheek.

Sam didn't try to hide her confusion. "Babe, it's not even ten o'clock."

"There's never a bad time for tacos, and you need to get something in your belly." He brought the plate down to eye level. It looked more like a science fair project gone wrong than a meal. Red and white sauces covered a cluster of taco shells stuffed with ground meat that had a pink hue to it.

"About that spare key..." Vincent had trouble stomaching Tyler at the best of times, and these were not the best of times.

Sam went back to looking for it.

"No worries, man. There are plenty of tacos to go around." Tyler moved the plate toward him.

The smell made him nauseated. "That looks so good, but I think I'm going to have to pass for now."

"Your loss, man."

"Here you go." Sam pulled out the key and handed it to

him. She turned around to look at Tyler. Whatever face she made or words she mouthed made the smile on Tyler's face fall.

"By the way," Tyler said. "Sorry about what happened. That really blows."

"It really fucking does, doesn't it?"

Vincent turned around and headed for the stairs. The door shut, but he heard Tyler say, "Ow, what was that for?" before Sam said something else in a hushed voice. Vincent didn't know what Sam saw in him.

He was so busy wondering how clueless someone would have to be to say a murder "blows" that he was at the top of the stairs before he knew it. His annoyance with Tyler dissipated when he reached the door. He had been in the hospital for so long it seemed like a separate existence that was detached from his real life, but once he stepped back inside, he would be returning to his old life. One without James.

Vincent might have taken up Sam's offer to hang out in her apartment if the car ride hadn't been so awkward and Tyler so insufferable. He unlocked the door. Forced himself to go inside. The apartment was freezing. He shut the door behind him, set his bag down, and went down the hall. Passing the kitchen on his left, he continued into the living room.

The window that went out to the fire escape was open. James must have cracked it before he'd met Vincent for the jog. The radiators often made the apartment unbearably stuffy in the winter. He was surprised Sam hadn't shut it when she came to grab his things, but she might not have noticed. He took out the wooden block that held the old window open and guided it shut before he locked it.

He went to their bedroom that was just off the living room. Their clothes were strewn all over the floor. James was a slob when he was in a hurry. Vincent could practically track his movements before their jog from where everything fell on the floor. His lab coat and dress clothes were in a pile at the door where he must have stripped down to his underwear. Then, a few clothes from their closet covered the carpet, marking where he started the search. He must have finished at their dressers. There was a massive pile of both of their clothes on the ground in front of them.

A lump formed in Vincent's throat that made it hard to swallow. He was the one who had made James go on a jog with him. The one who had shown up late and still insisted that they try to get in a few miles despite James's protest. The one who had frozen in the tunnel. All of it was his fault. He couldn't believe James was dead, because if James was really gone, then he was to blame.

Vincent wanted to curl up in a ball on the floor and die, but he couldn't. James was everywhere in this apartment. He could smell his musky cologne coming off the dirty clothes on the floor and see him lying in bed and studying at his desk.

Something between a scream and a sob escaped Vincent's mouth. He couldn't breathe. He needed to get out of there. His destination didn't matter; he just couldn't be in this apartment any longer.

He dug his spare car key from his dresser, grabbed his knife, tossed it in his bag with a few other belongings, and hurried out of the apartment. He hadn't reached the bottom of the stairs before Sam and Tyler's door swung open. Sam poked her head into the hall. "What's wrong?"

Vincent wiped away his tears on the cuff of his shirt. "Nothing. I just need to get out of here."

"You need to rest." She came into the hall, blocking the front door.

"I can't be here right now. I can't see all his shit and—" Vincent stopped himself before he completely broke down. "Please just get out of my way."

"How about you come inside and talk about it?" Sam reached for him, but he took a step back.

Tyler joined them in the hall. "What's going on?"

"Nothing." Vincent charged through them, grateful that they both moved aside for him to pass. He didn't have the strength to barrel through them.

"Where are you going to go?" Sam asked, following behind him.

Vincent pulled open the front door. "Anywhere but here."

Sam grabbed his arm. "What about school? And work?"

"It doesn't matter." He yanked his hand free, wincing at the pain that filled his ribs.

Sam stumbled back.

Tyler hurried over to him, chest puffed up like a rooster. "Hey, man, take it easy."

"Fuck off." Vincent slammed the front door behind him and started down the porch steps.

The door swung back open. Sam said, "Ignore him. Just

come talk to me. This is a lot, but we can get through it together."

Vincent didn't want to get through anything without
James. He couldn't. He continued down the steps, going as
fast as he could in his condition.

Sam still managed to pass him. She turned around at
the bottom of the stairs and threw her arms up to stop him
from getting around her. "I refuse to let you go off and do
something stupid. He's gone, but you are still alive, and
there's nothing you can do to change that."

Vincent didn't have any fight left in him. All that remained was the truth. "If he's really gone and those fuckers
are still after me, then I am as good as dead."

"Please stay," Sam said, but she let him go and didn't
follow.

Vincent didn't know how he made it to his car, which
was nearly a mile and a half away, but the next thing he
knew, he stood in front of the driver's side door. James's
empty car was still in front of him. He got in and started the
engine. He didn't know where he'd go, but that didn't matter. Nothing did, beyond getting the hell out of there.

CHAPTER SEVEN

GLASS TOMB

VINCENT PUT OAKLAND in his rearview mirror. He continued down Route 8 after that, to further distance himself from the city. A fog had settled over his mind, and while he reacted to traffic lights and signs, he had trouble focusing his thoughts. Only when he saw the sign welcoming him to Butler, "A Great Place To Live," did he realize where he'd taken himself. He drove to Elm Street and parked in front of the one-story house he had called home for the first eighteen years of his life.

Henry's truck was gone. He'd probably left for work a couple of hours ago. Good. Vincent couldn't deal with Henry right now. He just needed to rest. He took the spare key from under a fake rock in the front yard and made a beeline to his bedroom. He locked the door and lay down in bed. The comforter reeked of dust, but it was soft, and before he knew it, he drifted to sleep.

He awoke to the beating of a drum. No. Not a drum. Knocking. Fist on wood. Henry demanded that he unlock the door. Vincent didn't see much of a point in doing so. There was nothing Henry could tell him to change what he did and didn't do and everything that led to James's death.

The popcorn ceiling above his bed had turned to gold in the setting sun. How many hours of his life had he spent staring at those damn plaster hills and valleys? As a child, he'd looked for shapes and characters in the haphazard design. When he got older, he came to resent it. He saw it every morning and every night. Day in and day out for so long that the sight bookended every day of his monotonous life. Sometimes, it'd brought tears to his eyes. Knowing he'd have to get up the next day and face it.

Then, he went to college and met James, and for the first time in a long time, the ceiling didn't matter. What mattered was who was in his bed, holding him. Loving him. He didn't need to dread the next day because James was there alongside him to face whatever life threw at them. The details melted in the warmth of his love.

But here Vincent was again—watcher of the ceiling. Each line and crack in the plaster painfully clear. More knocking. Henry's voice rose to a roar. He'd break the fucking door down if Vincent didn't open it. He wasn't joking. He'd do it.

There was a bang, followed by the sound of splintering wood, but it seemed too distant to be his door. Maybe Henry had broken something else in his rage. He was prone to tossing a glass or leaving a fist in the drywall when he worked himself up enough. No, it was his door. Because Henry's heated face eclipsed the ceiling above the bed like a red moon.

"Do you know how fucking worried I was? Why didn't you answer me? Huh? Answer me!" His breath reeked of whiskey.

Even with Henry in his face, sweat dripping and spit flying, he seemed so far away. Vincent felt like he had fallen through the mattress and floor. Past the cellar and deep into the earth in a glass cylinder. Too far down to reach Henry now. So, he watched him through the glass and waited for him to leave so that he could return to his post. It'd be dark soon, and the ceiling would be covered in shadows.

Henry didn't leave. He continued to yell and even shake him—only to explode in rage when Vincent didn't respond. At some point, he left, and there was a crash and a string of curses before silence filled the air.

When the shadows gave way to complete darkness, he saw a flash, and the ceiling returned to its ivory color. Henry had turned on the light. He was back, veins bulging in his red forehead. The smell of whiskey was so sharp that Vincent might as well have sniffed it straight from the bottle. "You gotta get up, Vinny. You hear me? You aren't a kid anymore, and I won't do this again."

Again?

That was right. He'd taken on this role before. He'd kept watch of the ceiling after his mother had passed. So much of that time had become hazy in his memory. He couldn't remember how long he'd remained in bed or what had finally broken the spell. All that was clear was Henry's misguided attempts to scream him back into existence.

Henry lifted him into a seated position. There was pain, but it, too, seemed somewhere on the other side of the glass. Henry swayed back and forth. "You're gonna get up, or I'll, I'll call an ambulance. Have you 302'd. Remember what that is?"

Vincent's mother had been an ER nurse before she got sick. He remembered what getting 302'd meant. Involuntary evaluation and treatment to a psychiatric unit. A first-class trip to the funny farm. Or, more accurately, a bluff slurred from a drunk man. A part of him wondered if he needed it. If they could fix whatever had come loose in his mind after he learned what became of James.

"Fine. Have it your way, then." Henry let go of him, and he fell back on the bed. He felt the pain that time. Like someone had knocked the wind out of him. He coughed as tears filled his eyes.

Henry retreated. "Shit—I forgot. I didn't mean to—"

He fell backward, disappearing from Vincent's vision. *Crack.* Like someone hit a baseball out of the park. There was a dresser beside his bed. Henry could have smacked his head on one of the corners.

A hand grazed his arm and sank into the mattress. Henry pulled himself to his feet with a grunt. Vincent couldn't see him. He must have stood up by the headboard, out of Vincent's field of vision. Henry breathed heavily, but he didn't say a word. Something warm hit Vincent's face.

Drip.

Blood?

Drip.

Had Henry's skull met one of those corners?

Drip.

If so, he'd need help.

Drip.

Such an injury could be fatal.

Each time the warm liquid hit his head, he crawled a little farther from his glass tomb. Drawn back to his childhood bedroom to ensure that his inaction didn't result in another death. He just needed to turn his head back and check on Henry. Such a simple action seemed gruelingly difficult now. Like he was moving through quicksand.

He expected a dent in the back of Henry's head or a bloody hole above his ear. What he found was Henry, leaning over his bed, not covered in blood, but in tears. He wiped them dry with the cuff of his flannel. "I'm so sorry."

VINCENT AWOKE TO the sound of water hitting plastic. Thin drywall separated his bedroom from the bathroom. Henry must be in the shower. The morning light gave the ceiling a golden hue. His throat was dry, and he needed to piss, but more than anything, he wanted a cup of coffee.

He smelled it brewing in the kitchen. Strong motor oil coffee that he'd been raised on and made him think nearly all other coffee was watered down. It drew his sore body from his bed and down the hall to the kitchen.

All the mugs were still laid out on the counter. They used to be in the cabinet above the coffee pot, but when his mother's condition worsened and she required a wheelchair, Henry had modified the place to ensure everything was in her reach.

He'd made a whole weekend of it. Enlisting a few of his work friends to lend a hand with bribes of pizza and beer. Ramps had been crafted. Shelves had been built. Everything had been made accessible to her. Not that she'd enjoyed the modifications for long. Within a month, they had to move her to a hospice for round-the-clock care. She had passed away three weeks later.

She'd been gone for almost five years, and yet the mugs remained on the counter. They were covered in a layer of dust, and the cabinet above the coffee pot was still empty. Vincent hadn't thought much of it at the time, but he had walked up the ramp on the porch to come inside. And the living room was still arranged in a manner to make sure she could fit her wheelchair around the furniture.

Henry hadn't changed a thing.

Vincent grabbed an old mug shaped like a whale—the tail was bent back to form the handle. He ran it under the tap to rinse out the dust and poured himself a cup of coffee. The whole milk in the fridge had expired, so he drank it black. He'd nearly finished the cup when Henry, face red and shining from his hot shower and dressed for work, walked into the kitchen.

If Henry was surprised to see him, he hid it well. He dumped half the pot in a tall aluminum thermos. "You're up."

Vincent could see the white bottom of his mug through what little coffee he had left. "I am."

"Well, I gotta head out." He came closer, as if to pat Vincent on the back, before he thought better of it. "I'll pick up wings for dinner."

"Sounds good."

Just before he left the room, Henry stopped like he'd forgotten something. "By the way, tub's there if you want to clean up."

VINCENT GOT HENRY'S not-so-subtle hint. He finished another cup of coffee and went to the bathroom to asscss the damage in the mirror above the sink. His curly black hair was greasy and pushed to one side of his head. His skin was waxy and pale except the dark rings around his eyes. His cheeks were deflated like week-old birthday balloons.

The sour smell of his sweaty body hit him the moment he took off his clothes. He hadn't had a proper shower or bath since the attack. Cuts and bruises covered his skin, which hung a little looser than it had two weeks ago.

He looked almost as terrible as he felt. Had it not been for the smell, he probably would have skipped the bath altogether to see how long it would take for his outward appearance to reflect what he was experiencing beneath the surface.

He filled the tub with hot water. Steam rose in thin ribbons. He dipped his hand in, and it came out red from the heat. He got into the tub, wrapped his hands around his knees, and pulled them to his chest. He rested his chin on the tops of his knees. The water felt good on his sore body. He focused on the momentary relief it offered and let his mind wander. When the tub went cold, he filled it up again with hot water.

He had tried to take a bubble bath with James shortly after they moved in together. They never had the chance when they lived in the dorms. However, the tub in their apartment was so small that, no matter which way they tried to stuff themselves into it, one of them was left out of the water. After they had tried enough contortions to give the Olympic gymnastics team a run for their money, James had gotten out of the tub and sat beside him. He'd washed Vincent down with a sponge and rinsed him off.

James was usually so heavy-handed, but not then. He scrubbed Vincent like he was a china doll. Vincent would give anything to feel his gentle touch just one more time. He shut his eyes and lay back in the tub. He tried to picture James kneeling beside the bathtub with a steaming sponge in hand. He could almost feel him rubbing his chest with it in a slow, circular motion. Like James was in the room with him now, working his way down to Vincent's stomach.

Vincent let his fantasy die there. Thinking about it any longer would only devastate him when he had to return to reality, but the sensation didn't disappear. The sponge continued past his belly button. Vincent forced his eyes open.

James stood over him, smiling down at the water.

Vincent followed his gaze, expecting to see his own body submerged in the warm water. But the tub was no longer filled with water. Thick red blood had replaced it. James laughed, his hands covered in two red gloves of blood. Before Vincent could try to make a run for it, James grabbed his hair and dunked him in the blood.

Liquid flooded his nose and mouth. He dug his fingernails into James's hands, but his grip didn't waver. James pulled him back to the surface. Vincent spat the blood out of his mouth and struggled for air. "Please."

"You're not in a bargaining position." It wasn't James; it was the tall man. He'd found him to finish the job. Vincent was forced under again, and when he came up for air, the stocky man stood over him. Then the kid. And then back to James. He didn't let him come up for air this time. James held his head below the surface. He was going to drown him. Vincent fought against the inability to breathe for as long as his sore lungs could bear before he was forced to let the blood consume him.

HE AWOKE WITH a start. Somehow, he was still submerged, but there was no force holding him under. He sat up and hacked up water. Freezing cold water. No blood in sight. The relief was instantaneous, but before he let his guard down, he peered around the room, arms raised over his head to prevent an assailant from grabbing his hair.

The bathroom was empty.

He must have dozed off at some point and slid under the water, and his mind had found a creative way to incorporate it into his dream. It'd felt so real he was almost surprised to find his scalp didn't hurt when he ran his hands through his hair.

He drained the tub and finished washing up in the shower. Whatever clothes he didn't take with him to college were still in his dresser and closet. He put on an old French Club T-shirt and a pair of gym shorts before climbing in bed. He remained there until Henry returned with hot wings, but he didn't dare fall asleep.

DAYS PASSED, AND Vincent grew used to Henry's routine. Coffee in the morning. Some combination of bar food for dinner. Henry drank whiskey after dinner. Sometimes, just a glass or two. Other times, half a bottle. He fell asleep on the couch most nights, his bloated face changing colors in the TV light. Excluding a few minor variations, he stuck strictly to this schedule day in and day out.

Vincent joined him for coffee in the morning. Then, he napped until Henry got home a little after five with dinner. They ate in front of the TV, and Vincent returned to bed before Henry got too drunk. The mundane repetition of it all was comforting. He understood how people like Henry could spend their lives in an empty cycle.

Vincent considered returning to his apartment. He could create his own routine. Preserve all the relics James left behind. Stop time in the apartment so that he never had to live without him. But memories weren't the only thing waiting for him back in Pittsburgh. His attackers were still out there, probably searching for him.

He attempted to put the thought out of his mind. It didn't stop him from waking up drenched in sweat or jumping at any foreign sound, but it did enable him to make it through the day without falling apart. He almost got through dinner one night without thinking about it before the news report started.

The camera zoomed in on a grave-looking anchor who sat behind a news desk. Her hands were folded over a piece of paper in front of her. "The Pittsburgh Police are urging college students to be vigilant after two University of Pittsburgh students were attacked in Schenley Park in what is believed to be a gang initiation that involves targeting local college students. We have—"

Before she finished her sentence, the screen cut to a baseball game. Vincent thought there was some kind of technical error until he saw the remote in Henry's hand. "That's enough of that."

Vincent's chest felt tight. "Can you turn that back on?"

"I gotta check the score."

"It's three to seven. Change it back."

"What good is that going to do you?" Henry set the remote down on the coffee table. He dipped a hot wing in the puddle of ranch dressing on his plate and took a bite out of it.

Clutching his ribs, Vincent leaned over and snatched the remote before Henry had the chance to stop him. He flipped back to the news channel, but they were talking about traffic delays. He tossed the remote back to Henry and went to his room. He couldn't believe what they had said.

Henry must have turned off the channel before they explained what had really happened.

He pulled his phone out of his backpack. Of course, it was dead. He plugged it into the wall, and as soon as it had enough of a charge to turn on, he searched for the story online. He barely typed it in Google when his phone was overwhelmed with alerts. Texts from classmates and casual friends who expressed their sympathies. Emails from Pitt staff and faculty. Missed calls from his work supervisors, Sam, and Henry.

He ignored them and searched for the article. He hadn't missed much of the story. The police were actually going forward with the asinine theory that he and James had been attacked because they were Pitt students. He was ready to toss his phone. But then he remembered that Tillman had given him their contact information.

Vincent dumped his bag out on the floor and sifted through the mess. He found the small white card stuck between two pages of one of his schoolbooks. He copied the number into his phone and called. Each time it rang, he found the tightness in his chest getting worse. Had they listened to a single word he said? Clearly, they hadn't. They'd created a narrative and forced what had happened to him and James into it.

The call went to an automated voice mail. His blood was boiling. "Targeting Pitt students, are you fucking kidding me? Where the hell—"

"Vincent, is that you?" Tillman's voice filled his ear.

He was ready to scream. "Yes."

"What's going on? Are you okay?"

"I saw the news report. Pitt students. Really?" It was all he could say without exploding on her.

"As we discussed, we don't know their exact motive, so we are ensuring everyone's safety in the meantime."

Ralbovsky said something in the background that he couldn't make out. Tillman shushed him and said, "Is there anything else we can do for you?"

Vincent hung up. There was nothing they could do for him. Not when they treated him like a lunatic and dismissed anything that didn't fit the story they wanted to tell. He remembered why those fuckers had attacked them. He remembered covering James in dirt. He remembered James carrying him to the trail. He remembered how that person in his hospital room had wanted to strangle him, and he remembered seeing the man in the lobby.

He needed answers. The unknown would peck away at his mind until he went completely insane or ended up like Henry, trapped in a shrine of a past that could never be reclaimed. He couldn't depend on the police to help him, so he'd have to find his own answers. Everything seemed to go back to the night of the attack, but the only other person who knew what had happened was James. And Vincent's last memories of James didn't align with what the police told him.

He'd seen how Ralbovsky and Tillman distorted the motives of their attackers. They could've been just as inconsistent regarding how they had found him and James. Vincent didn't know why they'd lie, but they weren't being forthcoming with what they knew, which made him wonder what else they could have tailored to fit their story. The only problem was, besides the police, no one else had seen James that night.

Except whoever had identified his body.

CHAPTER EIGHT

A BAD IDEA

VINCENT CALLED SAM immediately. Only after she answered the phone and silence filled his ear did he think about how he'd left things with her when he fled from Pittsburgh nearly a week ago. He didn't know what she'd said in all those unanswered voice mails. Was she angry? Sad? Maybe she didn't want anything to do with him anymore. While any and all of those reactions were justified, each seemed to warrant a different approach to this conversation.

Fearing she might hang up on him if the silence continued much longer, he settled for "Sam, you there?"

"Yep." She wasn't giving him anything.

"I'm sorry. I feel like I'm always apologizing to you, and I'm sorry about that too. I've been a mess. I'm staying at Henry's," he rambled.

"I know. I called him when you ran off."

Of course, she had. He wondered how much she and Henry had talked about him. He knew they cared about him, but he couldn't help feeling embarrassed that they treated him like he needed to be cared for around the clock. Then again, maybe that was because he had since he'd woken up in the hospital. "How've you been?"

He wasn't sure if she had intentionally sighed loud enough for him to hear her or if her breath had just caught the microphone. After another moment of silence, she said, "Fine. Busy with school. What's up?"

Figuring out how to ask her what he needed to know was yet another thing he had failed to consider before calling her. "I, ah, have a question to ask you."

"Yeah?"

"Did you see him? After what happened?"

More silence.

"Come on! Are you blind?" Henry's screams about whatever game he was watching in the living room traveled down the hall.

Vincent shut his door and sat down in bed. "You there?"

"I didn't see him. His parents had a closed casket. The last time I saw him was the morning before it happened. I was in a rush to get to class. Barely said 'hi' and 'bye' before I ran out the door. Don't even remember what he was wearing."

Questions swarmed his mind. James's parents had a closed casket? That didn't make any sense. He'd seen enough episodes of *Six Feet Under* to know that morticians could work magic with all sorts of injuries, and James's parents didn't seem like the type to invite the questions a closed casket warranted, especially when they had plenty of money to throw at such a problem.

James's parents must have been the ones who identified the body because Sam hadn't seen him since—it hit him then. Not just the information about James, but what she'd said about the last time she'd seen him. He thought back to the pile of clothes in the doorway of their bedroom. "He had on that dark-blue dress shirt with a gray tie and matching pants. The ones that let everyone know he had a nice ass. Not that you could see it through his lab coat."

Sam laughed. "His ass did look nice in those pants."

"Right? I was ready to steal them myself." Vincent let out a laugh that was cut short by the sharp pain in his ribs.

"You okay?" Her voice was tinged with concern.

"Yeah." The pain sobered him. Reminded him there was a task at hand. "You wouldn't happen to know his parents' address?"

"I do. Why?"

Her reservation was justified. James's parents might be fine with turning a blind eye to their son's sexuality, so long as he took Sam to their annual Christmas party, but they had drawn the line at a boyfriend. Vincent had never met them, and he'd never intended to until now. "I just want to talk to them."

"You want to call them? I have their number," she offered, her words stilted.

Vincent knew they'd never answer his questions over the phone. They might not in person, but he was hoping the social niceties that governed much of James's youth would force them to talk to him. "I want to see them in person."

"I have Greta's number. If you—" Sam went quiet.

Vincent checked his phone. The call hadn't disconnected. "Sam? You there?"

"Sorry. I thought I heard something. Anyway, I have Greta's number if you want to talk to her?"

Greta was James's nanny and the family's maid, and as far as Vincent knew, she was the one who'd raised him outside of mandatory family dinners and other social events. He'd much rather talk to her. From what James had told him, she seemed like a lovely woman. That being said, he seriously doubted she'd identified the body. "I need to talk to his parents."

"I can come with you. I have class tomorrow at two thirty, but I am free after that until seven."

"I need to do it alone." He'd depended on Sam far more than he should've when he was in the hospital, and he couldn't ask James's parents about what he needed to know with her at his side.

The silence stretched on for so long that he checked the screen to ensure she was still on the phone. Finally, she said, "Okay then. Tell me when you're ready for it."

Vincent switched the call to speaker and opened Notes on his phone. "I'm ready."

"Let the record show that I think this is a bad idea."

He readied his thumbs to type in the address. "I couldn't agree more."

VINCENT STOOD ON the road in front of the house. This cul-de-sac had no sidewalks. There was a break in the lawn for the driveway leading up to a two-car garage and another path that wound its way up to the wraparound porch. The house looked nearly identical to every other one on the street except for the navy siding and maroon trim.

Vincent tried to picture James riding his bike in the driveway or rolling around in the grass as a child, but something told him James's parents probably didn't allow such nonsense.

He checked the time. A quarter after five. From what little James had told him about his parents, they only stomached each other's presences for family dinner at five o'clock. Whether or not they still upheld this tradition after James went to college wasn't clear, but it was the best chance he had to talk to them both at the same time.

He caught something moving out of the corner of his eye. A woman in the house next door watched him from a part in her lace curtains. When he made eye contact with her, she quickly drew them shut, but he could still see her outline standing in front of the window.

Was it so obvious that he didn't belong here?

His racing heart and sweating palms seemed to have come to that conclusion from the second he parked his beater in front of James's childhood home. Fox Chapel was only a twenty-minute drive from their apartment in Oakland, but it might as well have been a different planet. One alien to his life of cracked sidewalks and dilapidated houses.

It didn't matter if he didn't belong in suburbia. He wasn't here to settle down. He had come to get answers. No matter how disastrous the meeting would surely go, a lifetime of not knowing what had happened that night would be far worse.

He forced his body up the path to the front door. A little gold knocker was fixed to the door. He nearly used it until he spotted the doorbell. He pressed it, and windchimes rang out in the house.

From inside, a deep voice said, "Greta, get the door!"

Within a minute, the door swung open. An old Italian woman stood in the doorway. The top of her curly gray hair barely reached his chest. Her eyes lit up with recognition. James must have shown her photos of them together. She glanced over her shoulder before she shooed him back and cracked the door behind her. "What are you doing here?"

"I need to speak with them," Vincent said with as much authority as he could muster.

"No, you don't. You need to leave, trust me, *ragazzo*."

"Greta, what's going on out there?" a woman called from inside.

"I'm not leaving until I see them." He meant it. He'd give the woman behind the lace curtains next door a show before he left without answers.

Greta looked up at the sky, clutching the gold cross around her neck. "*Dio mi aiuti.*"

While he didn't know a word of Italian, he understood her sentiment. "Please get them."

"Greta, tell them we don't want whatever they are selling." The door opened. A tall, slender woman stood in the doorway. She had James's blond hair and his bright-blue eyes. She held a glass of white wine in one hand. "What's going on?"

"Nothing, Mrs. Beaumont." Greta turned back to Vincent. Her eyes bored into him, pleading with him to leave. "Like she said, we are good. Thanks for stopping by."

James's mother turned around and started back into the house.

Every molecule of his body told him to drop it and go back to Butler. Told him nothing good would come from this. But he couldn't. He refused to leave empty-handed. "Mrs. Beaumont, I'm James's boyfriend. I need to speak to you and your husband."

She stopped in her tracks. The glass of wine lifted to her mouth. He wasn't sure she'd heard him, and he was about to repeat himself when she said, "Greta, get rid of him."

The disgust in her voice was almost tangible.

"I just need a few seconds of your time. Please." He tried to walk inside after her, but Greta blocked the doorway.

"You need to go." She pressed a hand to his chest and pushed him back.

Pain exploded through his ribs. He barely noticed it. He didn't know what was worse—that James's mother dismissed him without a moment's hesitation or that she didn't have the decency to look at him when she said it. Like her eyes would rot out of their sockets if she saw such a disgusting excuse for a human being. He clenched his fists. "Look at me!"

"What's going on?" A man hurried into the entry from another room. He had the same tall lean build as James.

Mrs. Beaumont turned around. Her eyes were wet, and she glared at him with a hatred he had only seen in the eyes of their attackers. He half expected her to grab an aluminum bat so that her husband could beat him with it. The sound of metal hitting flesh rang in his ears, echoing off the tunnel walls. A face flashed before his eyes. Not James's mother. Another face. One wrapped in shadows and filled with disgust—the moment before a rusted crowbar sent him into the nightmare that had become his life since that night.

"Get the hell off my property, or I'll call the police," she said.

Greta rushed inside. "Nothing is going on, Mr. Beaumont. And we don't want to make a scene, Mrs. Beaumont. Why don't you two get back to dinner, and I'll deal with him? The alfredo is no good cold."

Before either of James's parents could answer, Greta stepped back onto the porch and shut the front door behind her. "You need to go now."

He couldn't hold back the tears. "No. Let her call the police if she wants. I'm not going until they talk to me."

Something in Greta's face softened. "Look, come back in an hour. I'll be on the back porch. Don't show your face until you see me. *Capisci*?"

"Okay," he managed to say.

"Then go. Get out of here."

Vincent hurried down the porch steps, clutching his ribs. There was movement again beside him. The woman peered out from her window once more with the interest of a child gawking at a monkey exhibit at the zoo.

"Enjoy the fucking show?" he mouthed to her.

The curtains snapped shut.

He was so mad he couldn't breathe. He needed to get out of here. He got in his car and drove off. He parked on a nearly identical street a few blocks away in the hope of avoiding nosy neighbors or the cops if James's mother actually called them. He barely got his key out of the ignition before he collapsed in a fit of tears.

She'd treated him like a criminal. No, something less than human. An animal. He wanted to hit something. Break something. Make something feel as destroyed as he felt. His chest stung with every sob, but he couldn't stop the tears from coming.

He didn't understand how James could grow up with such a terrible woman and still turn out so kind and generous. The answer was obvious. Greta. He couldn't imagine the person James might have become without her. How cold and detached he might have acted with his mother as his main role model. But Greta had raised him. And she was going to talk to Vincent in an hour. Maybe she had his answers.

GRETA WAS WAITING for him on the back porch, leaning over the railing. A silhouette in the light from a fixture above the sliding glass doors behind her. He was about to start up the stairs to meet her when she said, "Stay down there. Come stand in front of me."

He walked over to her. She looked older from this angle. Tired from a long life of hard work.

She pulled a pack of cigarettes and a lighter from her pocket. "I'm sure Mrs. Beaumont is watching me from her perch to make sure I don't throw a butt in her precious yard." Greta motioned her head behind her to what he presumed was a window. "She won't be able to see you with me standing here."

"Okay." Even thinking about her rubbed salt into the fresh wounds of her loathing.

Greta tapped out a cigarette and lit it. "This is my only smoke break, so you have until I finish this one. What do you want?"

There was a no-nonsense attitude about her that reminded him of James. He took a deep breath and held back a cough from the smoke in the air. "I never got to see him. After what happened. I just wanted to know what he looked like when they found him. Sam said they had a closed casket, so I figured whoever identified him was the only one who did."

Greta took another long drag. She blew the smoke out over his head. "Neither did I. His father identified the body. When he came home, he said they were having a closed casket, and that was that."

A flicker of hope. Maybe he didn't need James's mother to get his answers. "Do you think he'd talk to me?"

"No, he won't. She's the better of the two, if you can believe it."

Vincent couldn't imagine how anyone could be worse than the woman he met earlier, but Greta didn't have a reason to lie. His answers were inside the house. So close. And as aloof as the smoke that twisted and twirled through the night sky overhead. He wanted to stomp his feet like a child and scream until he got his way, but the reality that James's parents would never talk to him, that he'd never know what had happened that night, was too crushing for such anger.

Greta said something he didn't catch.

He tore his eyes from the smoke. "Huh?"

"Was he happy?"

Vincent thought back to before the attack. When James had returned from his classes and labs, excited to detail the latest thing he learned that day. When they'd cuddle on the couch and watch TV and hold one another. "I think he was. Yes."

"Good. I'm glad."

"He talked about you. Said he had you to thank for every success."

She smiled. A warm, loving smile. "He did, did he?"

"Yes, ma'am."

"Ma'am? Don't make me feel older than I already am. Call me Greta."

"Sorry, Greta."

"You're forgiven." She flicked her ashes, and they fell on him. "Shit. Sorry. Wasn't even thinking about what I was doing."

"Don't worry about it." He ran his hands through his hair and brushed off his shoulders. She was nearing the filter, and she didn't have what he needed anyway. "Thank you. For talking to me."

"My pleasure." She took one last puff and stubbed out the cigarette on the railing.

She was still breathing out the smoke when a window snapped open and yellow light poured onto the porch. Greta was right. She blocked the window from his sight.

Mrs. Beaumont's shrill voice stung his ears. "Greta, make sure you throw that butt away in the outside garbage. I don't want to find it in the lawn again."

Greta rolled her eyes. "Of course, Mrs. Beaumont."

"And make sure to lock the door when you come inside. *Someone* left the deadbolt unlocked last night."

"Yes, ma'am."

The window shut, and the light disappeared.

"*Puttana*," Greta said under her breath. She flicked the cigarette over his head and into the yard.

Vincent had a pretty good idea what that meant.

"He loved you, you know," she said, staring ahead at something he couldn't see. "Never shut up about you when he called. It was always Vincent this or Vincent that. If he was happy, then I have you to thank for that."

Vincent bit his lip to fight back tears. "I loved him so

much."

"If you want to say goodbye, they buried him in Green-wood Cemetery. First left when you drive in and another when the road forks in three. He's buried under the first pine tree on the right."

"Thank you."

"Goodbye, Vincent."

The tears came long before he made it back to his car.

CHAPTER NINE

LIES

VINCENT STARED AT the rows of bottles. Wine. Rum. Whiskey. Tequila. Vodka. Colored glass and vibrant labels. He gravitated toward the vodka and picked up a bottle of Smirnoff Green Apple—the larger of the two bottles available, which James used to playfully call "family-sized." Then, he checked out.

He'd tried to drive straight to Greenwood Cemetery. Pennsylvania law prohibited trespassing on cemeteries after sundown, but if he didn't go tonight, he'd never go. He'd made it halfway there when the thought of seeing that patch of unsettled earth sent him back the way he'd come. He didn't know if he'd intentionally driven to Fine Wine & Good Spirits or if the glowing white letters drew him in like a moth to a flame. Either way, he found what he needed.

As soon as he got back in his car, he twisted off the cap and took a shot. Liquid fire the whole way down. Another. Just as bad as the first. He clamped his mouth shut to keep it down. He twisted the cap back on, stuck the bottle between his legs, and started his car.

He'd known his visit with Mr. and Mrs. Beaumont wouldn't go well. He'd expected to be insulted and belittled. He hadn't expected the loathing. God, that look on her face. He was pretty sure he could drink the whole bottle and still see her expression when he closed his eyes. And he didn't even get any answers. He just got the location of where they'd buried James.

He took one more shot for the road.

Greenwood Cemetery was a few miles away. He followed the winding roads, putting the destination out of his mind. He focused on the warm feeling of the vodka settling in his stomach. Not necessarily a comforting warm. More of a burning sensation. A lit match that wasn't hot enough to distract him from the reality of driving to his boyfriend's gravesite.

James's gravesite.

He concentrated on the road.

Before long, Google Maps informed him he'd arrived. His headlights shone on a hinged gate that closed off the road to the cemetery. There were bronze plaques fixed to waist-high stone pillars flanking the entrance. Each read:

"Greenwood Cemetery, Incorporated in 1875."

A chain was wrapped around the end of the gate and an adjacent metal pole, held in place with a silver lock that gleamed in the headlights. The trees on either side of the pillars prevented him from driving around the gate. He considered backing up and trying to ram it open. He might have, if it weren't for the houses across the street from the entrance. He drove a little further down the road and parked on the shoulder.

He didn't realize how bad his hands were shaking until he let go of the steering wheel. He took another swig from the bottle in the hope of drowning the urge to flee. He'd come too far to turn back now. Clutching the neck of the bottle in one hand, he climbed out of his car.

Pain shot through his chest.

"Fuck."

Something about the way he'd stood up had pissed off his ribs. He leaned against the side of the car and fought to breathe. Six months. That was how long Dr. Carter told him it would take for his ribs to heal. He should have taken all the pain medicine he was offered when he had the chance. He'd give anything to feel that beautiful numbness again. The only thing he had now was the vodka, and it had barely affected him.

He walked along the side of the road to reach the gate. The porch lights and lampposts from the houses across the street provided enough light for him to see where he was going. In one window, a woman sat at a dining room table with a girl who was dressed in a school uniform. The girl's mouth was moving, and the woman motioned to the girl's plate. The girl ignored her, too focused on whatever she was telling her mom—probably about her school day.

Had he been so eager to tell his parents about his day when he was her age? He wasn't sure. For as far back as he could remember, he described his days in one-word answers like "long" or "boring." After his mother's diagnosis, he did his best to sugarcoat the horrors of high school. The sicker she got, the hungrier she became for details—like she was trying to gather as much information as she could about his life before she was no longer a part of it. As a result, his lies became all the more elaborate and sickeningly sweet until she was gone and a part of him wasn't sure what was the truth and what was a fabrication.

He didn't have a person who cared enough to ask him about his day until he met James. And with James, he didn't have to lie. He could leave in all his anger and frustration. They'd spend so much time talking about what had happened to them when they were apart that James could probably pass any of the classes Vincent was taking with flying colors. How strange it was to return to the silence. To know that he was the only person in the world who knew what had happened to him today. He needed to get used to it.

He was alone now.

He had almost reached the gate when something black darted across the ground in front of him. He stumbled back before he realized it was his shadow. He turned around, and a bright light blinded him. He squinted his eyes. The light split in two. Headlights. Someone was driving down the road. He stumbled into the cemetery through the space between the pillar and the trees. Dead undergrowth crunched under his shoes. He pressed his back against the pillar and crouched down as low as his sore ribs would let him.

His heart pounded, and his chest burned. The world swayed around him. He prayed that whoever was in the car hadn't seen him. The last thing he needed was for the cops to find him drunk in a graveyard at night. Rays of light shot through the gate and lit up the dirt road stretching out in front of him to the cemetery. He waited for the car to pass and the light to disappear, but it didn't. He could hear the engine purring as the car slowed to a stop.

Shit.

They must've seen him.

Any moment now, a car door would open, and someone would have questions for him to answer. He was so busy listening for the car door he almost didn't notice that the light had turned red. Vincent glanced around the side of the pillar. The car pulled into a driveway across the street. He remained where he was until whoever was in the car went inside the house.

He took another drink and set off down the dirt road. The farther away he got from the houses, the harder it became to see in the dark. His eyes eventually adjusted enough to make out his surroundings in the pale moonlight. There was another house down the road on the right. Probably belonged to the caretaker who must have gone to bed early. Not a single light was on in the house. Vincent stayed closer to the line of trees on his left in case he was wrong.

As per Greta's instructions, he made a left at the first road he came across. Down the path he went. He chugged more vodka. It made it harder to walk in a straight line, but it also dulled the pain in his chest and the soreness in his legs. Just when he was starting to think he'd gone down the wrong path, the road split in three. He took the one on the left.

The trees thinned. Graves swam around him, undulating like waves in an ocean. He kept blinking his eyes to focus them on the path. At some point, he spotted—or thought he spotted—a pair of eyes peeking out at him from a distant obelisk. They seemed too close together to be human. A small comfort. Maybe a deer. Or a coyote. Or a bear. Whatever it was, its eyes were on him, following his progress.

He took another swig and continued down the path a little faster. His legs felt heavy, but he forced them to move. One foot in front of the other. Over and over again. Rinse and repeat. And there it was—the pine tree. Swaying high above the sea of gravestones. The green needles blue in what little light the moon and the distant city provided. James was buried somewhere beneath it. Vincent took another gulp of vodka.

He didn't remember walking over to it. The next thing he knew, he was standing in front of the rectangular patch of dirt that was just outside of the ring of pine needles beneath the tree. He knew there wouldn't be a headstone. The earth hadn't had enough time to settle. But the little metal marker stuck in the earth at the top of the dirt looked so utterly pitiful. He drew a little closer and, with significant effort to slow down the rotation of the earth, he made out the two lines of text:

JAMES A. BEAUMONT

July 5th, 1994–February 16th, 2017

He took another mouthful of vodka. He was supposed to say goodbye. Come to some realization that James was really gone and return to what was left of his life. That was the whole point in him coming here, wasn't it? Closure? Something to make his existence more bearable. Staring at the little marker that danced in front of him, he felt no rush of certainty. He saw nothing in that frosted pile of dirt except a lie.

James wasn't in that grave. Vincent had covered James in mud. And James had carried him to safety. And—

Something crawled up his leg. He felt its little legs scurry across his thigh. He screamed and stumbled back, hitting his leg. He slipped in the dirt and hit the ground. The world blurred. If there was pain, he didn't notice in his rush to kill whatever was on him. He didn't see anything on his jeans. But he felt it, buzzing between the fabric and his flesh.

Not a bug.

His phone.

He let himself breathe. He sat up and pulled it from his pocket. He blinked his eyes until he could read the number. Ralbovsky and Tillman. Before he could decline the call, it ended, and not long after, a voice mail appeared on his screen. He clicked on it.

"Vincent. It's Detective Tillman," she said in a restrained manner. "We got a call from Mrs. Beaumont. Said that you were trying to break into her house and wouldn't leave. She's very upset. Wanted to make a police report—despite the fact Fox Chapel is outside our jurisdiction. We talked to her, and she is letting it go. But we need to talk to you. Call us back. In the meantime, you need to stay away from—"

"You need to shut the fuck up!" He wished it were a phone call so that he could say it to her. He tossed his phone away from him.

They were all part of the lie. James's dad had lied about identifying the body. Ralbovsky and Tillman couldn't stop lying to him to save their lives. No, James wasn't here. The marker. The grave. All of it was a lie. James was alive. Vincent had seen him with his own eyes in the hospital, and he trusted himself far more than any of those assholes.

He went to lift his hand up to open the bottle for another sip, but he must have dropped it when he fell. He found it in the dirt, cap missing and dirt coating the rim. The ground around it was dark from the spilled liquor.

Fuck.

He raised the bottle to the moon, praying he hadn't wasted it all. A third of it remained. After he wiped off the rim, he gulped down a mouthful and looked at the grave. If James wasn't buried in the ground, then who was? Was it an empty casket? He might not have gotten answers from Mr. and Mrs. fucking Beaumont, but he could answer this one. He just needed a shovel. He'd dig the thing up and give it a look-see. Show everyone they were a bunch of fucking liars.

He managed to get to his feet. The world tilted back and

forth like he was on that Noah's Ark ride at Kennywood. The one where everything moved too mechanically to properly imitate a boat on rough waters besides the resulting nausea. He stumbled to keep himself upright. He needed a shovel. *A shovel*. The word sounded strange in his mind.

Shovel.

No. He needed to focus. He looked around him. Graves and trees and nothing else in sight. He collected his phone and shone the flashlight into the darkness. Something moved behind a tree in the distance. Something big. No. Just the tree swaying. Tilting in Noah's Ark.

In the far corner of the cemetery, he spotted a small wooden structure. Maybe a toolshed. He started in that direction until he noticed the big silver lock on the door. He stumbled back to the grave.

Fuck it. He didn't need a shovel. He had two attached to his arms. He sat down in the dirt. He dug his fingers into the cold earth and pulled out handfuls. Good. This would take no time. He did it again. And again. But the earth was so damn cold it wouldn't budge after he had taken away a few clumps of dirt that were as hard as stone. He clawed at it. Pain flooded his hand. He pulled it up to the moonlight. Blood ran down his arm from his ring finger. He'd say from the nail, but there wasn't one there anymore.

His saliva felt thick. Stomach acid crawled up his throat. No. He clamped his hands over his mouth, but he couldn't stop it. Vomit shot from his mouth. The world needed to stop spinning so fast. He couldn't see straight in this merry-go-round from hell. His throat burned. That acidic smell. God, it was terrible.

He just needed to lie down for a minute to regain his strength. He pressed his cheek into the puddle of warm vomit. Shut his eyes and prayed for it all to end. More vomit shot from his mouth. He buried his face in it. The slimy texture filling the space between his skin and the earth was the last thing he remembered.

HE AWOKE WITH a searing pain in his head. He brought his hands to his temple, expecting to find the hilt of an ax. Just skin. His hand throbbed. He rubbed his tongue against the roof of his mouth and felt the grainy texture of dirt and vomit.

The night returned in flashes. He'd drunk at least half, if not more, of that bottle of vodka. He'd gone to Greenwood Cemetery. He'd tried to dig up the grave. Then, he'd vomited. He could still smell it on him. He lifted his eyelids. He was lucky. It was still dark outside. He waited for the moon and the stars to come into focus, but all that did was a cracked plaster ceiling.

He went to push himself up from the ground, but his hand went further into it. Soft. Like...a bed. He looked around him. Dark square shapes. He searched for details to ground himself. Anything to explain where he'd woken up. He wasn't at the cemetery or in his car. He was inside a house. But he wasn't at Henry's.

Two dressers came into focus, and an old wooden desk with enough books and papers stacked on it that it could topple over at any minute. It looked just like James's desk. And those dressers were the same as the ones in their apartment. It was their furniture, but they looked so strange in the shadows it took him a moment to realize that he was back in their apartment.

It didn't make any sense. He couldn't stand, much less walk or drive. Someone must have brought him back here. Who could have done it and why they had taken him here of all places were questions he didn't even know where to begin to find answers.

He heard it then.

The wood floors creaked in the living room.

He watched the bedroom door. It was cracked open. Must be Sam or Henry. He opened his mouth to call for them, but then another thought hit him. *How could they have known I was at the cemetery?* Greta could have told Sam, but why? And if they'd collected him, why take him to his apartment instead of Henry's house or Sam's apartment? He clamped his mouth shut.

Another memory flashed through his mind. He'd seen something in the graveyard. Behind that obelisk. And again, behind a tree. No, not something. Someone. Had the stranger brought him back here? The door started to open. There was no time left to think. He flopped back down in bed and swallowed the stomach acid that climbed up his throat. Maybe the stranger would let him sleep. Go back to wherever he'd been waiting in the apartment so that Vincent could try to figure something out. He just needed a few minutes to collect himself and think.

He listened and tried not to move an inch. It was hard to tell if the stranger had stopped in the doorway or come into the room. Unlike the living room, the bedroom was carpeted. A plush green carpet that muffled footsteps.

Something cold grazed his cheek. A hand. Fingers. Caressing him. He couldn't hold in the scream. He raised his arms to protect himself and focused on the man standing over him. Broad shoulders. A thin, muscular physique. Light hair that glowed in the dim light coming in from the living room. Not a stranger.

James.

CHAPTER TEN

WHAT MATTERED

"JAMES?" TEARS OBSCURED him, and Vincent wiped them away as fast as he could to ensure James hadn't disappeared. He stood over him. He wasn't a distant figure in a hospital lobby. He was right beside their bed. Alive.

Vincent couldn't think. Couldn't breathe. He jumped to his feet and wrapped his arms around him. His pain, his nausea—everything in the world melted away except for the man in his arms. Vincent nestled into his chest and sobbed and clung to him, his life raft after being lost at sea for weeks in the nightmarish hell that had become his life.

James kissed the top of his head. "It's going to be okay."

Vincent looked up at him. Stared into his eyes that caught the light coming in from the living room. Beautiful bright-blue eyes. He had always known James was alive, but everyone else had been so certain of his death he was starting to wonder if he'd ever see his eyes again. They were even more striking than he remembered. "Everyone said you were gone."

"I know," James said, his voice hollow. He pressed Vincent's head back to his chest and ran his fingers through his hair.

Questions swarmed his mind, sprouting and dying off in a matter of seconds. Why would the police say James was dead? Why would his father lie about identifying his own son's body? Vincent felt sick. Dizzy. He clung to James a little tighter.

That didn't matter. He could hear James's heart beating. They had the rest of their lives to figure out what had happened. What was important now was that James was back. Vincent just needed to relax and breathe. In and out. In and—the smell hit him then.

Beyond the dirt and vomit, there was an underlying scent of rot. He must have brought more than dirt and vomit back with him from the cemetery.

James lifted his chin so that he looked into his eyes. "You okay?"

"I just feel a little sick."

"Do you want to lie down?"

"No!" Vincent refused to let sleep separate them. "I just need to get cleaned up."

James backed away from him.

Vincent grabbed his hand. He wasn't letting him out of his sight anytime soon. "Will you come with me?"

James was looking right at him, but there was a glassy, distant look in his eyes—like miles separated them. Vincent was so happy James was back that he hadn't paid much attention to how he was acting. He seemed to be in shock. A reasonable reaction after all he'd been through, and they would work through it together. Vincent squeezed his hand, and he was about to repeat himself when James answered, "Of course."

James led him through the living room to the bathroom. He flipped on the light and started the shower. Once Vincent's eyes adjusted, he looked at their reflection in the mirror while they waited for the water to warm up. James was just as handsome as ever. Vincent, on the other hand, looked like the one who'd died. Dried vomit and dirt smeared his face and stuck in clumps in his hair. His clothes were filthy.

James must've thought his boyfriend had lost his mind. Vincent could barely believe what he'd tried to do himself. But that didn't matter now. James was back. Whatever rock bottom he had collided with in Greenwood Cemetery wasn't relevant in a world where James was still alive. Everything that had happened between him waking up in the hospital and now belonged to a different life where he was facing all this alone. Now, he had James. The world had righted itself, and they could return to the lives those bastards had tried to take away from them.

Vincent started peeling off his shirt. Pain shot through

his chest, and he stopped to breathe for a second, shirt covering his face.

"Here." James lifted it off him. He helped him out of his jeans and underwear before bending over to remove his socks.

Vincent had missed him so much. "Thanks."

Steam wafted out from behind the shower curtain. Vincent's aching body couldn't have asked for a better remedy. James had yet to undress, and he didn't look like he was in a rush to do so. Vincent asked, "Are you joining me?"

James paused, seemingly lost in thought. Vincent wished he could hug and kiss him until whatever preoccupied him disappeared, but he knew that wasn't possible. They had a long road ahead of them.

Vincent repeated himself.

"Yeah," James said after another moment. "I'll meet you in there."

Vincent stepped inside the tub, not giving the hot steam more than a passing thought. Scalding-hot water poured down his chest. He stumbled out of the range of the water, rubbing his red skin. "Shit!"

James pulled back the curtain, pants around his ankles but face determined to destroy whatever had made Vincent scream. "You okay?"

"Sorry. The water's hot."

James turned on the cold-water faucet to lower the temperature, but by that point, the water was the least of Vincent's concerns. James was naked, and there wasn't a single scratch or bruise on his body. Hell, after two gun-shots, he looked healthier and stronger than he had before the attack. The sight was so jarring that Vincent just stared at him until he hopped in the shower and closed the curtain. "What's wrong?"

Vincent ran his fingers over the skin on James's chest where the bullet had entered his body. The bullet hole he had packed with mud in the hope of saving him. There was nothing there now. The skin wasn't even pink from heal-ing—not that such a wound could heal in just a few weeks. He pressed his fingers into the skin, looking for tough scar tissue or a small indentation. Nothing.

James took his hand in his. "What happened to your fingernail?"

"You don't even have a scar." Vincent looked at the side of James's head where another bullet had grazed him, but there was no sign of an injury. It was as if he'd never been attacked. "How is this possible?"

James hadn't looked away from his hand. "Your whole fingernail is gone."

Vincent pulled his hand away, wincing as the bare flesh under his missing fingernail grazed the rough skin on James's hand. "Who cares about that right now? How did you heal so fast?"

James looked lost, searching for something in the dark. "I don't know."

The three weeks that had transpired between the last time he saw James seemed incredibly long and full of terri-ble possibilities. "What do you mean?"

"When I woke up, they were gone. There were lights and people. I ran." James looked down at his feet.

Vincent waited for more of an explanation, but James didn't say anything else. "Where have you been? Why didn't you tell everyone you were alive?"

James pulled him close. "Because they said I was dead."

A chill came over Vincent that had nothing to do with the temperature of the water. They had reported James dead. They had a funeral for him and everything. Vincent didn't know why the police or his parents would lie about such a thing, but whatever the reason, it wasn't good. Something far greater than just an attack had happened that night. Something well beyond the two of them.

Vincent tried to breathe. "What are we going to do?"

"We'll figure it out." He spoke with such certainty that Vincent almost believed him. Even the impossible seemed manageable with James at his side.

"I love you so much," he said, punctuating his words with a kiss.

James kissed him back. An intense, hungry kiss that was far more aggressive than his usual gentle pecks. "I love you too."

They had both been through a lot in the last few weeks. Vincent pushed everything else out of his mind except for the knowledge that the man he loved was still alive. He kissed him back. James grabbed his ass and pulled him closer, pushing their naked bodies together. His sore body hurt under the force of James's hand, but he ignored it. He could feel himself growing hard. He kept kissing him and grinding into James in spite of the pain.

After another long, rough kiss, Vincent pulled back to catch his breath and look into his boyfriend's eyes, hoping they had lost that distant look. But they hadn't. He wondered where James was and what had happened to him during those weeks apart. Would he ever get the James he knew and loved back? He shut his eyes and kissed him again. And ignored the smell of rot still lingering in his nostrils.

HE AWOKE TO a distant pounding sound. He'd fallen asleep with his head on James's chest, listening to his heartbeat, so it only seemed right that he'd wake up to it. Only, the pounding was inconsistent, and it sounded farther away. Like it was coming from the other room. Like someone was knocking on the front door.

Exhaustion pinned him to the bed. "James, I think somcone's here."

No response.

The pounding continued, joined by words he couldn't quite make out.

"James?" He lifted his head and turned around to shake him awake. The bed was empty. He lay on a pile of blankets. His eyes darted around the room that was full of afternoon light. James wasn't there.

He must already be up.

Vincent got to his feet and rushed into the living room. James wasn't on the couch or in the armchair. Panic overtook him. He tried to shake it off. James was fine. He probably heard the knocking and panicked and made a run for it. The only problem was that he'd have to go out through the front door to leave the apartment.

"I know you're in there!" Sam called from the door. "Your car is out front!"

Sam would have to wait. Vincent continued into the bathroom. Kitchen. Hallway to the door. James was nowhere in sight.

He tried to breathe.

Last night wasn't an illusion.

It was real.

Sam continued to pound on the door. "I'm not leaving until you let me in."

He just needed to think.

Bang.

There had to be a rational explanation for this.

Bang.

But every thought—*bang*—was cut short by that blasted pounding.

He went to the door and pulled it open. "What?"

Sam stood in the doorway, a glass casserole dish covered in tin foil in her hands. "Nice to see you too. Yes, I'd love to come in. Thanks."

Before Vincent could say a word, she slipped past him into the apartment. "God, what's that smell?"

"Sam, now is really a bad time." Sam walked into the

kitchen as if she hadn't heard a word he said. He looked out of the door. He knew James wouldn't be there, standing behind Sam on the stairs, but he had to be sure.

A cabinet slammed shut. "Remind me where you keep your plates?"

Vincent shut the door and joined Sam in the kitchen. She'd managed to find the right cupboard and taken out two plates. "What about a serving spoon and forks?"

"I could really use some time alone. How about you come back in an hour?" By then, he could figure out where James had gone.

"I spent all morning making my world-famous cheesy potato casserole. It's best when it's still warm from the oven. So, we are going to sit down and stuff our faces until we're sick. Then, I'll get out of your hair."

Her look of determination assured him he'd have to physically pick her up and carry her out of the apartment if he wanted to be alone. He knew he should be grateful that she was trying, but she was trying at the worst possible time. "The silverware is in the drawer beside the sink. I'll be right back."

He returned to the bedroom. He threw blankets and pillows off the bed to ensure James wasn't still asleep in the bundle. No luck. He got down on the floor, ignoring the protest of pain from his ribs, and looked under the bed. He pushed away old shoeboxes and discarded clothes. Legs appeared in front of him on the other side of the bed. He was almost relieved until he saw the toenails were painted black.

He rose to his feet, using the bed for support. Sam stood

by the door, her hand resting on her hips and her face pinched with confusion. "Whatcha doing?"

"I—ah..." For a split second, he considered telling her the truth. *I'm looking for James.* He wasn't sure why James hadn't already told her, but he must have had his reasons. Plus, Sam would probably think he'd gone insane if he didn't have James at his side to prove his claims.

"Well?" she asked, her expression unchanged.

"I can't find my phone."

She grabbed it from the bedside table, where it was in plain sight, and held it out to him.

Vincent took it, focusing on the empty bed. "Thanks."

"Food's ready."

Two steaming plates piled high with casserole were waiting for them at the kitchen table. He couldn't lie. The mixture of cheese and potatoes objectively looked delicious, but after a night of vomiting, the smell made him feel like there might be an encore. And his stomach was in knots over James. Sam watched him, waiting for him to take a bite. The faster he ate, the sooner Sam would be gone. He shoveled in a forkful and forced himself to swallow it.

Sam dug into her own mound. "Like it?"

"It's great." He took another forkful to push down the first that was threatening to come back up and used the silence of them chewing to think. Last night couldn't have been a dream. He'd dreamed about James before, but this was different. He'd touched James. Kissed him. Made love to him and stayed up for hours in his arms. There had to be another explanation.

A hand waved in front of his face. He looked up at Sam. "Huh?"

"I asked you how you're doing. Twice." Her annoyance gave way to concern. "You okay?"

"Yeah." Vincent stuffed more casserole in his mouth and took his time chewing it. "I just had a long night."

"I heard." Before he could ask her to elaborate, she said, "I talked to Greta."

Vincent searched for a change of subject. "Where did you get this recipe? It's awesome."

"From my mom. She makes it every Christmas. It's one of the three things she can cook without setting off the fire alarm. It was one of James's favorites."

Silence overtook them again.

James could have left this morning for some reason. Maybe he went to pick up Panera for breakfast. He'd done it many times in the past. It was just down the street. He could have already returned and hung back because he heard Sam.

"It's strange," she said, pulling him back to the kitchen table.

"What's that?"

"That people make casseroles when someone dies. When my grandma passed away in high school, my mom and I ate them for weeks."

Who cared about casseroles? James was missing. He might have taken a morning stroll, or something far worse could have happened to him. Someone could have taken him, and they were talking about fucking casseroles.

Vincent took a breath.

He needed to relax. James was probably waiting outside with coffee and bagels.

Sam's trying, he reminded himself. *She still thinks James is dead, and she's trying*.

"I guess carbs fill the void," he said.

She laughed. "I guess so. Look, I've been thinking. Maybe you could come stay with me and Tyler for a few days." Something in his face must have given away how little he wanted to do that, because she added, "Tyler's hardly ever there between his classes, practices, and games. And I don't like the idea of you being here all alone. And I could use the company. What do you say?"

He finished off the plate with a pang of guilt. She had no idea that James was still alive. He made a mental note to see why James hadn't told her yet. "I appreciate it, but I think I just need some time alone right now. Thanks though."

She took another bite, leaving only bits of cheese on her plate. "Of course. Here, let me wash these before I go."

"Honestly, I can take care of them." He went to grab his plate, but she already had both in her hands.

She headed to the sink. "This way, you don't have to worry about them."

"Thanks." He sat back in his chair. He'd waited weeks for James. Another few minutes wouldn't be the end of the world. He worried too much anyway. James could take care of himself.

Sam scrubbed the plates clean with a sponge. "No problem. Trust me, I'd much rather be doing this than studying. Have you talked to your professors?"

"Yeah, they've been really understanding," he lied. In all honesty, the thought hadn't even crossed his mind. Lectures and tests seemed so trivial compared to James's death, and now he had bigger issues to contend with than passing Myths, Legends, and Folktales.

"That's good." She placed the dishes in the drying rack beside the sink. She then covered the casserole dish. "This should keep you fed for at least another day or two."

She opened the fridge, and instantly recoiled, coughing. "Jesus, something—or a lot of things—have gone bad in here. When's the last time you've cleaned this out?"

"Since before the—yeah." That explained the persistent smell of rot he couldn't wash away last night.

She set the dish on the counter. "I can help you clean it up if you want."

Vincent didn't think he could wait much longer to figure out where James had gone. Every minute that passed without seeing him seemed to give more credence to the idea something bad had happened to him or Vincent had made him up. "You've done enough. Honestly. I can do it later."

"It'd be faster with two." She dragged the garbage can over to the fridge.

Vincent got up from his seat. "Really, it's fine."

Sam ignored him. She picked up a bag of kale that had liquified in the past few weeks and tossed it in the garbage can. She then pulled out a container of Greek yogurt and searched for an expiration date.

Vincent grabbed it out of her hands. "I got it. I appreciate your help, but I'm not helpless."

Sam bit the top of her lip. "I know...I wasn't saying you were. I just want to help."

She looked like she was on the verge of tears.

"Shit. Sam, I know that. I just—sorry." He cringed, waiting for her to tell him he was acting like an asshole, which would be completely accurate.

"Don't worry about it. I should get going before Tyler leaves for practice." She turned around to leave, but then she stopped, like she had just remembered something. She pulled a fat envelope from her pocket and tossed it on the table.

"What's that?"

"Started a little collection at school. Just to help you until you get on your feet. It was Tyler's idea. Anyway, I'll talk to you later." Sam set off down the hallway.

Even if the envelope was only stuffed with one-dollar bills, it was so full there was at least a couple hundred dollars in it. "Sam, I can't accept this."

She stopped. "It wasn't anything official. We just passed around some coffee cans. Couldn't give it back if we tried."

He didn't know what to say. He was grateful she had done so much for him, but he didn't know how he could even begin to return the favor. He hurried over to her. "Sam, thank you. Not just for the money. For everything. Sorry I'm such an asshole."

Sam turned around to face him. He wasn't sure if she was going to slap him or cry. Either option would be appropriate. Instead, she hugged him. "We're going to get through this."

Vincent ignored the pain flaring in his ribs and hugged her back. "Thanks."

AFTER SHE WAS gone, he tossed the yogurt in the trashcan and searched the house again. He had just pulled back the shower curtain in the bathroom to see if James was lying in the tub when he heard the floorboards creak in the living room. He stuck his head out of the bathroom door. James was closing the window to the fire escape.

Vincent let out a shaky laugh. James wasn't in trouble or a figment of his imagination. He was just waiting for Sam to leave as Vincent had predicted. Vincent walked over to him and pulled him into a hug. "You scared the shit out of me."

James wrapped his arms around him. He was freezing. "Sorry."

Vincent glanced at the window. He could have sworn it was shut, but maybe he'd overlooked it in his panic. "I'm just glad you're okay."

James watched the front door. "What did she want?"

"Just to help. Why haven't you told her that, you know, you're alive?" Sam was hurting, and they could end her suffering with a quick trip downstairs.

His gaze didn't leave the door. "I don't want to involve her in this mess. It's bad enough that you're caught up in it."

Vincent pressed his head against his chest. That explained why James had disappeared when Sam arrived and why Vincent was the only one who knew he was alive. What a relief. Vincent wasn't going insane. James was just protecting Sam. It all made perfect sense.

So why did he wonder whether Sam could see James if she walked through the front door right now? Why was his insanity far more plausible than James's survival? The doubt lingered in the room like the smell of rotting food in the fridge. He held tight to James. Whatever had happened or was happening, he had James back.

Nothing else mattered.

CHAPTER ELEVEN

GHOST

"I'LL GO. I'LL be back before you know it," James said as if he was a brave astronaut about to take a one-way trip to save the world.

"You can't. You're supposed to be dead, remember? We can't risk someone seeing you. It's not a big deal. I'll just stop at ALDI and come straight back." Vincent got up from the kitchen table to find a clean shirt. In truth, he would have much preferred to remain in the small oasis they'd created in their apartment. His heart beat a little faster at the thought of leaving James's side. But he didn't have much of a choice. Sam's casserole and what few foods of theirs that hadn't rotted had only kept them going for a few days.

James followed him into the bedroom. "What about the cash? We can order Chinese."

Vincent fished a fresh shirt out from his dresser. James must really want him to stay. He despised Chinese food and only put up with it for Vincent's sake on special occasions. Vincent was tempted, but the growing stack of bills outside their door made him think better of frivolously using the cash Sam and Tyler had raised. He still had a little money left in his bank account; he just had to spend it wisely if he was going to keep them going for a while. "Relax. Take a shower. I don't know if it's you, me, or this apartment, but something stinks."

James pulled him close and planted a kiss on his forehead. "Just be safe."

"I'm not going to war. I'm going to get groceries. Please release me." He'd have to leave soon if he was going to get there before it closed. It was already close to eight.

James let him go. "Love you."

"Love you too."

Vincent grabbed his keys and left before James tried to knock him out and go on his own. He snuck down the stairs. He hadn't spoken to Sam since she'd brought him that casserole, and at this point, he didn't know what to say to her. He hated knowing she was still mourning James's death, but James was right; involving her in this mess would only endanger her.

Thankfully, Tyler was blasting some sort of coverage of a game that announcers were hotly debating. Vincent could've slammed the front door, and Sam would be none the wiser. He didn't take any chances. He shut it quietly and snuck to his car.

He was so worried about running into her that he didn't even think about how unaware he was of his surroundings beyond the apartment until he got behind the wheel. He looked around. He didn't see anyone except for a neighbor down the street who was smoking on her porch, but that didn't mean someone wasn't somewhere in the night, waiting for him to let his guard down. He locked the car door before he set off for ALDI.

Silence filled the car so absolutely it was almost tangible. The last thing he needed was quiet time alone to mull over the events of the last few days. He was tired of overthinking everything. James was back. He should just be grateful instead of making more problems for himself.

He tried the radio. Flipped through the stations. A car commercial. An old country song. Some sort of church service about atoning for your sins. A pop song he used to belt out on his way to work. He kept it on. Tried to sing along to it. But the lyrics didn't sound carefree in his mouth now. They tasted hollow.

He turned off the radio and almost became resigned to suffering through the drive in silence until he remembered he had another option. He had a cassette he could play. One that James had found for him at a garage sale after learning that Vincent's car had a cassette player. Fleetwood Mac's self-titled 1975 album. He skipped to track four, "Rhiannon," and tried to empty his mind.

Even Stevie Nicks's vocals couldn't halt the onslaught of

racing thoughts. The store seemed farther away than he re-membered, each passing minute adding more distance between him and James and more time he'd have to be away from him. More than anything, he didn't like the idea of leaving James there alone. Despite being at his side day and night, James hadn't said much of anything since he'd re-turned.

Vincent had caught his distant stares more times than he could count over the last few days. Last night, Vincent had this terrible nightmare that he was falling down that slope off the trail, but he never reached the bottom. He just kept falling, smashing into underbrush, and catching pale faces peeking out from trees. He awoke around three in the morning, and when he turned to James to wake him so that he could hold Vincent until the feeling of falling dissipated, James was still awake, staring blankly at the ceiling. Like he was in a trance.

Vincent couldn't stop thinking of all the terrible things that could have happened to James in the three weeks they'd spent apart. His mind oscillated from the reasonable to the fantastic. From being a misidentified hospital patient to fall-ing victim to some strange experimental trial concerning super healing. He'd tried to broach the subject on several occasions, but James didn't seem to understand it any more than he did.

Vincent had a sinking feeling James was hiding something from him. That James remembered every second of those three weeks, and he was keeping it to himself because he didn't think Vincent could handle it.

He turned up the volume as high as it would go. The

bass vibrated in his aching chest. He just wanted their old lives back. While he knew it would take time and the important thing was that James was alive, James didn't seem like himself. He was so quiet. So withdrawn. Vincent would wait for him as long as it took, but living with him, being so close to him and yet knowing he was unreachable, only made Vincent miss him more.

The parking lot was packed. Vincent couldn't think of any sort of holiday that would prompt such business. Then again, he'd never gone to the store so late in the city. Maybe the avoidance of crowds in the day had created its own chaos at night. He got a shopping buggy and hurried into the store. The narrow aisles were filled with people chatting, reading labels, and staring at the rows of food. He maneuvered around them, snatching items from unoccupied shelves. After staples like lunch meat, cheese, and bread, he collected a pile of canned goods. He wanted to put off his next visit as long as possible.

He tried to think if he needed anything else, but he couldn't concentrate. There were too many people crammed into the store. He felt like one of the cans on the shelf, boxed in and waiting to be selected and consumed.

He gravitated toward the meat section. A man dug through a pile of chicken breasts beside him. His bulging muscles could make quick work of Vincent's neck. Not that such strength was needed to end his life. The little girl skipping around her mother could easily do it if she knew how to point a gun and pull a trigger. Hell, the older woman who was inspecting a can of soup farther down the aisle could pull a letter opener from her wicker purse and slit his throat.

Vincent wiped the sweat from his forehead, selected a pound of ground meat, and set off for the freezer section. He didn't know how people walked around the world so clueless to just how vulnerable they were to the whims of each other. He'd had horse blinders on, and now they had been snatched away, he couldn't help gawking at all the terrible possibilities around him. Every person in this store had the capacity to kill him.

He opened the first available freezer door and stuck his head inside, letting the frosted air cool his heated face. He leaned farther in, as if he was inspecting the frozen fish, and took a deep breath. The cold tickled his nostrils. He just needed to calm down. He'd been to the grocery store a million times without incident. There was no reason this time would be the exception.

A hand tapped his shoulder, and he jumped back, shielding his face in a sad attempt to defend himself as he slammed into the shelves of frozen food. The small older woman he'd spotted before stood behind him, her big eyes magnified in thick glasses. Hardly a trained assassin.

"Excuse me, young man. I didn't mean to startle you. Could you grab me a can of lentil soup from the top shelf?" She motioned to the cans farther down the aisle.

Several other shoppers had stopped to see what the commotion was all about. He tried to ignore them. "Of course."

He got her the can and retreated to his buggy. He didn't even have a chance to collect himself before one of the onlookers was on him. "Vincent, is that you?"

Vincent glanced up at the young woman. She was dressed in black with hair cut in a short blond bob. Jen. One of his classmates in Dr. Cowart's Myths, Legends, and Folktales class. "Hey, Jen. How's it going?"

"Fine. Just grabbing some late-night snacks to cram with." She raised the pita chips and hummus in her hands. "I've missed my...fellow rebel."

They spent most lectures messaging memes back and forth about Dr. Cowart and trying not to laugh. They often continued their bashings after class at G Door, formally known as Garage Door Saloon, where they'd order a few of the questionable yet completely delicious pickle shots. Everything had seemed so much simpler then. Another life, where he was young and the world was full of possibilities. Talking to her now was like seeing a ghost.

"Same." He could see her surveying him, eyes darting around to take in each cut and bruise.

She looked down at her food, her pale cheeks turning red. "So, ah, how are you doing?" She cringed as soon as the words left her lips.

Of course, she knew what had happened to him. Pitt was a big school, but between the police's warnings and Sam and Tyler's collection, word of his tragedy had undoubtedly traveled fast.

How long would it take for this spotting at ALDI to make its rounds? He could picture his classmates discussing how distraught he acted, flinching under the gentle touch of an elderly woman, and how terrible he looked. Jen meant well, but he doubted she would keep this chat to herself.

People fed on bad news like vultures on a dead carcass, tearing away at it until they picked it clean.

"I'm okay." He needed to get the hell out of this store. He looked down at his food in the hope of hinting that it was time to euthanize this awkward conversation. "Just getting a few things."

"Well, I should probably get going. If you ever need anything or want to chat, just let me know." With a halfhearted smile that dipped into a frown, she set off down the aisle.

He wondered if this would be the last time he saw her in person. Jen was originally from Washington, and she'd be graduating in spring with Sam and all the students in his year who'd managed to keep their shit together for four years. And he, well, he didn't know. That, like so many other aspects of his life, was a problem that could be later addressed if he survived long enough for it to become a more pressing matter.

"Excuse me, I just need to get some tilapia," a man said, cutting behind him to get to the freezer.

Vincent moved out of the way. He was ready to get back to the apartment. He dumped some frozen food into the buggy on his way to the checkout. The muscular man got in line behind him, and he was standing so close to Vincent that the man's heavy, stale breaths brushed the back of his neck and assaulted his nostrils. Vincent was never more grateful for an efficient cashier.

When he finally pushed his buggy through the automatic doors, he pulled off to the side of the entrance, just within the reach of the fluorescent lights inside the store, to breathe for a second. He was alone at last.

All alone in a dark parking lot. The space between the entrance and where he parked seemed incredibly long and full of shadows. Like the world had been wrapped in those tall tunnel walls where their attackers had been waiting to trap and kill them.

Vincent gripped the handle of the buggy in a vain attempt to stop his hands from shaking. He wished Jen were back at his side with awkward small talk to keep him from thinking about all the places where someone could hide in this poorly lit parking lot.

The first of the two sets of automatic doors opened behind him. The muscular man was walking out of the store with paper bags held in his massive arms. He was looking right at him. Vincent pushed the buggy forward into the darkness. He tried to walk at a normal pace, but when he heard the *swish* of the second set of automatic doors opening, he ran for it.

He grabbed his keys from his pocket when he neared, abandoned the buggy beside his car, and tried to steady his hands long enough to get the key in the lock. He missed a few times, scraping away faded blue paint to reveal the silver steel beneath it. He glanced over his shoulder. The man was walking right toward him. When, at last, he got his key in, he turned it so fast he thought it might snap. He pulled it out and jumped in the car. He went to put his keys in the ignition, but he dropped them on the floor.

He was reaching for them, hands clawing at the dirty mat on the floor, when a fist rapped on the glass beside his head. He froze. Forced himself to look up at the man, who towered over him. Only then did he realize that he never locked his door.

"Hey, man. Don't forget your groceries." The muscular man then continued to a Jeep on the other side of his car.

You've got to pull yourself together, he told himself in the rearview mirror. The only thing the man was guilty of was civil decency. He found his keys under the seat and got out of the car. The parking lot was starting to empty. He moved quickly, tossing groceries at random into the tote bags in his passenger's seat. Despite his interaction with the muscular man, he didn't want to have his back to the parking lot for long.

He was drenched in sweat by the time he'd emptied all the groceries into his car. He turned around to return the buggy, and he spotted the silhouettes of two people standing near the entrance. *Fuck no.* He left it in an empty parking space beside him—someone else could attend to it—and got back in his car. He peeled out of the parking lot as fast as his old car would take him; the bags banged against one another and the door. He rolled down his window and focused on the road ahead of him.

His heavy breaths filled the car. He knew he was acting paranoid, but there was a disconnect between what he knew and how he felt. He saw nothing except a world full of executioners, and he feared that the minute he stopped would be when one finally swung the ax down on his neck.

The light ahead turned red. He slowed to a stop and took a deep breath. Held it in despite the pain in his chest. *Relax.* He reached for the play button on his cassette player. Then, he heard himself exhale.

Only, he was still holding his breath.

What the...

The air slipped from his open mouth.

His body tensed.

He looked at the passenger's seat. Nothing except groceries. Of course not. He didn't expect anyone to be there. He was familiar enough with horror tropes to know where the killers hid. He pulled his eyes up to the rearview mirror, but all he could see in the blinding headlights pouring in from the car behind him was the headrests.

See? Nothing.

But if it was nothing, then he wouldn't have a problem craning his neck back to make sure he was right. Turn around and confirm that no one was hiding behind his seat, out of the view of the mirror. There was no point in doing it though. He was alone. The wind must have made a strange sound coming in through the window.

The light turned green.

The car behind him beeped.

He drove.

There was no time for a person to get in his car anyway. He didn't have automatic doors, and he always kept his doors locked. Even now, he could see the little tabs were pushed down. He may have been distracted in the parking lot, but he seriously doubted that someone could have climbed into his car without him noticing. This was just more fear giving birth to wild illusions.

Same as in the parking lot—the shadows playing tricks

on him.

Unless... Well, unless that uneasy feeling in the parking lot wasn't just a feeling. Unless he had accidentally left his door unlocked back at the apartment and those fuckers had tracked him down and snuck into his car and locked the doors and waited for him. Unless the small pressure in his lower back was the knees of a man crouched down behind his seat. Vincent wondered which one was in the car with him. The tall man, the leader, wouldn't stoop so low himself. It'd have to be the stocky man or the kid.

Vincent didn't understand why they wouldn't have just gotten it over with already until he thought about it. With him rushing in and out of the store, the assailant must not have had the chance to kill him before they were back on the road. The fucker wouldn't risk ending his own life for the sake of Vincent's. He'd probably wait until Vincent parked in front of his apartment before he slit his throat ear to ear.

Vincent didn't need to worry about random shoppers at the store. He needed to worry about the three assholes who had landed him in the hospital. The ones who believed Vincent was the only one who'd survived the attack and seen their faces close up. The loose thread that needed to be tied up before he could identify one of them in a police lineup. And he had been so oblivious that he walked right into their trap.

He couldn't lead them back to James. He should jump out of the car and try to tuck and roll away to safety. Or drive to a police station. Or, hell, even speed up and drive into something. Put them both out of their misery. He remembered hearing about a guy who did that once. Apparently, his car brakes had gone out at the top of a hill leading down to a crowded schoolyard. Instead of taking the risk of hitting one of the kids, he just ran into a brick wall and ended his life.

A noble thing to do. James wouldn't hesitate to do it if the roles were reversed. Vincent was coming up on one of the abandoned houses in their neighborhood. If he just cut the wheel, he could end it all and take one of those fuckers out with him.

He glanced in the rearview mirror again, hoping to catch the eyes of the asshole hiding in the back before he sent him on a first-class trip to hell. He didn't see anyone. Whatever surge of emotion and determination he felt immediately deflated. He couldn't see directly behind his seat. Right where the fucker was probably sitting, but he hadn't, after all, seen anyone. Just thought he heard someone exhale and thought he felt knees pushing into his back, which was still all screwed up from the attack.

And he was ready to go all Joan of Arc on a whim.

He laughed so hard his chest hurt and eyes teared. The absurdity of it all. That he was in a deathmatch with one of the attackers, and he was going to defeat them like some sort of action hero. He didn't stop laughing until he parked his car in front of their apartment. The bottomless pit of his imagination was playing tricks on him again. He'd made it all up.

He looked at the lights glowing in the windows of their apartment. The sight had a sobering effect. That nagging uncertainty—the one he'd been avoiding since Sam's last visit—returned. Was the man in his back seat the only person he was making up? After all, no one had seen James since the attack, and he managed to disappear every time someone came around. Maybe Vincent had lost it in that cemetery, and everything since then was just a strange collection of delusions.

No.

He needed to stop thinking and get the damn groceries.

Still, he moved faster than usual grabbing the tote bags, and no matter how much he wanted to, he couldn't bring himself to look in the back seat—even after he'd shut his car door. He made a beeline to the front door of the apartment building and shut it behind him.

Just then, a door pulled open. He screamed and dropped the bags in his hands. Sam stepped into the hallway as the food spilled onto the floor. His cry seemed to frighten her as much as she'd scared him. "You okay?"

Vincent laughed even harder. "Yeah, I just wasn't expecting you."

His reaction did little to ease the concern on her face. "Sorry. I've just been worried about you."

"You worry too much." He leaned over to collect the food, but his ribs had no intention of bending that way. He opted for kneeling instead.

"Here, let me help you with that." Sam dropped a pack of cheese back in the bag.

"Thanks." He collected the rest of the food, put one bag over his shoulder, and was about to grab the other one with his free hand.

"I got this one." Sam snatched it away from him before he could get a good hold on it.

Vincent was too tired to argue with her. He stood up. "Thanks."

Up the stairs they walked. Sam climbed first. She kept glancing back at him, her brows knitted with distress. He waited for the inevitable discussion of how he needed to take better care of himself. However, she didn't say a word. Not that she needed to with the look on her face.

Maybe Jen and Sam were onto something. Was he a fool for thinking he was doing fine? The events of the night were definitely working in their favor. He couldn't go to the store without falling apart, and the only moments of joy were when he was lying beside a man who he wasn't altogether sure was real.

James.

He didn't even think about him being up there when Sam offered to help. Even if James answered the door, he wasn't entirely sure that Sam would be able to see him. But there was that sliver of doubt—a raw slice of meat cut so thin you could see through it—that made him worry she might see James and compelled him to be somewhat proactive.

"I appreciate you helping me with all of this, Sam," he said loudly in the hope of tipping James off.

Sam stopped for a moment, as if she was going to say something, but for whatever reason, she didn't. She continued up to the door. In a tired voice, she said, "No problem, Vincent."

Vincent took his time with the keys. He feigned

ignorance of their location until Sam pointed out that she could see their outline in his pants pocket. He then accidentally relocked the deadbolt and turned the key the wrong way in the hope of giving James enough time to get the hell out of sight if he was, in fact, real. Sam reached forward with her free hand, twisted the key the right way, and pushed the door open.

The hallway was dark and empty. James might've just run off into the bedroom or bathroom to hide. Or he might never have been there at all.

"Thanks. I think I can take it from here." He held out his hand for the other bag.

Sam handed it over to him. "Vincent."

"Sam." He almost started laughing, but Sam didn't look in a humorous mood. Her heavy lids and pursed lips appeared solemn.

"Just take care of yourself. Okay?"

He focused on the bag. The stitching on one of the handles was fraying. It would snap one of these days. "You too."

Sam started down the stairs, and he shut his door. He expected to feel relieved. He'd survived his trip to the store. No such feelings came. Doubt plagued him. He was starting to understand why Jen and Sam appeared so concerned. He could see the headline in the *Pittsburgh Post-Gazette* a few weeks from now: *YOUNG MAN GOES INSANE WITH GRIEF. IMAGINES BOYFRIEND CAME BACK FROM THE DEAD.*

He set the bags down on the floor and flipped on the light.

James stood at the end of the hall. "Close one."

A knot had formed in Vincent's throat that kept him from responding. He hurried down the hall, arms outstretched. James met him halfway. Held Vincent in his arms. Ran his hands through his hair as he cried. "Babe, what happened?"

Vincent looked up at him. "Nothing. Just missed you."

James kissed him. "Missed you too."

The door creaked open. "Look what rolled into my apartment."

Vincent turned around. Sam stood in the doorway, holding a can. She dropped it the second her eyes focused on them. She opened her mouth to speak, but she seemed to have lost the words. After a moment, she managed to say, "James?"

James was real.

Sam could see him.

The reality of that statement hit Vincent with the force of a falling anvil.

Fuck.

Sam sees him.

Tears ran down her face. "How…how is this even possible?"

Vincent looked to James to answer her, but he seemed to be at a similar loss for words. "We can explain."

Sam backed away, knocking into the doorframe. "But we buried you."

She looked like she was going to faint. Vincent took a step toward her. "Sam, just breathe."

Sam pointed a shaking finger at James. "We fucking buried you."

Before Vincent could do or say anything, she ran down the stairs. Her words lingered in the empty doorway.

We fucking buried you.

CHAPTER TWELVE

SOMETHING'S WRONG WITH HIM

THE CERTAINTY, THE fear in Sam's words, had stopped Vincent midstride in the hallway.

We fucking buried you.

Her steps echoed in the stairwell. Bare feet on hardwood, growing more distant by the second. Maybe she just needed time to process what she'd seen. *Slap.* Then again, she could tell Tyler about it. *Slap.* Or call the police. *Slap.* Silence filled the air for an unbearable moment before her door opened and slammed shut.

In truth, he wasn't sure what she'd do.

"Fuck." Vincent turned to James for answers to the terrible questions filling his mind. James was frozen in place. His slack expression was strangely devoid of emotion, as if her words had hollowed him out. "Are you okay?"

"Huh?" James's eyes focused on him.

Vincent rubbed his arm, trying to thaw him out. "You okay?"

After a long pause, James managed a "Yeah" that only confirmed he was far from it.

Vincent was on his own with this one.

"I gotta go talk to Sam before she—" Vincent stopped himself. James had enough to manage without being provided with a detailed report of all the ways their predicament could end badly. "Well, I'll be right back. You stay here, okay?"

"Okay," James said. Vincent wasn't sure if James had understood him or was merely repeating what he'd heard, but he couldn't wait for a more concrete answer. He had to get to Sam before she talked to anyone about what she'd seen.

He hurried down the steps to her door, one hand cupping his sore ribs and the other clinging to the railing. Images swirled in his mind of government workers in white hazmat suits poking and prodding James with metal instruments. When he reached the door, he didn't bother knocking. He twisted the knob and went into the apartment.

Sam and Tyler's apartment had the same layout as his and James's. He rushed down the hall into the living room. Tyler didn't materialize to throw him out. Neither did Sam.

The lights were on in the living room, but it was empty. Had Sam gone out the front door? The bathroom door was open, and the light was off, which left the bedroom. The door was cracked, but he didn't hear anything.

"Sam?" he called.

No response.

Oh God, had she already told Tyler? Was this silence from the shock of the news? He pushed open the door. Sam's back was to him. She was riffling through a stack of papers on her desk. Tyler was nowhere in sight. A fleeting moment of relief, lasting the lifespan of a shooting star. He didn't have to deal with Tyler. Just Sam.

He approached her. "Sam?"

She didn't say a word.

"Sam, we need to talk."

"Can't," she said in a surprisingly level tone.

"Look, what you have to understand is—"

She whipped her head around to face him. Her cheeks were red and wet with tears, but her jaw was clenched. "I don't have time for this. I have more important shit to deal with." She brushed past him to search another pile of papers on a nightstand beside the bed.

Shock? Denial? Vincent wasn't certain, but he couldn't let her leave until he was sure she planned on keeping James's survival to herself. "How about we just sit down and chat for a minute?" he started, and when she tried to interrupt him, he spoke over her. "Just for a minute. I know—"

Sam tossed aside the papers in her hand. "I was supposed to leave an hour ago to go study. I have an exam tomorrow—not that you'd care. So, I'm leaving as soon as I find my fucking notes."

Vincent raised his open hands in an attempt to show her he came in peace. "Listen, I know you're upset, and you have every right to be. But what you saw up there, you can't tell anyone about it. Something happened, and until we figure out what, we can't risk it."

Sam rubbed her temples. "Why would I tell someone about that? That's crazy. I lost it for a moment—we both did, but he wasn't real. He can't be. James is dead." Tears flooded her eyes, and her breath hitched.

She wasn't making any sense.

"Sam, we both couldn't have imagined the same thing at the same time. That's impossible."

"I need to leave. I'm not going to fail out of school in my last semester. I am going to study. And you? Well, you can go enjoy your fantasy or whatever the hell is going on. You clearly don't need me." She resumed her search.

The sharp edge of her words took him aback. This was a lot to handle, but he wouldn't let her lie to him. He snatched the papers from her hands. "He's alive. You saw him."

"Listen to what you're saying," she said, her voice wavering. "I mean, I went to his funeral. Put a rose on his casket. Watched them pile dirt on it."

James, covered in blood and dirt in Schenley Park, flashed in his mind. He pushed the image away. "Did you see him? At the funeral?"

"No. It was a closed casket, but—"

"Exactly. 'Cause he wasn't in there."

"Why would they have a funeral, then? Huh? Did he fake his death? Does he have some sort of amazing life insurance? Were those men in on it too?" She took her papers back.

Vincent didn't even know how to respond to that. James wasn't some maniacal villain; he was a victim. "Do you really think he'd do this to me? I mean, look at me. Look!"

Sam surveyed his broken body. Something close to pity flickered in her eyes. "What does he say happened?"

"He doesn't know."

"Well maybe you should find out." She set the papers back on the nightstand and knelt to look under the bed. She pulled a black plastic box from under it, set it aside, and reached back under.

He chewed on her words. James wasn't lying to him. He had been through a lot, and he couldn't remember it all. Hell, Vincent could barely remember what had happened that night. And while they argued, James was staring off into the distance upstairs, his mind lost in who knew what. "You don't understand what state he's in."

"You're right; I don't," she said, still under the bed. "Because no one bothered to tell me he's alive."

Vincent's blood pulsed in his ears. She couldn't even face him. He'd had about as much of Sam as he could take. "Get up!"

Sam froze.

"Get the fuck up!" The anger, the forcefulness in his voice surprised even him.

Sam got to her feet, her eyes wary. "What?"

"First of all, he didn't tell you because he wanted to protect you from the shitstorm that has surrounded us since that night." Vincent wiped away the tears blurring his vision. "And second, you're supposed to be his best friend, his sister. And he needs you. He needs us. Because he's alive. And he's not okay."

"I...I can't" was all she managed to get out before the tears overwhelmed her.

Vincent waited. He wanted to hear why she'd rather mourn James than help him.

"What the fuck is going on?" Tyler stood in the doorway. He had a gym bag over one shoulder, and his skin shone with sweat.

Sam was crying too hard to answer him.

Vincent looked down at his bare feet. Even someone as daft as Tyler could put together Sam's tears and Vincent's presence. Still, he said, "Nothing."

Tyler shrugged off his bag, and it fell to the ground with a deafening thump. "I think it's time we had a talk."

But Tyler didn't look like he wanted to talk. He looked like he wanted to strangle him. His nostrils were flared, and his eyes were narrow. Vincent fought against the urge to make a run for it. Even before the attack, Tyler could've caught him, and he stood between Vincent and the door anyway.

"Tyler, don't," choked Sam between sobs.

Her words only seemed to add to his fury. He advanced, a rabid attack dog ready to sink his teeth into Vincent's Achilles tendon. "You know what I don't fucking understand? Why is it that Sam goes above and beyond to help you, and she always ends up in tears? Huh?"

Tyler was so close to his face Vincent could smell his sweat. Made it hard to breathe. What could he say that wouldn't piss Tyler off more? He might've snapped at Sam when she brought over that casserole, but this was different. A misunderstanding that had been blown out of proportion. One he couldn't explain to Tyler without revealing that James was alive. But Tyler wanted answers, and he looked like he was ready to break open Vincent's jaw and forcibly extract them if necessary.

Vincent took a step back. He was shaking so much he was surprised he could carry his own weight. "Sam?"

"I'm talking to you!"

Tyler's words were so close, so loud, Vincent stumbled back, attempting to distance himself from a strike that was sure to come. Whatever he stepped on shot out from under him. He fell. He screamed as he bashed his head on something before he hit the floor and the pain exploding in his chest silenced him.

Papers rained down around him from the desk that was now overhead.

"Stop!" Sam cried.

"I didn't even touch him." Tyler threw his hands up in frustration. "The klutz fell."

Vincent rubbed his chest and tried to breathe. Through the blur of falling paper, he saw a pair of legs in the bedroom doorway. Sam and Tyler must have noticed the person, too, because they'd fallen silent. The papers cleared. Vincent propped himself up on his elbows to find James stepping into the room.

"James?" Vincent tried to process the scene playing out in front of him. James was supposed to wait upstairs. They couldn't risk anyone else learning the truth. But Vincent had fallen over, and he had screamed, and here James was, his eyes locked on the man standing over his boyfriend.

Tyler looked from Vincent to James and back, as if he was ensuring he wasn't the only one seeing the man in the doorway. His jaw dropped, and Vincent readied himself for a scream, but when Tyler spoke, it was barely above a whisper. "What the fuck?"

James didn't say a word. His face was carved from stone, cold and unemotional. He marched over to Tyler, grabbed him by the collar of his jersey, and somehow lifted him into the air. "If you ever lay a hand on him again, I'll end you."

"James!" Sam reached out a hand like she wanted to do something to stop him but wasn't sure what she could do.

Tyler kicked and screamed, struggling in vain to break free. He didn't look so intimidating now. In fact, he looked like a scared little boy. A dark spot expanded from the crotch of his gray sweatpants and ran down his leg. James shook him. "Understand?"

"Yes!" Tyler said through tears.

James let him go. Tyler hit the ground hard with an awful moan before he curled in on himself like a dead bug. Sam checked on him. Vincent had been so caught up in what was happening that he'd forgotten himself for a moment. The fog dissipated, and it was clear to him that he needed to get James out of there. Now.

Vincent scrambled to his feet. He almost slipped on some papers, but James caught him. Vincent looked into his eyes. "James, we need to go."

James didn't respond. He was lost in that far-off place again.

"Now!" Vincent grabbed his hand and pulled him toward the door. He didn't stop or look back or try to explain anything. The situation had escalated far beyond words. The best thing he could do now was put distance between them and Tyler until everyone had some time to cool off.

He'd almost made it to the hall when the metallic click stopped him in his tracks.

Somewhere behind them, Sam screamed. "Oh God! Tyler, stop!"

Vincent turned around. The black box that Sam had set aside before was open. Tyler held a deep-blue pistol in his hands, and it was pointed right at them. "Nobody move!"

Vincent was no longer in their bedroom. He was in the tunnel, clasping James's hand, staring into oblivion. Only, the man holding the gun in front of them wasn't full of disgust; he was full of fear. The gun shook in Tyler's unsteady hand, the blue metal shining in the light. Vincent and James had survived death once. He doubted they could slip through its grasp a second time.

"What the fuck is going on?" Tyler said. "You're supposed to be dead."

Vincent tried to explain, but he couldn't get enough air in his lungs to speak. Sam's words were unintelligible between her sobs. James was silent. He let go of Vincent's hand and stepped toward Tyler. Vincent grabbed him. They needed to get the hell out of this apartment before Tyler killed them both.

Tyler backed away toward Sam. "You stay the fuck away from us."

James was getting closer, pulling Vincent along with him. Vincent had to put an end to this now, or they'd both be dead. He forced air into his aching lungs and managed, "He's James."

Tyler started to lower the gun, but after a moment, he raised it again. "No. James couldn't do that. Something's wrong with him or it or whatever that is."

"Put the fucking gun down!" Sam pushed the barrel toward the floor.

Vincent leaned back so that his entire weight pulled on James, sending pain ripping through his chest. "Stop!"

James halted, turned around. His eyes focused.

"We need to go!" Tears ran down Vincent's face. They didn't have a choice in the tunnel. But they did now. They could leave. He wouldn't lose James again.

Finally, James relented. He backed away. Followed Vincent out of the room and down the hall.

"You okay?" James asked him.

"I will be." Once they were far away from Tyler and behind their locked and deadbolted door. Once he could sort out what had just happened and what could happen now that Sam and Tyler knew the truth.

They were almost out of the apartment when Tyler yelled from the bedroom, "Stay the fuck away from us!"

Vincent slammed the apartment door shut behind them.

He didn't look back.

CHAPTER THIRTEEN

BREAKING NEWS

"TILT IT DOWN a little." Vincent sat on the floor in the hall-way. The image on his phone shifted from the wall across from their apartment door to James, who stood on a chair in the doorway, staring up at the camera he held in place. His eyes glowed white in the footage. Like some sort of phantom or ghost.

"I think that's good." Vincent pocketed his phone and handed James a screwdriver. His ribs whimpered from the movement. They'd been even sorer since his fall. He gritted his teeth and passed the screws up to James as he needed them. After three sleepless nights, momentary pain was well worth the relief of having a security camera that streamed a live feed of the front door to his phone.

Soon, he wouldn't need to wonder whether the sound he heard in the dead of night was or wasn't anything; he could just check the feed and go back to sleep. Hopefully, James would get some sleep too. Between Vincent's drive home from the store and their catastrophic reunion with Sam and Tyler, they'd both spent most nights lying awake in bed, too stubborn to get up and put on the coffee until the morning light came in through the bedroom windows.

James finished turning the last screw and got off the chair. An alert appeared on Vincent's phone to inform him that motion was detected in the range of the camera. He opened the app that came with the camera, and a still image of James, pulling the chair inside, appeared on his screen. He went to the live feed, where there was nothing except their welcome mat.

He could be lying in bed right now and know for sure that the commotion was nothing more than James. The relief was so immediate he might have kissed the camera if he could reach it. For the longest time, they'd been reacting to what happened to them, but for once, they were being proactive. Whether or not they were home, they'd have a set of eyes on the only door in or out of their apartment.

Vincent shut and locked the door behind them before he followed James into the kitchen. "Want to see the fruits of your labor?"

James pushed the chair in at the kitchen table. "Okay."

He sounded about as enthused as the welcome mat.

Vincent presented his phone to James. No "oh?" or "nice" or anything of the sort. There wasn't even a flicker of relief in his eyes. He just mumbled something along the lines of "hm" and went back to adjusting the chair.

For an awful moment, Vincent wanted to grab James and shake him until he broke free from whatever had taken hold of him. Scream. Cry. Do something to snap him out of it. He'd give anything to see those eyes focus on him. See that stone face move. James's best friend refused to believe he was alive, and her boyfriend had pulled a gun on him, and James hadn't done more than bat an eye. Not even staring down the barrel of a gun had jolted him awake. He just walked toward the gun like he was some sort of superhero. Like he couldn't care less whether he died and left Vincent alone in the world.

Vincent rested his chin on James's shoulder. "You okay?"

"Yeah," James said distantly.

In some dark recess of Vincent's mind where he'd tried and failed to stash them away, Tyler's words resurfaced: *Something's wrong with him or it or whatever that is.*

Vincent didn't know why. His words were so clearly bullshit, spoken by an asshole who'd sooner pull a gun on a friend than celebrate that he was alive. James might have lifted him into the air and dropped him, but he'd thought that Tyler had attacked Vincent, and after what they'd been through in that tunnel, you could hardly blame James for being overprotective. And people were capable of all sorts of miraculous strength when they feared for the lives of their loved ones. Mothers pulled cars off their children and what-not. No, Tyler's words were nothing more than a reminder of how little he and Sam cared about James.

There was no denying James was different from the man who'd jogged into Schenley Park, but that wasn't because of some nefarious plot. James had faced death. He'd spent three weeks alone during which who knew what did and didn't happen to him. James wasn't gone. He was just lost somewhere inside himself.

And those three weeks are the key to getting him back.

Vincent hadn't gone near the subject in days—trying to give James some time to process everything that had happened with Sam and Tyler—but the longer he avoided it, the longer James would suffer.

Vincent stepped back from him. "You hungry?"

"Are you?"

"I could eat. How about I whip us up some sandwiches for dinner, you find something to watch on TV, and we can just cuddle and talk?"

Hardly a subtle proposition, but James didn't seem to find it all that strange. He just said, "Okay," and headed into the living room.

Vincent made two turkey sandwiches. He went light on the meat and cheese in the hope of stretching their supplies a little further. Once he'd smashed the halves of each sandwich together, he cut them in fours—like his mother used to when he was a child. He remembered asking her why she did it at one point or another, and she just laughed and explained, "They're much fancier looking, aren't they?"

They are, he supposed.

He didn't know why he could remember stupid shit like that while the sound of her voice and the smell of her favorite perfume were lost to the endless march of time. He stopped himself. Now was not the time to fall down that rabbit hole. Not while James was in this state.

They sat down on the couch to eat as the evening news came on. James hadn't changed the channel since last night. Apparently, it had been a slow news day. The first story concerned the red stars on school bus taillights and how some Christian organizations thought they were inappropriate and satanic in nature.

Vincent turned his attention to James. He'd hardly touched his sandwich. Not that he ate much of anything these days. With the curtains drawn shut, the lights from the TV gave his eyes that same ghostly look as before. Vincent set his plate down and curled up next to him. "Whatcha thinking about?"

James tore his gaze away from the TV. "Nothing. Why?"

Something about his blank expression and parted lips seemed so innocent and childlike that Vincent felt the sudden urge to shield him from the horrors they'd experienced. Hug him and kiss him and never go near the dreadful few weeks they'd spent apart.

But, he reminded himself, *this isn't James*.

Right now, he was little more than a shell. And the silence that had filled the apartment since their reunion had already become unbearable. He couldn't keep creating excuses. It was time to rip off the Band-Aid and hope the wound beneath it wasn't as bad as he thought.

He took James's hand and interlocked their fingers. "You know what I've been wondering?"

James watched their hands. "Hm?

"Well, when I was in the hospital—and when I went back to Butler. What were you up to? I know you said everything was hazy, but don't you remember anything more specific? I mean, I thought I saw you in the hospital lobby when I was leaving, and I don't even know if I did or if I was just seeing things."

James's grip tightened.

Silence.

"If you don't want to talk about it, that's okay," Vincent said without thinking. *Shit*. He'd given James an out before he'd even given him a chance to respond. Quickly, he added, "I just think it might help you. Help us. To talk about it."

James sat there for some time. Just when Vincent expected him to shut down again, he said, "I was...trying to get back to you."

James pulled him into a hug. He shook in Vincent's arms like he was silently crying.

Vincent rubbed his back. He wished he could do something to help him, but James wasn't ready to broach the subject. And forcing him to talk about what had happened before that time came would only hurt him more. All Vincent could do was be there for him.

Vincent breathed through the stinging pressure of James on his chest. With each short, pained breath, a faint, unpleasant smell infiltrated his nostrils. Soon, he recognized it as one of decay. They'd already scrubbed the apartment down twice, and yet, it lingered. They'd have to comb through the fridge and cabinets again, and, if nothing else, hope that a third round of cleaning would rid them of the stench.

On TV, the devilish school buses had given way to a story about a kitten who'd protected a sleeping woman from an intruder. Then, the picture faded to blue and "Breaking News" flashed on the screen in silver lettering. A video of the Allegheny River appeared with a line of text across it that read, "Breaking News: Missing Student Found."

Vincent grabbed the remote and turned up the volume.

The screen cut to a news anchor who had his hands folded on a desk. "Missing undergraduate student from the University of Pittsburgh, twenty-three-year-old Damien Wright, was found in the Allegheny River earlier this afternoon. Wright, last seen at Cruze Bar, was missing for over a month. This afternoon, Pittsburgh Police Assistant Chief Laura Anderson held a press conference to discuss the case and the ongoing investigation."

Vincent dropped the remote. It clattered on the hardwood. James got off him to see what was going on, but the weight on his chest remained. *Damien Wright.* He'd been missing for a week before his talk with Dr. Cowart. And during that meeting, his professor had asked him about Damien missing class. With everything else going on, he'd forgotten all about it, but—*oh God*—Damien had been gone all this time. And now, he was found floating in the Allegheny River.

Vincent tried to focus on the TV. A Black woman with angular features stood at a podium in front of a sea of reporters. In a controlled monotone, she said, "The person recovered from the water was identified as Damien Wright by way of physical evidence by the Allegheny County Medical Examiner's Office. Until their examination is completed, additional information concerning this death investigation cannot be released. I would like to express my sincere condolences to the Wright family. At this time, I can open up to questions. Keep in mind that what we can tell you is limited at the moment."

"Can you comment on whether or not there was any sort of trauma to the body?" asked a reporter off-screen.

"Not at this time."

A reporter directly in front of the podium waved his hand. "Do you suspect that alcohol was involved in what happened?"

The police assistant chief sighed. "Allegheny County Medical Examiner's Office is examining Damien, and we will get additional information after that examination has concluded."

"Is there any reason to believe this is related to the attack in Schenley Park a week after his disappearance?" another reporter asked.

"Not at this time, no."

Someone off-screen thanked everyone and informed them they wouldn't be taking any more questions at this time. The news anchor returned. He said something about the story—Vincent heard him, but the words turned to garbled sounds in his mind—before transitioning to the local weather report.

Vincent stared at the TV, trying to manage all the new information that attacked his mind. Damien Wright, another gay Pitt student, a nerdy kid who Vincent had slept with a few times freshman year, dead in the Allegheny River. He'd disappeared a week before they'd been attacked. They hadn't examined his body yet, but there were too many details aligning for mere coincidence.

Vincent felt dizzy. The meteorologist spoke too loud and too fast for Vincent to understand him. The Doppler weather radar map behind him looked more like a terrifying impressionistic painting, yellow and green tentacles squirming across the screen.

James grabbed his unsteady hand. "You okay?"

Vincent had almost forgotten he was beside him. "I don't know. I just...don't know."

James scooted closer. "What can I do to help?"

"It's too similar, isn't it?" Their attackers had wanted to cleanse the world of people like them, and Damien Wright was dead.

James fell silent, perhaps trying to think of another explanation that wasn't so terrible. Finally, he admitted, "It is."

"If Damien Wright was murdered..." Vincent's thoughts raced too fast for his mouth to keep up. Then, well, they probably weren't the first victims to look down the barrel of the tall man's gun. They were just the only ones lucky enough to survive these fuckers. And with the police tying

the crimes to Pitt students and their attackers evading discovery... "We aren't the only ones in danger."

He didn't know what to do, but he felt like he needed to
do something. He couldn't just sit there. And yet, he was
pretty sure that if he tried to stand up now, he'd faint. His
phone vibrated in his pocket. He answered it without even
thinking.

"Vincent?" said a familiar voice he couldn't place.

"Yeah?"

"This is Detective Ralbovsky. We'd like you to come in
to take a look at some more photographs tomorrow if you
can. Say around two or three?"

Vincent straightened up on the couch. "Ah. Okay. Two
works for me."

"See you then." Ralbovsky hung up.

"Who was it?" James asked.

Vincent set his phone down. "The police."

The call had been so short he hadn't even thought of
asking Ralbovsky about Damien Wright until now. Surely,
the detectives couldn't chalk all of this up to them being Pitt
students any longer. Not when another gay man had
disappeared two days before they'd been attacked.

Then again, they were all Pitt students, and he wouldn't
put it past Ralbovsky and Tillman to cling to that idiotic theory like a drowning man grasping at straws. The thought
that they'd dismiss what had happened to him and James,
what had happened to Damien—sweet, goofy Damien—was
too infuriating to even consider.

No, they had to be smarter than that. He needed to relax. As far as he knew, the detectives might've narrowed down the suspect list based on something relating to Damien, and that's why they wanted him to come in to look at photographs. A perfectly reasonable possibility that, given his previous interactions with the detectives, was unlikely.

For better or worse, he'd know by tomorrow afternoon.

CHAPTER FOURTEEN

PHOTOGRAPHS

VINCENT HAD SPENT most of the morning on the couch with James, trying to focus on reruns of random '90s sitcoms amidst reality TV. Every hour or so, he checked to see if there had been any updates about Damien online, but nothing had come out since the press conference yesterday afternoon. Eventually, he showered, scrounged up a clean outfit, and forced himself to eat half a sandwich. A little after one, he stopped dragging his feet and searched for his car keys.

They weren't in the metal dish by the door. Or in the pockets of the pants he had on last night. He might've dropped them in Sam and Tyler's apartment, but he decided to check with James before he even allowed himself to go down that unfortunate road.

James was still on the couch, his sandwich untouched. It was hard to tell if he was engrossed in the episode or out of it again. Both options could've caused his zombie-like stare. Vincent opted for the former, if only to calm his nerves about leaving him alone. "Hey, have you seen my keys?"

James looked down at his lap. Little silver and gold bits stuck out from one of his clenched fists. His eyes widened— like he was just as surprised as Vincent that he had the keys.

Vincent held out his hand. "Where'd you find them?"

James drew his fist to his chest. "You shouldn't go."

The intensity with which he spoke took Vincent aback. "What?"

"They can't be trusted," he said, as if that explained everything.

Vincent searched his eyes for anger or fear. They were impenetrable. Lifeless glass marbles. He took a seat beside him. "I don't trust them any more than you do, but—"

"They said I was dead."

"I know, but we don't know if they were the ones who did that," Vincent explained. They'd been over this more times than he could count. "They could be as much in the dark as us, or they could tell us something that might help us piece together what the hell happened that night. We won't know for sure unless you give me the keys."

He hoped his words sounded more convincing to James

than they did to himself. He'd actually been up all night worrying about it. He couldn't wash it away with hot water or stuff it down with food. If the detectives knew that James was alive and at their apartment, then Vincent was possibly walking into a lion's den. However, if he didn't show up, that'd be just as damning, and if, by chance, the detectives didn't know the truth, he didn't want them to start looking at him in a suspicious light and discovering James.

There were a lot of "ifs" to contend with. Thankfully, James didn't put up much of a fight. He relented and passed Vincent the keys. They felt heavier in his hand. "I'll be back soon. Who knows, maybe they've suddenly become competent and found those fuckers."

James didn't need to say or do anything for Vincent to know he found that unlikely.

"Love you." Vincent kissed him on the forehead and headed out.

He was in the doorway, listening to ensure that Sam and Tyler were nowhere to be found, when James appeared behind him.

"Miss me already?" Vincent said.

"I'm coming with you."

Vincent looked back at him. Nothing about his blank expression suggested he was joking. "No, you're not."

His whole body was tense. "You can't go alone. Too dangerous."

James meant well, but there was no way in hell Vincent was going to let him tag along. "Coming with me is only going to put us both in more danger. What if they spot you in the car? No. You need to stay here. I got this one."

James didn't respond. His gaze was fixed on something in the distance. Vincent didn't bother checking to see if there was anything on the wall behind him; he knew only James could see it. "If I'm not back in a few hours, you are more than welcome to storm the station and rescue me, deal?"

James pulled him into a tight hug. Vincent stumbled back, wincing at the pain that pulsed in his ribs. His phone vibrated in his pocket to inform him motion was detected at the door.

"Deal?" he managed to choke out.

James let him go. "Deal."

THE DRIVE TO the police station did little to placate his fears. Whatever brave face he managed to put on for James crumbled within seconds of leaving the apartment. The back seat was empty, and no cars lingered too long in the rearview mirror, but there were so many moving parts to the organism that was the City of Pittsburgh he just wanted to crawl into a dark place where he only needed to contend with himself and his own actions.

The closer he got to the police station, the harder it became to breathe. He took deep breaths, but the air never seemed to reach his lungs. The whole ordeal seemed like it was out of some absurd espionage film. Only he wasn't an international spy who had the training and tact to get information out of two detectives who might or might not be on his side. He was just some kid. And he couldn't imagine Ralbovsky and Tillman being infamous villains—that'd be giving them far more credit than they deserved. However, James had a point. Someone in law enforcement had lied about his death, and they were a piece in the puzzle of that night.

He reached the station early. He didn't realize how wound up he was until he had to forcefully pull his white-knuckled hands from the steering wheel. A quick look in the rearview mirror only confirmed that fear and anxiety was written all over his sweaty face. He couldn't go in there looking this way. He'd make Ralbovsky and Tillman suspicious before he said a word.

He checked the time on his phone. A quarter to two. He tried deep breathing until five minutes had passed, and the only discernible change was that his fingers and toes were growing numb from the lack of oxygen, which only worried him more.

In an attempt to distract himself, he focused on his phone. With James at his side, he hadn't had much use for it. No new missed calls or text messages since the last time he checked it. His email notifications, on the other hand, had grown significantly. He didn't even want to think about how many of them were from Dr. Cowart and his other professors at Pitt.

Instead, he went to his photos. Little squares filled his screen. Random memes, pictures of food, nature shots from his jogs. And pictures of him and James. A couple of weeks before the attack, they'd both had a little too much wine and decided to have a photoshoot. There were pictures of them laughing, kissing, and cuddling on the couch in various stages of undress.

The pictures reignited his memories of that night, which had been lost in the blur of booze. The taste of the dry wine. The warmth radiating off their connected bodies. He tried to remember what had been running through his mind then, but he came up empty-handed. All he knew was he had been happy. Maybe that's what happiness was—when the moment you're in is so great that you lose yourself.

He clicked on one of James. He was shirtless and downing the rest of his glass of wine. His hair jutted out in every direction like a porcupine. His lips were red from kissing Vincent all over. There were lines forming in the corners of his mouth. If Vincent had taken the photo two seconds later, James would've had a big silly grin on his face from trying to keep the wine in his mouth as he laughed.

Vincent hadn't seen James smile, much less laugh, for a long time. All these photos seemed like they were from someone else's life. Vintage stills of long-dead strangers that are sold in antique shops for a quarter.

That's why you're doing this, he told himself. To get back the life that had been stolen from them by their attackers. To get back James.

His eyes wandered back to the time. Almost two. He pocketed his phone and got out of the car. His fears and anxieties hadn't left him. But there was something else there now. Anger. It slowed his breath and steadied his hands. He went into the police station. He'd do far more than face Ralbovsky and Tillman to get James back.

THEY WERE ACTING strange.

Vincent noticed it as soon as they collected him from the front desk. Ralbovsky greeted him with a tight smile and a firm handshake, and Tillman, black binder under one arm, thanked him for meeting with them on such short notice. They were on their best behavior, and the reason escaped him.

They led him down a series of short, tight hallways to a wooden door that Ralbovsky held open for him. Inside was a windowless room with a metal table and three chairs. Two on one side one, one on the other. An interrogation room if Vincent had ever seen one. Panic jolted his system—was this why they were playing nice?—and he must not have hidden his concern well because Tillman said, "We figured this would be free from distractions. We can certainly find another room, though, if you'd like."

A part of him wanted to ask to go somewhere else to see if she was bluffing, but there was no reason they would be interrogating him. This was just nerves. After all, if they were involved in what had happened to him and James, they'd probably take him somewhere less conspicuous than a police station. The photo of James resurfaced in his mind, and he breathed. "This is fine."

He took a seat, and they sat down across from him. Tillman set the binder on the table. "Thanks again for coming in. We know this isn't easy."

"Want some coffee? Water?" asked Ralbovsky without a hint of sarcasm.

"No, I'm okay. Thanks though." He might not be getting

interrogated, but they were up to something. This wasn't like the last time he had talked to them in the hospital—wait, there was also that phone call. The police had issued that idiotic warning to Pitt students, insinuating that was why he and James had been targeted, and Vincent had called Tillman to let them know how he felt about it. With everything going on with James, he'd forgotten all about it. Maybe they were trying to play nice.

Makes sense. But something told him that wasn't the whole story.

"Well, let's dive in then." Tillman absently raised her hand to her ear, as if to tuck any stray hairs behind it, but there weren't any out of place. "Same as in the hospital, we compiled mugshots based on the physical descriptions you provided of men who have been involved in comparable activity and crimes. Take your time. If you have questions or if anything comes back to you, please don't hesitate to let us know."

Vincent waited for an "and" or an "also" that would explain the real reason they'd wanted him to come in. None came. He drew the binder close to him. Maybe they really did just want him to look through mugshots.

He opened to the first page. Four square photos of bald men stared back at him. An archaic form of the application on his phone. He studied each one. Some had tattoos of numbers—one on the right spot of his head—but none of them looked familiar. It was strange; he couldn't remember the faces of his attackers well enough for a sketch artist to properly portray them, but he was sure that if he laid eyes on one of them, he'd know.

More pages. More faces. Young men with blond hair and angry glares. Dead, glassy-eyed men with stocky builds. What constituted comparable activities and crimes? How many of these men looking back at him would've killed him if they'd come across him in Schenley Park? He wasn't sure what was worse, feeling their gaze, or knowing the detectives were watching him like hawks.

He leaned back in his chair and rubbed his eyes, grateful for the momentary darkness.

"We know this can be a frustrating process," Tillman said before he'd reopened them. "Do you want to take a break?"

"I don't know about you, but I could use a coffee myself. Little afternoon boost. How about we take a break? Let's take a break." Ralbovsky stood up.

"No," Vincent said, perhaps too sternly from the way the detectives froze. He just wanted them both to stop whatever the hell it was they were doing and tell him what was going on. The question almost left his lips, but he was afraid to know the answer. No, he needed to finish the last few pages of the binder and go. "I'm fine to keep going."

Tillman studied him. "You sure?"

"Yeah."

With a longing look at the door, Ralbovsky sat down. "If you insist."

Vincent tried to focus on the photos again, but he hadn't had the chance to give the first photo a good look when, out of the corner of his eye, he caught the two exchanging looks. *Focus*. He didn't want to miss one of these fuckers because of them. He scanned the page. More strangers. He flipped to the next one.

"Feel free to take your time. Really look at them," Tillman said.

"Not a race," Ralbovsky added with an empty laugh.

Vincent resisted the impulse to chuck the binder at them. He turned back to the previous page. Took a minute looking at each one. And, as he knew, still nothing. He didn't know what to tell them; he didn't recognize any of the men in the photographs.

He turned to the last page and only found more strangers in a crowd. Maybe his attackers were never meant to be in the binder. Maybe this was some test, and the photographs were all random lookalikes, and he was the one being studied. He felt like a monkey in a zoo. Any minute now, Tillman would shove a fistful of stale Cheerios in his face and tell him to eat up.

He rubbed his temples.

Tillman leaned closer to him. "How are you doing?"

"Fine." He was ready for James to storm the station and rescue him. She was treating him like an unstable child—oh, that was it! They didn't think he was a suspect. They thought he was made of glass. A child who required coddling. He didn't need their faux concern or canned reassurance. He needed them to drop the act and do their job. He shut the binder.

Ralbovsky straightened up in his chair. "All done?"

"Yeah."

"This can be a frustrating process," Tillman chimed in, "but your boyfriend. He'd be proud of you."

Even Ralbovsky had trouble refraining from rolling his eyes at that one. "Thanks for coming in, kid. We can lead you out of the maze."

As much as Vincent wanted to put a continent between him and them, he didn't want to go. Nothing had been accomplished. "Is there anything else I can do?"

"Not at this time," Tillman said.

"So, what are you going to do?" The question came out before he could stop himself.

"Our job," answered Ralbovsky, getting to his feet.

Are they even going to mention Damien?

"We know you're probably—" started Tillman again.

Vincent couldn't listen to another inspirational quote. "It's just...they're still out there, and we're still in danger."

Ralbovsky paused. "We're?"

Fuck.

He hadn't said *I'm*.

He'd said *we're*.

"I, ah," Vincent said, trying to think in spite of someone having sucked all the oxygen from the room. He could feel his face growing hot. "We. People—like me. I saw on the news that Damien Wright's body was found. Did you know he was gay?"

"We can't discuss details of other cases," Tillman said, her expression unreadable.

Sweat ran down his back. "Well, I guess that's that."

Vincent got to his feet, nearly knocking over his chair in the process.

Ralbovsky didn't seem all that suspicious. Just annoyed. "Yep. We should be getting back to *our* jobs. Follow me."

Not another word was said until they reached the entrance. Halfhearted goodbyes were exchanged with promises from Tillman to have some more photographs for him to look at soon. Vincent had to force himself not to run to his car. He rolled down his windows as soon as he got inside and breathed in the cold spring air.

He couldn't believe how close he'd come to giving himself away. He didn't even want to think about what could've happened if he hadn't used Damien as an excuse. Sure, now the detectives were pissed that he'd tried to tell them how to do their jobs, but they needed help if they couldn't see the clear connections between their case and what had happened to Damien. Pulling random mugshots until the end of time wasn't going to catch these fuckers. The only thing he'd learned today was that neither of them was capable of putting a stop to what was happening.

WHEN VINCENT MADE it back to the apartment, he expected James to be waiting for him at the door, but he wasn't. The apartment was dark, and the only sound was that of the TV. He found James on the couch, watching the news. Vincent plopped down beside him. "The jury is still out on whether or not we can trust them. They sure as hell aren't going to help us though."

"We should leave," James said, his gaze fixed on the TV.

"What? I mean, it's not like they're onto us or anything. They're just incapable."

"A CMU student went missing."

The weight of his words and all they implied pushed Vincent further into the couch. He checked the TV, but the anchors were discussing some political scandal. He pulled out his phone and searched for the story online.

Sure enough, freshman CMU student, Todd Caldwell, had gone missing. No one had seen or heard from him in three days. Last time he was spotted, he was going for a late-night walk. His family was offering a $5,000 reward for any information about his disappearance.

Vincent looked him up on Facebook. The profile picture was of a young wiry man with rainbow streaks across his frcckled cheeks. On his "About" page, he explained that he was bisexual. A crowbar would make quick work of such a small thin build. They might not have even needed to use a gun.

Vincent set his phone down. "Fucking hell."

"That's why we need to get out of here," James said. "Before we go missing."

His head was spinning. "Where would we even go?"

"Anywhere."

James used to talk about moving to Boston when they both graduated. He told Vincent it seemed like a good place to start over. Was that what he had in mind? Vincent tried to imagine them in a new city, but there were too many problems with that picture. "Everyone thinks you're dead, and I don't even have a college degree. I haven't worked since before the attack. What will we do for money?"

"We'll figure it out. We'll be together. And safe." His distant look and monotone voice had disappeared. He was with Vincent in this moment, and he was determined to protect him.

"The detectives refuse to see what's really going on."

James squeezed his hand. "All the more reason to leave."

Todd's picture was still on his phone screen. Would he be found in a few days floating in one of the three rivers? How many more people would have to die before law enforcement did something?

Vincent might have agreed to leave before he'd gone to the police station, but the detectives weren't going to help them. It wasn't just about him and James any longer. "People are getting killed, and more are going to die while those fuckers are still on the loose."

"But—"

"No. We can't just let this happen. We have to stay and try to get to the bottom of what the hell is going on. And stop these fuckers." Tears ran down his cheeks. He knew he sounded absurd, but he didn't care. They couldn't hide in this apartment or run away for the rest of their lives. They had to do something. And maybe then they could return to their old lives.

James rubbed his back. "What do you want to do?"

That was the question.

Vincent dried his eyes. "Whatever we have to do to end this."

CHAPTER FIFTEEN

SOMETHING

VINCENT WENT OUT of the side door to the deck. The flashing lights from inside the bar came through the tall windows and colored the crowd and smoke outside in an array of blues, pinks, and greens. At least out here, he could hear himself think. And smokers were usually more open to chatting than those grinding on the dance floor. He started to his left, skipping over patrons he'd talked to on previous nights.

The first new face he found was that of a young Black man. He leaned against the railing, lighting a new cigarette off the one he'd just finished. He was dressed in a tight white T-shirt and black skinny jeans. With a short, red mohawk that looked like the plume of a Roman helmet and gauges the size of Oreos in his ears, he didn't look like the usual clientele of Cruze Bar. He also didn't appear in a particularly talkative mood, but Vincent had gotten better at fighting against the urge to flee at every glaring look over the last few nights.

Vincent sipped his water—wishing it was something stronger—and approached him. "How's it going?"

The Roman soldier took a long drag and looked him up and down. "No offense, but you're not my type."

"I was actually wondering if I could ask you a few questions."

A guarded look. "Why? You a cop or something?"

"No, and I'm not a reporter either," he said to answer the next question that usually arose.

"What's it about?"

"I'm just wondering if you've had any trouble lately. Like people threatening you or trying to hurt you."

"I'm a gay Black man who looks like this," he said, motioning to himself. "What do you think?"

He had a point. Pittsburgh might have more accepting, or perhaps indifferent, residents than a small town like Butler, but it was hardly a utopia. "Were any of them a tall, bald man with a number tattooed on the side of his head? Or a short, stocky guy? Or a young, bleach-blond kid?"

Vincent felt strange not turning his phone to show the guy the police sketches. That's what he and James had done when they first started going to gay bars around town to ask people if they'd run into their attackers. But the sketches were so general and so many more questions arose because of them that they'd stopped using them last night.

The Roman soldier thought for a minute. "Not that I can remember. Why?"

Why?

The question Vincent dreaded most, and the one nearly every person he talked to had naturally asked him. "They attacked one of my friends for being gay. Tried to kill him."

The distance of the lie did little to stop his heart from beating faster at the thought of that night and those three assholes whose faces were lost in shadows, but whose actions were crystal clear in his mind.

"Shit, I'm sorry." The Roman soldier tapped his pack of cigarettes against the railing. "Want a smoke?"

Vincent did, but he told him that he was all right. He was pretty sure if he started smoking again now, he'd devote the rest of their depleting resources to cigarettes. "Thanks anyway."

"No problem."

Vincent continued around the deck, enjoying the secondhand smoke.

He knew the chances of finding someone who not only came across their attackers, but also survived them and happened to be at the same bar as him and James were slim. However, he'd be lying if he didn't admit that another night of answers in the negative was disheartening. One guy did explain that a bald man had screamed, "Faggot," at him from the window of a moving pickup truck, but that was hardly a lead. Vincent would need more than two hands to count the number of times something similar had happened to him and James in the city.

Vincent headed back inside to check on James's progress. He was standing against the wall on the other side of the dance floor with a baseball cap pulled down low on his forehead. Hardly an elaborate disguise. Just a precaution in case they ran into someone from school or had the misfortune of crossing paths with the detectives. Both possibilities were relatively low in a gay bar—most of their acquaintances happened to be straight—but it made Vincent feel a little better about James being out in public.

James made eye contact with him over the heads of the three men standing around him. Vincent started around the edge of the dance floor toward him. He clutched the knife in his pocket as he squeezed through the crowd, comforted by the thought that if someone tried to hurt him, he wouldn't be defenseless.

James was describing their attackers to the group when Vincent reached him. James didn't need to make much of an effort to get men to talk to him. Vincent wasn't sure if it was his looks or the mysterious air about him, but people were drawn to him. He could stand in one place for most of the night and talk to at least half the bar.

Vincent leaned against the wall and surveyed the room while he waited for James to finish. There was a man and woman in the center of the dance floor. Eyes glazed with booze, they dripped sweat as they groped and kissed each other to the beat. He was fine letting James talk to them when he was done.

His eyes wandered through the crowd. Unfocused bodies. They probably looked like a sea of squirming mealworms from an aerial view. If some giant lifted the roof off, the monster would surely shrink back in horror at the sight. That's what Vincent did when Henry presented him with a container of the bait on one of the few occasions he'd tried to get his son interested in fishing. But Vincent had also accidentally knocked the container out of Henry's hand, sending the worms straight over the side of the dock and into the pond.

A younger guy with curly hair and circle glasses appeared in front of him. "Let's dance."

Before Vincent could answer, the guy dragged him toward the middle of the dance floor.

"Oh, that's okay. I'm not in the mood," Vincent yelled over the blaring techno music as he dug his heels in the floor and tried to pull his arm free.

"Come on!" The guy tugged him forward. Hard. Vincent lost his balance and slammed into him.

The pain that shot through his chest was so sudden and intense he lost his grip on his water. He glanced down to see where it landed, and the next thing he knew, the guy had let go of his hand and was sprawled out on the ground in front of him. James stood at his side, fists clenched and chest heaving.

James had knocked him on his ass.

The man scrambled back on his elbows. "What the fuck?"

James ignored him, his attention on Vincent. "Babe, are you okay?"

Vincent looked up at him. His face was unreadable. The words on the tip of Vincent's tongue dissolved when he saw the crowd looking back at them. James was supposed to keep a low profile. He was supposed to be dead. And yet, a circle was forming around them and the man. Some guy said, "Oh shit!" A woman held her hand over her mouth in surprise. Someone else asked what was going on, and a man who could barely stand up straight chanted, "Fight!"

Vincent searched for an opening in the crowd through which he and James could flee. There didn't appear to be a break in rank among the flashing bodies that were starting to look more like the bars of a cage.

"Are you okay?" James asked a little louder.

Vincent didn't get a chance to respond. A tall, muscular bouncer dressed in black pushed his way into the circle. His eyes went from the man on the ground to James. The story told itself. Without hesitation, he marched up to James. Inches from his face, he said, "Get the fuck out of my bar."

James didn't flinch, much less move.

The man grabbed him by his forearm. "Let's go."

James yanked his arm free. He pulled his other arm back, his fingers tightening into a fist. *Shit, he's gonna hit him*. Vincent didn't have time to think of anything else. He threw himself between the two men. "We're going!"

The bouncer didn't move; he just watched James over Vincent's shoulder. "Then go."

"Sorry," Vincent said to him. He turned to James, who was locked in a staring contest with the bouncer. He snapped his fingers in James's face until he looked at him. "Let's go."

Whatever spell had come over James broke. He took in the scene and tugged down on the visor of his hat to further hide his face. "Okay."

The bouncer led them out, letting them know at the door that they weren't welcome back. Vincent hurried down the sidewalk, and when they turned the corner down the block, he stopped to face James.

He was ready to demand to know what the fuck James thought he was doing. Remind him that the goal was not to have every person in the bar look too closely at him. Let him know that the small pool of gay bars where they could talk to people had now significantly shrunk. Make him realize just how screwed they would have been if that bouncer had called the cops.

But when he opened his mouth, all that came out was a choked sob.

James pulled him close. "What's wrong?"

"I don't know." It was the truth—he felt lightheaded. No matter how hard he tried, he couldn't stop the flood of tears. And only after they were streaming down his face did he realize he'd been holding them in for days.

James stepped back to examine him. "Are you hurt?"

"No," Vincent managed between sobs.

"Come on." James led him down the street to the car.

He helped Vincent into the driver's seat.

Vincent focused on the people stumbling around the corner from the bar. Eventually, the tears slowed. He searched his mind for some explanation of what had set him off. The confusion of the fight certainly pushed him over the edge, but that wasn't it. There was more to it.

They'd gone out nearly every night for a week, and they had nothing to show for it.

He might feel less discouraged if that was all they had tried, but it wasn't. There were hours of online searches into attacks against minorities in Pittsburgh. Unreturned calls to local news agencies. Questions posted in local LGBTQIA+ social media groups, which led them to going out to talk to people at gay bars. After all of it, they were no closer to figuring out what had happened than they were last week. Damien was still dead, Todd was still missing, and their attackers were still on the loose.

To make matters worse, they couldn't keep this up forever. Rent and utilities needed to be paid if they were going to continue living in their apartment. Vincent had enough money in his bank account to cover another month or two, and they still had that envelope of cash from Sam and Tyler (which he was determined not to touch unless completely necessary), but what would they do after that? Every night, it was becoming clearer that they couldn't continue this way for long.

"I just don't know if we're fighting a losing battle," he said, drying his face with a tissue from the glove box.

"What do you want to do?"

"That's the thing. I don't know what else we can do. It's not like we're detectives or anything. We're just trouble-shooting in the dark and praying something works."

James patted his thigh. "It's something."

That had become Vincent's motto over the past week. After every night when they collapsed in bed utterly exhausted, he'd reminded James that doing something was far better than hiding in their apartment. He thought he'd been saying it for James's sake, but now he wasn't so sure. "You're right."

They had no idea what they were doing, but they were trying. It was something.

DAYS PASSED IN a blur. They branched out to other bars. Stayed out later. Became nocturnal animals who drifted to sleep when the sun started to rise in the early morning. Vincent usually awoke sometime in the afternoon, covered in sweat from the latest horror show his subconscious had cooked up for him. Then, he showered, ate dinner, and waited to head out.

His cuts and bruises were healing. James, on the other hand, was as distant as ever. Every once in a while, Vincent caught a glimpse of his old boyfriend. James smirked at a joke he told or kissed the back of his neck when they cuddled on the couch. And for a moment, Vincent was taken back to a time before the attack. Then, James retreated into himself again, and he was left with the bitter taste of their old lives in his mouth.

On Saturday, they went to Blue Moon Bar, which was having a drag show centered around '80s divas. The first performer went on at midnight, and the place was already filling up by the time Vincent and James got there at ten thirty.

Patrons had embraced the theme. Gravity-defying hair-styles. Acid-washed denim. Neon accessories. They'd been transported back in time. Under different circumstances, Vincent might've had a lot of fun tonight. He could've forced James into some ridiculous matching outfit, thrown back a few vodka tonics, and enjoyed the show.

Unfortunately, these weren't different circumstances, and while a vodka tonic would make the prospect of questioning a room full of strangers less daunting, he had to keep his head clear and focused. They couldn't afford to be downing drinks. They were here to get answers.

James had already started talking to the people hanging out around the stage—he was assigned to the more populated front of the bar. Vincent got himself an ice water and went down the hall, past the bathrooms, to the back room where there was a pool table and lax smoking rules.

A less rambunctious crowd was divided into small groups who sat at high-top tables along the walls, smoking, drinking, and chatting. A few women were playing pool in the center of the room. He didn't think he recognized a single person, but it was hard to tell when half the people were done up in '80s garb and smoke filled the air.

Vincent took as deep of a breath as his ribs would allow.

It's something, he reminded himself.

After a week and a half of doing this, he was getting better with crowds. There was still that nagging doubt when people brushed past him that they could easily pull out a blade and plunge it into his stomach, but such possibilities seemed more outlandish in gay bars, and knowing he had a knife in his pocket to defend himself kept his thoughts from spiraling too far out of control. Plus, James was just one scream away from rushing to his side and demolishing anyone who tried to hurt him.

He went clockwise around the room from table to table. He'd gotten through half of them with no more luck than he'd had the previous nights when his phone buzzed in his pocket. He stopped where he stood between two tables and checked it. He had a notification from the security camera. Motion was detected at the front door.

He went to the live feed. He wasn't sure what he expected, but he was surprised to find Sam knocking on the door. He hadn't seen her since the night Tyler had pulled the gun on James. For the first few days after that, he kept expecting her to reach out to James to apologize and see how her oldest friend was doing. After two weeks, he was pretty sure that wasn't going to happen. James didn't seem to be too bothered by it, but there was no way it wasn't affecting him.

Was that what she was finally attempting? A half-baked apology?

Just then, something slammed into his stomach. The force was so concentrated and sharp he thought his worst fear had materialized. He jumped back and dropped his phone to search the folds of his sweater for the blood that'd be gushing from the wound.

His sweater was dry. He looked up to find the source. No attacker wielding a knife. Just a heavyset woman with a scrunchie in her side ponytail and a pool cue in her hands. "Sorry, hun. I didn't realize you were right behind me."

"Sure, Liz," one of her friends, whose hair was teased into a mound of blonde hair, said before erupting in laughter.

"Ignore her," Liz said. "I wish I could say Kat was drunk, but that's just her personality."

"You're fine." He knelt to pick up his phone. He'd learned pretty early on that he wouldn't be bending over until his ribs healed. The landing was empty. Sam must have retreated. He closed the app and pocketed his phone. He still had the women's attention. "Can I ask you and your friends a few questions?"

"As long as you aren't some confused Jehovah Witness, sure."

Vincent went through his spiel. Had anyone threatened them or tried to hurt them? No. They hadn't come across a tall man, a stocky man, or a blond kid, had they? No, they hadn't. Why did he want to know? He told them the lie. An automatic response by this point. Almost as if it had created an alternate history that he could explain without even thinking about it. He appreciated them taking the time to talk to him anyway. He started back over to the next table along the wall when Kat said, "Wait a minute, Liz. What about your car?"

Liz thought for a moment and took a swig of her beer,

which was sweating on the edge of the table. "We don't even know who did that, and I think it had more to do with where I was than anything."

"What's that?" Vincent forced himself to remain calm. Nothing anyone else had said so far had led to anything. There was no reason that this would be the exception.

"Oh, some asshole fucked up my car," she said dismissively.

"Did more than that," Kat said.

Liz shot her a glaring look before focusing her attention on Vincent. "I doubt this will help, but if it'll shut her up, I might as well tell you. So, my shit-for-brains brother bartends now and then at this dive bar in West Oakland. End of January, I had to pick him up because his ride fell through—he doesn't drive."

"He can drive. The dumbass got his license suspended," Kat said, as if it was an essential detail to the story.

"Anyway," Liz continued, ignoring her friend. "It was like almost two in the morning, and I was out front beeping and beeping, but he never came out. So, I parked my car and stormed in. Found him trying to talk up this busty bartender. And when I finally dragged him back to the car, someone had keyed it. I have a rainbow Star of David on my bumper, and they carved 'undesirable cunt' across the door. Never found out who did it though."

Undesirable.

The word echoed in his mind.

Not in her voice.

In a deep, gravelly voice.

The tall man. He'd called them that. *Undesirable filth*. Of all the things those fuckers had called them, this one stuck out because it was so uncommon. Strange. Stranger still that it'd been carved into a car less than a mile or two from Schenley Park within a month of the attack. There was no denying that, despite the coincidences, their chances were slim, but it was the closest thing to a lead they'd gotten since they'd started. "What bar was that?"

"Rob's. But I wouldn't go around there if I were you. Most of the men there are looking to fuck or fight. Not a place for a nice boy like you."

"Thanks. Sorry about your car." He started backing up. He needed to get James. Tell him what he'd found.

She shrugged. "Just a car. Sorry about your friend."

It took him a second to realize that she was referring to the lie. "Thanks."

"Hey," Kat said, her face brightening. "Wanna play the loser? We suck, but after a couple beers, you won't be able to notice."

"Thanks. But I gotta go."

"Be careful out there," Liz said.

"You too."

Vincent rushed out of the room. It could be nothing. Someone else with similar sentiments to those three fuckers could have used that word...or the tall man could have spotted Liz's rainbow Star of David in the parking lot and decided to leave her a little present.

He found James at the bar, chatting with a seven-foot-tall Whitney Houston. "Hey, can I talk to you?"

James turned to him, his eyes widening with concern. "You okay?"

"Yeah, I'm fine. Listen, it's not much, but I think I found something."

CHAPTER SIXTEEN

ROB'S

ROB'S WAS ON the corner of a deserted residential street. They wouldn't have found it without Google Maps. The paint on the sun-bleached sign over the long rectangular building was peeling, leaving only "b's." The gravel lot beside the building was filled with cars, trucks, and motorcycles in various stages of rust and decay. Everything about the place warned of trouble.

James stared out of the window at the entrance. "You sure this is it?"

"Yep." Vincent parked at the end of one of the rows next to the road in case they needed to make a speedy escape.

He'd relayed Liz's story to James, who'd agreed that they should head straight there from Blue Moon, but Vincent had omitted her comment about the regulars wanting to either fuck or fight. James was guarded enough.

"We're just gonna go in there and see if we recognize anyone. If we do, we'll leave and call the cops. If not, we'll ask around a bit. No big deal," he said, as if they hadn't discussed the plan at length on their way over.

"No big deal," James repeated without any of the false enthusiasm Vincent had injected into the phrase to mask his rising concern.

The whole thing was a long shot, so he wasn't sure why it made him so nervous. This would inevitably lead down another dead end like everything else they did. It wasn't like they were going to go in there and find the tall man finishing off a lager. The scenario was so preposterous he couldn't even picture it in his mind.

What was less preposterous, however, was the connections between Liz's story and their own. *Undesirable.* The hate had dripped off each syllable. As hard as it was to picture their attackers outside of dark tunnels and sketchy alleyways, he supposed this looked like a place the tall man might frequent.

There's a chance, he admitted.

Wasn't that why a rush of excitement came over him when he heard the woman's story? Because there was a chance Vincent and James could find them. A chance their attackers' hatred could have started with keying a car with a rainbow Star of David at a local bar and escalated to taking care of those who they deemed undesirable. A chance they could end this strange limbo they had been floating in since the attack. An amazing chance...until he realized it involved facing those bastards again.

Vincent would face them, though, if it meant getting their old lives back. He turned to James. "You ready?"

James must've come to a similar conclusion about crossing paths with their attackers. His pensive expression had gone grave; forehead wrinkled and lips drawn in a thin line. "You should stay here."

"No," Vincent said without hesitation. There was no way he was letting James go in there alone. Ever since the attack, James had been ready to fight anyone who looked at either of them the wrong way. If he tried to pull that in a place like this, he could get himself killed.

"It's not safe. You should—"

"I know it's not safe," Vincent interrupted. "I'm going."

"They think I'm dead. They won't be looking for me."

Vincent opened his mouth to dismiss him, but he couldn't find a simple way around that point. "I don't care. I'm going. Let's go."

Vincent got out of the car before James could say another word. James didn't stop him, but he didn't look happy about it. They crunched through the gravel to the front door. Shards of glass and cigarette butts littered the ground. The windows that weren't boarded up with plywood were lined with posters and signs giving no hint to what they were to expect inside.

Vincent gripped the handle. There was a small chance they would find what they were looking for, and whatever risk was involved in that chance was worth taking if it meant ending this nightmare.

He steeled himself and pulled open the door. Smoke rushed out to greet them. Through the haze, dim lights hung over a bar that stretched across the length of the building. To their left was a small table filled with bikers dressed in leather and denim. To their right was a busted pinball machine and a group of men throwing darts at a bullseye on the wall.

Vincent searched for bald heads and stocky frames—the kid seemed too young to be allowed in such a place. He managed to examine and dismiss the bikers and the men playing darts in a matter of seconds. Too short. Too thin. Too much hair. No tattoo. He was having a little more trouble with the men who were sitting with their backs to them at the bar.

An old man who was hunched over in his seat glanced back at them. A crooked grin spread across his face, revealing yellowed teeth and black gaps where some of them must've rotted away. He tapped the man beside him who was too large to be either of their attackers. The man looked at them and chuckled. It was clear Vincent and James didn't belong there. The age gap between them and the mostly silver-haired patrons was only part of it. These were grizzled, working men, and two gay fresh-faced college students didn't fit into that equation.

Vincent spotted an opening at the end of the bar behind the table of bikers. Maybe they could fit in a little better over there. He led James to the corner. If one of those fuckers was at the bar, he didn't want them spotting him and James before they identified him.

The red-haired man beside them was tall and thin. Another no. Vincent craned his neck to look down the bar. He'd made it through half of the faces when the bartender, who seemed to be one of the few women in the place, interrupted him.

"Hey, baby dolls, what can I get you two?" Her face was covered in lines that contrasted the taut flesh sticking out from her low-cut shirt.

"Waters would be great," Vincent said.

"And?" She tapped her acrylic nails on the bar. Just a water wasn't going to fly here.

"And…" Vincent repeated to give himself a minute. The red-haired man beside them had his scabbed knuckles around a bottle of Pabst Blue Ribbon. "And two Pabst Blue Ribbons."

"Bc right up."

By the time she returned with two bottles, Vincent had gone down the bar and back, and he was pretty sure their attackers weren't there. None of the men coming in or out of the bathroom matched their descriptions either. He didn't know if he was disappointed or relieved. Probably a little bit of both.

The bartender set the beers down in front of them. "That'll be six bucks."

"Thanks." Vincent handed her a ten.

"Thank you." She stalked off and didn't return with his

change.

Vincent tried his beer and had to force himself not to spit it out. He didn't think he'd had a beer since he snuck a few from Henry in high school, and something told him this wasn't the cream of the crop. Swallowing hard, he turned to James. "I don't think they're here."

James held the bottle, but he didn't bring it to his lips. "Neither do I."

"Well, we should probably make this worth our while, then." They couldn't, however, take the same approach as they had at the gay bars. Not in this kind of place. "We can at least see if anyone knows them or has seen people in the bar who fit their descriptions."

James turned around to face the bikers. A fight that started with a crude comment and ended with him and James getting dragged down the street on chains attached to the back of motorcycles played out in Vincent's mind. He leaned in close to James. "Maybe we should do this together."

James turned back around. "Okay."

Vincent started with the redhead. "Excuse me, I was wondering if—"

"No," the man said without looking up from his drink.

They went a little further down the bar and tried again with similar results. Several men were noticing them. Whispers were exchanged. They didn't blend in well with this crowd, but did it go deeper than that? Could these men somehow tell they were gay by the way they held themselves? He didn't want to wait to find out.

He set his beer down on the bar. "We should go."

"We should," James agreed.

Only when they were back in the car with the doors locked did Vincent speak again. "You know, I wouldn't be surprised if they came here."

"Me either," James said.

"But it's not like we can just wait around for them here." Liz was right. Those men looked like they were asking for any excuse to hit something.

A car pulled up behind them. The headlights flooded the car, blinding them with yellow light. Neither of them spoke until they saw that the driver's hair was too long to be the tall or stocky man.

"We could watch from the car," James said.

Vincent thought it over. Sitting in the parking lot each night. Looking over the patrons as they made their way inside. "We could, but wouldn't people get suspicious after a little while?"

"They would." James looked down at his lap.

Vincent could see the cowlick on the top of his head. The same vantage point he got of Sam in the security footage— her messy blonde hair pulled into a bun that bounced as she knocked on the door. "I meant to tell you Sam stopped by the apartment earlier."

He opened the app and showed James the clip. James's face didn't betray whatever he thought or felt about it. Vincent watched the footage again. The answer to their problem was so obvious he wasn't sure how neither of them had thought of it sooner. "We don't have to be here every night to see who's coming and going."

They just needed a camera.

THE FIRST HURDLE was a power source. It wasn't like there was an outlet on the side of the building beside the dumpster they could use to plug in a camera, and even if there was, it'd hardly go unnoticed. They needed to find something else to see who was coming and going from Rob's parking lot.

A few quick internet searches brought Vincent to game cameras. He didn't know why he didn't think of it before then—Henry had one he used during hunting season back when his knees bothered him less. Unlike Henry's camera, which needed to be taken down and manually uploaded to a computer, there were several newer game cameras that could send images straight to Vincent's phone like the security camera outside their door. He found one with infrared night vision that took footage and images without using a flash. It also had a battery life of a few weeks. The camera was kind of pricey—a little over a hundred dollars—but well worth it.

He ordered the camera that night, and in two days, it arrived in the mail. He was surprised by how small it was. A little camo box he could easily hold in one hand. They tested it in the apartment at night with the lights off. The scope captured so much of the room they only needed to place it waist high to get everything in the frame. The video was lower quality than the images, so he set it to take a picture each time motion was detected. The images were somewhat grainy, but it would be easy to identify a face or a license plate with it, which was the goal. If they could identify the tall or stocky man along with their license plates, they could take the pictures to Ralbovsky and Tillman and wash their hands of the whole mess.

The bar closed at two in the morning. They drove past at three, but there were still a few vehicles lingering in the gravel parking lot. By four, it was empty. They parked next to the side of the building that faced the parking lot.

The headlights shone on a rusting, army-green dumpster and a stack of wood pallets beside a steel door marked, EMPLOYEES ONLY. The door and the surrounding brick wall of the building were covered in graffiti. A royal-blue peace symbol. White cursive letters that were illegible. A tiny black alien in a flying saucer. Not a lot of places to hide a camo game camera.

They got out of the car to look around. The dumpster was the obvious choice because of the color, but when it was emptied, the camera could be easily damaged or trashed. Vincent was a little worried about hiding it in the pallets in case the employees used them for shipments or something, but the ice frozen to the top of the stack indicated that they weren't used too often.

Just then, a car passed, bathing the parking lot in light. *Shit*. Vincent grabbed James and crouched behind the dumpster. The car continued on without stopping, but they waited another minute or two before they stepped back out in the open. He didn't want to know how many laws they were breaking, and he'd rather not have Ralbovsky and

Tillman tell them.

Even if the driver didn't see them, someone else could. They worked fast after that. James lifted the top third of the pallets, and Vincent strapped the camera to the wood. Once James put the stack back down, he readjusted it so that the lens looked out of an opening in the grates. Then, he turned it on and waved his hand to test it.

No flashing lights or sound. A few seconds later, he received a notification. A green photograph of him and James. They stepped back to where the car was parked. Their faces were still identifiable, and the license plate was easy to read. It had taken five more pictures by the time they got back in the car and drove off.

"At least we know it works," Vincent said.

IT WASN'T LONG before the number of images became overwhelming. Hundreds upon hundreds. Cars coming and going. A stray cat skittering across the gravel. Blank photos that, at least according to Vincent's superficial Google searches, might've been caused by a heavy wind. Nights were far worse, naturally, when business picked up at the bar.

The first few nights, Vincent tried to balance continuing to visit gay bars with checking the images. But with each night at bars bringing no new leads, and the number of new patrons shrinking, they agreed to focus on looking through the images. They worked on the couch, passing Vincent's phone back and forth every couple of hours to give their eyes a break.

James had just given it back to Vincent one night when there was a knock at the door. A notification appeared on his phone from the security camera. He opened the live feed. Sam stood on the landing.

"It's Sam," Vincent said.

James got to his feet. "I'll get it."

"You can't," Vincent said automatically. He had to remind himself that, unlike the rest of the world, Sam already knew he was alive. "Sorry. Force of habit. Yell if you need me."

His phone vibrated. A new image from the parking lot. He opened it. A still of an old man getting back in his beater. He'd been there since the bar opened at four, and he had to be smashed by this hour, which was a little after ten. In the next image, his silhouette could be seen through the back window of his car, and then the car had just about disappeared out of the frame.

Another notification from the front door. Vincent went to the live feed without thinking. James stood out in the hall with Sam. It was strange going from static green images to live footage in color. Sam's hands moving as she spoke almost looked uncanny. James might as well have been in a picture—he just stood there, his back to the camera, listening. Vincent hoped something more productive came from this meeting than the last one, for James's sake.

A new image from the bar. A light-colored truck, probably white, was pulling into the spot the other guy had just left. The driver was backing into it, so no license plate. Quite a few patrons at the bar backed into the unofficial parking spots that were formed by other cars in the gravel lot. He'd been wondering if they should get another camera to deal with this problem. There was a tree beside the sidewalk where they could easily conceal it. He probably would've already bought another one if money weren't an issue.

He switched back to the live feed of the front door. Sam was hugging James and whispering something in his ear. The moment seemed too intimate to intrude upon. He closed the app. As terrible as Sam and Tyler's reactions were to the news that James was still alive, James could probably use as many friends as he could get at the moment. Maybe having Sam's support might help him return to his old self.

Another image from the bar. A man stepping out of his truck. He was so short that only the top of his hair stuck out from the open door. Another image. He was walking toward the building. He must've been moving fast because his image was blurred. Vincent didn't need the details to recognize him though. Broad shoulders. Solid build. He'd seen him before. Watched his shadowy figure advance on them in Panther Hollow.

The stocky man.

He was at Rob's.

Vincent went to get up to collect James, but he couldn't move. His body was fused to the couch. And his heart—it was racing so fast he expected to have a heart attack any second now.

Oh God, we found him.

He brought his hand to his chest to keep his heart from

bursting through his ribcage.

Images flooded his mind. Not of the stocky man at the bar. But him on the trail. His shadowy smile. His hands wrapped around the crowbar. Bringing it down on James in the tunnel.

The front door shut.

Vincent looked over the back of the couch at James. The horror must have been written all over his face. James ran down the hall to him. "What's wrong?"

"I found one of them." He held up the phone so that James could see him.

James's face darkened. "We should call the police."

"We should." Vincent looked at the image. "But it's not clear, and we don't have his license plate."

"Does it matter? He's at the bar now."

"He is but..." But after his last meeting with the detectives, he was pretty sure it did matter. He had a feeling they wouldn't send the cavalry just because he told them he'd found one of their attackers in a blurred image from a game camera they had illegally set up in the parking lot of a dive bar. Plus, they didn't have his license plate. If his truck was gone when the police got there, then they'd be back at square one, and the detectives would think he was even crazier than they already thought. No, they needed the license plate at the very least if they were going to catch this bastard.

Vincent forced himself to his feet. "We have to go."

"There is no way you are—"

"I'm just gonna take a picture of the license plate, and we can leave. We don't even have to get out of the car." Vincent didn't wait for an answer. He started down the hall to get his keys from the dish beside the door. He wasn't going to let him get away. They were going to finish this tonight.

James followed behind him. "It's too dangerous."

"There's no time to argue." Vincent plucked his keys from the dish. "You don't have to come with me, but I'm going."

James bit back whatever he was thinking. "Let's go."

CHAPTER SEVENTEEN

SILHOUETTES

"YOU SHOULD SLOW down." It was the first time James had spoken since they'd gotten in the car.

Vincent checked the speedometer. They were going twenty over the speed limit, but it seemed like they were crawling down the street. He had this sinking feeling that he'd soon receive a notification showing the stocky man driving out of the parking lot, taking any chances of catching these assholes with him. But getting pulled over for speeding would only ensure that they'd never get there in time. He begrudgingly let off the gas pedal.

The next light they reached was red. Vincent slowed to

a stop. They were only a few minutes from the bar, and, as if to counter his momentary relief, his phone buzzed in his pocket. He brought it eye level and steadied his hand as best he could. A new image from the game camera. *Of course.* He opened it. A biker with a long, braided beard was captured midstride in front of the white truck, which was still parked.

"We're okay," he told James, whose expression didn't change. Vincent knew James was nervous, but they were so close to ending this he could taste it. The reward far exceeded the risk.

The light changed, and he took off down the street. He only slowed down when they arrived at the parking lot. His headlights pierced the darkness, lighting up the graveyard of cars. A shirtless man with red lipstick smeared on his face raised his head from the back of a car. Vincent cut his lights and continued through the lot until he reached a black Jeep parked directly behind the truck. He drove past the Jeep, then reversed to try to get a good view of the stocky man's license plate, but the Jeep was parked so close to the truck that he couldn't see anything.

Shit.

They'd have to leave the safety of the car if they were going to get the picture. He glanced at the door of the bar. It was just around the corner from the truck. A few feet away at most. If the stocky man walked out while they were taking the picture, he'd be on them in a matter of seconds.

We don't have a choice, he told his racing heart. *We'll be fine.* The stocky man was probably still working on his first beer. They just needed to do it. Now.

Vincent unbuckled his seat belt and grabbed his phone.

"What do you think you're do—" James started.

"I'll be right back. Just keep an eye on the door."

James unbuckled his seat belt. "No, I'll do it. Give me the phone."

"Watch the door." Vincent got out of the car before he thought better of it. He hurried around the Jeep. His ribs burned, and the cold air refused to enter his lungs, but he didn't care. He'd worry about it after he got the license plate. He wedged himself between the Jeep and the truck and snapped a picture.

No flash.

He fumbled to switch it on. An engine roared to life somewhere behind him. He looked back. A car was pulling out of the back of the lot, headlights shining through the parked cars. Perhaps whoever they'd caught in that car when they'd arrived was leaving. He focused on his phone. A little white lightning bolt icon in the corner of his screen was supposed to control the flash. Despite how many times he pressed it, the flash refused to turn on.

"Come on!" He closed his camera app and reopened it.

All of a sudden, the music and chatter from the bar became far louder and clearer than it had been a moment ago. The front door. He hadn't seen anyone walking over to it from the parking lot, which meant someone was leaving the bar. He checked for a warning. James motioned that it was all right. That didn't mean the stocky man couldn't be right behind whoever had just left.

He took another photo. Still no flash. He fought against the urge to chuck his phone into the dumpster and run for it. *Work, you bastard, work!* He smashed his pointer finger into the screen and lost his grip on his phone. He lunged to grab it, but it fell through his fingers, and he lost his balance. Something hit him hard in the face. It took him a moment to realize he'd fallen face-first into the hatchback. Before he could even get back on his feet, the taillights flashed, and the alarm sounded.

Beep! Beep! Beep!

Pain radiated from his nose, and something hot and thick gushed from his nostrils. *No, no, no.* He knelt as low as he could between the two cars, searching through the rocks for his phone. Footsteps on gravel. Getting closer. He was a dead man.

"What happened?" James stood over him.

There was no time for relief. The stocky man would be coming for them any second now.

"I dropped my phone. Help me find it!"

James got down on all fours and pulled it out from under the Jeep. "Here. Come on."

"One second." Vincent unlocked the phone and tried the flash button one more time. The lightning bolt turned yellow. It was on. He took a picture of the license plate. James grabbed his hand, and they were running.

"Hey, stop!" screamed an unfamiliar voice behind them.

Vincent didn't turn around. He ran to the car, and as

soon as James was beside him in the passenger's seat, he peeled out of the gravel lot. His phone vibrated nonstop in his pocket from the crowd that must've formed outside of Rob's.

The stocky man would be among them.

How close had they come to crossing paths with him again? Vincent didn't want to think about it. He needed to drive. They weren't out of the woods yet. He turned at random until even he couldn't remember how they'd gotten to the residential street they were on. He parked his car by the curb and took a breath for what felt like the first time in minutes. Only then did he realize he could have easily just copied down the license plate number in his phone, but that didn't matter now.

"We did it," he said, laying his head on James's shoulder. Their plan had quickly dissolved into chaos, but they had gotten the picture and made it out of there relatively unscathed.

James handed him a tissue to clean the blood from his face. "We did."

ONCE VINCENT HAD gotten his breathing under control and decided how he wanted to frame their discovery, he called the detectives. The phone rang. And rang. He checked the time. Close to ten thirty. Not exactly early, but this couldn't wait until morning.

The call went to voice mail. He hung up and redialed. Wasn't it bad enough that they had to find these fuckers on their own? Did they really have to track down the detectives too? Just when he expected it to go to voice mail again, someone answered the phone.

Silence.

"Hello?" Vincent said.

A garbled cough. "This is Detective Ralbovsky."

He sounded groggy. They'd woken him up.

"I was out, and I saw one of them. The stocky guy. He's in a white truck at Rob's bar in West Oakland. I don't know how much longer he's going to be there, so you guys should hurry. But I got his license plate. Let me know when you're ready for it." Vincent switched his phone to speaker and pulled up the image in preparation.

A long pause. Vincent assumed he was grabbing something to write with until Ralbovsky said, "Vincent?"

"Yes, I—"

"Where are you?"

"I'm in my car. I drove off as soon as I saw him. I'm safe. Are you ready for the license plate?"

He yawned. "Have you been drinking?"

"What?" Was he even listening? "No, we found one of them."

Indiscernible sounds of movement came through the line. "We'll look into it. You should, ah, head on home."

"I have the license plate," Vincent repeated for what seemed like the millionth time.

"That's right. Good. I have my notebook. Ready when

you are." There was something in his tone—a false eagerness that you might use with an upset child—that convinced him Ralbovsky hadn't moved from his bed.

Vincent fought the urge to scream into his phone. "Are you sending people out to the bar?"

"We'll look into it."

That wasn't an answer.

"It's him. I'm sure," Vincent said.

"I believe you."

The implication was hardly disguised. *I believe that you believe, but that doesn't make it true.*

"Why would I lie?" Vincent said before he thought better of it. James put a hand on his thigh, but he shook it off. He was tired of placating these idiots.

"I didn't say you were lying," Ralbovsky said.

"Are you even sending anyone out to the bar?"

"Vincent, we'll look into it. Trust us."

He didn't. "But?"

"But we can't go rushing around every time someone thinks they see someone. There's a lot of stocky guys in Pittsburgh. We will look into it. I promise. So how about you tell me that license plate and head back home? It's late."

Vincent ended the call.

They'd done everything. Risked their lives. And even now, the detectives refused to do their jobs. A thought burrowed its way into his brain. A question. Because they couldn't be that incompetent. Because someone in law enforcement had been involved in what happened that night. Because, despite the funeral and grave, James was still alive.

Could Ralbovsky and Tillman be involved?

And if they were, who could he and James trust?

Vincent's phone continued to vibrate. Ralbovsky calling him back amid further notifications from the game camera. He ignored the call and focused on the images. Men standing around, checking their vehicles. The back of the stocky man, inspecting his truck and talking to another guy. They had him, but what was there to do if the people tasked with protecting them weren't going to step up to the plate?

"We could go to a news agency," Vincent said. "I know they haven't called us back before now, but what if we hand them the license plate and a picture of the man who we know attacked us? Let them know just how helpful these detectives have been."

James mulled it over. "Then they'd have to do something."

Vincent flipped back through the images for one of the stocky man. The best one they had was still his unfocused figure walking to the bar. A green photograph clearly taken with a game camera. They couldn't give them this shot. Beyond how unclear it was, it'd raise too many questions about how exactly they'd acquired it. "We need a picture though. Not with the game camera. With my phone."

"Then, we can end this," James said. His gaze never left the windshield, but he seemed to grasp the gravity of what they'd been working toward this whole time. There was a light at the end of the dark tunnel they'd been trapped in since the night of the attack, and they were close to reaching it. They just needed to hang on a little longer.

Vincent leaned over the center console and wrapped his arms around James. "One more picture, and we can end this."

VINCENT TYPED THE address for Rob's into Google Maps. He'd made so many turns that eventually contradicted one another he hadn't put more than a mile between them and the bar. The plan wasn't elaborate. They'd wait for the stocky man to leave and snap a picture of him from the car. Then, Vincent would fly out of there like a madman. They'd be long gone before the stocky man got the chance to climb into his shitty truck.

A notification from the game camera appeared after he made the first turn in that direction. Vincent clicked on it. A couple walked toward the bar. He went back to the map. He picked up the pace a little after that. But when another image came through, he was still a few streets away from the bar.

He clicked on it. The stocky man stood with his back to the camera, his hand stuck in his back pocket where he must have been shoving his wallet. He was leaving. He probably just went inside after his alarm went off to finish whatever he was drinking and close his tab.

Vincent floored it. Another image came through, but he didn't waste time looking at it. He blew past a stop sign and continued onto the street of the bar.

The stocky man's white truck pulled out of the gravel lot ahead of them.

"Fuck!" Vincent hit the steering wheel. They'd lost their chance. He'd been an idiotic klutz who couldn't even take a picture without setting off a car alarm and scaring off the stocky man, and now, they were back at square one.

"Follow him," James said.

"What?" Vincent must have misheard him. James wasn't actually suggesting they trail a homicidal maniac. It was too dangerous.

"Follow him," he repeated. Not so much a suggestion, but an order. James looked through the windshield, but his eyes were focused on something tangible. The truck. There was a hunger in his eyes. A need only Vincent could under-stand.

We could end this tonight.

Follow him to wherever he was going and get a picture when he reached his destination. No more waiting. They could send it to the papers first thing in the morning. Start the day thinking of something other than these monsters and their crimes.

The truck turned right at the end of the road.

Vincent sped up and did the same. He tried to turn onto the next road right before the stocky man turned onto the following. The white truck was easy to keep track of, even at night. Vincent was about to close out of Google Maps, which was trying to redirect him to Rob's, until he recognized the value of an aerial view of the roads around them. He left it on the screen. A nice preview in the event the stocky man realized he was being followed and pulled into a winding driveway or a dead-end street.

Not that he gave any indication he was on to them. He drove fast and didn't signal before making turns, but that just seemed to be the way he drove. There were no sudden cuts of the wheel or dashes to evade them. He wound through the streets of West Oakland, seemingly unaware that he was part of a cat and mouse game where he was the prey.

This side of Oakland, which Vincent had been warned by local students to avoid at night, wasn't all that different from where they lived. Older houses were sectioned off into various apartments with minimal upkeep. Mixed colors of siding and cheap patches on roofs. There were, however, fewer students milling about at this hour.

Every once in a while, when his eyes weren't glued to the back of the truck, he spotted residents. Smokers on a dark porch, their gaunt faces glowing in the embers of their cigarettes. A group of kids who scattered from the street when his headlights shone on them. An old man hunched over a garbage can with a bag of aluminum at his feet. They reminded him more of rougher parts of Butler than the city. He wondered if there were places like this all over the world or if something about this area drained the life out of people.

The stocky man slowed down on Allequippa Street. They watched him from the stop sign at the intersection. Just when Vincent was sure the stocky man had noticed he had a shadow with headlights following him, the truck turned onto what Vincent thought was a driveway until he consulted his phone and realized it was a side street that branched off into two other roads. To the right was a dead-end road and to the left was a narrow road that ran parallel to Allequippa for a block before rejoining it.

Vincent hung back until the truck's red taillights were only a faint memory. Either the stocky man lived on one of these streets, or he was trying to lure them into some trap. Vincent turned off his headlights before he followed him. The stocky man had stopped in front of a house halfway down the road to their left. Vincent couldn't make out many details outside the scope of the truck's headlights shining down the road. The only streetlamp in sight was at the other end of the road, across from the cluster of houses far away from the spot where the stocky man had parked his truck.

His red taillights glared back at them for a moment before they blinked out of existence. The stocky man had stopped, and there was no way they were making it down the road without tipping him off. Vincent backed up and parked on Allequippa Street. He turned to James to ask him if he was okay going over there on foot. Before he said a word, James opened his door. They were on the same page at this point; they were getting that fucking picture.

The stocky man had already made it inside when they reached the narrow road. Lights glowed from the windows on the first floor. Vincent tried to ignore the weight of disappointment pressing down on him. They hadn't gotten there fast enough to take a picture while he was still outside. "He might be leaving again soon. It could be a friend's house or even a dealer's place or something."

"Yeah," James said, "we should take a closer look."

They hurried down the road at a fast walk that only mildly annoyed Vincent's ribs. As they got closer, he realized the sheer pink and white materials covering the windows were various bedsheets. One had a pattern of Strawberry Shortcake on it. Silhouettes could be seen inside, and the glowing light enabled him to make out more of their surroundings.

Vincent might have assumed the house was abandoned if it weren't for the lights. The right side of the house was covered in lime-green siding, and the front was just exposed wood. It was so close to a dilapidated red brick building on the other side of it that, from the angle they were standing, he couldn't tell if they were connected. Either way, a shoulder-high chain-link fence went around both buildings. Garbage cans and blue barrels littered the yard among pieces of tarp and other bits of garbage and old toys.

They slowed when they neared the house. There was a large tree just off the road, a few feet from the fence, that they could easily hide behind. Vincent took a moment to catch his breath when they reached it. The night air chilled the sweat beading on his forehead. He wiped it away. "Now, we wait."

They watched the house from either side of the trunk. A light turned on in one of the upstairs windows. Then another. The lights remained on for a few minutes until someone turned one of them out. Vincent's heart pounded in his chest. He readied the camera on his phone. Any minute now, the stocky man would come walking out of the house, and they'd have him.

Silhouettes passed the windows on the first floor. He focused the camera on the front door. He would get the most light when the door was still open, so he needed to be quick. But the door didn't budge. Lights turned on in the back of the house. He stayed in place until five minutes had passed and the likelihood of the stocky man leaving soon diminished. "What if this is his house?"

James poked his head out from around the tree so that they could see each other. "We could come back."

Vincent turned back to the house. He didn't want to return on another day. The anticipation would eat him alive. There was a lot of light shining into the backyard. More windows. Maybe they didn't have enough bedding to cover every one of them, and the back windows seemed like the best ones to leave bare—on the other side of the fence in the back was just a patch of woods. "Do you want to check around the back? See if we can get a picture through a window or something? I just want to finish this tonight."

After a moment of consideration, James said, "Okay."

They crept along the fence to the backyard. Paint peeled back from the rusting metal, making it look like it had thorns. Once they were far enough back, Vincent could see the other side of the house. Yellow light poured out of several windows on the first floor, illuminating the yard. While nearly every window was covered with some sort of fabric, the square window in the top half of the back door was bare. They could see right into the house if they were close enough.

The fence was too high to climb. Vincent found a gate in the back right corner. James lifted the latch and opened it. He waved Vincent through before shutting it behind them.

A thought hit him immediately: *What if he has a dog?* Some big, foaming dog that'd give Cujo a run for his money. But Vincent hadn't heard anything barking when the stocky man got home or now, so they were probably fine.

James drew close and whispered, "What's wrong?"

"Nothing. Come on." Vincent started through the knee-length grass toward the house.

A red pickup truck without tires rusted in the middle of the yard, between the two houses. Among other bits of trash strewn about the yard was an equally rusted lawnmower and a large, curved piece of porcelain that must have come from a toilet. They snuck up to the truck and ducked behind the tailgate, which had partially sunk into the earth, to get a better look at the back-door window.

The back of the house was covered in green siding. Similar to the brick building beside it, the house didn't have a back porch. Stacked cinder blocks served as steps. Vincent peeked around the side of the truck at the window. He could make out a stove and wooden cabinets behind a small collapsible table that had three empty plastic chairs around it.

"I don't see anyone," Vincent whispered.

James looked over the top of the truck. "Same."

Vincent took out his phone and lifted it over the top of the truck until he got a good view of the kitchen on his screen without his whole phone being out in the open. His hands were shaking, distorting the image, but hopefully the camera would autofocus when the moment came.

Someone passed by the window. Vincent readied himself. An emaciated woman set a plate covered in tin foil and a glass of milk on the table. The stocky man sat down in front of the plate, facing the window. They couldn't get a better shot if they tried. Chubby cheeks. Beady eyes. A thick unibrow and a narrow, pointy nose. Thin lips turned up in a disgusting little smile.

Vincent clicked on the screen to focus the image. *Say cheese, motherfucker.*

He was about to take the picture when the stocky man looked away. A girl who couldn't be older than four or five, in a large pink T-shirt that she wore like a dress, hopped onto the stocky man's lap and took a sip from his glass of milk. The stocky man pulled the glass away from her, snickering as he ruffled her hair.

Vincent prayed it wasn't his daughter. No child deserved the misfortune of having such a sorry excuse for a human being as a father. The stocky man faced forward again, and Vincent snapped the picture. Light flashed from his phone. The stocky man looked up. Vincent dropped to the ground.

Shit!

He'd never turned the flash off.

The stocky man saw it.

They were trapped in his backyard.

"We need to go." James helped him to his feet so that Vincent was squatting beside him.

Vincent didn't have enough breath to say anything.

Darkness descended on them. Vincent poked his head over the top of the truck. The stocky man stood in the doorway, blocking out most of the light from inside. A silhouette with a shotgun in his hands. He looked down at them. A pause of recognition. "What the…"

He aimed the shotgun.

CHAPTER EIGHTEEN

RUN

VINCENT STARED AT their executioner.

Fuck, we're going to die.

He wondered if all final thoughts were so ineloquent. Garbled curses at a world that was cruel enough to give you a warning when it was far too late to do anything about it.

James yanked him to the right, and he crashed to the ground near the front of the truck.

Bang!

Shotgun pellets blasted the truck and kicked up a cloud

of dirt.

"Run!" James ordered. He pulled Vincent to his feet, forced him forward, and somehow, his legs carried him. They ran toward the fence on the other side of the truck. The girl cried somewhere inside. The stocky man screamed out in frustration. There were footsteps behind them.

He was chasing after them.

He was going to kill them.

They were going to die here.

Become part of this wasteland.

The reality of just how much trouble they were in ate through his shock all at once, like a colony of starved termites had burrowed into his mind and torn it to pieces. He realized James was pushing him toward the fence behind the brick building. But he couldn't climb it. Not with his ribs in their current condition. Hell, he could barely run. They needed to change directions. Run for the gate. He looked back to try to communicate this to James, and he spotted the stocky man standing in the dust behind them, aiming the barrel of the shotgun at them.

Bang!

James slammed into him, and they smashed to the ground. The fence shook as the pellets hit it. Pain exploded in Vincent's chest. James was on top of him.

Oh God, the stocky man had killed him. Shot him dead. Something between a scream and a moan escaped Vincent's throat. That fucking monster had killed James, and he was next.

But then the weight was gone, he was pulled to his feet, and James pushed him to the fence and screamed, "Climb!"

James was alive—he must have tackled Vincent to the ground before the pellets reached them. But there wasn't time to celebrate that or try to redirect him toward the gate. Vincent grabbed the top of the fence and attempted to pull himself up.

The stabbing pain in his chest cut so deep that his strength evaporated. Before he had the chance to tell James to save himself, James wrapped his arms around Vincent's waist and lifted him into the air. Vincent swung his legs over the top of the fence and dropped to the ground. A shock wave shot up his legs and struck him in his chest.

James landed beside him.

The stocky man charged toward them, fumbling with the gun. *Reloading.* The fence wouldn't protect them from the blast of a shotgun. They needed to keep going.

James grabbed his hand and took off for the woods behind the fence. Each step sent pain rippling through Vincent's system. He focused on the tree line. If they slowed down now, then they were as good as dead. Muscle memory, forged from years of jogging, took over, and he ran alongside James despite the pain.

"Get back here, you fuckin' faggots!" the stocky man screamed.

They had just crossed into the tree line when he fired the next shot. Twigs and bits of bark sprayed the air. Vincent shut his eyes and raised his free arm to shield his face. The ground sloped down. His foot caught on something on the ground; then he and James were falling. They tumbled down a hill that only seemed to be growing steeper by the second, smashing through undergrowth and bouncing off trees and who knew what else.

When they finally came to a stop, he was face up on the ground, and his body burned so hot with pain he felt like he'd fallen right into a cremation chamber. The stocky man fired another shot, but it sounded far more distant than the last one. He screamed something, but that, too, was somewhere above them.

Footsteps beside him. He forced his eyes open. In what little light came from the stars above, he could make out James's figure over him.

James knelt at his side. "Are you hurt?"

"I don't know," Vincent managed. He coughed, and pain pierced his chest. "I just—need a minute."

"We have to go." James slipped an arm under Vincent's armpit and around his back and pulled him to his feet before he could object. The second Vincent tried to put weight on his left foot, the pain radiating from his ankle made his leg give out. He stumbled, but James held him upright.

"I must have twisted it or something." He tried to inspect his leg, but he couldn't see it well in the dark.

Snap.

A twig broke, and it didn't sound all that far away. Any number of small creatures could have caused the sound in this patch of woods, but all Vincent could think about was the rage in the stocky man's voice. He was angry enough to fire a shotgun at them in a residential area, and Vincent doubted he'd give up on the opportunity to kill them just because they'd run into the woods. James was right. They had to move.

Vincent grabbed onto James's shoulder and whispered, "Let's go."

James helped him along. Vincent battled against the grunts and breaths that forced their way from his mouth each time they took another step forward, but between them and his heavy tread, he was far from inconspicuous. Sweat poured from his body, and stomach acid crawled up his throat. The only thing keeping him going was the thought of that barrel pointed straight at them, held in the hands of a man determined to kill them.

Thankfully, in a few more steps the trees thinned, and they were out in the open. The outline of a house stared down at them, undoubtedly lit up from a streetlight somewhere behind it. A growl filled the air. Chains rattled. A light fixed to the back of the house snapped on, and through the spots clouding his vision, Vincent caught sight of a large black dog running at them.

It was less than a foot from them when it was suddenly yanked back with a yelp. It had reached the end of its metal leash. Still, it leaned forward, barking and snapping as it choked itself. A light turned on in one of the second-story windows of the house. Skeleton branches of tall shrubs lined either side of the yard, but there was a gap to their right. James led him along the edge of woods and through the opening to the next yard.

Whether it was the pain or the knowledge that fucking dog was leading the stocky man right to them, Vincent wasn't sure, but when stomach acid shot up his throat again, he couldn't stop it. He bent over and vomited into the grass. The pain from the action made him vomit again.

"Quiet," called someone behind them, and only when the barking stopped did Vincent understand that whoever had said it had been talking to the dog.

Vincent managed to take a breath. "I need a break."

James pulled him forward.

"I said I need—" Vincent started until he looked up and saw that James was leading him toward a shed at the edge of the yard.

Once they were on the other side of it, James helped him to the ground. "You okay?"

Vincent didn't feel okay. He felt like he'd been ground up in a blender. Examining himself did little to dispel this theory. His clothes were ripped and torn, covered in some combination of blood and dirt and whatever else he had smashed through in the woods. His body shook from exertion, and he was pretty sure he'd undone any progress his ribs had made in healing in the past month.

He didn't know what they were thinking. They'd presented themselves on a platter to a psychopath who had already tried to kill them once, and they'd done so without any means to defend themselves. He'd been so blinded by the need to end this nightmare that he'd forgotten to turn off the flash on his phone. An idiotic mistake that still might cost them their lives.

"I'm so sorry." He held back the tears.

James leaned down and hugged him. Half his face was caked in leaves and dirt, and his shirt was ripped all over. He didn't look all that much better off than Vincent, but whatever injuries he'd sustained had to be superficial. He had enough strength to practically carry Vincent to this point; he could probably make it back to the car and get out of there in a matter of minutes on his own.

Vincent pulled his keys from his pocket. "You should go. Get the car. There is no way I'm making it back there before he finds us."

James pulled away and stared at him like he had three heads.

"You can come back and get me," Vincent offered weakly.

After what felt like an eternity, James said, "No. It's not safe. We need to go."

He pressed the keys into James's hands. "I'll just slow you down. Go."

"I can't," James said. "I love you."

I love you.

The movement of the lips, barely visible in the darkness—Vincent had seen it before. It had been the last thing James had mouthed to him in the tunnel before those monsters had shot him and tried to kill Vincent. And all he could think about after he'd woken up in that hospital bed was how he might have prevented what happened in that tunnel if he'd listened to James. Maybe if he hadn't been so scared then, he could have run for it when James told him to, and in the ensuing confusion, James might have made it out of there as well.

Somehow, James had survived. But here Vincent was, putting his life at risk all over again. James wasn't going to leave him here, and all he was doing was giving the stocky man more time to find them.

He pocketed his keys and reached out a hand. "We should get moving, then."

The pain didn't disappear. Neither did the sweat and nausea. By the time they'd made it across two more lawns, he'd vomited again—pure stomach acid this time—and removed his coat to find his shirt completely drenched in sweat.

He kept moving until they made it to a road. He opened his phone and pulled up Google Maps. They were two blocks down from Allequippa Street. A far way for Vincent to go in his current condition, but he gritted his teeth and kept moving. He'd rather die of exhaustion than live knowing his inaction had gotten James killed.

They had made it up one block when the sirens started. Red and blue lights passed by on the street ahead of them. Someone had called the cops. A relieving development until Vincent considered that, depending on what the stocky man told them, the police could be looking for him and James before long. They picked up the pace. When they made it back to the car, four separate police cruisers had pulled onto the side street where the stocky man's house was located.

The moment they got inside, Vincent locked the doors and twisted the keys in the ignition. The engine roared to life. Somehow, they had made it out of there. He was so relieved he might have cried if he had the energy. Even though he'd been stupid enough to take a picture in the middle of the night with the flash on, they were safe.

The picture.

In the madness that had ensued, he'd almost forgotten all about the reason that'd brought them there in the first place. He took out his phone and pressed the home button. An empty battery appeared on his phone. Dead. Between Google Maps and the pictures, he'd drained the battery. He'd lost his cigarette lighter adapter, so he wouldn't know if they'd gotten the picture until they got back to the apartment.

"More reason to get the hell out of here," he told James, who was watching the screen.

After the sirens faded, an overwhelming exhaustion took hold of his body. He turned up the volume on the Fleetwood Mac cassette to keep from dozing off. He mindlessly mouthed the words to "Monday Morning," the picture consuming his thoughts. He was almost positive he'd gotten a clear one, but if the flash had reflected off the glass of the window, then all their efforts could have been in vain.

The ten-minute drive back to their apartment felt like an hour. Vincent didn't think he'd ever been happier to see the faded green sign for their street. He pulled into the right lane to turn onto the road, but James grabbed the wheel, keeping him in the left lane and forcing him to drive past the street.

"What the hell are you doing?"

James didn't answer. He was focused on the

passenger's side mirror.

Vincent checked the rearview mirror. A matte-black truck was coming up the road behind them, too far behind to see who was inside. "Are they following us?"

"Don't know," James said, without looking up at him.

Had the stocky man called his friends? Made sure that, even if he was arrested, someone would track them down. Vincent turned down the music. They approached a red light. He stopped—naturally, turns on red were prohibited at this intersection. The truck got closer, but its high beams were on, sending nothing but light through the back of the car.

The streetlight turned green.

No other cars were on the road.

He was too exhausted to drive around for hours, hoping the truck was just happening to take the same route. He cut the wheel left and made a U-turn. He hardly gave the road out the windshield more than a passing glance, his eyes focused on the truck behind them. It continued down the street.

"Thank fuck." Vincent didn't think he could deal with anything else tonight. Just to be safe, he turned on the street before theirs and cut through an alleyway to get to it. He also parked a few houses down from their apartment. The longer walk was well worth a little peace of mind, and the prospect of seeing the picture made the pain of limping the distance almost bearable. He did, however, have to take a breather when he made it up the front porch steps.

"Come on!" Tyler screamed in exasperation. Vincent

jumped, looking around. Tyler was nowhere in sight. He must be in his and Sam's apartment on the other side of the big stained-glass window out front that was covered in dark curtains.

"I'm not going to say it again. Just go have fun," Sam responded in a low, sharp voice from inside, confirming Vincent's assumption.

"We should get going," he told James. They were too close to figuring out whether or not they'd gotten the picture to get wrapped up in whatever was going on with Sam and Tyler. Plus, their current conditions would only raise questions. They made it through the main door and to the stairwell when Sam and Tyler's apartment door flung open.

Fuck. Vincent stopped, one foot on the hallway floor and the other on the first step. He looked back down the hall, which was still empty.

"I have to go study," Sam said, still inside. "But go party if you want to party. I'm leaving."

Vincent turned to James, motioning for them to hurry up the stairs. They still might go unnoticed. He held on to the railing, and with James supporting him, he hopped up the steps.

"It's not a party," Tyler said. His words were ever so slightly slurred. He was drunk. "We are fuckin' celebrating. Everyone has their girl with them but me. Come on. They all know I came back for you."

"Which is why I texted you to not waste the Uber ride. I have to study. Go have fun." Insincerity coated her words.

Vincent and James were almost halfway up the stairs.

"Fine," Tyler said.

"Fine." Sam's voice was far clearer than before.

Vincent looked back. Sam pulled open the front door and stormed off without even noticing them. Tyler stumbled after her, falling into the wall across from their apartment door. He stood up and stuck his head out of the front door. "Well, maybe I just won't come home tonight, then!"

"Have fun," Sam said, farther away.

"I will." Tyler slammed the door.

The sound made Vincent jump. He lost his balance for a second and had to hop to keep himself on the step. Tyler looked up at them. "Can I fuckin' help you?"

Vincent faced forward. To James, he said, "Let's go."

James didn't move.

Tyler burped. "That's what I thought."

James turned around to look down at him.

"Needa somethin'?" Tyler slurred.

"Let's go," Vincent said, more forcefully. He refused to let a drunken Tyler further delay them. He tried pulling himself up the next step, but he didn't have enough strength. James snapped out of it and helped him.

"Smart choice. You don't want a second round with me. I'd be your funeral for real this time," Tyler said. He waited a moment to see if he'd get a reaction out of James. When he didn't, he stormed out of the front door.

Vincent looked up at the ceiling, tempted to ask the universe what else it could throw at them tonight. He kept it to himself for fear it might answer with some other obstacle. He didn't stop for another break until they'd made it up the steps, into their apartment, and down the hall to their bedroom, where he plugged his phone into the charging cord lying across the bedside table. It would take a minute or two for it to get enough of a charge to turn on. In the meantime, James helped him down to the bed.

Vincent didn't lie back for fear that he'd pass out immediately. Instead, he remained in a seated position and waited, looking down at his feet. His left ankle had swollen to twice the size of his right. No wonder he couldn't walk on it. He turned to James, who still stood over him. "Can you grab me something from the freezer to put on this?"

"Yeah." He hurried out of the room. The back of his jacket was covered in holes but, thankfully, the wounds didn't seem that deep. Only a little blood spotted the fabric among the dirt and other remnants from the woods. Tyler must have been pretty smashed not to notice the condition they were in. Or he just didn't care. Vincent wasn't looking forward to showering and seeing just how bad all the wounds covering his body were.

He tried the home button on his phone. Still dead.

James returned with a bag of peas and helped him out of his shoes before wrapping the bag around his swollen ankle. The cold bag started to numb it immediately, and he let out a breath of relief. A memory of his mother sitting at the kitchen table, her bare feet planted on bags of frozen vegetables after a twelve-hour shift at the hospital, came to mind, but he pushed it away. Now was not the time.

"Thanks," he told James. He tried his phone again. The

screen lit up. "It's on."

James sat down beside him. Vincent unlocked his phone and went to his camera roll. The stocky man stared back at them. The flash had created a glare on the window, but it wasn't near his face.

They had him.

Vincent leaned against James, tears welling in his eyes. "We can send it out tomorrow morning. And then, we're done."

James didn't say a word.

Vincent looked up at him. No relief or joy. His expression was inscrutable. "What is it?"

"We should keep this to ourselves."

CHAPTER NINETEEN

THE STRANGER

"WHY?"

"He saw our faces," James said, as if that explained it.

Vincent waited for more details, but James didn't elaborate. "Which is why we need to go to a news agency. Get the police to lock up him and the others for life. End this."

James stared at the wall. "What if they don't go to jail? Or they get out? They will know who put them there."

Vincent was going to tell him there was no way those fuckers were getting out anytime soon after attacking him and James and probably killing two other men, but the more he thought about it, his certainty wavered. They'd watched enough news over the last few days to know that justice wasn't as straightforward as it appeared on hour-long police procedurals. Furthermore, their attackers could have other friends who'd be more than happy to take care of him and James. "We could move away—like you wanted."

James's gaze fell to the floor. "They could track us down."

A brief glimpse of a future where they were always looking over their shoulders, using cash for purchases, and living out of seedy motels filled Vincent's mind. Hardly a life after all they'd been through. "Well, what do you think we should do?"

More silence.

Finally, James said, "When someone is diagnosed with cancer, you have to get rid of it before it has the chance to spread."

The matter-of-fact way he said it, like he was spouting off an answer to one of his board exam prep questions, and the implications that hung on his words sent chills crawling across Vincent's body. *Get rid of it.* He waited for some explanation that would assure him he'd somehow misconstrued the point James was trying to make. None came. James wouldn't even make eye contact with him.

"You don't know what you're saying." Vincent went to rub his back, but the dried blood made him think better of it. James was in shock. He was afraid. Mad. He'd feel differently in the morning.

James looked up at him, his heart-shaped lips

disappearing in a thin, grave line. "They wouldn't hesitate if it were the other way around."

"We aren't them. And I know you want this to be over as much as I do, but we don't know that our plan isn't going to work."

"But he saw our faces."

He'd already made that point, and Vincent was about to remind him of that until the full meaning of James's words hit him, and it tore holes in his plan that seemed so perfect only moments before.

He saw our faces.

His *and* James's. He knew James was alive. If the police were compelled to arrest the stocky man because of a news agency, then the bastard's report of their interaction in his backyard would surely raise suspicions, which was only more troubling considering they didn't know who they could trust in law enforcement. That was, of course, presuming that any reputable news organization would believe them in the first place.

"He saw our faces." Panic filled Vincent as he spoke. Those fuckers had already killed Damien and probably Todd. And they'd keep killing others until someone stopped them. They weren't innocent men. They were monsters. Cancers to society. And with them gone, Vincent and James could figure out what else had happened that night without fearing every car in the rearview mirror harbored men who were determined to end their lives.

"No," Vincent said to put a stop to the train of thought that was far too intoxicating and terrible to entertain. They'd both been through a lot tonight—and he was too tired and afraid to think straight. "We aren't killers."

James took his hand. "We will never be safe while they're still alive."

Vincent turned away from him. He didn't want to see him or consider his words. He focused on James's desk, which hadn't been touched since before the attack. Books and papers stacked in neat piles.

How many nights did Vincent lie in bed and watch him study and know that if he fell asleep before James turned in for the night, he'd wake up in his lover's arms? When was the last time he'd gone to bed without worrying about who might try to kill them in their sleep? Vincent had been holding his breath since the attack, and if those fuckers were gone, then he might be able to exhale. Figure out the rest and return to their old lives where death was a lifetime away.

"We aren't killers," he said again, more to himself than James. "And even if we could cross that line, we'd just get ourselves killed. I mean, look at us. We barely made it out of there alive tonight."

"We weren't prepared. We could—"

"We should get cleaned up," Vincent said, cutting him off. He couldn't handle any more tonight. "I'm exhausted. Let's sleep on it. Talk in the morning after we've rested."

Without another word, James got up and helped him to the bathroom. Once Vincent peeled off his ruined clothes, he stepped into the shower. The water pressure was too strong for his raw skin. He pressed down the divider and filled the tub with steaming water. James didn't join him.

Vincent pulled back the shower curtain to see what was taking him so long, but the bathroom was empty. James must've realized he could use some space.

The water grew opaque as he wiped away the worst of the gore. His skin was varying shades of pink and purple along with deep-red cuts, which seemed particularly vibrant in the brown water. How many paints would an artist have to mix to match these shades? Would they ever be as vibrant as they were now? Stupid questions that didn't serve their sole purpose of stopping him from replaying their conversation in his mind.

He drained the tub, wrapped a towel around his waist, and limped out of the bathroom. James sat on the couch, looking at the blank TV screen. Vincent stopped behind him. "Bathroom's all yours."

He'd just gotten to the bed when he heard the shower turn on. It wasn't long before James crawled into bed beside him. Vincent felt like he could sleep for a decade, but the gears in his mind refused to stop turning. Snippets of their conversation filled the silent room.

He saw our faces.

Get rid of it.

We aren't killers.

We will never be safe while they're still alive.

He wrapped his pillow around his ears, but that didn't stop them. *Get rid of it.* The room was so warm. *He saw our faces.* The air thick. *We will never be safe while they're still alive.* He couldn't breathe. He got up and stumbled out of the room. While the swelling in his ankle had gone down a little, he could barely walk on it without pain shooting up his leg. But the living room was just as suffocating. He opened the window and stuck his head outside, over the fire escape.

Cold wind whipped at his face and whooshed past his ears. He closed his eyes and inhaled. The crisp air filled his lungs. He wanted to take a deeper breath, but his ribs warned against it. He was just happy to be out of that room. It was starting to feel more like a casket than a sanctuary. He took another breath, and smoke filled his nostrils.

For a moment, he thought he'd imagined it. An old memory from when he'd first tried to quit smoking and occasionally snuck a cigarette on the fire escape. But when he looked down, a pale face stared up at him. He almost screamed until he realized it was Sam, wrapped in a blanket, sitting on the steps below with a cigarette in hand.

She forced a smile. "Hey."

"Hey." He tried to think of an explanation for what he was doing. Nothing came to mind.

"You, ah, want a smoke?"

Vincent should say no. Go back inside. Try to get at least a few hours of sleep before their big talk in the morning. But he didn't think he could bring himself to go back to bed so soon. The cold air was far too inviting. And after the night he'd had, he could use a fucking cigarette. "Yeah, I do."

Sam tapped the empty space beside her on the stairs. "Come sit."

Easier said than done. Vincent swung his good leg out of the window, grabbed the railing, and pulled out the other. The cold metal soothed his aching feet. He'd only dragged himself down a few steps when Sam appeared to realize he wasn't exactly in fighting shape. She set her cigarette down in an ashtray on the step above her and rushed up the stairs. "Oh my God, are you okay?"

"Yeah," Vincent said through short breaths. "Just twisted my ankle earlier. Makes stairs a little bit of a hassle."

"You should've said something. Let's just sit here." Sam helped him down and went back to retrieve her ashtray. She wasn't in a particular hurry, but she moved so effortlessly down the steps that he burned with envy. No cracked ribs or twisted ankles or who knew what else. He couldn't remember the last time he took a breath, much less a step, without hurting. He should've appreciated the ability to run as fast and as far as he wanted while he still could do it. He'd give anything to rush down the steps and just keep running until he couldn't breathe and all his worries melted away in the euphoria of exhaustion.

"I'm such a bad premed student." Sam plopped down on the step below him. She relit her cigarette, which had gone out, with a small pink lighter. In the light spilling out from the window above, he could make out the dark bags under her eyes. She must not be sleeping well either.

"Your secret is safe with me."

"Well, to ensure your silence, please accept this cancer-inducing bribe." She offered him the pack of Camel Crush Menthol and the lighter.

"If you insist." He took the pack. A smile broke across his face at their pointless banter—it seemed like it belonged in a life that was separate from the one he'd soon have to return to inside his apartment. He slid out a cigarette, crushed the butt to release the menthol, and lit it. He inhaled slowly and blew out the smoke as soon as his chest started to hurt. He hated how much he missed smoking. He took another smaller puff and handed the pack and lighter back to her. "Thanks."

"Sure." She looked him over. "Aren't you freezing?"

Vincent wore an old T-shirt and gym shorts, but the cold soothed his warm, wounded skin. "I'm fine."

"So, how'd you twist your ankle?"

Vincent took another drag to give him a moment to think. "Oh, it was stupid. We, ah, went for a walk. I fell."

Sam exhaled smoke through her nostrils. "Must have been a pretty bad fall to get all those cuts and bruises."

"Yeah." Vincent looked down at the empty street to avoid her gaze.

"You know, you can tell me to mind my own business if you don't want to tell me what you and James are up to at all hours of the night, but at least respect me enough to make up a better lie."

His mouth went dry. It had nothing to do with the cigarette. He coughed, and his chest seared with pain. "Sorry, we were actually searching for the Holy Grail. We made it past the beheading blade trap and the false floor trap, but I fell on the leap of faith trap, so here I am."

"Isn't that from *Indiana Jones and The Last Crusade*?"

"Pure coincidence."

"I'll accept it, then." Sam stubbed out her cigarette in

the ashtray and lit another.

Vincent took a drag. "What brings you out on this lovely spring night?"

"Passing time. Tyler and I—I guess it doesn't matter. I'm just killing time so I can pretend I'm asleep when he gets home."

"Oh," Vincent said, trying to sound surprised. Tyler must not have gotten a chance to tell her about their little talk earlier.

"I should be studying for finals, but here I am, brooding. Can't concentrate."

"Want to talk about it?"

"Sure don't. How's James doing?"

Vincent shrugged, taking a long drag despite the pain.

"I tried talking to him earlier. I don't know if you were there or not or if he mentioned it to you, but he didn't really say much."

Vincent had almost forgotten she'd come to the door. Somehow, this was the same, never-ending night. "He's had a lot on his mind lately."

Something moved below them, and he dropped his cigarette. It fell to the cement between their building and the one beside it. A raccoon scurried out from behind their garbage cans along the side of the house with something in its mouth and made a beeline for the backyard.

Sam handed him the pack and lighter. "You both seem to have a lot on your minds lately."

"A lot has happened recently." Vincent lit another

cigarette and gave them back to her.

They smoked in silence for a while.

Sam eventually said, "It's just strange...not talking to him. Before, I had to turn my phone on Do Not Disturb in class because he texted me so much. Now, he acts so...different."

Vincent looked at her, but she was focused on the ashtray. "What do you mean by different?"

"I don't know. Out of it. The lights are on, but nobody's home, you know?"

Vincent knew more than he could ever tell her. "Yeah."

When someone is diagnosed with cancer, you have to get rid of it before it has the chance to spread.

"I guess I just miss him." Sam flicked the ashes from the tip of her cigarette. "I miss you both. And I have so many questions. And I'm trying to give you two space. But I went to his funeral, and now he's back, and, like, do the police even know he's alive? What have you two been doing? Who gave you those cuts and bruises?"

"We're just trying to figure out what happened. Same as you." The most honest answer Vincent could give without involving her.

Sam stubbed out her cigarette in the ashtray. "I used to know him better than anyone, even Tyler. Now, he's a stranger."

Her face fell into her hands, and Vincent couldn't tell if she was crying. No comforting words came to mind, so he just rubbed her back.

"Thanks. I'm just tired. I think I'm gonna call it a night. I'll deal with Tyler in the morning." She stood up. Her face was dry. "Need anything before I go?"

"No. Thanks for the smoke."

"No problem." Sam retreated to her apartment.

A stranger.

The word lingered in the air like the smoke emanating from the tip of his cigarette. He wanted to refute her words. Chalk it up to her limited interactions with James. But he'd been by James's side since the night in the graveyard, and James was different. Before the attack, he'd been working toward becoming an ER doctor and prolonging the lives of as many assholes as he could. He never would've suggested killing someone, even a person as disgusting as the stocky man. What happened to them had clearly changed James, but had he become someone else, a stranger? And if so, what was this stranger capable of?

Even after Vincent finished his cigarette, went back inside, shut and locked the window, and returned to bed, he wasn't any closer to answering those questions. In all honesty, he wasn't sure what either of them was willing to do to end this nightmare.

VINCENT STOOD IN front of a well. Behind him, down a long, tree-lined path, a dark figure ran toward him in the moonlight. He didn't know who it was until he heard the hoarse, mischievous laugh. He could run around the well and continue down the path, but something told him he couldn't outrun his assailant. Down the well, stones jutted out from the walls, spiraling down like stairs into the darkness. There was no time to think it through. He started down them.

The farther he descended, the more spaced out the stones became and the harder they were to see in the dwindling light from above. He kept going until the next stone disappeared beneath dark water. All of a sudden, everything was dark. Above, the silhouette of a man leaned over the top of the well and obscured the light. There was no way to know who it was for sure, but the spiky hair assured him it wasn't the stocky man.

"Help!" came a familiar voice below him.

Vincent looked down, and a black hand reached up from the water. Wait. It wasn't water. It was mud. Dark, shining mud encasing the hand. Whoever was down there, the poor bastard was far beyond any help that Vincent could provide. He started back up the steps, but another hand shot up from the mud and grabbed his ankle.

He screamed. Stumbled back. Somehow, his outstretched hands managed to grab hold of the stone wall for support. They were trying to pull him under. Drown him in the mud. Another hand took hold of his other ankle—the fingernails of whoever or whatever it belonged to cut into his flesh. Another latched onto his thigh. His cries filled the well. He kicked and punched and tried to break free, but it was no use. They had him. They pulled him down into the mud, and the last thing he saw before he was dragged below the surface was the dark figure watching him overhead.

VINCENT WOKE UP and grabbed his pocketknife from under his pillow to cut away at the hands. But no one was touching him. And he wasn't covered in mud. Just sweat. He was in bed. James stirred beside him. *You're safe.* Just another nightmare. He was about to breathe a sigh of relief when the scream came again, louder this time, from somewhere below.

"*Help*!"

For a moment, he thought he was still dreaming. Awakened from one nightmare into another, but then he recognized the voice. He had never heard her so distressed, so terrified, but there was no doubt it was her.

Sam.

CHAPTER TWENTY

NIGHTMARE

VINCENT JUMPED OUT of bed. His left leg gave out, and he toppled to the ground. The pain stripped away the grogginess, and as much as it hurt, he had to move. Sam was screaming. They needed to get to her. James pulled him to his feet and tried to help him from the room, but Vincent waved him off. "Go. I'll be right behind you."

By the time he reached the hall, knife still clenched in his fist, James had headed out their front door and down the steps. Vincent used the wall for support and limped down the dark hallway. He stopped for a moment at the door to catch his breath. Sam's cries floated up the steps. Now wasn't the time to rest. He pushed through the pain and kept going. James stood in the doorway at the bottom of the stairs leading out to the front porch. She was outside. The porch light was on, but he couldn't see past James.

Vincent grabbed the railing and stumbled down the steps. His thoughts raced. James was just standing there in the doorway. Sam sounded like she was hurt. Why wasn't he helping her? Did Tyler do something to her? No, he couldn't. But he was so angry when they'd crossed paths with him earlier that night. And drunk. Vincent couldn't imagine how much worse he'd be at this hour. He didn't know the exact time, but the sun was still down. He couldn't have been asleep for more than a few hours at most. And Sam was hurt.

"What's—going—on?" he said between breaths when he reached James.

James looked at him, but his eyes were unfocused. A lost child.

Vincent stepped around him. The sight was so awful it took a moment to accept this wasn't just another nightmare. This was real life.

Sam sat on the top step of the porch with Tyler cradled in her lap. She was covered in blood, rocking back and forth. Tyler was pale; white compared to the dark blood that poured from his stomach. Sam's hand was pressed into the wound, but it didn't seem to be working. Blood ran down the steps. His eyes were wide. Lifeless.

Dead.

Vincent wanted to rush to Sam's side, but he couldn't move. "What—what happened?"

"I don't know. I heard a gunshot, and he was on the sidewalk, and he was alone. He was alone and cold, and someone shot him. Someone fucking shot him! But the ambulance is on its way, and he's going to be fine, aren't you?" She brushed his hair out of his face, smearing blood across his forehead.

Someone shot him.

Sirens blared in the distance. Vincent looked around them. The street looked empty, but it was hard to know for sure. The light from the porch only extended so far into the night. Anyone could be lurking in the shadows.

James grabbed his arm. "We need to go."

Vincent shook him off. He wasn't leaving her here alone. "Sam, we need to go inside."

Sam pulled Tyler closer. "No! The ambulance is on its way."

James grabbed him again. "It's not safe."

Vincent whipped his head around. What was wrong with him? "We need to get her inside."

"We are in danger," James said, motioning between them.

His words sank in through the panic. *We.* He and James. All the pieces of the shooting fell into place so suddenly Vincent didn't know how he hadn't made the connection before now. Tyler had been shot outside their apartment building. The place they'd fled to straight from the stocky man's house. They thought they'd lost that truck, but maybe they hadn't. Maybe the stocky man or one of his friends had staked out their building and mistook Tyler for one of them and shot him. Maybe the assailants were still out there, waiting for him and James to show their faces so that they could riddle the porch with bullets. He and James were in danger; Sam was only at risk by association.

Fear wrapped its hands around his throat and choked him.

He struggled for air.

The sirens were getting so loud it was making it hard to think. First responders would be there any minute to help Sam. James couldn't be there when they arrived. As terrible as it was to leave her here alone, Vincent couldn't think of any other way to ensure both Sam and James's safety.

"I'm so sorry," he said to her, backing up toward the door. "We have to go."

If Sam heard him, she didn't respond. Vincent turned around. James gave him his shoulder and helped him climb the steps. Vincent didn't look back at them over his shoulder. He didn't need to. The sight of Sam, holding Tyler's lifeless body in her arms, was burned into his memory.

As soon as they were through the door of their apartment, James locked it behind them. Their attackers had found them. The police would be there any minute. They couldn't just wait until the scene outside dispersed. They had to leave, possibly for good, and from the ever-growing sound of the sirens, they didn't have very long to pack.

James was faster. Vincent turned to him. "Grab my backpack by the dresser. Dump out whatever's in it. Get my wallet, my phone and charger, and my car keys—I think they are still in one of my pants pockets from last night. And a change of clothes for both of us. And anything else you can think of. I'll get the envelope." He'd put Sam and Tyler's envelope of money in a kitchen drawer so that he didn't have to look at it every time he walked past the table where it'd sat for some time. He meant to put it somewhere safe, but he'd never gotten around to it.

James hurried down the hall to their bedroom. Vincent limped to the kitchen. The light over the stove made it easy to see. He yanked open the drawer and pulled out the envelope. There was no other envelope that would be stuffed like this one, but he made sure it was full of money before he made his way to their bedroom. They wouldn't have a chance to return anytime soon.

The light from the bedroom leaked into the living room. Vincent hobbled down the hall toward it. Something was off. The whole place was freezing, and there were far too many dark corners where a gunman could easily hide. They needed to get the hell out of there.

Someone rushed out of the bedroom and ran right into him. Vincent screamed. James grabbed him before he fell over. "Sorry."

Vincent got his footing. "We gotta go."

James looked past him into the living room. "The police are here."

Outside, red and blue lights colored the brick wall of the adjacent apartment building. The front door was no longer an option. They could, however, use the fire escape. They just had to hurry if they were going to reach his car down the street before the police started searching for the gunman. And if the sirens hadn't scared them off, whoever shot Tyler was still out there.

Not just shot—killed, his mind corrected. But he couldn't go there now. They needed to move.

James helped him over to the living room window and pulled it open. He guided him onto the fire escape. Outside was chaos. Flashing lights and blaring sirens. On the metal stairs, they were out in the open. Anyone who looked around the corner of the house could easily find them. Vincent struggled to keep up with James's pace down the steps. His heart pounded, body ached, and he could hardly think straight, but the possibility of running into anyone else tonight kept him moving.

Right before they reached the bottom of the steps, his foot connected with something solid. He only realized it was Sam's ashtray when it shattered on the pavement below. The sharp sound echoed off the sides of the buildings, loud enough to hear over the sirens.

James pulled him down the last few steps and ducked behind their garbage cans. A flashlight shone down the space between the two houses, spotlighting a wide-eyed raccoon that dashed around the back of the building. The light disappeared. James peered around the garbage cans. The coast must've been clear. He pulled Vincent to his feet and led him toward the backyard.

They crossed through the next two yards. Thankfully, there were no fences. Vincent hardly noticed anything else around them. He was focused on the car. Only after he started the engine did he look back at the mess they'd narrowly escaped. An ambulance and several cop cars blocked the road in front of their apartment building. He pulled out and drove slowly down the street. His body was so tense that if James touched him, he might shatter. Any minute now, someone would scream or shoot. Or a police car would whip around and pull them over. But when he turned at the end of the street, no one followed. Vincent sat back in his seat. Thanks to James, they'd evaded death for a second time that night.

"WE'RE FUCKED." VINCENT sat on the edge of the bed. The relief of escaping immediate danger only lasted until they found a Motel 6 that was still open and booked a room. All that remained was the undiluted panic at the reality of their situation.

James paced in front of the large window beside the door looking out to the parking lot. They'd parked around back, but he kept peeking through the drawn lavender curtains to make sure no one had tracked them down. While they'd paid for the room in cash, they had to give the woman at the front desk a card to put on file in case of damages to the room. Vincent wasn't nearly as concerned about that detail as James. They had bigger problems.

"They found us. They killed Tyler. And Ralbovsky and Tillman are going to want to talk to me." Tears ran down his face. They were facing opposition on all fronts. "And we just left Sam there. Abandoned her."

James pulled himself away from the curtains and sat down beside him. "We didn't have a choice."

That didn't make him feel any better.

"They'll keep coming after us until they kill us." The weight of that knowledge made it hard for Vincent to breathe.

James rubbed his back. "I won't let anyone hurt you."

Vincent knew James meant it, but he couldn't promise such a thing. Vincent wanted to get back in their car. Keep driving until they ran out of money to refill the tank. Start a new life wherever they ended up. But he knew that wouldn't be living. That'd be surviving. Ever since the attack, all they'd been doing was surviving. They were no different from that raccoon who picked through trash in the hope of finding something to get it through the night.

And it wasn't just about them. Those fuckers had already killed Damien, and Vincent was pretty sure that Todd's body would be discovered any day now. They'd killed Tyler, too, and why? Because he had the misfortune of living in the same building as Vincent and James. Not injured. Not terribly maimed. Dead. Dreamless sleep forever.

Tyler's lifeless eyes appeared in his mind.

He looked up at James. "They'll never stop."

James pulled him close. "They won't."

They'd never stop, and the police wouldn't do anything about it. Vincent couldn't imagine killing someone—causing another person's eyes to glaze over with death—but they didn't have a choice. They couldn't let those fuckers hurt anyone else. "I don't know how the hell we are going to do it without getting ourselves killed, but we have to try to stop them. We have to end this."

James sat back, and Vincent could see the determined look in his eyes. "We will."

CHAPTER TWENTY-ONE

THE QUESTION OF HOW

LIGHT. BLINDING WHITE light. Vincent shut his eyes against it, still too drunk on sleep to know what was happening. He took his time reopening them. Eventually, his eyes adjusted. But the ceiling over their bed had changed. It wasn't plaster with cracks and lifted squares where their landlord had patched leaks. Instead, the white surface was smooth with a metal vent that blew warm air down on him.

He wasn't in their apartment.

He was in a motel room.

The momentary displacement reminded him of awful mornings freshman year when, after drinking himself into oblivion the night before, he'd woken up on a random couch or, worse, in a stranger's bed. Unlike those mornings, the previous night was not a mystery to him. He remembered everything.

Sam's screams.

Tyler's body.

James's promise.

We will.

They'd lain down in bed not long after their talk. But, even nestled in James's arms, Vincent hadn't been able to fall asleep. Every moment that had brought him and James to this point had raced through his mind. A long series of dominos that had started in Panther Hollow and ended in their motel room.

Something about their decision to take the law into their own hands had felt inevitable—like it had been transcribed in one of those massive volumes of ancient tales he was forced to read in his Myths, Legends, and Folktales class. But this wasn't some old story that had been passed down for generations. This was their lives, and they only had one option left if they were going to survive this nightmare: kill or be killed.

Vincent wasn't sure when he had finally drifted to sleep. He was still awake when the morning sun had crept in around the edges of the curtains. He didn't expect it to still be light out when he woke up. For a moment, he wasn't sure if he'd slept through a whole day and night. His exhaustion, however, assured him he hadn't been out for very long.

James still seemed to be asleep, lying motionless beside

him. Vincent couldn't even hear him breathing. He turned away from the ceiling to check on him. All he found was a pile of bedding and pillows that was far too small to conceal him.

He sat up.

James wasn't by the window either.

Or in one of the two chairs on either side of the table next to the door.

The bathroom door was cracked. "James?"

No answer.

Vincent climbed out of bed and limped over to the door. "Everything okay in there?"

Once he got closer, he realized the light was off. He checked inside anyway. The bathroom was empty. Panic stabbed at the edges of his mind. James was gone. Vincent stumbled back into the main room. There was no note or indication of where he'd gone. Vincent turned out the pockets of his pants that he'd tossed on the floor last night. James hadn't taken his knife, phone, or, more importantly, car keys.

Vincent went to the window and peeked through the curtains. He didn't know what he expected to find. There were just a few parked cars. James could have left for any number of reasons. He could have gone to grab a drink or snack from one of the vending machines in the office. Or he might've gone to pay for another night. The problem was that Vincent didn't know how long he'd been gone.

Why didn't he wake me up before he left?

Terrible thoughts rose to answer his question. James could've noticed someone loitering outside their room. Maybe he'd gone out to confront them, and they'd overpowered him. Dragged him into the black truck that had been tailing them last night. Beat him bloody with a crowbar and blasted him out of existence with a shotgun.

A woman passed in front of the window. Vincent jumped back before he realized she was dressed in a maid's uniform. He tripped over himself and fell on his ass. Pain rippled through his sore body. *Fuck.* He had to pull himself together. He could've woken up right when James stepped out. He just needed to give it a few minutes.

He went to the bathroom and splashed cold water on his face. Fear filled the eyes looking back at him in the mirror over the sink. *Relax.* If James had stepped out and their attackers had gotten him, then they would have taken the key card for the room and gotten Vincent too.

Unless James didn't take a key card with him.

Just then, the sound of rattling metal pierced the silence. He looked out of the open bathroom door at the motel room door. The handle shook, and a shadow blocked out the light coming into the room around the curtains near the door.

Or they just realized that James had the key card on him.

And they'd come to kill him.

The deadbolt that prevented even someone with a card from getting in the room was not locked. He started across the room for it. He hadn't made it more than a few steps when a beep rang out, which indicated that someone had stuck the key card in the door.

He needed to run back to the bathroom and lock himself inside, but his legs wouldn't move. On the ground at his feet were his pants and everything he'd taken out of his pockets. He just had the chance to grab his pocketknife and flip out the blade before the door swung open.

He held the knife out between him and the door.

James stood in the doorway, haloed in afternoon light, with several bags of groceries in his hands. His stone face brightened at the sight of Vincent until he took in the whole scene. He rushed over to him. "What's going on?"

Vincent still had the knife pointed at him. He dropped it. "Why didn't you wake me up before you left?"

The question came out far harsher than he intended.

"Sorry." James pulled him into his arms. "I thought you'd want to sleep."

Vincent took a breath. They were safe. "No, I'm sorry. I was just worried about you."

"Next time, I'll wake you."

"Sounds good." Vincent snuggled into his chest. He should feel relieved that he could still hear James's heartbeat, but the fear of losing him again to those fuckers stayed with him long after James had locked the deadbolt and led him over to the table.

James laid the groceries out between them along with the envelope of cash that had thinned even more since they'd booked the room last night. "You should eat."

Vincent leafed through the bags. The gas station down the street had a few more options than the vending machines, but not many. Prepackaged deli sandwiches. Bags of chips. Chocolate candy bars. Plastic bottles of water and pop. Vincent was itching for a cigarette more than anything, but he settled for some potato chips. He opened the bag and shared them with James.

They ate in silence. They needed to talk about last night. Make a plan to end this once and for all. But every time Vincent tried to focus, his mind returned to him standing in the motel room alone with nothing except a pocketknife to defend himself against whoever walked through the door.

The idea that a pocketknife would do anything against men with crowbars and guns was almost laughable. What had he been thinking? He'd hardly let it out of his sight since the attack, clinging to it like it was some magical artifact that could defeat their worst adversary. Useless—that's what it was. If their attackers had come through that door, then he'd be dead.

James watched him. "Are you okay?"

Vincent set down the chip in his hand. He felt like he was going to vomit if he ate any more. "Yeah."

"You aren't—"

"No." Vincent wasn't having second thoughts. "I just don't know how we are going to do this. I mean, they outnumber us. They have weapons. Guns. What do we have? A pocketknife. I want to end this, but I don't want to get ourselves killed in the process."

James watched him. He looked like he was about to say

something, but then he swallowed the words.

Vincent took a drink of Diet Coke to get the taste of the chips out of his mouth. "What is it? Just talk to me."

James reached into his back pocket and set something wrapped in white cloth on the table. There was no mistaking the shape. A handgun.

Vincent recoiled. "Where the hell did you get that?"

James wouldn't make eye contact with him.

Vincent waited for an answer. "I doubt you got it at the gas station."

"I didn't" was all James said.

Vincent followed his gaze. He was looking right at the envelope. Vincent had just assumed it was significantly thinner because it had mostly been stuffed with smaller bills. Maybe James had made more than one stop on his trip this afternoon. "Who did you buy it from?"

James's head turned toward the bed so fast that Vincent expected to see someone standing across the room. Nothing looked out of the ordinary. After a moment, he heard it. *Buzz. Buzz. Buzz.* Not a hornets' nest. His phone was vibrating on the floor. The screen lit up with an incoming call.

He went over and picked it up. A number he instantly recognized. The detectives. He ended the call. He had five missed calls before this one. All from the detectives. He almost threw it back on the floor until something occurred to him. Could the police track them down using his cell phone? He wasn't sure. Just to be safe, he turned it off.

Back at the table, he told James who'd called. "They

were probably pulled into what happened last night once the police realized it was our apartment."

James paused. Concerned. "Would Sam tell them about me?"

Vincent almost reminded James that she was his friend and he would know her better than Vincent, but James hadn't talked to her much since the attack. "I don't see why she would. I think she'd have been more concerned about Tyler."

While it was hardly a comforting answer, it seemed to put James at ease.

Fleeing from a crime scene and dodging calls wasn't a good look though. Especially given what they intended to do. "Can anyone trace that gun back to us?"

"No."

The plain way he'd said it made Vincent believe him. "Why didn't you tell me about it before now?"

James pocketed the gun. "I didn't want to upset you."

"What?" Why would James think that? The last time Vincent had seen a gun was when Tyler had his pointed at James. Vincent hadn't exactly reacted well in that moment, but he thought his response was justified given the situation, especially compared to James, who'd acted unfazed. "I don't like guns. I don't like any of this. But a pocketknife isn't going to work against them. At least this might give us a fighting chance."

Vincent took another gulp of pop. "Now we just need a plan."

James didn't have any off the top of his head. Vincent stared into the bottle, searching the dark, fizzing liquid like the bubbles would align to form an answer. *We are planning a murder over a gas station meal.* The absurdity of their situation almost made him want to laugh. Or, perhaps, cry. He wasn't sure at this point.

Over the span of a few weeks, they'd gone from two happy, albeit stressed, college students with their whole lives ahead of them to this. James should be getting ready for another board exam. Vincent should be scrambling to pass Dr. Cowart's class. Instead, they sat in a motel room, planning to murder three men.

Three monsters, he corrected himself.

Three monsters who'd started all of this. Vincent and James had just been minding their business. They hadn't been hurting anyone. They'd kissed. A simple peck on the lips. And those fuckers had tried to kill them for it. Vincent and James were planning a murder, and the world would be a better place when those fuckers were buried six feet under.

Vincent capped the bottle and decided that laying all their cards on the table was probably the best place to start. "So, we know where the stocky man lives, but that still leaves the other two."

"We don't want to face them all at once," James said. "They outnumber us."

"Agreed. But what I mean is we still have no clue where to find them. And if they realize that the stocky man is dead before we get to them, then they'll be ready for us." Killing them now seemed close to impossible, even with a gun. If those fuckers knew what he and James were planning to do, then their chances of succeeding significantly diminished. One of their only benefits was that their attackers underestimated them.

James's eyes lit up with an idea. "We could make him tell us where they are. Take care of the others before they know he's dead."

The stocky man didn't seem like the loyal type, especially if he had a gun to his head, and doing it in quick succession was probably the only way to take them all by surprise. A plan was emerging. "We know where to find the stocky man, but where should we do it?"

James looked at him like he didn't understand the question. "We know where he lives."

They did. And they'd probably have a greater chance of avoiding detection if they did it on that secluded side street than anywhere else. There was, however, only one problem with that location. "What about the woman and girl? I mean, they'll be better off without him, but they can't be there when it happens."

"So, we find a time when he's alone."

Vincent didn't know if the woman worked, or if the girl was old enough for school, but surely the stocky man had to be there on his own at some point. "Maybe we should give it a day or two for everything to calm down, and then we can start keeping tabs on them. See if we can find a time when the woman and girl are gone."

James agreed.

They would need to iron out the details, but they had a

plan. The ease with which they were able to develop it disturbed Vincent. How many other murders had been planned so simply over the course of human existence? Had their attackers had a similar discussion before they'd come across him and James in Schenley Park?

But planning was only half of it. Coming face-to-face with those fuckers again and surviving would be the hard part. The very thought made him feel sick, and yet, strangely relieved. He could see it in James's eyes as well. Through this mess was an end in sight. They would kill them or die trying. Regardless of what happened, they'd soon be freed from the constant fear of wondering who might be waiting for them on the other side of a door.

CHAPTER TWENTY-TWO

DRIVE

TONIGHT, WE ARE doing it.

We are going to kill them.

The words weighed on his mind.

Vincent wasn't sure why the gravity of what they were about to do hit him now as he and James watched the stocky man's house from behind a tree along the road. They'd been there for the previous two nights, staking out the house and tracking the movements of its inhabitants—during which time, he'd had no reservations.

But he'd known they had no chance of enacting the plan

then. Tonight was different. He took a breath and mentally cursed the heatwave that had hit Pittsburgh. While the warmer temperature made the hours they'd spent outside far more bearable, he wanted the cold back. The freezing air seemed to reach his sore lungs in a way the warm air couldn't.

He wasn't having second thoughts about killing them. He was ready to get rid of those cancers of society. What he couldn't stop thinking about was losing James in the process. A possibility that seemed far more tangible tonight. They'd taken every possible precaution they could, given the circumstances, but it'd only take one stray bullet to kill him.

The crescent moon shone brightly enough for Vincent to see James's profile sticking out from around the other side of the tree. He prayed that, even if he didn't survive the night, James would. James could make it without him. He was strong. Even now, he watched the house like a hawk without even a hint of concern coloring his face. Nerves of steel.

Like clockwork, the porch light turned on just after six thirty. Vincent ducked behind the tree, meeting James in the middle. He leaned against the trunk and tried to breathe. They couldn't risk the woman or girl spotting them tonight, and he and James didn't need to watch them leave. The woman and girl had left the previous two nights around this time and returned about an hour later. Unlike those other nights, the stocky man was actually home. Vincent and James had watched his silhouette through a sheet-covered window on the left side of the house, where he sat on what looked like a couch in front of a TV that sent erratic flashing lights through the room.

"He hasn't moved," James whispered to him.

Something about the regularity with which the woman and girl had left and returned made Vincent think they were going to some sort of lesson or class, which neither he nor James thought the stocky man would attend. They were right. The stocky man would soon be alone. They couldn't ask for a better opportunity.

Vincent closed his eyes and gripped the knife in his pocket. A useless safety blanket that somehow calmed him. He wouldn't need it. James had a gun. And they had the element of surprise. And the stocky man had probably already finished the twelve-pack he'd carried into the house when he got home an hour ago.

We are going to be fine.

They would get him to divulge the location of the others, kill him, and finish off the other two before the fuckers caught wind of the stocky man's fate. By morning, they'd be safe again. Free from the constant fear of being tracked down and slaughtered.

Tires on asphalt and a humming engine tore him away from his thoughts. He opened his eyes. Headlights shone down the road. The light would reach him in seconds. James pulled him around the trunk to avoid it, his focus never leaving the house. The Uber driver pulled up behind the stocky man's truck, and James guided Vincent back to where they were standing out of view.

Ever since the night they'd tracked the stocky man down, his truck hadn't moved from where he'd parked it on the road in front of his house. Both he and the woman had been using Uber to get around. A logistical nightmare in that any car driving down the road could harbor the stocky man, but Vincent and James had managed to avoid detection.

Vincent caught sight of the handle of the gun sticking out of James's back pocket. He couldn't see it without thinking about the tunnel. The gun pointed at James's chest. The barrel pressed into his own skull. James knew the effect it had on him, even before Vincent did, which was why Vincent hadn't laid eyes on more than its handle since he'd learned about it. The sight was almost comforting tonight though. This time, they weren't the victims. They were the executioners.

A car door slammed shut.

Vincent jumped.

James turned to him, as if to ask if he was all right. His surveying eyes seemed to ask another question: *You aren't having second thoughts, are you?*

"I'm fine," Vincent said, probably a little too fast.

James had become rather obsessive about their plan over the past few days. He'd stayed up most of the day and night in a manic state that Vincent thought was solely reserved for tortured artists. At several points, he'd tried to get Vincent to agree to stay at the motel while he dealt with the attackers. A suggestion Vincent had vehemently protested until James had dropped it. They were doing it together or not at all. Still, he was pretty sure James was looking for any excuse to leave him behind, so he tried to look unfazed.

The car continued down the street. Time to move. They

only had an hour, possibly less if they came back sooner for some reason. James led him to the gate in the backyard. Each step made his feet feel heavier. His sprained ankle had healed over the past few days. This was different. He felt like someone had injected wet cement into his heart, which was pumping it out to his extremities. Rationally, he knew the cards were stacked in their favor. However, a more primal part of his brain refused to believe it. All it saw waiting for him in that house was danger. Vincent continued forward in spite of it.

Once they made it through the gate, they crept over to the old truck. James peered over the top of the truck to make sure the kitchen was empty.

The stocky man, aiming a shotgun at them, raced through Vincent's mind. But even if the police hadn't confiscated the stocky man's weapons, James would have his gun trained on him long before the fucker would have a chance to react.

James turned to him. "Ready?"

The stocky man must still be on the couch. Everything was going according to plan. Vincent took a breath that only seemed to highlight the cement setting in his chest. "Yep."

James pulled two ski masks out of his pocket. He handed one to Vincent, who slid the coarse fabric over his face until he could see out of the eye holes. The stocky man knew who they were, but his neighbors didn't, and Vincent didn't want to risk anyone linking the murders to them. James pulled on his mask. His eyes looked like they were made of glass. Distant. Unemotional. Vincent hoped his appeared just as impenetrable and that the fear flooding his system was disguised beneath the mask.

James didn't seem to notice. He started around the truck. "Come on."

Vincent followed him to the door. James tried the handle. Unlocked—as it was the night before when they'd tested it in the early hours of the morning. At first, Vincent hadn't been able to explain why the stocky man was acting so carelessly until he'd considered who they were dealing with. Even though they'd tracked him down, the stocky man didn't view them as a threat. They were little more than pests to him. Ones that needed to be eradicated—not feared. After all, why would a man like him fear two faggots who weren't even brave enough to tell the police they'd found him?

An oversight that'd be his downfall.

James waved him through the back door.

After Vincent stepped inside, there would be no going back. They'd have to follow through with their plan. As terrified as he was to put himself and, more importantly, James in harm's way, Vincent was ready to end this nightmare. One terrible night stood between them and their freedom from these monsters. He wasn't going to freeze. He was going to be brave for both of their sakes. He walked through the doorway and into the kitchen.

A blaring TV echoed through the house, filling his ears with some sort of sports commentary. The announcer spoke so fast his words mashed together in a jumbled mess that sounded more like a frantic auctioneer than anything else.

James shut the door behind them, closing them in the

house with the stocky man. He pulled the gun from his back pocket and started over to the dark hallway off the kitchen. Vincent surveyed the room in passing. Random details logged in his mind. Pizza boxes. Dirty plates. A half-empty sippy cup of milk. The hall was the only other way out of the room besides the back door. A small comfort. The stocky man couldn't sneak up on them.

Light flashed in the passage from a room toward the end of the hall on the left where the stocky man was watching TV. James advanced down the hall toward it. Vincent stayed close behind him. The hardwood creaked beneath their feet like it was crying under their weight. He almost grabbed James to tell him to be more careful, but the stocky man wouldn't be able to hear it. Vincent could barely make it out over the sound of the TV. The closer they got, the louder the TV became. Vincent could make out the words— someone had struck out, ending the first inning. The stocky man would never hear them coming.

They were halfway down the hall when the lights and sound went out at the same time. They both stopped. For an awful second, Vincent thought the stocky man had heard them or this was some sort of trap where he would appear behind them from one of the dark doorways they'd already passed and blast them with his shotgun. Then, a commercial started, and the hall filled with light and sound.

James looked back to check on him.

Vincent was glad he was wearing a mask. Even in the limited light, James would probably be able to see how the blood had drained from his face. He motioned for James to continue forward. There was a commercial, and while it was a relief the stocky man hadn't become suspicious, a commercial meant he might get up to grab a drink or run to the bathroom. Vincent had never seen Henry move faster than during a commercial break in a game. With the TV volume turned up so high, they wouldn't get a chance to be ready for him until he was standing right in front of them. The thought made Vincent get out his knife. Useless against a shotgun, but far better than his fists if the stocky man surprised them.

James slowed to a stop right before the doorway.

The cement coursing through Vincent's veins was starting to harden, making it difficult to breathe. His face and hands were numb. He squeezed the handle of the knife harder and tried to focus. He couldn't lose it now. He refused to let his inaction endanger James again.

James leaned around the corner to look into the room. He pulled his head back so suddenly Vincent thought the stocky man must've seen him. But James didn't raise the gun. And nothing came out of the room except the sound of another commercial. James turned back to face him. The hall was too dark to see if he was mouthing anything. Vincent could, however, make out his hand, which waved for Vincent to follow him.

They crept into the room. The light from the massive flat-screen TV that hung on the wall to their right was so bright Vincent had to force his eyes to remain open. Directly in front of the TV was a couch. The back of the stocky man's head stuck out from the top of it. Littered around the carpet leading up to him was an assortment of trash and toys. Aside from a small end table beside the couch with an unshaded lamp that was turned off and several crushed aluminum cans on it, the room was empty. The whole place reeked of beer and sweat.

The TV went dark for a second before the game came back on. James took slow, calculated steps toward the couch to avoid stepping on anything on the floor. Vincent followed in his footsteps. His heart was beating so fast he wondered if there was any truth to the concept of being scared to death. Maybe his heart was just getting in as many beats as possible in case he died tonight. He tried to take quiet, deep breaths to avoid fainting.

"Come on!" The stocky man threw an empty beer can at the TV.

Vincent instinctively jumped back. He landed on something small and round. Panic erupted through his body like a string of firecrackers, and before he could even get his balance, the toy beneath his foot lit up in an assortment of colors as a chorus of children sang "Humpty Dumpty." He stomped on what appeared to be a rubber egg, hoping to either stop it or break it, but it kept going.

James glanced back at him. Vincent couldn't turn it off, and even if he could, it was too late. They were screwed. He could dump a piggy bank into a wishing well, but that wasn't going to stop the stocky man from hearing the song. The TV was loud, but there were enough random silences between the announcer's words the song filled with its haunting melody. He stared at the back of the stocky man's head, waiting for his reaction.

The stocky man looked down. The TV went silent. He must have muted it. The only sound in the room was the children singing. He leaned over and flipped on the lamp.

Light flooded the room.

"You're supposed to be in bed." He craned his neck back to look behind him. Vincent heard the words, but they didn't make any sense. Who did he think they were? The exasperated smile on the stocky man's face disappeared when he saw them. "What the fuck?"

The stocky man leaned forward. Vincent couldn't see he was reaching for—the couch was in the way. James aimed the gun at him. "Freeze, or I'll shoot."

The man rose and turned to face them, his hands empty.

James took a step closer, aiming the gun at his head. "Where are the tall man and the blond kid?"

The toy finally stopped making noise, leaving them in silence.

The stocky man glared at him. "You even know how to use that thing?"

James came around the couch. Pressed the gun into the side of his head. "Where are the men you were with the night you attacked us?"

"Us?" the stocky man tried to say nonchalantly, but his voice wavered. Fear. He wasn't so brave without a crowbar or a shotgun. "We killed one of them. And I'd know that fag with or without the mask"—he nodded his head toward Vincent—"so who the fuck are you?"

Their attackers didn't know James was still alive.

"Answer the question!" James pushed the gun into his

temple.

The floor creaked behind him. Vincent turned around, pointing his knife out in front of him. The little girl stood in the doorway. She was dressed in an oversized pink T-shirt. Her nose was bright red, and her eyes were wide with shock.

What the fuck was she doing here? She was supposed to be with her mother. Off at some mother-daughter afternoon activity. Far away from the house and what Vincent and James were planning to do to the stocky man.

"James," Vincent said, at a loss for words.

"Hey, she's just a kid," the stocky man said. "Leave her out of this!"

James took a step back, the gun still aimed at him. "Tell us what we want to know, and no one gets hurt."

But that wasn't the plan. The plan was to kill him after he told them where to find the other two. They couldn't let him live. He'd warn the others. But they couldn't kill him. Not in front of the girl.

"Go back to bed," Vincent said to her, trying to steady his voice.

The girl just stared at him.

Vincent turned to James for guidance. The very second James looked at him was when the stocky man lunged for something in front of the couch. James must have seen the movement out of the corner of his eye because he turned back and lowered the gun to aim it at the stocky man.

"No!" Vincent screamed.

Bang!

The bullet tore through the stocky man's chest. Blood sprayed the plain white wall behind him. He collapsed to the ground in front of the couch. James pointed the gun at the ground where the stocky man must've landed.

"Daddy!" The girl let out a blood-curdling scream and started around Vincent for her father.

Everything was happening so fast.

Vincent managed to step in front of her and grab her shoulders to stop her.

"Where are they?" James demanded, pulling Vincent's focus back to him.

A garbled "Fuck you" was the stocky man's only response.

Bang!

The girl screamed even louder, falling to the ground with her hands over her ears.

This couldn't be happening.

The next thing Vincent knew, James had grabbed him by the wrist. "We need to go."

What was he talking about?

They couldn't leave the little girl here alone with her father's corpse.

But James didn't wait for an answer. He pulled Vincent past the girl and into the hall.

Vincent had to stumble forward to keep from falling. "Wait!"

James ignored him, dragging him into the kitchen. "We

don't have a choice."

Vincent planted his feet firmly on the vinyl flooring and yanked his arm back. James's grip didn't loosen. A bomb of sharp needles detonated in his chest, sending stabbing pain through his body. "Stop!"

James kept pulling him toward the back door.

"I said fucking stop!"

James froze. He whipped around and drew close to him. "We need to go. I'll carry you if I have to, but we are leaving."

His words were low. Cold. But his eyes were wild in a way that Vincent had only seen in photographs of crazed, shell-shocked soldiers in history class. James looked like he'd do far more than carry him if Vincent didn't cooperate.

"Okay, let's go," Vincent told him. He fought against the urge to run in the opposite direction. There would be no point. James seemed like he'd sooner dislocate his arm than let him go.

Vincent followed him through the backyard. James flung the gate open when they reached it and pulled him around the front of the house. Would the police later lift his print from the latch when the house became a crime scene? Where would they find the girl? He hoped she'd run to her room and hide underneath her blankets and imagine that what she saw was just a terrible nightmare.

They continued onto the street, close to the tree line. James only released his grip when they reached the car on Allequippa Street. "Drive."

Vincent rubbed his throbbing wrist. The skin had

broken out in red and purple blotches. He unlocked the doors, got into the car, and started the engine because he wasn't sure what James would do if he disobeyed. James took off his mask and instructed him to do the same before they drove off. Vincent focused on the road, tears streaming down his face as he tried to process everything that had just happened.

He kept waiting for James to say something, but he didn't say a word. When they hit a red light several blocks away, Vincent glanced over at him. His face was tinted red in the traffic light, but his expression gave no hint to what he was thinking or feeling.

The light changed.

"Drive," James ordered.

Vincent drove.

CHAPTER TWENTY-THREE

TICK, TICK

THE BRUISES ON Vincent's wrist were darkening. Black and blue ovals spreading like ink in water. His wrist was swollen, and it throbbed with pain as he gripped the steering wheel to keep his hands from shaking. He tried to focus on the road ahead of him, but his eyes kept falling to the marks on his skin.

James had caused these bruises.

He'd dragged him from the room like Vincent was a rag doll.

Snapped at him.

Vincent wanted to believe that James had just reacted poorly in a terrible situation. That he'd been so consumed with rage he'd killed the stocky man without even considering that his daughter had been watching. That he'd been so afraid of being caught by the police he'd been unaware of how much he'd been hurting Vincent. But, even after there was time for the shock of what they'd done to dissipate, he didn't seem overwhelmed with emotion. In the passenger's seat, he stared off into the distance, his expression blank. Like he hadn't just killed a man in front of his daughter.

Ever since James had returned, Vincent thought his boyfriend had been lost in himself and, once they were free from the attackers, he'd get the old James back. But what if James hadn't been lost? What if he'd been fighting to contain the madness and anger that was bubbling just below the surface? And, more importantly, what would happen the next time he lost control?

"Where are you going?"

Vincent jumped at the sound of his voice. He hadn't even thought about their destination. They were on the Boulevard of the Allies, entering a world of concrete and asphalt. The same route they'd taken back from the stocky man's house since they'd started staking it out. In the evenest voice he could muster, Vincent said, "The motel."

James drew closer. "What?"

Vincent fought against the urge to move against the car door to create some space between them. Regardless of what he'd done, James would never intentionally hurt him. Vincent knew that. Or, at least, he told himself that. He squeezed the steering wheel. Let the pain pulse through his wrist and empty his mind. When he spoke, he made sure to be loud and clear. "The motel."

James pulled away from him, and Vincent hated the relief that came with the distance. James said, "Pull over."

They were on the highway. No exit in sight. Their only option was the side of the road, and there was barely enough walking room outside of the white line. Half of the car would be sticking out in the right lane, which was sure to draw attention. "Won't that seem suspicious?"

James reached for the wheel. Vincent cut it right, and the car swerved off the road. The driver in the car behind them honked his horn before cutting into the left lane to speed past them. Vincent barely noticed. The car bounced on the uneven asphalt, kicking up dust in its wake. He pressed the brake pedal to the floor, and the car skidded to a stop.

Vincent turned on the four-way flashers.

Tick, tick.

Tick, tick.

Tick, tick.

A bomb counting down to detonation. The only other sound in the car was Vincent's heavy, strained breaths. He stared out the windshield. The headlights illuminated a flattened pack of Marlboro Lights and an empty bottle of Pepsi, both of which floated in a puddle on the side of the road.

James placed a hand on his shoulder. "I didn't mean to hurt you, but you weren't listening."

Vincent couldn't stop himself from shivering under his

heavy touch. The James he'd known and loved would never say such a thing. He was a healer. A guide to Vincent in the darkness of his life. Not some unstable monster who'd hurt anyone who didn't follow his orders. Something was truly wrong with him.

James withdrew his hand. "We have to finish it."

That was the plan. After getting the location of the other two men from the stocky man, they were going to kill them before the fuckers realized one of their own had been murdered. But nothing had gone according to plan. "We don't even know where to find them."

James held out a phone. "I took this from him."

The screen was black. "What about the password? And it's not like we can go back and get his fingerprint to unlock it." Vincent regretted the words as soon as they left his lips. He wouldn't put it past James to suggest breaking into the morgue if that was what it took to finish off the tall man and the blond kid.

James pressed the home button, and the phone opened. No password. He handed it to Vincent. "Find them."

Another order.

Vincent didn't even know where to start. The pages of apps looked like a rabbit hole they shouldn't go down while on the side of the road. "How about we look through it when we get back to the motel?"

"No. Now," James said.

A car rushed past them.

Vincent ignored it. A message appeared on the screen

from Ashley.

Make sure she's sleeping.

Another followed.

Needs rest if she's gonna feel better.

The girl must be sick, which explained why she'd been left at home. And the woman's name was Ashley. Wherever they'd been going each night, it clearly wasn't a mother-daughter class. He prayed Ashley would be home soon for the girl's sake. Whether or not the police had already arrived, the girl would need her mother. She'd need a lot more than that. He was tempted to message Ashley to tell her to hurry home, but James was watching the screen.

Find them.

He went to the stocky man's text messages. Below his conversation with Ashley was a group chat with two other people. Mathew and Caleb. They were planning on "riding around" later tonight when the stocky man was free. Caleb was going to head over to Mathew's around eight, so the stocky man should let them know when he was ready.

Their attackers.

Riding around in search of us.

The thought sent chills down his spine.

Mathew and Caleb.

He had their names.

Vincent opened his Facebook app. The stocky man

looked back at him in his profile picture. The wry smile on his face didn't look all that different from the way he had looked at them when he stepped onto the trail holding a crowbar on the night of the attack. Vincent went to his page. Gage Moulder—that was the stocky man's name.

Vincent searched his friends for Caleb. Only one friend with the name. Caleb Peters. The blond kid. Vincent clicked on his profile picture. His hair looked white in the flash of the camera. Vincent didn't know how he'd forgotten the kid's strong nose and thin reptile lips. The few glimpses of the kid's face that he'd made out in the tunnel resurfaced. The kid pointing the gun at them. Wrestling with James on the ground for the gun. Aiming the weapon at James's chest before he shot him.

The sound of the gun firing, magnified by the tunnel walls, filled his ears.

Vincent went back to the stocky man's friends. Searched for Mathew. He had quite a few friends with the name or slight variations. Mathew. Matty. Matt. Only one of them was bald. Mathew Baker. Vincent clicked on his picture. Ice-blue eyes. Pig nose. A tattoo on the side of his head—14/88. The tall man. The leader of the trio. The one who'd brought a crowbar down on Vincent's skull.

Tears filled his eyes at the memories that were no longer a mystery. He could remember every moment of that night with alarming clarity. His hands were shaking so much he dropped the phone in his lap. *Gage, Caleb, and Mathew attacked us*. The names were far too ordinary for the terrible things their owners had done. He didn't want to know their names. He didn't want to know anything about them. He just wanted all of this to be over.

James took his hand. Vincent looked at him. His eyes were filled with concern. Vincent hugged him. Whatever James was going through, he loved Vincent. And despite everything that'd happened, James was right. They had to find them tonight if they were going to have any chance of killing these fuckers.

"Okay." Vincent pulled away to dry his eyes. He couldn't fall apart now. They didn't have the time. He picked up the phone. "We have their names. And we know the kid is going to be at the tall man's around eight. Now we just need to figure out where he lives."

Naturally, neither of their addresses was in the stocky man's contacts. There also hadn't been any saved addresses or recent searching in his Google Maps, which made sense after Vincent thought about it since the stocky man probably didn't need a GPS to get to his friends' places.

But he hadn't been driving his truck for a while. He'd been using Uber to get around for the past week. Vincent opened the app. No favorited addresses, but all his previous rides were saved under Your Trips, which provided the starting and ending points as well as the date and time of each trip. Some addresses were easy to dismiss. A beer distributor. A strip club. Random bars. The residential addresses were far more difficult. They could drive around town all night without ever knowing if any of them belonged to the tall man or the kid.

An idea came to him at the thought of them. He went back to their group chat. Scrolled through their earlier messages. If he could find a time when the stocky man had planned on going over to either of their places, then he might be able to match it to one of his Uber trips. However, they hadn't communicated very much via text since the night the stocky man had discovered them in his backyard. On the night in question, he'd texted the group, demanding that one of them call him back immediately. According to his recent calls, the tall man had reached out to him within minutes.

With Vincent and James traveling back to their car on foot, the tall man would've had plenty of time to get in his matte-black truck and hightail it over to the stocky man's place. Maybe the kid had come with him. Regardless, they'd followed Vincent and James back to their apartment, where those fuckers would later kill Tyler.

Tyler.

Another mystery of that night unraveled in his mind. When they'd confronted the stocky man, he hadn't known James was alive. In fact, he seemed to think Vincent had an accomplice. One he'd spotted in his backyard when he'd shot at them. *Then, the others went to our apartment and found Tyler.* They must have thought Tyler had been helping Vincent. A mistake the stocky man had only seemed to realize when he found two masked men standing in his living room.

Vincent felt like he was going to be sick. They hadn't just killed Tyler because they'd mistaken him for Vincent or James. They'd killed him because they thought he'd been in the stocky man's backyard that night. Somehow, knowing how deliberate Tyler's murder had been made it all the more apparent how much of his blood was on Vincent's and James's hands.

If he didn't know us, then he'd still be alive.

"What's wrong?" James studied whatever expression was on Vincent's face.

Vincent almost explained it to him, but he wasn't positive it mattered at this point. James knew their attackers had killed Tyler. Their motivation didn't change that, and it wouldn't help them find the others. "Nothing."

He turned his attention back to the phone. Hours after they'd fled from the stocky man's house, but long before he'd woken up to Sam's screams, the stocky man had taken an Uber to an apartment building on the other side of West Oakland.

At first, the trip made no sense to Vincent. Why would he go there when the tall man had already tracked them down to the apartment? Vincent didn't expect to find any trips that night. He'd assumed the stocky man had been forced to deal with the police while the others had hunted them down.

But he wouldn't want to miss out on finishing them off. Not after they'd already slipped through his grasp in his own backyard. And after the police had been crawling around his house, maybe the others had been hesitant to pick him up. Maybe they'd met up at the tall man's apartment to plan their next move, which brought them back to Vincent and James's apartment building only hours later.

A possibility, but Vincent was reaching. He checked the other trips the stocky man had made to the address. He'd returned to the apartment building the following afternoon, right after another short call with the tall man. "I think I found something."

Vincent told James what he'd discovered, adding, "The only problem is that we don't know which apartment might be his."

James didn't seem to think that was a major hurdle. "We can scope it out when we get there. The kid isn't supposed to be there until eight, right?"

"Yeah." Vincent checked the time. Close to seven thirty.

"If we don't find anything, we can follow him inside. Come on. Let's go."

Vincent put the address into Google Maps and got back on the road. Their ETA was seven forty-five. He hoped the kid wasn't early.

Vincent turned around at the next exit. The apartment building was on the far side of West Oakland, and only when the neighborhoods started looking familiar did it occur to him they'd be passing within blocks of the stocky man's house to reach their destination. The very place they'd just fled from to avoid the police who were surely swarming the area.

Shit.

There wasn't enough time to find an alternative route. He tried to remain calm and keep his eyes peeled. He wished his old engine weren't so damn loud so that he could listen for sirens. But, even when he neared Allequippa Street, there were no flashing police lights or bellowing sirens coming from the direction of the side street. A relief until the implications of their absence became apparent.

No one had called the police.

The thought of the girl, lying on her father's bloody chest, pleading with his corpse to wake up, plagued his mind.

"Left here," James said.

Vincent made a sharp, tire-screeching turn. As terrible as it was to think of her there alone, they couldn't help her now. He had to focus on the task at hand. Her mother would be home soon, and the nonexistent police presence meant they had a far better chance of getting away with what they were about to do.

They got to the apartment building at seven forty-five on the dot. It was a modern gray structure with small square windows that looked out of place among the rotting Victorian houses around it. Vincent parked behind a line of cars on the opposite side of the street. He didn't spot the black truck in passing, but that hardly mattered at this point.

After making sure the kid was nowhere in sight, they got out of the car. Vincent followed James up the cement steps that led to the building, his aching ribs the least of his worries. James tried the front door handle. Locked. He tried it again with no success.

To the left of the door was a metal box with six white buttons and six red labels beside them—1A, 1B, 2A, 2B, 3A, and 3B. Vincent turned to James to tell him about the door buzzer. James yanked back the handle. Grinding metal and *snap*, and with that, he ripped open the door.

Vincent stared at him in shock. Then horror. His rage had taken over again, and he'd somehow managed to break through a metal lock. When James faced him, his expression was unreadable. In an eerily calm voice, he said, "After you."

Vincent hurried inside. He looked around the frame of the door in search of whatever James had just broken. He didn't see anything out of the ordinary. "What did you do to it?"

James followed him inside. "Doesn't matter. We have to hurry. The kid will be here soon."

Vincent's mind whirled. He looked around them. There was a stairwell to their left, and a short hallway leading to the first-floor apartments to their right. It wasn't like they could go door to door, asking after their attackers without creating a whole building of witnesses. And after what'd happened with the girl, Vincent refused to involve anyone else in this mess. Not when James had a gun and anger coursing through his veins.

There were, however, six little metal mailboxes along the wall at the bottom of the stairs. Each one had a keyhole as well as a small handle. Below the boxes were the apartment numbers. James had made quick work of the door. These little boxes shouldn't be a problem for him. "If we can check their mail, we can see who lives in each apartment."

James started with 1A. He ripped it open with ease. There was a gas bill for Mr. and Ms. Wise. Whoever lived in 1B didn't have any mail, and the handle for 2A came off in James's hand. No mail for 2B. A fat envelope informed them that 3A belonged to Kevin Jackson. One to go. James tore it open. In 3B, there was a bill for Mathew Baker. The tall man.

"Got him," James said, stuffing the letter back in the

box. They attempted to make the mailboxes appear untouched. Then, they snuck back out of the building and returned to their car right before eight. Not that they were risking a run-in with the kid. He didn't ride up to the building on his bike until a quarter after. He rushed up the front steps before calling up to the tall man, who must've buzzed him in. He didn't even seem to notice that the door was broken.

A lamb to the slaughter.

Had the kid thought something similar when he and James had run into the tunnel on the night of their attack? He supposed it didn't matter. Those fuckers had started the chain of events that had led him and James to this apartment building. They had to die. What concerned Vincent was the risk that came with this final confrontation. Two against two. He and James had the element of surprise, but they had no idea what'd be waiting for them in the apartment.

James handed him his mask. "Ready?"

Vincent put it on—it reeked of sweat. He was as ready as he'd ever be to face them.

James pulled him into his arms and squeezed him a little too tight. "It's almost over. After we kill them, we'll be one step closer to getting our old lives back."

Vincent wished that were true. But even if they managed to survive the night and figure out why the police were claiming James was dead, they'd never be able to return to their old lives. James loved him, but he'd changed. Turned into someone who could snap at Vincent one minute and comfort him the next. A stranger who could be filled with enough rage to rip open a metal door and then, seconds later, calmly wave Vincent through the doorway. Wrapped in his arms, Vincent was well aware of how easily James could crush him if something set him off.

"We need to go," Vincent told him through shallow breaths.

"We do." James released him and put on his own mask. He led Vincent back to the building, where he held the door open for him. Vincent slipped inside, and James shut it behind them.

Whatever happened tonight, death would be joining them in apartment 3B.

CHAPTER TWENTY-FOUR

APARTMENT 3B

Two flights of stairs. All that separated them from their attackers. Stone painted white with thin, silver railings. Vincent stood at the bottom of the stairs. He didn't want to climb them. He wanted to run out of the front door of the apartment building and keep going until he collapsed from overexertion. The destination didn't matter so long as it was far away from these men and all the terrible possibilities that were waiting for him and James in apartment 3B. Knowing they had to do this did little to prevent the beautiful possibility of leaving this all behind from taking root in his mind.

He considered trying to convince James to leave. He

could acknowledge what a terrible idea it was and do it anyway. As much as it seemed like this was their only option, they didn't *have* to do anything. They could just turn and run. He looked over at James, who stood beside him. But whatever sudden mania had afflicted Vincent hadn't seemed to make its way to James. His resolute expression assured Vincent he was only ready to finish this once and for all.

Because we have to finish it. We have to try.

Just about any other option seemed preferable at this point, but that didn't change what they needed to do. Vincent started up the stairs. He didn't let himself stop, but the closer they got to the third floor, the weaker his legs became and the harder he had to grip the railing to keep himself upright. Bloody, gruesome visions of their attackers overpowering them—finishing the sadistic torture he and James had gotten a preview of in Panther Hollow—infected his thoughts. When they reached the top of the stairs and James took the gun out of his back pocket, Vincent drew his knife. He might actually have to use it if they planned on making it out of this one alive.

Apartment 3B was to their right. Metal music blared from inside—hoarse, indiscernible screams with a thunderous bass Vincent could feel in his chest. They stopped at the door. James looked over at him. A final check-in. Vincent hid the fear that was drowning him. They had to finish it.

James pulled him close. Kissed him. Vincent kissed him back, praying this wouldn't be the last time he felt James's lips on his own and hoping that, even if they could never get their old lives back, they could find some form of happiness on the other side of this nightmare.

Then, it was time. James cocked the gun. He tried the doorknob before he pounded on the door with enough force to make the metal 3B hanging on the door jump. Someone lowered the volume of the music. Vincent could hear his heart pounding in his chest.

James knocked again.

"I'm coming," came a gravelly voice from inside.

The same voice that had ordered the kid to kill James. The tall man. Vincent tightened his grip on the knife and readied himself.

"About fucking time." The tall man swung open the door. His muscular build filled the doorway. "Kid's on two wheels, and he managed to—"

He stopped midsentence, his eyes growing wide with the realization that the two men standing at the door, faces covered in ski masks, weren't who he was expecting. He reached for something down the back of his pants, but before he found what he was looking for, James fired.

Vincent jumped back at the sound, crashing into the wall across from the door. Something clattered to the ground in the apartment. The tall man ran at James, arm streaked in blood. James fired another shot into his chest. The tall man collapsed to the ground. Motionless.

Everything had happened in the span of mere seconds, and Vincent, leaning against the wall, tried to process it. Just like that, James had killed him.

Their leader was dead.

"Grab his gun," James ordered, stepping over him and

walking into the apartment.

Vincent didn't have any more time to think about it. They had to keep moving. He pushed himself back into a standing position. He followed James inside, shut the door behind him, and quickly stepped over the body on the ground. The black pistol James must have shot out of the tall man's hand lay a little further into the apartment. Vincent pocketed his knife and scooped it up, nearly dropping it because he'd underestimated its weight.

They were in a living room. There was a leather couch to their left beside a lamp that lit the room in cold, white light. The music was louder in here, where it erupted from two speakers on either side of a flat-screen TV across from the couch. It wasn't loud enough, however, to cover the crashing sound from the hallway to their right.

James stormed down the hall after it.

Vincent kept close behind him. His hands were shaking so hard any shot he fired would surely miss. Not that he was sure how to operate it beyond pointing and pulling the trigger. Henry's numerous tips at the local firing range from when he was a boy escaped him now. Still, he held the gun out in front of him to provide the illusion that he had some control over the chaos unfolding around him.

James stepped into the doorway to his left and quickly came back out, seeming to find no one inside. In passing, Vincent noted it was the kitchen. There was a door to their right a little farther down the hall and two more across from one another at the end. All of them were closed.

James opened the next door and disappeared inside.

Vincent stayed where he was, waiting for a shot to fire and praying James was the one who fired it. Seconds later, James reappeared and hurried down the hall to the last two doors.

Vincent didn't have time to feel relieved. The kid was in one of those rooms. He followed behind James. The room James had just inspected was a bathroom. James went to the door on their left. Vincent kept his eyes on the one across the hall, waiting for the kid to come barreling out of it, firing at anything that moved the moment James opened the other door.

James tried the handle. Locked. He pulled his leg back and landed a kick to the center of the door. The wood splintered around the lock, and a scream of shock came from inside, but it didn't open. Someone or something must be behind it, keeping it shut.

James took a step back and ran at the door, trying to shoulder it open. He landed hard against it, but the door barely budged. He went at it again. And again. Over and over, throwing himself against it like a rabid dog. Vincent didn't know what to do except keep out of his warpath. James looked like he'd keep going until he broke the door or every bone in his body. The next time he ran at it, there was a loud crash, and the door opened enough for him to get inside.

Vincent couldn't stop to consider the mangled door or how much force it must have taken James to break it open. He had to keep going. He slipped in the door behind James. A large wooden dresser lay on the ground in front of the door. Every drawer had been removed, and the contents were scattered about the room on the bed and the other furniture. The kid stood against the opposite wall with a knife held out in front of him. He must've been searching for a gun, but all he found was a knife, no larger than the one in Vincent's pocket. The window was open beside him, but he made no attempt to go near it. From three floors up, the fall was hardly an option. He was trapped.

James aimed the gun at his head, and the kid dropped the knife. In an uneven voice, he said, "I don't know what you want, but take it all, man. I won't say a fucking word. Not a word."

The kid was shaking even more than Vincent. James stalked over to him, the gun aimed at his forehead. When he was less than a foot away from the kid, he removed his mask. What little color was left in the kid's pale face disappeared. He looked like he'd seen a ghost, and as far as he knew, James was one.

Vincent took no satisfaction in the look of fear on his face. The kid had already been trying to hold it back in a similar manner on the night of the attack. The only differences now were that the tall man wasn't there to give him the orders and there was more light. The kid was young with a lanky, juvenile build. There was no way he was even out of high school.

"You shot me," James said without a single ounce of emotion.

The kid looked from James to Vincent and back. He decided something, and his face hardened. "Do it."

James pressed the gun into the kid's forehead. The kid

shut his eyes, sending tears cascading down either side of his face. James was ending it. He was killing the last of their attackers, and all Vincent could think was that this wasn't right.

This kid had done terrible things, and he would have put a bullet right through Vincent's skull if that gun hadn't jammed, but he was a kid. A kid under the authority of two terrible men. How long ago had he been the same age as that little girl who they had left alone with her dead father? He deserved to pay for what he did, but he didn't deserve to die.

Vincent ran toward them. "James, wait!"

James ignored him. He pulled the trigger, the knuckle of his pointer finger turning white with the effort. But nothing happened. The slide stuck out the back of the gun. One of Henry's first lessons resurfaced. *If the trigger won't budge and your pistol looks like this, then you're shit out of luck...and bullets.* But, in the overhead light, that wasn't the only thing Vincent saw. The gun was deep blue. He'd only ever seen one gun like it.

Tyler's gun.

Vincent froze. He dropped the gun in his hands.

James has Tyler's gun.

Without a second's hesitation, James raised the weapon over his head and brought it down on the kid's face, hitting him squarely in the nose with the butt of the gun. The kid fell back, and James grabbed the collar of his shirt to hold him up. He hit him again, and this time, there was a horrible, cracking sound that pulled Vincent back to the room.

Blood gushed from the kid's nose. He grabbed at

James's hand, but there was no stopping him. James hit him again and again with the same, animalistic force he'd used to break down the door. The kid's nose sank further into the pool of blood that was his face with each hit, and James didn't look like he was going to stop until he reached the kid's brain.

He was going to smash that boy's face in with Tyler's gun.

Vincent couldn't just stand there. No matter how James had acquired that gun, Vincent had to do something before James killed the kid. He let his thoughts fall to the wayside. If he thought about what he was going to do, then he'd never do it. His legs were weak, but they would carry him. He ran at James. He had no calculated plan. Just the desire to end this bloodshed.

James raised the blood-soaked gun in the air for another strike, and Vincent reached out and grabbed James's arm with both hands. His ribs burned, and his wrist throbbed, but he clung to him for dear life, screaming, "Enough!"

James ripped his arm free, and Vincent stumbled backward. His body tensed, preparing to slam against the wall, but just when he anticipated the collision, his waist hit the windowsill and his torso went out of the window. There was no time to think. Wind rushed around him, and his stomach dropped. He reached out in front of him to grab hold of something, but he was too far out to seize anything except the cool night air.

He went from looking up at the window to seeing the night sky before the world turned upside down. He screamed. Just when he thought the only thing that would stop his fall was the sidewalk below, hands wrapped around his ankles and grabbed him. His back slammed into the stone exterior, knocking the wind out of him. He didn't even have time to cough before he cracked his head on it. White-hot fireworks filled his vision, and his head exploded with pain. He brought his hands to the back of his head, half expecting his brain to spill out of his shattered skull. Miraculously, the back of his mask was dry. He wasn't even bleeding.

The next thing Vincent knew, he was on the floor again. James sat him up against something, removed his mask, and felt the back of his head. "You okay?"

Even though James was bent over him, he sounded like he was across the room. His face was covered in blood splatter, his eyes unhinged and furious. He looked like he was going to kill him. "What were you thinking?"

Vincent felt like he was drunk. He couldn't focus his vision on James. He heard something beside him. The kid lay on the ground, seizing. His arms and legs flailed violently as blood sloshed around in his caved-in face.

Vincent looked back at James. Blinking in an attempt to focus his mind and vision, he said, "You...you have to—"

Bang!

A hole burst from the center of James's chest, spraying warm liquid all over Vincent, who cried out in sheer terror. James fell to the ground beside the kid. The tall man stood in the doorway. He was pale and covered in blood, but he was alive. He had a silver revolver he must've picked up somewhere else in the apartment.

"Fucking faggot." The tall man aimed the gun at him.

Vincent raised his arms in front of his face—as if that would stop the path of a bullet. This was it. *He killed James, and I'm next.* But then, James lunged forward and grabbed the black gun Vincent had dropped. The tall man disappeared down the hall as James fired two shots in his direction. They tore through the door across the hall.

Vincent went to reach for James to see if he was okay, but, somehow, James was already on his feet, running out of the room after the tall man. *How could he even sit up?* Vincent must have seen it wrong. He couldn't move like that with a gunshot to the chest. Everything was happening too fast.

Another gunshot went off.

"James?"

There was no response. Heavy footsteps came down the hallway. They were getting closer. Vincent shut his eyes, rubbing his pounding head. He might have been mistaken about where the bullet had hit James, but he wasn't imagining things now. He could hear the tall man's heavy breaths as he approached. Vincent was going to die. He searched his mind for some thought worthy of his last, but before he could think of anything, the gun went off once again.

The acrid smell of a fired gun filled his nostrils, but he felt no pain. Vincent opened his eyes. James stood over him—the black gun in one hand and Tyler's in the other. The kid lay dead on the ground beside him. A bullet to what was left of his head. James was breathing hard, but no matter how many times Vincent blinked, the wound remained in the center of his chest.

"He got away." James said it as an accusation.

Vincent didn't know how to respond. He stared at James's wound. The dark blood leaking from it had already started to congeal to the consistency of pancake batter. "What the hell is going on?"

"I just want to protect you, but you won't let me." James leaned over him. He grabbed Vincent's bruised wrist and pulled him to his feet.

The room span. "James. Please. Stop."

"I hear sirens. We have to go." He pulled Vincent out of the room.

His eyes wouldn't focus on the world around him. He caught a glimpse of the living room and the stairs. Drops of blood led to the front door of the building where the tall man had escaped. *How is James still walking?* He was shot almost directly in the center of his chest, and he acted like he didn't even feel it. Shock and adrenaline couldn't keep off the effects of that kind of gunshot wound, and they didn't explain how it was already clotting.

Outside, the cool night air roused Vincent. "We need to get help."

If James heard him, he ignored it. When they got to the car, he snatched the keys from Vincent's pocket, shoved Vincent in the passenger's seat, and got behind the wheel. Vincent could hear the sirens now, and in the rearview mirror, the police lights were already flashing in the distance.

James started the engine and backed into a parked car behind them. Vincent bounced off his chair and flew forward. His outstretched hands hit the glove box before his face did, but the force sent a new wave of pain roaring through his body. James sped off down the street. Vincent had enough sense to buckle his seat belt before James swerved onto the next street.

Vincent was still trying to piece together everything that'd just happened. Fat tears came at the thought of the kid's sunken-in face. He had tried to stop James, but he couldn't. "You killed that kid."

James blew through a red light without stopping. "I was trying to finish this, and you tried to stop me, and now he got away. He knows we're after him, and he'll be after us."

Vincent massaged his temples, considering his words. "I thought they were already after us?"

James said nothing.

But Vincent didn't need an answer.

He knew the truth.

James beat in the kid's face with Tyler's gun.

Tyler was dead, and James had his gun.

Memories of Tyler's bullet-riddled body flashed in his mind between those of the kid. His thoughts returned to the night he'd woken up to Sam's screams. They'd rushed downstairs to see what was wrong. And when they'd realized they were the reason for the shooting, they'd rushed back to the apartment. Packed. Something had been off. The apartment had been freezing. And James had pulled open the window to the fire escape and helped him out. He hadn't unlocked it. Just pulled it open.

Which didn't make any sense because Vincent had locked the window when he'd come inside from his talk with Sam. He was certain. He'd flipped the lock. Double-checked that the window couldn't be pulled open before he'd gone back to bed. And yet, it had been ajar, filling the apartment with cold air. Like someone had gone back outside...

Someone who'd needed a weapon. Someone who'd wanted to convince Vincent to murder their attackers. Someone who could've killed Tyler and slipped back into bed beside Vincent before Sam had the chance to discover the carnage waiting for her outside.

James.

The certainty came with the swift brutality of a punch to the gut. He struggled for air, unsure if he was going to faint. Or cry. Or scream. Or be sick. He rolled down his window and vomited.

Oh, God.

There was no denying it. No other explanations fit what'd happened. James had killed Tyler. This wasn't just rage. James was far worse than Vincent could've ever imagined. Tyler had seen it. *Something's wrong with him.* So had Sam. *He's a stranger.* Vincent had been so happy that James was alive he'd explained away every glaring warning sign until they'd killed two people.

He had to get away from James. Give himself some time to think and figure out what to do. No ideas came to mind. With his ribs and ankle still healing, he could barely outrun a tortoise. James was faster. Stronger. Even if, by some stretch of the imagination, he managed to get away from him, where would he go? The police would rightfully arrest him. He doubted Sam would even answer his call after they'd deserted her. And Henry would sooner lock him up in the looney bin than believe James was back. He had no one else except James. A thought that had once brought him comfort, but now, only dread.

Vincent needed to hear him say it. He needed to hear the truth. "James, how did you get Tyler's gun?"

"You know how I got the gun," James said, with hardly more than a glance in Vincent's direction as he sped onto Boulevard of the Allies. "He threatened us. I didn't have a choice."

Tears streamed down his face. "You killed him."

"To protect you. All I ever wanted to do was keep you safe. I will always keep you safe. Even if it's from yourself."

A threat.

He'd shot the stocky man in front of his daughter. He'd bashed that kid's face in. He'd killed Tyler and made Vincent believe their attackers were after them. James had done all of this, and now, he was threatening him. Vincent looked at his blood-stained face, searching for the man he loved, but all he saw was a monster. "What does that mean?"

James didn't answer.

If James was going to kill him, Vincent didn't know why he didn't let him just fall out of that window. He had no idea what James had in store for him when they got back to the motel, but he didn't want to find out. There was nowhere he could go and no one he could turn to for help. His only real option was to unbuckle his seat belt, open his door, and let the pavement finish him.

Death had to be better than whatever James had in store for him. Vincent could end all the pain right now. What did he really have to live for at this point? He clutched the door handle. He gritted his teeth together so hard he thought they'd break to pieces.

Just do it.

He gripped the handle.

Finish this.

He let it go.

Fuck.

He couldn't do it.

He didn't want to die.

Despite James's crazed driving, they made it back to the motel in one piece. After James parked, he got out of the car, went around to the passenger's side, and opened Vincent's door. "Come on."

Vincent stared at their motel room door. "What are you going to do to me?"

James grabbed him by his wrist. Vincent unbuckled his seat belt just in time to be yanked out of the car. James led him to the door. Vincent didn't struggle. There was no use. James could do whatever he wanted to him. Vincent's vision had cleared, and he wished it hadn't. He didn't want to see what James had planned for him.

With one hand still wrapped around Vincent's wrist,

James unlocked the door. He pulled Vincent inside and kicked the door shut behind him. He stuck his arm through the loops in the grocery bags on the table, then grabbed one of the chairs. He dragged it across the floor, pulling Vincent toward the bathroom. Only after James pushed him inside did Vincent realize what he was doing.

"Wait!"

James threw the bags of groceries inside and shut the door. Vincent tried the door handle, but James must've already put the chair in place because it didn't budge. Vincent banged against the door. "James!"

"No one is ever going to hurt you again."

"James, I don't want this!"

"I am going to find him and kill him. Then, I will come back for you."

"Please. You don't have to do this!"

"You won't ever have to be afraid again." His voice was growing fainter.

"James!" Vincent pounded his fists into the bathroom door.

"I'll always be there to keep you safe."

Even if it's from yourself.

James slammed the motel room door shut behind him.

CHAPTER TWENTY-FIVE

TRAPPED

VINCENT BANGED HIS palms against the door. He was no longer trying to get James's attention. He'd heard the car peel out of the parking lot minutes ago. Now, he was just trying to open this damn door before James got back. His wrist and chest begged for relief, but he kept hitting it.

A flash of Tyler's blood on their front porch raced through his mind. The sound of the kid's nose crunching filled his ears. When his palms grew hot and swelled, he resorted to pressing against it. The door bent, but it wouldn't give way or break.

The walls were closing in on him, forcing what little air

was left in the room out through the bottom of the door. Soon, they'd collapse against him until he was pressed into a small box. A present James could open when he returned. He didn't know how he was going to break down this door, but he needed to get the fuck out of here.

He searched his mind for a solution, and the memory of James kicking in the door at the tall man's house rose to the surface of his mind. Vincent wasn't half as strong as James, but maybe one good kick could knock the chair out from under the doorknob.

He drew his leg back and landed a kick in the center of the door with as much strength as he could muster. Pain rippled through his body like electricity, flaring in his ribs. He stumbled backward.

The door stood impassively in front of him, unchanged beyond a black scuff mark.

"Fuck!" He sat down on the toilet, clutching his ribs. That door might be a thin piece of shit, but he wasn't getting through it. He wiped the sweat from his forehead, and the back of his hand came back smeared with blood.

What the hell?

Vincent clambered to the mirror above the sink. James's blood was still splattered across his face. Dark thick blood that had already dried to brown, crusting flakes where his sweat had not dampened it. He rubbed his face, and flakes drifted into the sink. He turned on the water and scrubbed his skin.

He'd be convinced he had imagined James's bullet wound if he weren't covered in his blood. Maybe James had somehow gotten lucky enough that the bullet missed every vital organ in his chest. Vincent doubted it. Even if that was the case, James should've lost enough blood from a shot to the chest to at least faint. But it had congealed almost instantly.

James was never injured. Not even when he'd first returned. His body had been spotless then as well. No patches of healing skin or even scars. Good as new. Maybe better. And Vincent had chalked it up to another aspect of that night he'd never understand until he'd watched a shot to the chest do little more than infuriate him.

Vincent washed his face with hot water until the only red thing on it was his irritated skin. It might take James some time to find the tall man, but it was only a matter of time. Then, James would be back to collect him.

James probably wouldn't kill him outright. Somewhere in his delusional mindset, he still thought he was protecting Vincent. But what would happen the next time Vincent didn't follow his orders? Would he crush his other wrist? Take the butt of Tyler's gun to Vincent's nose? Slowly destroy him until he begged for death?

He had to get out of here. The door wasn't an option, so the next obvious choice would have been the window above the toilet if it were larger than a cinder block. A small child would have trouble wiggling their way out of it, much less Vincent.

He could just scream. The motel rooms were on top of each other. Someone would hear him and complain to the front desk. The only problem was that someone might also call the cops. They definitely would if they saw his bloody clothes, and after being an accomplice to two murders, the police were the last people he wanted to see.

You're fucked.

He sat back down on the toilet. Tears welled up in his eyes. As much as Vincent hated to admit it, he was incapable of getting out of this bathroom on his own. Hell, if he was honest with himself, he was incapable of doing anything on his own. Nothing had changed since the attack in the tunnel. He'd only survived this long because James had been there to protect him. He was delusional if he actually thought he had a chance of saving himself. As always, he needed help.

He wiped away his tears and took out his phone. He had two missed calls from Henry and three voice mails from the detectives. Vincent deleted the voice mails before he did something stupid. He was so helpless he almost listened to what they had to say.

What if he came completely clean with them? Called them up and told them James was alive and on a murder spree because the police were incapable of finding three men who Vincent and James had tracked down without any formal training? They'd probably send him to the funny farm—if he was lucky. They could assume he was behind all the murders and lock him up. Trade one jail for another. James was dangerous, but the thought of jail with men like their attackers was a far worse death sentence.

Vincent looked through his contact list, hoping to find anyone other than the obvious choice to help him out. Alas, he reached the end of the list with no other options. The truth was there was only one person who could help him.

One person who'd believe James was back and he'd murdered those people. She'd seen James and had figured out that something was wrong with him long before Vincent had even noticed.

Sam.

There was no way she'd answer his call. Vincent didn't blame her. After everything she had done for him and James, they'd left her on their front porch alone.

He would also have to explain what happened to Tyler. He couldn't tell her the truth. He could barely think about it himself.

Besides, she didn't need to be further involved in this mess. The police might be watching her, and she could lead them to the motel room. The reasons not to call her went on and on, but the prospect of waiting for James without exhausting every possible option compelled him to at least try.

He called her. The phone rang. One ring. *Come on. Pick up.* Another ring. *Please, Sam. Just pick up your damn phone.* It went to voice mail. *Shit!* He hadn't realized how desperately he wanted to hear her voice until she didn't answer. He hung up and tossed the phone. It bounced across the room, landing facedown near the door.

Fucking useless. He could do nothing but sit here and wait for James to get back. He should just take the grocery bags off the floor and chow down on some chips because it was probably his last meal.

What a fucking way to go.

Vincent buried his face in his hands and cried. His sobs echoed in the empty bathroom, and hearing how pathetic he sounded made him cry harder. If he hadn't stopped for air, then he might not have heard his phone buzzing on the floor. Clutching his ribs, he leaned over and grabbed his phone.

He turned it over in his hand. A crack snaked down the center of his screen, and the right side was now black. Still, on the left side, he could make out the beginning of a number. Maybe Sam was using her house phone or something. He answered the phone and put it to his ear.

"Hello?"

"Vincent?"

He knew the voice, and it didn't belong to Sam. Tillman. He needed to hang up. He didn't know if detectives could track telephone calls or if the scope of his case warranted such efforts, but talking to them wouldn't do him any good. He pulled the phone away from his ear.

In an urgent voice, like she sensed he was going to hang up, Tillman said, "Vincent, listen to me. We can help you. Just talk to us."

Vincent hung up and set his phone on the counter. His heart pounded in his chest.

The phone vibrated again. Undoubtedly another call from the detectives. He only wished they had worked this hard to track down their attackers in the first place. He let it ring. The point where they could've helped him had come and passed a long time ago.

It kept ringing. He should probably lift the seat and toss his phone in the toilet before the detectives tracked him down. But then he wouldn't have any chance of getting a hold of Sam, and as unlikely as it was, she might call him back. This could be her now. He was acting like an idiot. He grabbed the phone. The incoming call was coming from one of his contacts. There was an *S* just before the point where the screen wasn't working. He answered the call.

"Sam?" He didn't hear anything. Hopefully, the audio wasn't broken. "Can you hear me?"

"What's wrong?"

"I wasn't sure if my phone was working. I've—"

"I meant why are you calling me? I assume you need me, or you wouldn't call."

She wasn't wrong. "Sam, I wanted to—"

"What is it?" There was an edge to her voice.

He should say how sorry he was for deserting her, but he had a feeling she'd hang up on him any second now if he didn't get to the point. She was, after all, right. He needed something from her. "I'm in trouble."

"Is James busy or something?"

Vincent tried to think of the simplest way to explain everything, but he couldn't tell her everything. At least not over the phone.

"You were right. Something's wrong with James. He's done terrible things. He trapped me in the bathroom of our motel room, and I don't know what he's going to do to me when he gets back." He tried to breathe. He felt tears coming, and he tried to hold them back. Saying it aloud had somehow made everything more real. All the pain and death of the past week flashed before his eyes. "I've been an awful friend, and I don't blame you if you never talked to me again, but I need you."

Sam didn't say a word. Vincent looked at the half of his screen that was working. She was still on the line.

Finally, she said, "What's the address and room number?"

Vincent managed to give her the information before the tears started. "Thank you."

Sam hung up.

Vincent set his phone on the counter. At some point, the tears became ones of relief. Sam was coming for him. She'd help him escape.

But then what? How was he going to tell her what James did to Tyler? How was he going to protect himself? He needed to take each problem as it came. Getting out was the first step. However, not thinking through what would happen next was what got him here in the first place.

By the time he heard the front door opening and Sam thanking someone for letting her into the room after she'd foolishly locked herself out, Vincent had decided he would tell Sam everything. She deserved the truth. It was the least he could do before they parted ways.

There was an exasperated grunt outside the bathroom door before the clattering of a chair on thin carpet. The door swung open. Sam stood in the doorway. He wanted to hug her, but her cold stare stopped him in his tracks.

"You look like shit," she said.

"Feel way worse," he said, trying to smile.

Sam's expression didn't soften. "You all right?"

"I've been better."

"You're a fucking asshole."

"Couldn't agree more. How are you?"

Sam sighed. "Okay—all things considered."

She looked about as okay as Vincent, with puffy red eyes and a raw nose, but something about her demeanor made him believe her. Like an old lighthouse, she was weather-beaten but strong.

She seemed to be waiting for him to say something, and when he didn't, she said, "So, what the hell is going on?"

James could be back soon. "How about we talk in the car?"

"Where are we going?"

"Anywhere that's away from here."

"SO?" SAM SAID when they had put a few blocks between them and the motel.

Vincent turned away from the side mirror where he'd been watching out for any car that looked like his 1995 Ford Escort. "Yeah?"

"So, talk."

Where should he even start? Sam looked over at him, and she blew through a red light. His body tensed, waiting for a car to smash into the side of them. Thankfully, the road was clear.

"Can you park somewhere?" he asked.

"Why? Are you going to vomit or something?"

"No, just to chat." Nothing good would come out of her receiving the news while driving.

She pulled over to the side of the road. "Talk."

He told her everything. From the attack until the bathroom. "And then he just left. I'm so sorry, Sam. I would have tried to stop all this if I had known where he got the gun, but everything got out of control so fast."

Sam stared straight ahead. He kept waiting for her to scream or cry. Demand that he get the hell out of her car. But she just sat there. No tears. Nothing. After several minutes of silence, in which Vincent realized there was nothing he could say, Sam opened the car door and left.

Vincent unhooked his seat belt. "Where are you going?"

She walked around the front of the car and continued down the side of the road. Someone beeped as they flew by, but she paid no attention. She'd get herself killed at this time of night. Vincent took the keys out of the ignition, got out of the car, and followed her.

He clutched his aching chest as he walked through the puddles on the roadside. "Sam, come back!"

She kept walking.

Another car shot past them.

He picked up his pace. He was only a few feet behind, but he couldn't catch up. Breathless, he pleaded, "Stop. Please. I can't breathe."

She stopped.

He walked up to her, sucking in air, but she didn't

acknowledge him. Even with him at her side, she continued to stare down the road.

"It's not safe out here," he said.

She opened her bag, took out her pack of cigarettes, and lit one. The embers glowed orange in the darkness surrounding them. She smoked it clear to the filter and lit another. After exhaling a plume of smoke, she said, "James killed Tyler."

She seemed to be saying it for her own benefit. Like she was testing out the idea. She stood there, continuing to smoke.

"Want to go back to the car?" he asked.

"I knew something was wrong with him. Knew it from the moment he came back."

"You did."

"I just never imagined..."

"I know."

"I should have done something." Her hand shook as she raised the cigarette to her mouth.

"You couldn't have. I was with him every day, and I didn't know." He wanted to hug her. Comfort her. But she didn't look sad; she looked pissed.

"I've known him since fourth grade. Practically my whole life, and I knew something was wrong, and I did nothing, and now Tyler's dead."

"You couldn't have stopped him. If anyone could, it's me, and I didn't. So, if there's anyone to blame, it's me."

He hadn't realized how culpable he was until he said it. A part of him always knew something was wrong with James. Something far worse than the aftereffects of shock. But he'd ignored it until Tyler was murdered, that little girl watched her father die, and that kid had his face smashed in.

James had wielded the gun, but Vincent had helped him every step of the way. He was just as guilty as James. Ralbovsky and Tillman would probably be more than happy to lock him up.

Sam took another long drag, quickly burning down her cigarette. "We have to run."

"We? There is no we. James isn't after you. I wouldn't have even involved you in this mess if I wasn't trapped. You need to drop me off somewhere and get back to your life. This isn't your problem."

"What do you plan to do?"

Vincent hadn't gotten that far yet. "I'll figure something out."

"I have a gun."

"What?"

"Tyler got it for me. After what happened with James, he started carrying his with him. I already had a stun gun, but he said he'd feel better knowing I had something with a little more power to protect myself when he wasn't there. It's in the glove box," she said, motioning back to the car with her cigarette.

She wasn't understanding him.

"Sam, I'm not dragging anyone else into this, and it's not like a gun is going to stop him. A bullet to the chest didn't even slow him down."

"Maybe one to the head will."

The coldness of her words took him aback.

"What?" Sam asked.

James needed to be stopped. Something deep inside him had soured after the attack, but they couldn't just kill him. "It's James."

She tossed the cigarette into a puddle, and it fizzled out. "This just doesn't make any fucking sense."

"Sam."

"Don't fucking 'Sam' me! He didn't have a scratch on him after the attack, and now, what, he can take a bullet to the chest without even blinking?"

"I don't know what to make of it either." His head swam every time he tried to think about it. "But I saw it with my own eyes."

"I'm not saying you didn't, but I went to his funeral. Watched them bury his casket. Then, he was just back, and I guess I was too fucking happy to ask too many questions, but I should have."

"Something else is going on here. I mean, someone in law enforcement pronounced him dead. And his father lied about identifying his body." The implausibility of what he was saying only hit him when he saw the confusion on Sam's face.

"That doesn't make any sense," she said. "Why would

the police do that?"

"I don't know."

"And his father wouldn't lie about something like that."

"Why wouldn't he?" Vincent wouldn't put anything past either of James's parents.

"Don't get me wrong. They're fucking assholes. They treated him like shit when he was alive, but they acted like they were burying a saint. His mother barely got through the service without wailing, and his dad acted like he just had a lobotomy." She grabbed another cigarette, but she dropped her lighter on the ground. Vincent started to bend over to grab it, but she waved him off, saying, "I got it."

"If they aren't lying, then how is he still alive?" He didn't know James's parents well enough to say what they were capable of doing, but Sam couldn't argue with facts.

Sam put the cigarette back in the pack. "Does it really matter? He's a fucking murderer."

"You're talking about shooting him in the head. I think it fucking matters."

"Did you know the only reason Tyler could afford to go to Pitt was because he got a hockey scholarship? His loans wouldn't cover tuition without it."

Vincent had to stop himself from asking what that had to do with anything.

"His parents are loaded, but they wouldn't give him a cent for college. They didn't think it was a 'wise investment.' He struggled, but he was always good at math. He wanted to become a teacher and coach at some high school. He said hockey had gotten him to this school, and I'd met him at a game, so he even credited it with bringing us together."

"I didn't know that," Vincent admitted.

"Why would you? You always hated him. So did James."

"Hey, I—"

"He's dead, Vincent. His whole life fucking gone before it started. If everything you are saying is true, then you can't help him. You need to come with me and let me do what I have to in order to protect us, or you're going to get yourself killed."

Vincent couldn't. "There's more to it. You said yourself this doesn't make any sense. The funeral. The way he healed. Don't you want to know what's actually going on?"

"He locked you in that bathroom. Look at your wrist. Why are you defending him?"

"I just want to know what happened." He couldn't tell in the dark if she believed him, but he didn't have another answer. Despite all the terrible things James had done, he couldn't bear the thought of losing him again. There had to be another way. "What if something happened to him between the attack and when he showed back up? Something that made him this way."

Sam lit another cigarette, and in the flame light, he could see pity in her eyes. He wasn't sure who it was for: him or herself. "Let's run through this. You're attacked. He's pronounced dead. His dad identifies the body. He shows back up at your apartment, uninjured and not acting right. Then, he starts killing people." She stopped. Not to take a drag, but to collect herself. "Our James would never do something like that."

"I know. He's changed."

"But...what if he hasn't?"

He wasn't following her. "What?"

She sucked on her cigarette. The embers burned in her frantic eyes. "Think about it. There are two possibilities. Either something happened to change him completely. Or..."

"Or what?"

"Or he isn't James."

Maybe she needed more oxygen. "What are you talking about?"

"Either he has changed into this psycho killer, or this psycho killer isn't him."

Had she lost her mind? "Sam. That's crazy."

"Crazier than being bulletproof?"

"He was shot. I think he just got lucky."

"Bullshit."

The gunshot wound was unbelievable, but that didn't mean everything unbelievable was possible. James couldn't be someone else—Vincent would've noticed. And this wasn't some soap opera. James didn't have an evil twin. He wasn't some sort of robot or clone. He had just changed.

"Look, you want to know the truth. There's only one way to figure out what's actually going on."

"The casket." It was the last piece of the puzzle. The only way to know who they'd buried. It wasn't James, but his father had identified someone, and they had buried that person in the ground. Vincent had already tried and failed to dig it up once. But then, he'd been alone and drunk. And the ground had been frozen. Now, he had Sam, and the warmer weather had thawed out the earth.

"If someone else is there, or it's empty, then you can do whatever you want to do. But if not, you're coming with me. And we are going to kill him."

Sam was angry and grieving and probably still in shock. Digging up the grave, if they could even manage it, wasn't going to change what happened to Tyler or anyone else. But Vincent wanted to know who was in that casket. He wanted to know the truth. "Fine, but I'm driving."

Sam put out her cigarette on the road. "Why?"

"Because your driving is going to get us both killed. And I know the way."

CHAPTER TWENTY-SIX

SIX FEET UNDER

THE DRIVE TO the cemetery was far shorter than Vincent anticipated. Every road ended too soon, every red light was too brief, and every green light was too long until he was only minutes away from Greenwood Cemetery. He wanted to know the truth and figure out exactly what was going on, but at the same time, some possibilities were far too terrible to even imagine. He couldn't shake the fear that, unlikely as it was, Sam could be right, and if James was actually in that casket as his father had claimed, then who the hell had he lain beside in bed for the past month and a half?

He'd know the truth soon enough. He just hoped this

didn't unearth more questions than answers.

Sam was too pensive to read. In the rare instances when he found himself at a stop sign or a red light, he looked over at her. She looked out of the passenger's side window, hands in her lap, the fingers of her right hand twisting a ring on the pointer finger of her left in a rhythmic, unconscious manner. Vincent had never noticed the ring before now. Had Tyler given it to her, or perhaps James? Half of James's belongings were gifts he'd acquired from Sam over the course of their friendship, so there was no way to know for sure.

A few streets away from the cemetery, the streetlight turned yellow as they approached. Vincent slammed on the brakes, grateful for a little more time. The beige van behind them skidded to a stop. Sam jolted from her trance and shot him a look that informed him he had little room to comment on her driving from this point forward.

"Sorry." He checked the rearview mirror.

Surprisingly, even though their vehicles had to be less than a foot away from each other, the driver of the van didn't honk. The windshield was tinted, and he squinted his eyes, trying to get a good look at the two shadowed faces inside. He could have sworn tinted windshields were illegal, but he had seen an SUV with one as well when he'd left the hospital.

The light changed, and the faces inside the van were illuminated in the green light. Tillman in the driver's seat, and Ralbovsky beside her.

What the fuck?

He couldn't do more than stare at them. He'd only managed to tear his gaze from the rearview mirror when

Ralbovsky made eye contact with him.

"Green means go," Sam said, pointing at the light.

Vincent stepped on the pedal, and they lurched forward. The air in the car felt stale and warm as he tried to force it into his lungs. He rolled down his window to let the wind hit his face, but it did little more than fill his ears with frantic whooshing sounds. They were following him, and he had nothing except questions. How long had this been going on? What had motivated them to start, and, more importantly, what had they seen?

At the next street, he was supposed to turn right, but he continued straight.

"I think you missed a turn there," Sam said. "Hello?"

Her waving hand appeared in front of his face, and he batted it away. "I know I missed the turn."

"Then—what the hell is going on? You look like you've seen a ghost."

"The detectives. The ones who are investigating the attack. They're in the van behind us." He forced himself to focus on the road.

"What?" Sam turned around in her seat.

"Don't look back! Pretend you didn't see them!"

Out of the corner of his eye, he saw her face forward again.

"Why would they follow you?"

"I have no fucking clue," he said, but his mind was trying to work through it, piece together all they must know. Depending on how long this had been going on, they might've seen him and James staking out the stocky man's house. Then, they'd know about the murder as well. No wonder they didn't have time to find their attackers. They were too busy following him.

At the next light, he made a quick turn without signaling, and the van followed. "Fuck."

"What should we do?"

"I don't know, but we can't go to the cemetery with them on our asses."

"I mean, I got that much."

Vincent needed a plan. He couldn't drive in circles forever, and he couldn't exactly lose anyone in Sam's white Beetle. What he didn't understand was why they hadn't already arrested him yet. Why leave him all these messages when they knew exactly where he was and what he'd done?

Unless they hadn't seen the worst of it. Maybe they didn't know Vincent and James were at the motel until he'd answered Tillman's call in the bathroom, or they'd followed Sam. Those possibilities were far too good to be true. The detectives were probably still collecting information, and they didn't want him to know they were following him until they got what they needed to put James and him away.

Sam kept an eye on them in the side mirror. "Got any ideas?"

"Working on it," he said.

The only thing he could think to do was call their bluff. Pull in somewhere, park, and see if they followed him. They might have seen everything they needed to in order to arrest him, but they hadn't tried to pull him over yet. Even if they were just waiting for him to stop, he'd rather they arrest him now than force him to keep wondering when they'd do it. Plus, if they backed off, he might be able to get to the cemetery before they knew where he and Sam went.

Vincent explained the plan to Sam. He hoped she'd tell him there was a much better way to go about it, but she just said, "I don't know what else we can do."

Vincent made a U-turn at the light and started toward Wine & Spirits—one of the few businesses he knew was out this way. Naturally, the van followed behind him. After a few more turns in which the van kept on them, the white sign came into view down the road on the left.

When he approached it, he put on his turn signal and slowed to a stop to wait for the opposing traffic to pass. He watched the van in his side mirror, his turn signal lighting up the front of it in brief flashes. A camera going off, capturing each second that seemed to expand to lifetimes as he waited for their turn signal to join his. A car drove past, and without another in sight, he turned left into the parking lot, watching the van behind him so intently he almost hit an old political sign that was stuck in the grass alongside the road.

The van remained in the street. Like they were deciding on whether to join them. Beads of sweat trickled down Vincent's back. *Just drive away*. Then, the van started moving again. Too slow for Tillman to have done more than let her foot off the brake. The van continued down the street, rolling out of sight. He blinked his eyes to ensure he hadn't imagined it—he didn't think his plan would actually work, but it had.

"They're gone," he said, almost laughing with excitement.

"Let's get to the cemetery before they come back."

He turned around in the parking lot, and, once the van's taillights had disappeared down the street, he made his way to the cemetery. This time, he thanked every green light they hit. Leaving a white Beetle on the side of the road would be a clear indication of where they were if the detectives came across it, but that couldn't be helped. He only hoped they got their answers before the detectives found them—if they found them. He didn't know whether he was ready to see who, if anyone, was in that casket, but never knowing was a far worse possibility.

Sam cleared her throat. "Do you think they know what you and James did?"

He knew what she was actually asking him. *Are you afraid they'll arrest you?* That was exactly what he was trying not to think about right now. "Let's just focus on the task at hand, okay?"

"Sure."

Before long, they made it to Greenwood Cemetery. Vincent parked on the shoulder, and Sam followed him around the gate and down the road to the path on the left. No cars came down the street this time to force him into the thicket or behind a pillar. The quiet absence of any life was just as unnerving as it was relieving. The graveyard was too quiet. No animals stepping on old leaves or wind whistling through the trees lining the cemetery. No anything beyond rows of gravestones that glowed in the moonlight. The quiet before a storm or some other cliché that didn't properly convey how strange it was to hear your own breathing and steps so close to downtown Pittsburgh.

As they walked down the trail, he kept waiting for a SWAT team to surround them with assault rifles and demand they get on their hands and knees for the crimes he and James had committed. He'd beg them to just open the damn casket before they carted him off jail, and they would laugh at his poor attempt at an insanity plea.

The thought helped motivate him to move as fast as possible just in case the detectives found Sam's car sooner rather than later. It was too dark for him to see more than Sam's bowed head. She seemed to be pretending his slow pace was natural. She shortened her strides and fell back anytime she got too far ahead of him. How strange to focus on such a trivial matter on the way to dig up a grave. He supposed that was the point—better to worry about that than think about what they were actually going to do.

Their destination was the toolshed he'd noticed the last time he'd come to the cemetery. There had to be shovels in it. He'd thought it was locked then, but he hadn't given it a good look. He could've been wrong, or there could be a window they could easily break to get inside.

Vincent passed James's grave and kept walking toward the shed that was tucked into the corner of the cemetery farther down the path, but the light footsteps behind him faded. He turned around. Sam stood in front of the grave, looking down at the marker.

He went to her side. He couldn't make out the writing in the dark, but he knew what was written on the marker.

Whether or not it was accurate was the question he wanted to be answered. Sam knelt and shone her phone flashlight on the grave. There was an orange cigarette filter set at the base of the marker, stood up on one end as if it had been intentionally placed there. It wasn't Sam's brand, and he searched his mind for another visitor before he realized the obvious. Greta. Probably left it there to ensure James knew she'd come to visit him.

Vincent could use a cigarette right about now, but there was no time. Their answers were waiting six feet underground, and it wasn't going to be easy to dig them up. "We should get moving."

"Who do you think is down there? If anyone?"

"I guess we'll find out." He didn't want to think about it anymore. He just wanted to dig.

Sam followed him to the toolshed. Same as the previous night, the door was closed, and a silver lock held it shut. Vincent pulled at the handle, hoping the lock would just magically disappear, but it held the door shut. "Shit."

"Wait." Sam reached for the lock and twisted it. Whoever had put it on hadn't actually closed it.

"How did you know?"

"I didn't, but my mom was always afraid of locking us out of ours, so she just made it look locked. The sight of it is usually enough to deter people." She took off the lock and opened the door.

He supposed it'd worked on him.

Sam handed him her phone to use the flashlight. He

stepped into the toolshed. The smell of dirt and old wood filled his nostrils. A shovel hung on the wall. He handed it out to Sam and searched for another. The next best thing he could find was a trowel in the back with a few other gardening tools. This was going to take a while.

He started out of the door, and Sam stepped inside and put her hand over the light on her phone. Darkness enveloped them.

"Hey," he started, but Sam shushed him.

He didn't need to ask why. Footsteps and hushed voices came from the back of the shed. "I'm telling you, man. I heard something."

"Quit acting so fucking paranoid," a second voice said.

Both voices were masculine, and he was grateful neither of them matched the detectives, but that still didn't explain who the hell they were. Groundskeepers? If that was the case, then they'd have the police here in no time. Vincent's body stiffened. The woodshed was full of things that would surely make a ruckus if he backed into them. The voices were growing louder. They must be coming around the front of the toolshed.

The door was still ajar, and what little light the moon provided crept into the shed through the opening. Vincent wished Sam would just pull it shut, but he knew the sound would give them away just as much as an open door.

"I think there's still one more hit on this," the second voice said. "Take it. You need to relax."

"Fuck you," the first one said. "That shit is all ash. I'll start the next one. But I'm telling you, I heard someone.

Maybe we should like go back to your house."

The click of the lighter. The smell of skunk and smoke wafted into the shed. A cough. "And risk Gary catching us? Come on, let's just go back into the woods. I'm telling you, man, you're hearing shit."

"When the fuckin' Slender Man takes you, I'm telling you I told you so."

"Nah, you'll be too busy screaming like a little bitch," the other said with a hoarse laugh.

There was a response, but Vincent couldn't make out what was said. They were going back from wherever they came from. Just some potheads. He'd never thought he'd be grateful to smell weed, but he'd take it over groundskeepers or policemen any day. He and Sam waited in the shed for another few minutes before they went back outside. In hushed whispers, they'd agreed to work by the moonlight to avoid bringing any more attention to themselves.

Sam led the way back to the grave. "What if they hear us digging and come back?"

"I have a feeling they'd be afraid of messing with grave-diggers. Plus, they can't call the cops; they're high." If they had to run into anyone, those two kids were the best option.

"We'd better get started, then."

The dirt was far softer than it had been the last time he was here, but it had started to settle. Sam took the shovel, and he went about loosening the dirt with the trowel. He planned on offering to switch her at some point, but even doing this sent tremors of pain through his ribs.

They worked in silence. Just heavy breaths and the sound of metal piercing dirt. Vincent focused on these sounds to keep his thoughts from racing. They only stopped working when the giggling of the two boys made its way from the woods, and they started back again a few minutes later. The work had a hypnotic effect. Stab. Twist. Then, Sam would take the shovel to the loosened dirt. They had made it nearly two feet down when Sam tossed the shovel aside and sat on the grass, her feet resting in the hole they had carved out.

The shovel hitting the ground woke him from his trance. He wiped the sweat from his forehead and took a seat beside her. Sam pulled a pack of cigarettes from her back pocket. It was thin. Almost empty. She pulled out two, lit one, and handed it to him.

His hands shook with strain, and he squeezed the cigarette tighter to avoid dropping it. As hard as it was for him to breathe, he probably shouldn't smoke it, but covered in dirt and sweat at James's grave, he didn't really give a shit what he should or shouldn't do. He needed a smoke. "Thanks."

"No problem."

They weren't even halfway done, and they had been at it for at least an hour. He checked the time. Almost eleven, which meant they'd been at it even longer. They needed to dig up the casket and get it back in the ground before sunrise. Already, he was exhausted, and so was Sam from the looks of her. Her skin shone with sweat. They were going to have to pick up the pace.

Once they finished their cigarettes, they went back to

work. Vincent's fingers hurt. His chest throbbed. He kept going. Stab. Twist. Sam lifted shovelful after shovelful of dirt from the rectangular hole they were digging. Lower and lower they dug until the rest of the graveyard disappeared and four dirt walls surrounded them. A part of him felt secure in these walls. They were out of the elements. In a protected little space, like a basement or bunker, below the earth. However, they were also trapped. If anyone came across them, then they'd be sitting ducks in this hole.

Vincent brought the trowel down again, but this time it hit something solid, and there was a scraping sound when he tried to twist the tool further into the dirt.

"We're here," he said, looking up at Sam. He hadn't realized how dry his mouth was until he spoke. He tossed the trowel to the side and went about clearing away the dirt with his hands before he asked for Sam's phone flashlight to get a better look at the casket.

Rather than a wooden exterior, the light illuminated gray cement. He knocked his fist against it. Solid. Like someone had put a sidewalk underground. "What the hell is this?"

"It's a container. I think someone called it a vault at the funeral. They lowered the casket into it."

Vincent wanted to scream. "How the fuck are we supposed to get through cement? Why didn't you say something before now?"

"Relax. They didn't seal it. They just like placed the lid on top. I think it lifts off."

"Well, we're going to have to dig out around it then if we are going to be able to get it off." He handed her phone back to her, took the trowel, went about loosening more dirt. Sam took the shovel to it as he went. He didn't know why it angered him so much. Perhaps it was because it added yet another step to this seemingly impossible task, or perhaps because, regardless of who, if anyone, was buried here, he should have known what they did or didn't put around James's casket.

They dug out around the edges. Another few inches until the black line that separated the cement top from the rest was uncovered. Then they dug out around it to give them places to stand. Sam took the bottom of it, and Vincent took the top. He gripped the edge with his sore fingers, willing them to work just a little longer. After they got into this casket, they could fall off for all he cared.

"On three," Sam said. "One, two, three."

Vincent sucked in air and lifted. The cement slab moved a centimeter, but the strain of trying to hold it up ran from his fingers to his ribs and back. His tendons and muscles felt as though they would snap like overstretched gum bands if he held it any longer. "Fuck, I've got to drop it."

They let go of it, and it fell back into place.

"It's too damn heavy," Sam said.

It was, but they'd have to find a way to remove it. "We can't quit now."

"I'm not suggesting we do. Here, take this." She handed him the shovel. "Come here. I'm going to try to lift this fucker up again, and if I can get it up high enough, stick the shovel in it. We can use it like a lever."

The handle was wooden, and he had a feeling it would

snap before they got this lid off, but it wasn't like he had any better ideas. "Ready when you are."

Sam bent down and pulled up on the end with an angered grunt. The cement slab barely moved, but it was enough for Vincent to get the tip of the shovel in the space. "Got it."

"Thank fuck." Sam let go, and a grinding sound erupted from where the blade prevented the box from closing.

Both Vincent and Sam pushed down on the shovel, and to Vincent's amazement, the slab began to lift. When the lever had raised the lid as high as it was going to go, Sam went to push the slab up further, and after she'd gotten a good hold on it, Vincent joined her. He pushed. Sweat poured down his body. His ribs burned like they were on fire, but he kept pushing, disregarding the pain. Before long, they had it upright, and with one final push, it fell against the wall of earth with a thud, sending a plume of dirt around them.

Once the dust had cleared, he saw the glossy dark wooden casket within. He rubbed his hand against it to wipe away the thin layer of dirt. The wood was so smooth and cold it almost felt plastic, and there was a thin horizontal line down the center where, presumably, the top and bottom half of it could open. They were lucky the cement slab was resting at the end of the longer, bottom half. He almost wanted to cry out of happiness. They had done it.

He looked at Sam. "Ready?"

She pointed her flashlight at the top of the casket. "Open it."

Vincent grabbed one of the iron handles on the side and pulled up on it, but it didn't open. He tugged on it again with the same result. He tried the other side with the hinge, just in case he was wrong, but it, too, didn't open. Sam pointed the flashlight along the side. There was a large golden buckle where the two halves of the casket joined. At the center was a hexagonal hole. He ran his hands over the cold metal. A lock.

"It's locked. It's fucking locked," he said, pulling hopelessly at it.

"Shhh." Sam patted his back in a soothing manner.

Vincent shook off her hand. "Give me the shovel."

"Vincent..."

"Give. Me. The. Shovel."

She handed it to him. He raised the shovel and brought it down on the lock, so hard that pain surged through his sore and broken body as he hit it. He lost his balance, and the casket came up to meet him halfway. Chest to casket. The pain was so sharp it took his body a minute to inform him just how much it hurt.

"Are you okay?"

Vincent pushed himself up and pulled on the side of the casket. Still, it hitched on the lock. He picked up the shovel again.

"Vincent, we can come back. We'll figure something out."

"No." He lifted the shovel and brought it down again. Metal on metal. A spark. More pain. He was pretty sure he had broken a few more ribs or at least shattered the ones that were already broken. He didn't care anymore. He'd keep going until he was a pile of broken bones and skin if that's what he had to do to get into this damn casket.

"Enough!" Sam was pulling at the shovel, her phone light darting around them as she moved.

Vincent didn't have the strength to hold on to it much longer. "Please, I need to do this."

"You don't."

He did. He had been through too much to quit now. Whoever was in this casket, he was going to find out. Not tomorrow or in a week when he might be sitting in a jail cell. Tonight, because it might be the only chance he'd get.

"Just put the light on it. Sam. Please."

"Jesus Christ." Sam let go of the shovel and shone the light on it again. The lock looked like it was hanging out a little farther than it had been when he first laid eyes on it. He couldn't be certain. He very well could be imagining it because if it looked unscathed, he didn't know if he could bring himself to go through the pain of another strike.

Vincent sucked in air and brought the shovel down again with all his might. No spark this time. Just a crunching sound. The shovel sank into the dirt next to the casket, beside a square box that had been the lock. He let go of the shovel. His face was wet and body shaking. He didn't know if the cause was exhaustion or tears, but it didn't matter. He brought his unsteady hands to the side of the casket and pulled it open.

Sam steadied the light on the pale face within. His eyes

were closed. Skin waxy. Hair parted and pushed to the side like some sort of politician. He was so perfectly preserved that if Vincent hadn't dug him up himself, he would have sworn the person lying below him was still alive. That and the smell. One of rot and chemicals that forced its way up his nostrils as he stared down at the body.

James's body.

CHAPTER TWENTY-SEVEN

MONSTER

NO.

It couldn't be him.

Vincent looked up at Sam, hoping her face would assure him he was just seeing things or this was a trick of her phone flashlight. James couldn't be buried here. He had come back to their apartment. He had been with him every day since then. Almost every hour. James had killed those men. He had locked Vincent in a bathroom.

He couldn't be dead.

But Sam's face only reflected the sinking feeling that

was bubbling up inside him. Eyes bulging, mouth pulled to-gether into a thin line like she was trying to contain something, she stumbled back into the dirt wall, dropping her phone as bits of dirt fell on top of her head.

They were consumed by darkness when her phone hit the ground, but there was enough moonlight for him to see James's pale face. The face he had kissed and loved for three years that now looked far too well-preserved after nearly two months in the ground.

Vincent's legs were shaking. They'd buckle any moment now. He sat down on the closed bottom half of the casket, examining James's waxy face. It almost looked like a Hal-loween mask. He reached out a hand, expecting it to feel like rubber, but when his fingers rested on James's forehead, they met skin—firm and cold, but still skin. He pushed back James's hair, and he could feel the uneven bumps of stitches where the bullet had grazed the side of James's head during the attack. There were probably more stitches closing up the hole in his shoulder.

No mask or costume. This wasn't an episode of *Scooby-Doo* where he'd pull off the disguise to find the culprit to be an old curmudgeonly man. The monster was real, and he wasn't in this casket. He was out there, and James, his James, was dead. He'd been dead since the attack.

Something between a wail and a scream erupted from somewhere inside him. He leaned over so that he was face-to-face with him. Pressed his forehead to James's and tried to ignore the putrid smell of chemicals that was radiating off him.

James hadn't come back to the apartment. He hadn't

lain in bed beside him. He hadn't murdered Tyler or killed the stocky man in front of his daughter or smashed in that kid's face. He hadn't hurt Vincent or threatened him or locked him in a bathroom. He'd been dead. Of course, he'd been dead. James couldn't have done those terrible things. The attack hadn't turned him into a monster. It had killed him. Left him buried in a casket that Vincent had foolishly dug up, thinking it would be someone else, who would be the key to solving some grand conspiracy.

And all this time, while James had been buried in Greenwood Cemetery, Vincent had been with someone else. Jesus, he'd slept in bed beside him. Made fucking love to him. Helped him murder people. He'd done terrible, unimaginable things for a future with a man who had been dead, and he'd dismissed every bit of evidence that clearly showed this wasn't the man he'd come to know and love. All so he could live in a fantasy world where James was still alive.

He felt like he'd had the wind knocked out of him, and all he could do was sit there, consumed in his own emptiness.

He wanted to climb inside the casket, shut it, and have Sam bury them together. Drift to sleep when the air ran out and lie there with him forever. The possibility was more tempting than any drug, but he couldn't do it. He couldn't hide while this man who looked like James hurt other people. He had to be stopped.

Vincent kissed James's forehead in the same manner he had after he woke up on that hill and packed his wounds with mud. One kiss that would never be long enough to bring James back or fill the void of his loss.

Vincent got to his feet. He stood up because if he spent one more second with James, he didn't think he would ever be able to leave his side. He shut the casket lid and forced himself to look away from the dark wood. Sam still stood against the wall, her expression unchanged.

He stepped away from the casket. "You were right."

"I was," she said without the slightest ounce of satisfaction.

Vincent picked up her phone and checked the time. Nearly five o'clock. "The sun's going to come up soon."

He handed her the phone, and she pocketed it. "Then we need to get to work."

First, however, they needed to get the stone back over the casket. Sam suggested just dropping it on there, but the sound of the colliding cement would be far too loud. He didn't like the idea of potentially cracking the lid either. He knew worms could burrow through more than dirt, and he didn't want to leave them any openings.

Each taking a side, they pulled down on the stone. As soon as it started to tip, Vincent thought it would just crush them both, but somehow, they were able to support it. They slowly knelt in unison, calling out frustrated orders to try to stay at the same level until the stone was back in place.

Dripping in sweat that was grainy with dirt, Vincent looked at the walls around them. Steep and solid. They might as well be two stories high because they seemed too impossibly tall for him to climb over. Without exchanging a word on the subject, neither of them would stand on the vault, regardless of how much easier it would make the climb. They'd just have to use each other.

He helped Sam out first, and in turn, she helped him. However, even with her assistance, pulling himself out of the grave was far more painful than he had anticipated. His cracked ribs felt like they were separating into small, piercing bone shards, and his wrist was in a bidding war with them for the most pain-inducing injury. When he finally got out, he lay on his back, clutching his chest and trying to re-introduce his lungs to air. The morning sky had already begun to chase away the moon.

Sam was just as out of breath as he was, but she wasted no time on a break. He hadn't been on the ground more than a couple of seconds when the sound of the shovel piercing dirt filled his ears. He was too exhausted to even react to it. He lay there, listening to the dirt and rocks rain down on the vault like hail on a tin roof.

He had to get up. She couldn't do it alone. He stole a few more breaths and staggered to his feet to help her. The small trowel was of little use at this point, so he scooped the dirt up in his hands and tossed it into the hole. When his arms tired, he pushed mounds in with the side of his shoe. He felt like he was fighting with it, punching and kicking it. Beating it until it fit back into the hole in the earth they'd created.

The ever-brightening sky was enough motivation to continue working without speaking or taking a break. By the time Sam was patting the top of the filled grave with the back of her shovel, it was light out. Vincent brought the shovel and trowel back to the woodshed and came back for Sam, who had stayed at the grave, staring at the marker.

"I guess we got our answer," she said, lighting a

cigarette. She crumpled up the empty pack and stuffed it in her back pocket.

"More questions than answers," Vincent said. His worst fears had come true. Not only was the man he had been with for almost two months not James, but they were also no closer to the truth than they had been last night.

Sam held the cigarette out for him. He took it and inhaled deeply on it, letting the smoke fill his aching lungs, before he exhaled. They needed to leave. He wasn't sure what time groundskeepers started their day, but it wasn't safe to be here, in front of a grave, covered in dirt.

But there was less urgency now. Perhaps exhaustion had calmed him, or he just didn't know what the hell they were going to do when they left, and he wanted to delay it.

"None of this makes any sense," he said, passing the cigarette back to her. "How could someone look exactly like him?"

"I don't know. I don't think I could even believe it if I didn't see it for myself."

He wished he'd just imagined it all and that he and this imposter hadn't left a path of destruction in their wake. "And how could he be impervious to bullets and incredibly strong?"

Sam shrugged. "What if he isn't a person, but a thing?"

Vincent looked up at her, waiting for a smirk to reveal that she was joking, but she just took a drag of the cigarette and handed it back to him.

He'd considered this man a monster for the terrible

things he'd done, but he'd never actually thought he was a literal monster. The only monsters in the real world were people like the stocky man and the tall man whose heinous acts inspired legends. They became immortalized in bedtime stories people read to their kids to prepare them for the evils of the world.

But people in the real world didn't have the strength to pull open locked metal doors without breaking a sweat. People in the real world died when they were shot in the chest. Sam was right. Whoever or whatever they were dealing with, it didn't seem to come from the real world, but from some story he'd read in his Myths, Legends, and Folktales class.

That's when it hit him. He sucked on the cigarette and handed it back to her. "I think I know someone who can help us."

"Yeah?" The cigarette was close to burning out. Sam took a small drag and passed it back.

"Dr. Cowart. He's one of my professors. He teaches about this kind of stuff." He'd planned on avoiding the man for the rest of his life, but he was the only person Vincent could think of who might have the slightest clue about what was going on.

"Works for me."

He took one last drag on the cigarette, twisted it into the dirt to put out the flame, and set it beside Greta's cigarette butt at the base of James's marker before they left.

HE STARED AT the poster on the door. The same one he'd

read the last time he'd waited outside Dr. Cowart's office:

I've always preferred mythology to history. History is truth that becomes an illusion. Mythology is an illusion that becomes reality. —Jean Cocteau

The irony wasn't unappreciated. He knocked on the door. No response. Through the opaque glass, he could see the silhouettes of two people sitting across a desk from one another. Probably another student whose meeting Dr. Cowart refused to interrupt. Vincent took a seat on the floor across from the office door and propped himself up against the wall.

He switched between rereading the poster and watching the silhouettes to keep his mind from wandering back to Greenwood Cemetery and to fight the urge to fall asleep. He'd been up for over twenty-four hours at this point. After leaving the cemetery, he and Sam went back to her mother's house in Fox Chapel to clean up. They both thought returning to their apartments would be a mistake. Plus, her mother left for work before six o'clock and wouldn't even notice that they'd come and gone.

Vincent showered first, and there were an oversized T-shirt and a pair of jeans waiting for him when he got out. Apparently, some previous boyfriend of Sam's mother's hadn't gotten his shit out of the house. He looked deflated in the clothes and needed to borrow a belt to keep the pants up, but at least he was no longer covered in dirt.

Once Sam had washed up, she dropped him off outside Posvar Hall. She offered to come with him to the history department on the third floor, but he needed to do this alone. He had a feeling what little sympathy Dr. Cowart had for him would completely diminish if he needed a friend to hold his hand through their meeting. Still, as the voices in the office crescendoed and the silhouettes raised from seated positions, he wished she'd joined him.

He hadn't seen Dr. Cowart since the day of the attack when he'd gone to him for help on his final project. His professor had been far from sympathetic then. Add all the unanswered emails he had from him, and there was no way this visit would go well.

Who cares? he told himself. *You need information from him. Nothing else matters.*

Dr. Cowart opened the office door. "Just try reading it with that in mind. If you still have trouble, then come talk to me after class tomorrow."

"Will do. Thanks again." A young woman, who had the nervous, overwhelmed eyes of a freshman, hurried out of the office and down the hall.

Dr. Cowart had a faint smile on his face, and it fell when he spotted Vincent, lowering his coarse rigid goatee with it. "Vincent?"

Vincent blanked on whatever introduction he'd prepared. He got to his feet with a stifled grunt of pain and said, "Hi. Ah. Do you have a minute?"

The professor looked back into his office, apparently searching for an excuse. "Sure. But I have class in half an hour, so you'll have to make it quick."

"Great." Vincent walked past him into the office before he could shut the door in his face. The morning sun blinded his eyes, and he was quickly reminded that the opposing wall was made up of three floor-to-ceiling windows. Black spots clouded his vision, and he blinked them away, taking a seat in one of the chairs in front of his desk.

Dr. Cowart cracked the door and sat down. He looked expectantly at Vincent, as if to say, "Well, get on with it."

Vincent looked down at his lap. Whatever subtle way he'd devised to gently bring up the question he needed to ask had escaped him. His hands were shaking, and he interlocked his fingers to steady them. He had just dug up a casket. This should be a piece of cake. But there was no way he could ask what he wanted to outright without sounding as mad as he probably looked. "Do you, ah, believe in legends and myths and whatnot?"

"In what sense?"

Vincent tried to think of another way to phrase the question. "Like do you believe these stories might have some truth to them?"

"Of course," Dr. Cowart said, shifting his weight. Vincent almost got his hopes up until his professor finished his statement. "As you should know from class, even the most fantastic of tales contains a kernel of truth."

"I mean like beyond morals," Vincent said, unsure of how else to say it.

Dr. Cowart looked over his head. Vincent followed his gaze to a clock hanging on the wall. Dr. Cowart cleared his throat. "Look, I have to be in class in twenty-five minutes and that includes the two blocks between here and there. So, if you have a point, I'd get to it."

He had to just come out and say it. "Do you know of any

myths or legends about something that is strong and invincible? Looks like someone who passed away."

Dr. Cowart's brow furrowed. "Like a ghost?"

"No, a physical being." Vincent searched his mind for any characteristic that might make this a little clearer. He'd been with this imposter for almost two months. There had to be something else strange about the way he acted. "One that's very protective."

"Is this somehow connected to your final paper? Because, as I discussed in my emails, between your absences in class and incomplete assignments, I don't think turning in this final would keep you from failing. I'm not sure if you got them, though, since I never received any responses."

Vincent wanted to dive across the desk and wipe that self-righteous look off the prick's face. Let him know just how little he cared about his fucking class. But he squeezed his fingers together and took a few deep breaths instead because he still needed this asshole's help.

"Sorry I haven't responded to your emails. Been a little busy lately. A lot has happened." He tried to sound sincere, but even he could hear the anger seeping into his words.

Dr. Cowart sighed and leaned back in his chair. "I understand, Vincent, I do. But it's not fair to the other students who have been working all this time for you to get a pass when I've done everything in my power to accommodate your situation."

Fuck you.

The words were on the tip of his tongue. Like a dog in a cage, they whined for freedom. He could just tell him to fuck off and leave. There was no way Dr. Cowart was going to help him anyway. His professor couldn't see anything outside the scope of his class. That's when he had an idea, and he wanted to ignore it because Dr. Cowart deserved every obscenity that Vincent wanted to call him, but he had to try. He owed it to James to do everything he could to stop the creature who'd stolen his appearance.

Trying to steady his voice, he said, "I want to finish the final anyway. I don't care what grade I get on it. I need to finish this for me. Please?"

Dr. Cowart glanced at the clock again. "Okay, but let's make it quick. What do you want to know?"

"I'm looking for a story about a being that's strong and invincible. One that is very protective and can look like someone else who has passed away. One of my articles talked about a creature that had those characteristics, but it didn't name it or the legend."

"Wasn't your paper on *Hansel and Gretel*? I'm failing to see the connection between the fairy tale and what you are describing."

"Long story. I just need a little help figuring out where this monster comes from to complete my paper. Please."

"Those are fairly vague parameters. I honestly can't think of anything that would have all those characteristics, especially imitating the looks of someone who has died."

"What about the strength and protection?" He was reaching, but he needed something. Anything that could help him stop that thing.

"The idea of protection makes me think it might be a

gorgon."

"A what?"

"They're believed to have originated in Greek mythology. They're often carved into objects, like shields or sacred buildings, for protection because their gaze can turn men to stone. This is all information that you can find if you research them."

"Like Medusa?" That didn't sound right. If that creature was one of them, Vincent would have been a statue when it first appeared in his apartment.

"She is considered a gorgon, yes. I should be going." He got up to leave.

"But I don't think that's what I'm looking for." The desperation was apparent in his voice.

Dr. Cowart sat back down. "Maybe a gargoyle?"

Vincent knew that one. The imposter didn't have wings so that didn't seem right either. "More human-like, if that makes sense."

Another glance at the clock.

Vincent wanted to smash the damn thing to pieces.

Dr. Cowart tapped his fingers against the desk as he thought. His eyes were unfocused. He seemed to be searching through his mind for another answer as if his knowledge of myths and legends sat on bookshelves—like the ones behind him—and he was running his brown fingers over the spines. He must have found his answer somewhere in there because his focus returned to Vincent, and he said, "It might be a golem."

"I don't think I've heard about that one."

"Then you'll have to research it. I'm out of time." He picked up a worn leather briefcase from beside his desk and stuffed a stack of papers inside it before getting to his feet.

Vincent remained seated. "What if it's not a golem?"

Dr. Cowart grabbed the coat he had hung over the back of his chair. "Email me then. Let's go."

He waved Vincent toward the door.

Vincent stood up. He didn't want to leave without a definitive answer, but he didn't have much of a choice. He had a feeling that any email he sent would surely be ignored—if only to teach him a lesson about all his unread correspondence. "Could I call you?"

"I don't hold office hours over the weekend, but you can leave a message, and I'll get it Monday morning." He led Vincent out of the office and turned to lock the door behind him.

"It's just that this is time-sensitive. I want to get it done this weekend. Please. I'm trying."

Dr. Cowart turned back around to look at him. "I don't give out my personal number to students. Email me, and I'll get back to you. Excuse me."

"Thanks." Vincent stepped aside.

"Better be one hell of a project," Dr. Cowart said, walking down the hall to the elevators.

More than you'll ever know.

A student rushed past Vincent to the escalators at the end of the hallway. Tired as he was, he didn't want to ride down on one of the elevators with Dr. Cowart, so he opted for the escalators. He had just stepped onto it when his phone vibrated in his pocket. He took it out and, seeing the beginning of Sam's name on the half of the screen that was still working, he answered it. "Hey, I'm coming out now. Don't know if I got much—"

"Shut up. Just stop talking. Listen to me." Sam's voice was stern, but there was a hysterical edge to it that made him freeze in place. "James—that thing—is here. I don't know how he found us, but he just walked into the building. Vincent, you there? Hello?"

The monster, whatever it was, had found him.

CHAPTER TWENTY-EIGHT

TIRED

"VINCENT, DID YOU hear me?" Sam's voice grew more frenzied with each word.

"Yeah." He had heard the words she spoke, but his brain was still processing their meaning. Somehow, this monster had found him. He tried to think if he'd seen his car at any point this morning, but he couldn't remember. He had been so physically and mentally exhausted that preparing for his talk with Dr. Cowart and keeping his eyes open had occupied most of his thoughts on the way there. How this thing came across them didn't really matter now. Not when he was in the same building with it.

Vincent was grateful he hadn't ridden down the elevator with Dr. Cowart. That thing would probably be waiting for him when the elevator doors opened. He needed to find a way out of here, but he didn't know this building well enough to know how many entrances and exits it had. Before he found a solution, Sam interrupted his thoughts.

"I have my gun. I'm coming in. In the meantime, you need to hide or run until I get to you. Where are you?" Her breaths were heavy like she was running.

"No! This is a college campus. You can't fire a fucking gun. And you know it won't do shit." A bullet would just piss the thing off, and the last thing he wanted was for James to hurt anyone else. "I can get out of here. Just get the car ready so we can get the hell away from this thing when I do."

"I'm not going to leave you alone—"

"I know a way," he lied. "Just have the car running out front. I don't have time to argue. Just be ready for me!"

Vincent hung up. Most stairwells had an emergency exit at the bottom of them. He wasn't sure about escalators. The creature was probably riding up the elevator now though. He could sneak out, and it would be none the wiser. Grabbing hold of the railing, he pulled himself down the escalator. He got to the second floor and was about to go down to the first when he saw it coming up from the first floor. James—that thing—was there. Its face was spotted with blood, and its dead eyes were focused on him.

Fuck.

Vincent fought against the urge to freeze. *If you freeze now, you'll die.* The monster could snap his neck without even breaking a sweat. He had to move. Now.

He turned around and ran up the escalator that was going up to the third floor, taking the steps two at a time. The taste of copper flooded his mouth as adrenaline surged through his veins. He could feel the pain in his ribs, but it seemed like an afterthought. Nothing mattered except getting to the third floor. There wasn't an exit up there, but it would put more distance between him and that thing. He heard its footsteps on the escalator behind him. It was stronger and faster than him, but he still had a lead of nearly a floor.

Vincent reached the third floor, and he—it—yelled after him, "Vincent!"

The hallway was uninhabited, but there were enough faint voices of professors and students that they had to be in meetings within the cracked office doors. He stumbled down the hall toward the elevators and stairwells at the other end, knowing full well that thing would catch him long before he reached Sam's car. He needed time to devise a plan, but there was no time to think. He had to act now.

He wished there were benches or racks he could tip over to deter it, but there was nothing except cork boards and office doors covered with posters for classes and events around campus. He needed something to give him a little more time to get ahead of it.

He was barely halfway down the hallway when he felt eyes burning into the back of his head and turned around to see that thing standing in front of the escalators, its broad chest expanding and contracting as it panted.

Vincent looked around him. There had to be something he could use to slow the creature down.

That's when he saw the red square on the wall beside him. The fire alarm. He pulled it down without hesitation. The alarm blared, and flashing lights filled the hallway. He caught a glimpse of its glaring face before people filed into the hall.

"Fire," he managed to scream in the hope of inciting panic before he hurried down the hall to the stairwell. He wasn't scot-free yet. That thing could very well pummel through the people in the hall or go back down the escalators and get to him before he reached Sam.

He burst through the door to the stairwell. No one must've made it to this stairwell yet because it was empty. He ran down the stairs, ignoring the sharp pains in his chest. He was grateful to find an emergency exit at the very bottom of the steps.

Not even wasting a second to see who or what might be coming down the stairwell behind him, he ran out of the building, weaving through people who had either already evacuated or had stopped on the sidewalk to see what was going on, and didn't stop running until he ripped open the passenger's door of Sam's car. He was shaking so much from some combination of fear, adrenaline, and exhaustion that he practically collapsed into the seat before locking his door and breathlessly screaming, "Drive!"

Sam stomped on the pedal. The car sped forward. People were funneling out of the building, but he spotted the creature pushing past people to get through the front doors. Its glaring eyes locked on the car, but then Sam made a sharp right turn, and the building disappeared from view.

"Where are we going?" she asked.

He didn't turn away from the side mirror, waiting for that thing to appear in it. They needed to get the hell out of Dodge. "Butler."

"What?"

"I'll explain on the way, but we need to get as far away as we can from that thing until we figure out what's going on." Whatever had kept the pain at bay in the building was dissipating, and he clutched his ribs, trying to take short breaths, as the stabbing sensation that he'd come to know all too well consumed him.

Sam turned at the next light to head in that direction. "What did your professor say?"

"Not. Much." He took a few more shallow breaths. "Thinks it might be a golem."

"What the fuck is a golem?"

"That's what I want to know."

When they were out of the city and the worry of James reappearing diminished, he asked for Sam's phone so that he could look it up online. She handed it to him, and he searched for "golem legend" on Google.

The first result was a Wikipedia page. He clicked on it, and an image of a brown creature roughly resembling the body type of the Hulk appeared on the screen. Not exactly promising, but at least it didn't have snakes for hair or bat wings. He read through the first few paragraphs. Seemed like most stories of golems came from Jewish folklore. They were creatures created from clay or mud, made to serve and protect their creators. How they were made depended on the story. Some were brought to life by a mystic who put a scroll into the mouth of the creature. There were other stories where the creature was brought to life by a word that was etched into its forehead.

The image of James lying on the side of the hill, covered with dirt, flashed in Vincent's mind. He had packed more dirt onto him in order to stop the bleeding. He had kissed him too. On the forehead in the same way he had when he was leaning over his casket. But James was underneath that mud, and Vincent wasn't a mystic. Still, there were enough parallels to give him pause.

"What are you finding?" Sam asked.

"Not sure yet."

Vincent kept reading. According to the article, most golem stories followed a similar arc. After being created to protect a persecuted group from harm, the monster either fell in love or became violent and turned into a deadly predator that went on a rampage and killed innocent people. Chills crawled up Vincent's neck like an army of tiny malevolent spiders. These were stories and legends, but they matched too perfectly to what Vincent was experiencing for him to dismiss them. All this imposter claimed to want was to protect him. And when it was shot in the chest, could that have been mud coming out of the wound? Had Vincent somehow created a monster?

"You okay?" Sam asked.

Vincent relayed the information to her and the odd similarities between these tales and his life. "But this imposter doesn't look like a mud monster, and I didn't write any words on its forehead."

Sam seemed to take the information better than he had. Maybe the shock of seeing James's dead body made everything else, even myths and legends, easier to digest. "And it's not like you made a complete clay person from scratch. James was in there. It just doesn't sound like something that can happen accidentally, if at all, in the real world. Do you remember anything else about what you did or said when you were in Schenley Park?"

"Not really. I was so out of it, and I was crying and trying to stop the bleeding. I mean, it's not like I stuffed a scroll in his mouth."

"A lot of this does sound familiar though. Does it say how they're defeated?"

Vincent kept reading. "It depends. They took the scroll from the mouth of one, and they rubbed a letter off the word on the forehead of another so that it meant something else, which apparently killed it."

"Does it describe any other ways?"

"Let me do a little digging."

Vincent went through at least a dozen more articles. He found one source that claimed magicians created golems by dancing around the creature while singing. The only way to destroy a golem created this way was to reverse the song and dance. He found loads of information that was just as useless and inapplicable as this story.

"The only thing I'm getting is that golems can be made and destroyed in a number of ways," he told Sam, exiting out of the page he was on. "None of which are any help to us."

"So, we are back to square one?"

"Looks like it. I can email Dr. Cowart, but I would be shocked if he got back to me anytime soon." He had a feeling his professor had suggested an email so that Vincent got out of his office, and he doubted Dr. Cowart would even check it until next week.

"Better than nothing."

Vincent logged into his email on her phone and drafted an email for Dr. Cowart. He detailed the research he found and how golems seemed to be a close match, but he explained that not all the specifics matched up with his sources. He also let him know that understanding how golems were defeated was necessary for the parallels he was creating between these tales and *Hansel and Gretel*.

He included his cell phone number in the email, welcoming Dr. Cowart to call him if it would be easier for him to respond over the phone. He couldn't imagine Dr. Cowart would ever actually call him, but he didn't think it'd hurt to offer. The only problem with telling Dr. Cowart this information was for his final project, which he'd already failed, was that it didn't underscore the true stakes at hand and just how desperately he needed those answers.

He sent it and looked out of the window. They were nearing Butler with no plan beyond hiding from the creature and hoping that Dr. Cowart actually got back to him. Seemed pretty close to a lost cause at this point.

You're doing this for James, he reminded himself.

But that lifeless body in Greenwood Cemetery didn't know what was going on. James was dead. The creature was running rampant in Pittsburgh, and all signs seemed to be pointing to Vincent being its creator. A monster who looked like the love of his life. And he was responsible for stopping it.

He could barely defeat a flight of stairs in his current condition, much less an indestructible monster. And he was tired of fighting. He was tired of trying to survive in a world that grew grimmer by the day. There was no happily ever after waiting for him on the other side of this monster. His happy ending had been taken away from him nearly two months ago. So why was he still fighting this? Why did he keep glancing at the side mirror, praying his car wouldn't appear?

He didn't have an answer, and by the time Sam made it to Butler, the adrenaline rush had died down and given way to a sleep-inducing calm. Sam seemed to be feeling it, too, blinking her wide eyes repeatedly to keep them open. He couldn't remember the last time he had slept, and he was going to be useless if he went much longer without rest.

Henry was still at work when they got there. Sam parked two blocks down to ensure no one followed them, and Vincent left a message for Henry that he was coming home with Sam and he'd explain everything later when Henry got back.

Henry's house was a shack compared to Sam's mother's, but she didn't seem to notice. He wasted no time on a tour. He made sure the deadbolt was locked and collapsed in his bed. Sam plopped down beside him and, before he knew it, he was drifting to sleep. His last thought was a vague hope that he'd wake up to find some concrete way to defeat this monster, and, if not, at least the will to try.

CHAPTER TWENTY-NINE

HAPPY BIRTHDAY

WHEN HE WOKE up, someone stood over him at the end
of the bed, blocking out the morning light. He assumed it
was Henry until, rubbing his eyes, James came into focus.

No.

Not James.

The monster.

It was breathing heavily and sweating so profusely the
blood drops streaked down its face in dark-red lines. The
drops clung to its chin for a moment before they fell,
splashing onto the blue quilt he and Sam had their feet

tucked under. When he was in middle school, his mother had made him the quilt from various squares of soft blue fabric. The quilt wasn't blue anymore. It took on a purple color as a growing pool of sweat and blood soaked into it. Oh God, that thing must have been standing there for a while, watching them sleep and waiting for one of them to wake up.

He found Sam's hand and squeezed it in the hope of waking her, but she didn't move. He stole a glance beside him. Her back was to him, but her head was turned the complete way around so that her open, empty eyes bore right into his. There were dark-purple marks around her neck. It had killed her. Snapped her neck, and Vincent was next.

Hands dug into his legs as that thing crawled up the bed, arms outstretched, reaching for his throat. Vincent tried to roll off the bed, but it was pinning him down. He turned to face it. Instead of looking into the bloody face of his imposter, he was staring at James's dead pale face. James smiled, flashing the stitches that kept his mouth sewn shut.

A scream rang out, but Vincent wasn't the source. It came from beside him.

Sam.

VINCENT WOKE UP covered in sweat. He searched the room for that thing or James or whatever was trying to kill him, but the rays of afternoon light were the only thing in the room with them. It was just a nightmare. Sam was curled in a ball beside him, her eyes shut as she cried out in terror.

He shook her awake. "Sam, wake up. You're just dreaming. You're okay."

Her eyes snapped open, and she reached for the gun in her pocket before she realized what was going on and stopped, her face reddening with embarrassment. "Sorry."

"Don't worry about it. I wasn't having a great dream either." He wondered whether they had the same dream. He doubted it. She was probably dreaming about Tyler. Still, the thought, unlikely as it was, unsettled him. At this point, nothing would surprise him, but if that was the case, he didn't want to know.

"Everything okay in there?" came Henry's voice from the hall.

Both Vincent and Sam jumped.

"Jesus," Sam whispered, bringing her hand to her chest.

"Yep. Be out in a minute." Vincent checked his phone. No missed calls, voice mails, or emails from the looks of it. He could see it was around four o'clock, but the minutes were lost in the broken half of the screen. He quickly changed into an old shirt and a pair of shorts before they left his room.

Henry was waiting for them in the hall. He had a stern expression, like he was playing the role of a disapproving parent. What exactly he was disapproving of was lost on Vincent, who could think of little else but injecting coffee into his veins.

"Vinny, I need to speak to you. Alone," he said.

"I'm going to use the bathroom if you don't mind,"

Sam said.

"Not at all." Henry's tone lightened. "Nice to see you again. It's in here to your right." He pushed open the bathroom door.

When Sam closed the door behind her, Henry's expression darkened. He turned around and went to the kitchen. Vincent was to follow him, and so, he did. Without turning around, Henry asked, "Coffee?"

"Yes, please." Vincent had a feeling this wasn't what he wanted to discuss.

Henry must have already gotten the pot ready because he just pressed the power button and it started to heat up, hissing to life. He turned around to face Vincent, rubbing his forehead like he had a migraine. "What kind of trouble are you in?"

Henry didn't ask if Vincent was in any trouble. He asked the question like he already knew something was going on. Vincent played dumb. "Sam had a nightmare. That's all."

"Don't bullshit me." His voice raised automatically, and he lowered it. "I had two detectives here, asking me all sorts of questions the other day. About James and the attack and whatnot. Questions about you. Now, you randomly show up here, looking like you had the shit beat out of you. What's going on?"

Vincent felt nauseous. They'd been investigating him. Not just tailing him but interviewing people. The detectives had to know way more than he'd feared. Why else would they be asking Henry about James? A million questions were born and died before he managed to ask, "What did you tell them?"

"The truth. That I didn't know what the hell they were talking about. Vinny, what's going on?"

Shit, shit, shit. As if he didn't already have enough to deal with, now he had the detectives breathing down his neck.

"Hey, I asked you a question."

Answering Henry was the least of his worries. What Vincent didn't understand was if the detectives knew James was alive and had gone after the attackers, why hadn't they arrested him already? None of this made any sense, and there was no way in hell Henry would believe a single word of the truth. Even with Sam there to back up his story, his father would assume they'd both gone insane.

But Henry was waiting for an explanation. Vincent strung together the loose details that Henry already knew into a story. "I got into a fight. Someone said something shitty about James, so I hit him, and he hit me back. And the detectives want to talk to me about it, but it's not like it's connected to the case or anything. They're just overreacting."

"*You* were in a fight? Jesus. Vinny, you need to meet up with them. They were talking about you like you were a criminal. You got to tell them this asshole started it."

"I know. I will. I need a little time to process everything." Vincent went to retrieve two mugs from the counter so that he could compose himself outside of Henry's careful gaze.

A criminal.

He took his time selecting the mugs. When he turned back around, he made sure the only look on his face was one of mild exasperation.

"Everything okay in here?" Sam stood in the doorway.

"Hope so," Henry said.

"Cream?" Vincent asked Sam, grateful for the change of subject.

"And sugar." Sam snuck past Henry and took a seat at the kitchen table.

Henry said something about picking up wings for dinner, but Vincent wasn't paying attention to him. He dumped a little half-and-half into each of the mugs, which barely lightened the strong coffee, spooned in some sugar for Sam, and took a seat across from her at the kitchen table.

Vincent sipped his coffee, hopefully giving the appearance of listening to Sam and Henry's small talk as he thought. The only reason he could think of to explain why he wasn't already behind bars, even with the detectives interviewing people like Henry, was that, similar to the conclusion he'd drawn when they were tailing him, the detectives hadn't gotten everything they needed to put him away.

They were still searching for something. Perhaps the last nail in the casket before they buried him. But how, in a court of law, would they explain that James had seemingly returned from the grave? What did they even need to in order to arrest Vincent for the murders? He hoped they didn't know what to make of this mess any more than he did.

Henry stepped out of the room, and Sam leaned across

the table. "What's going on?"

Vincent took a large gulp of coffee. It burned down his throat. "The detective came to interview Henry about me and James."

"Shit," she said, a little too loud.

"My thoughts exactly."

In a hushed voice, she asked, "What did he say?"

"Nothing. He doesn't know anything."

"We'll figure something out," Sam said, rubbing his arm.

Vincent appreciated the sentiment, but he didn't believe her for a second. If he survived this monster, then he'd still have to answer to the detectives. With the imposter nowhere to be found, all the murders would fall back on him. He'd been there for each of them. He'd barely tried to stop James, so if he was charged with murder, could he really argue his innocence? He didn't think he could, and he knew he couldn't run from them forever.

At some point, they'd arrest him, and claiming that a golem had murdered their attackers was hardly a sound defense.

Henry walked into the kitchen, holding a bouquet of flowers. "Picked these up on my way home from work. Got off an hour earlier today so I could take them up to the cemetery before dark. I can pick up dinner on my way back."

It was a huge bouquet of yellow and purple roses. Mom's favorite. Couldn't have been cheap, especially out of season. It had to be a special occasion. Wasn't their anniversary. That was in August. She died in December, so that couldn't explain them either.

Her birthday, however, was at the beginning of April, and a wave of guilt washed over him at nearly forgetting about it. "That's a nice birthday gift."

"I'm still waking up, but you two should go," Sam said, like Henry had asked for company.

Vincent shot her a glaring look. What was she doing? He had enough to figure out right now without adding quality time with Henry at North Side Cemetery to his seemingly never-ending list of problems.

"Well, Vinny, I'm going now if you want to come," Henry said.

Vincent didn't have to see his face to know that Henry wanted company; he could hear it in his voice. "Get the car running. I'll be out in a minute. I just gotta pee first."

"Make it quick." He shut the front door behind him.

Vincent was ready to scream. "Sam, what the hell?"

"What? Henry didn't look like he wanted to go alone."

Vincent's facial expression didn't change.

"We can't do shit until your professor gets back to you, and you'll worry yourself sick just sitting around. You better get going. He's waiting."

Vincent knew she was right, but it annoyed him no less. He needed time to think. "Next time, let me decide that."

Henry honked his horn.

"If you gotta piss, you better get to it," she said.

"You and I both know that was just an excuse to chastise you in private."

"Such a gentleman." Sam flipped him off.

Vincent returned the favor before leaving.

Henry already had the engine running. His truck had seen better days. Henry had patched and spray-painted rust holes in several places, but there were so many other ones that he must've given up at some point. Vincent got in the passenger's seat beside him. The truck reeked of booze. He rolled down the window and watched behind them in the side mirror while Henry drove. The cemetery was only a few minutes away, and he was grateful his car hadn't appeared behind him in that time.

The wrought-iron gate was open, and Henry pulled into the North Side Cemetery. His mother was buried toward the back. No grandiose gravestone. Just a small headstone plaque beside an empty plot that Henry would one day occupy. Different roads wound through the graveyard, but as far as Vincent knew, the wrought-iron gate was the only way out. He hoped that thing was still in Pittsburgh. He couldn't think of a worse possibility than coming face-to-face with it in North Side Cemetery with Henry at his side.

Henry parked on the side of the road near her grave. "You okay?"

Vincent pulled his gaze from the mirror. "Yeah."

"It's never easy. Even after all this time. Thanks for coming with me."

Vincent had been so preoccupied with keeping an eye out for that monster their destination had barely registered in his mind. He was visiting his mother's grave on her birth-day with Henry. He hadn't come here in years. And he hadn't been here with Henry since the burial.

Vincent followed him to the grave. Henry white-knuck-led the bouquet, which shook in his hand. Henry was often overwhelmed with rage, but rarely sadness. Vincent could count the number of times Henry had cried on one hand, including his last visit home, and he didn't think he could handle a sobbing Henry right now. But when they reached her grave, he saw that Henry's face was dry.

Vincent read the plaque.

In Loving Memory of Kathleen Vicar. 2/27/1970 - 12/15/2013. Beloved wife and mother.

There was a weed growing over one corner, and Henry pulled it out and wiped away what little dirt had accumu-lated on the plaque before setting the flowers behind it.

"Happy birthday, hun." He stood up, and his knees cracked.

Vincent didn't want to think about his mother now. He had enough to worry about between the monster and the de-tectives, but memories of her sparked in his mind like lightning bugs on a dark summer night. The smell of bleach that permeated the hospice facility. The way her skin hung from her bones toward the end. How dry her lips felt on his cheek when she kissed him goodbye for the last time.

Not that he knew then it'd be the last time he'd ever see her alive. He remembered how strange she looked at the viewing with powder-white skin and pink lipstick that she'd never worn in her life. Thinking about it, she just looked like she'd been sleeping. He'd wanted to shake her awake so badly, but he'd known she wasn't coming back.

James's face had been even paler than hers.

And he wasn't coming back either.

"Going on five years." Henry stared down at the plaque.

"Yeah."

Vincent didn't believe in an afterlife. He knew these graves were more for him and Henry than his mother, but something about standing here made him think she could hear him, even if he just thought the words he couldn't say in front of Henry. He wanted to think of something eloquent to tell her after being away for all this time, but his thoughts were jumbled.

I'm sorry. That I haven't come back sooner. I just...I don't know. I'm not good at this. I hate myself for thinking this, but a part of me is glad you aren't around so that you don't have to see what a mess I made of things. If you were here, though, I bet you'd know what I should do. You always did.

Happy birthday, Mom.

Vincent stopped there before he made himself cry. He looked out on the rows of graves and thought of all the brokenhearted people who'd visited their loved ones here. All the tears that must've dampened the soil of this cemetery over the years. "How does anyone survive this—losing people?"

Henry wrapped his arm around him. "I wish I knew. She talked about you a lot, toward the end, you know. Told me that, ah, she was more worried about me than you." His voice wavered, and he stopped for a second to collect himself. "Said that you were quiet, but...well, you were a fighter."

Vincent couldn't see anything through his tears. He wiped them away with the back of his hand. "Thank you."

"Do you remember when..."

Vincent didn't hear the rest of Henry's sentence because his phone vibrated in his pocket. He pulled it out and looked at the half of the screen that was still working. Pittsburgh area code. Could be the detectives with a different number. Or Dr. Cowart. "Sorry, I have to take this."

He walked out of earshot before he answered the phone. "Hello?"

"Vincent, it's Dr. Cowart. I found what you needed to complete your final. It has to do with the *circular narratives* of these tales." He emphasized the words, "circular narratives," like he was reading it out of a book or something.

Circular narratives sounded vaguely familiar. He was pretty sure they'd discussed the subject during one of the rare classes he'd attended at the beginning of the semester, but Vincent wasn't sure what story structure had to do with defeating this creature. "What do you mean?"

"I can't explain it over the phone. It's too complicated. You'll have to come in."

He had to be kidding him. "Please, this is time-sensitive. I just need a clear answer."

"Don't forget that I'm doing you a favor. I'll be here late tonight grading. Come in if you want your answers."

He hung up.

Son of a bitch!

Of course, Dr. Cowart would make a simple fucking answer a test of Vincent's commitment to show up in person. He didn't know that Vincent was out of town or that he had barely escaped that thing at his office only hours before, but he didn't even give him a chance to explain the situation.

The monster would have no reason to believe he and Sam would return to Dr. Cowart's office, but Vincent wasn't looking forward to going back there so soon after a narrow escape. Especially for no other reason than to prove just how desperately he needed Dr. Cowart's help.

Vincent pocketed his phone. He felt like he should be excited that they had a lead, but he wasn't even sure he wanted to face that thing. James was gone. Dead. Like his mother. What reason did he have to keep fighting? Wouldn't the detectives arrest him either way?

Maybe his mother was wrong.

Maybe he wasn't a fighter.

He walked over to Henry, who was pushing back the grass around her plaque with a small trowel he must've brought with him. The sight extinguished the anger that was rising inside Vincent. He didn't think he'd seen Henry so focused on a task that didn't involve drinking since before his mother died, and the worst part of it was it was still for her. Even after all these years, his life revolved around her to the point that he'd leave work early and bring flowers and gardening tools to her grave for her birthday.

Vincent didn't want to end up like Henry. He knew

fleeing Butler when his mother died and then running back after the attack wasn't much better, but at least he wasn't twisting a knife made of yellow and purple roses into the wound of his loss. There had to be a better way. He just didn't know what that would even look like, or if, between the creature and the detectives, he'd even get the luxury of trying to figure it out.

Henry got his feet when Vincent neared, pocketing the trowel. "Everything all right?

Vincent wanted to tell him it wasn't. He wanted to be a kid again where he could take all his problems to his parents and let them tell him what to do. He wanted to stay at his house with Henry and Sam and ignore all the terrible things that were happening in Pittsburgh.

But he wasn't a kid anymore. His mother was gone, and his life was in ruins. He couldn't fight this creature for James's sake, or he'd end up like Henry, whose whole life revolved around someone who was never coming back.

He had to go to Pittsburgh and talk to Dr. Cowart and try to find some way to stop this thing because he'd created this monster, and he couldn't stand by and let it hurt any more innocent people while he hid from his problems. He didn't owe it to James. He owed it to anyone else who crossed paths with the creature.

"The detectives called," he told Henry. "They want me to come in, so I think Sam and I are going to have to return to Pittsburgh sooner rather than later."

Henry dusted his hands on his jeans. "Well, we better get going then."

Vincent got back in the truck. He didn't know how he was going to deal with the loss of James, but this creature wasn't James. Something else was hurting people. Vincent would return to Pittsburgh, and once he got the information he needed from Dr. Cowart, he'd face it.

He'd kill the monster, or he'd die trying.

CHAPTER THIRTY

ENSNARED

VINCENT FOUND SAM on the couch in the living room, watching the evening news. She turned off the TV when he came in and asked, "How's it going?"

"We gotta go," he said, and upon her questioning look, he added, "I got that call. From the detectives. They want me to come in for a chat." He shifted his eyes to where Henry was standing beside him in the hope she'd play along.

The confusion on her face changed to one of understanding. She got to her feet. "Oh, good. We should get going, then."

Vincent walked to his room to collect his things before

he realized he hadn't brought anything with him. The only evidence that he and Sam had been there at all was the un-made bed. When he came out into the living room, Sam was hugging Henry goodbye.

"You watch out for him," he told her.

Sam laughed. "You know I will."

The sight seemed like it was from an alternate life. One where he dated a girl like Sam, and they visited Henry on weekends during which she pretended she'd never heard any of the stories Henry retold her about his late wife. Week-ends where Henry showered her with Vincent's embarrassing childhood photos, and she took pictures of them on her phone to later taunt Vincent when they got back to Pitt.

A part of him envied that other life. If he could love a girl like Sam, then he would've never been the target of the likes of the stocky man and the tall man. He and Sam would've walked out of Schenley Park like the other couple who'd witnessed the attack. He wouldn't be running from the detectives or trying to defeat a murderous creature who looked like James. His life would be far less complicated and probably closer to what his mother had envisioned for him before she passed away.

The only problem was that he could never love a girl like Sam. He wasn't straight. He couldn't choose who he loved, and even if he could, he couldn't imagine a life where he didn't have three years with James. Three years of waking up in his arms and knowing that no matter what happened, he'd been lucky enough to find someone who loved him. Even if he'd known when he met him that James was going to die, he wouldn't trade the time he had with him, however unfairly brief, for anything. Freedom from this nightmarish life wasn't worth the loss of those memories.

Sam walked over to him. "Ready?"

Vincent didn't have time to think about a different life now. He still needed to survive this one. "Yep. Thanks, Henry, for everything. I'll be back soon."

Henry lingered for a moment, looking at him. Whatever he wanted to say seemed on the tip of his tongue. Vincent almost asked him what it was, but he feared the answer would be an admission that his father had seen right through his lie. Henry forced a meager smile, appearing to swallow the words, and walked them to the door. "Let me know what they tell you."

"I will." Vincent didn't look back at him. He was too afraid the lie was written all over his face. The idea of talking to the detectives now made his skin crawl, but it was better Henry thought that than knew the truth about what was actually going on.

Once they were back in the car, Sam started up the engine. "So, what did he say?"

"Not much. He said he'd found a way to stop it, but he wants me to come in so he can explain everything in person." Vincent waved goodbye to Henry, who was waving back from the porch.

"What?" She glanced over at Vincent, her forehead wrinkled with concern.

"Just drive. I'll explain as we go." He hoped Henry couldn't see her face.

She waved goodbye to Henry and drove off. "Why would he want you to come in to chat? I thought he hated you."

"Prick probably just wants to make me work for it. He sounded so formal on the phone—like I was a stranger or something." Dr. Cowart seemed determined to ensure Vincent was constantly aware that any kindness on his part was an abnormality.

"What do you mean, formal?" She pulled onto Main Street and turned in to Dunkin' Donuts. "Also, I don't know if you're hungry, but I need a sandwich or something or I'm going to pass out."

Vincent couldn't remember the last time he ate. "Sure. And I don't know. The way he spoke just seemed off. He said the answer had to do with the 'circular narratives' of these stories in this weird way—like it was a riddle."

"That sounds sketchy." Sam pulled up to the drive-thru intercom and relayed her order before asking for Vincent's. He got a sandwich and an iced coffee.

Had he misinterpreted his call with Dr. Cowart? He couldn't think of what else could be going on with his professor, but the moment the buttery smell of the croissant wafted from the paper bag Sam handed him, he couldn't think of anything else except the bottomless pit of hunger that was his stomach. He devoured the sandwich in a matter of seconds, washing it down with several gulps of iced coffee. Wiping his greasy fingers on his lap, he revisited Dr. Cowart's call. Sam was right; the call was strange, and he couldn't just dismiss it as unusual. That's how he was blindsided by the creature.

What could be the worst possible reason for a strained formal call from a professor who hated him yet asked to meet with him in person outside office hours? Lately, the worst possible outcome seemed to be the most accurate way to predict what was going to happen next, and that's where he found his answer.

"Do you think this is a setup or something?" The detectives had been tailing him and interviewing people about him and James. What if they'd gotten everything they needed to lock him up, but he was suddenly nowhere to be found? Could they be working with the professor to arrest him? That would explain why Dr. Cowart sounded so strange on the phone. Maybe he wasn't reading from a textbook, but a script drafted by Ralbovsky and Tillman to lure Vincent to his office so that they could ambush him when he walked through the office door.

Sam thoughtfully chewed on a mouthful of her sandwich. "Maybe. I just don't get why he'd make you come in to meet him in person when he could just tell you over the phone, especially if he hates your guts."

"Shit." The sandwich felt like a weight in his stomach. An even worse possibility hit him. "What if it's the creature?"

"I don't think so," Sam said without hesitation.

"Why?"

She set her sandwich on the flattened bag covering her lap. "I was watching the news while you were gone. They talked about the murders."

She paused there, her gaze glued to the road.

Had they talked about the little girl watching her dad die at the hands of two intruders? He blocked out the memory of the little girl's screams. "Yeah?"

"Yeah. They think it might be gang related. There was a breaking news segment of a shootout in the Hill District this afternoon. Probably right after we ran into him—it. Witnesses reported hearing gunshots and then seeing an old Ford take off down the street with two men in it. This golem thing seems a little too busy to be worrying about your professor, but who knows."

The creature had done it, then. He'd killed the tall man. All their attackers were gone. Vincent thought he'd feel relieved, but he was in as much danger now, if not more, than when all three of their attackers were out there. He just hoped no more innocent people had gotten in the creature's way before it'd found the tall man. "Did anyone else get hurt?"

"Not from what they reported, but it was a developing story, and I turned it off when you and Henry got back."

Vincent searched for the news story on Sam's phone. According to the two videos he found, no one else had been hurt at the hands of the creature he'd created. The fact that a lack of fatalities came as a relief to him only underscored just how low his standards had plummeted. At least the creature was too busy with the tall man to create a trap. "I don't think I mentioned Dr. Cowart to that thing anyway, so I think you're right. It must have followed your car to Posvar Hall. Has to be the detectives."

"Do you still want to go?"

Do we have a choice? He needed that information. Without it, he might as well be locked up because that would be the only way he'd be safe from that creature. But then, who would stop that thing from hurting other people? "I mean, it's a risk, but we need that information."

"You sure?"

"I am." Even if there was a ninety-nine percent chance this was a trap, then the one percent chance it might bring this monster down was worth the risk. They still had another half an hour before they reached Pittsburgh. Plenty of time to think of some way to ensure that, if this was a trap, he didn't get ensnared in it.

SAM SLIPPED INTO an empty parking spot a street away from Posvar Hall. Vincent shook his legs, chomping on a stick of gum that had lost its flavor long before they'd reached Pittsburgh. The plan was simple and low risk, but he didn't like the idea of waiting around while Sam went in there alone. Unfortunately, as Sam pointed out, this was the safest way to ensure Vincent wasn't walking into a trap.

Sam put her gun in the glove box beside her Pepto-Bismol-pink stun gun and tossed him her keys. "Dr. Cowart? Third floor?"

"Yeah." He didn't like this at all. "You sure about this?"

Sam groaned. "I'm not donating a kidney to a stranger. Just relax. You're making me nervous. What can they actually do to me?"

Vincent knew that they could do very little to her, but

something about this seemed wrong. Sam grew smaller in the side mirror until she turned onto the next street. Even if the detectives saw through her lie that she'd accidentally gone into the wrong professor's office, they couldn't exactly arrest her. The worst they could do was follow her back to her car, and she'd text Vincent if that happened so that by the time she got back, he'd be long gone. That was even if the detectives were there in the first place.

He needed to relax. All his worrying had actually fogged up the passenger's side window. He turned the key in the ignition and rolled down the window. Even though the air was warm, there was a nice breeze.

He tilted the side mirror, so he had a perfect view of the corner Sam had disappeared around, and he took his phone out of his pocket so that he could answer it quickly if she called or texted him. He was probably overreacting, but they were so close to figuring out how to defeat this creature he couldn't help but worry. If Ralbovsky and Tillman locked him up, then all this work would have been for nothing, and this monster would continue to hurt other people while he rotted in jail.

We're too close to stop now.

Minutes passed. She was probably going up the elevator, or maybe she'd already gotten to his office. He could almost hear her knocking on his door, and Dr. Cowart's dry response along the lines of "Intrude," because he thought it was Vincent. She'd apologize for the mistake, saying she must have gotten off on the wrong floor or something before taking a look around and leaving. Any minute now, she'd come back around that corner and tell him the coast was clear.

But she didn't come around the corner. Ten minutes went by, and the knots in Vincent's stomach twisted so tightly he was sure they'd break. Sam hadn't called or texted him, which left only one possibility: the cops were waiting for him. Sam probably tried to leave, but they stopped her, and were grilling her on what an incredible coincidence it was that she happened to appear in a trap they'd set for Vincent.

Fuck.

They were ruining everything. The least they could do was get out of his way so that Vincent could do their job undeterred. There was no doubt in his mind that if he tried to get in contact with Dr. Cowart, then they'd have him locked up before he could apply any of the knowledge he had obtained. Without Dr. Cowart, they were screwed. That was, of course, if Vincent managed to evade the detectives. He had a feeling dancing around James while chanting would do little more than get him killed.

Vincent climbed over the center console and sat in the driver's seat in case Sam came running around the corner, waving for him to get the car started before the detectives caught up with her. He checked his phone for the umpteenth time. Still nothing. He wanted to call her, but if she was in a place where she felt comfortable calling him, then she already would have done it. He opted for a text message, which ended up being harder than it appeared with only half of his screen working. Just from memory of the other half of the keyboard, he managed to text her, *OK?* after a few failed attempts.

She didn't respond. And as the time since she left mounted to almost twenty minutes, emphasized by the falling darkness of night chasing away the last rays of the afternoon sun, he started to trust that bad feeling he had.

Even with the detectives asking her questions, she should already be back unless they had somehow detained her. Sam would probably tell him to drive away if she could use her phone so that he could meet up with her after she managed to shake the detectives, but he couldn't just desert her. What if they didn't let her go? Any trouble she might be in was because of him. He had to go in there and face them.

His mind was set, but his resolution did little to calm his nerves. As he climbed out of the car, stomach acid climbed up his throat. He managed to force the bile back down, and he started down the street, clinging to his phone so that his trembling hand wouldn't drop it. He wasn't running away anymore, but actively walking into a trap was far from a solution. Still, he kept walking toward Posvar Hall, praying the phone would start vibrating or he'd run into Sam on his way.

As much as he wanted to prolong reaching Dr. Cowart's office, his body was too sore to walk across the building to the escalators. The elevator came down from the third floor, and it dinged when it opened. He looked around. The lobby was empty. Everyone must've called it a day after the fire alarm went off.

The doors started to close, and he reached out his hand to stop them. When they opened, he stepped inside and pressed the button for the third floor. The elevator dinged when it passed the second floor and again before the doors opened on the third. When he'd first gone to talk to Dr. Cowart before the attack, he'd compared the dings to the beating drums of a funeral march. They sounded even more like them now.

He got out and walked down the hallway to Dr. Cowart's office. The same hallway he had fled down to escape James. He couldn't believe that had only happened this morning.

Dr. Cowart's office door was closed, and yellow light leaked out from under the door, but he couldn't see any silhouettes inside. Maybe because the room wasn't backlit from the wall of windows. He lifted his shaky fist and knocked on the door.

There was murmuring; then Dr. Cowart asked, "Who is it?"

He was walking right into the trap, and he had no other choice but to play along. Whatever moisture was left in his mouth evaporated. He rubbed his tongue against the dry roof of his mouth. "Vincent. Vincent Vicar."

"Come—"

Dr. Cowart was cut off by Sam, who screamed, "Run!"

Something crashed in the office, and before Vincent could even process her words, the door flung open, and James—or the creature in James's form—stood in the doorway. Its face was streaked red with blood that stained its disheveled hair. One of its hands was wrapped around Dr. Cowart's throat, holding him in the air so that his leather shoes barely touched the thin carpet. Behind them, Sam lay on the floor in front of the desk, clutching her face as she writhed with pain.

Dr. Cowart's eyes were wide with fear as he clawed at the creature's hand to no avail. "I'm so sorry. I had no idea that it was rea—"

The creature's grip on his neck tightened, and Dr. Cowart was silenced. The veins in his head swelled. The creature smiled—James's lopsided smile—and stepped aside. "Won't you join us?"

Ralbovsky and Tillman were nowhere in sight. The creature had lured him here, and he had walked right into his trap. A creature with James's face and smile and who called him babe. "You're not James."

The monster pulled the tall man's silver revolver from its back pocket and pointed it at Sam. "Get in here now, or I'll kill her."

The casual tone in its voice chilled Vincent to the bone. It wasn't bluffing.

"Get out of here!" Sam cried, crawling back toward the windows.

Every bone in his body pleaded with him to run, but Vincent wouldn't let anyone else die for him. It was time he faced his creation. He stepped into the office, and the monster kicked the door shut behind him.

CHAPTER THIRTY-ONE

PANTHER HOLLOW BRIDGE

VINCENT RAISED HIS hands in the air and tried to breathe through the terror that was shredding his insides to pieces. Any sudden movement could make the monster snap Dr. Cowart's neck or shoot Sam in the head. "Please. Let them go."

"He was trying to kill me," it said plainly, inspecting the professor's ever-reddening face like it was a fascinating display in an art museum.

Vincent needed a plan. Something to stop this creature. But it was choking the only person who knew how to defeat it. He needed to think of something. Now. Or Dr. Cowart would die. He couldn't move without risking their lives, so his only option was to somehow convince it to stop. "He didn't have anything to do with it. I went to him for help. It was me. Leave them alone. It's me you want. I wanted to kill you."

The creature stared at him with a blank expression on its face like Vincent had spoken to it in a foreign language. It shook its head as if it was trying to knock the thought loose from its mind. "No. You need me. It was him, and we don't have to worry about him anymore."

"It was just me!"

"Shut up!" The creature tightened its grip on Dr. Cowart's throat, stepping back toward the floor-to-ceiling windows on the other side of the room and raising the professor in the air above him.

"James, stop!" He hated even calling it that name, but he couldn't think of anything else to do. "Please!"

It ignored him.

Dr. Cowart clawed at its hand and kicked the monster— his struggles reflected in the window—but it didn't even flinch.

Vincent realized what the creature intended to do only moments before it drew the professor back and tossed him at the wall of glass panels.

"*No!*" Vincent started to run forward in the hope of grabbing one of Dr. Cowart's outstretched hands, but he forced himself to stop. Its gun was still aimed at Sam, and it wouldn't hesitate to kill her.

The glass shattered. A hoarse scream erupted from Dr. Cowart as he disappeared into the night. Then, the deafening collision of flesh and bone against cement filled the air before the glass rained down on the sidewalk three stories below.

The creature turned its back to Vincent and leaned out of the window to see what had become of Dr. Cowart. In its momentary captivation, Sam ducked out of the aim of its gun and dove at the monster.

But it was faster. In one swift motion, it turned toward her and smashed the butt of its gun against the side of her skull. She stumbled backward, smacking her head on the wall and collapsing facedown on the ground. The wall clock fell on top of her, but she didn't react to it. That didn't satisfy the monster though. It crossed the room, the gun aimed at the back of her head.

Vincent wouldn't let it kill her. He jumped between them, raising his arms out to block the creature from her. It didn't lower its gun, but he didn't move. He stared into its blank eyes, daring it. It'd have to shoot through him if it wanted to get to Sam. "Enough!"

"Step aside."

A low, breathless groan came from behind him, and he'd never been happier to hear someone in pain because it meant Sam was still alive. "No."

"I said step aside!" The anger in the monster's eyes returned, burning bright and hot at his defiance.

Vincent wanted to cower away at his rage because he knew he could very well become its next victim, but he wouldn't let it hurt Sam. "Why can't you just stop? No one is after us. You've killed everyone. Just stop!"

"Not everyone." The way it spoke made it seem like he wasn't talking about Sam.

Before a question could even form in Vincent's mind, a distant scream came from somewhere below. Another cry followed it, asking for someone to call the police. They'd found Dr. Cowart. The creature no longer had the luxury of time. Any minute now, the sirens would start, and they'd be trapped here.

"It's over."

The creature lowered its gun.

The action was automatic. Had he somehow found a way to make the creature follow his orders? Before relief could even enter his system, he got his answer. It wrapped its free hand around his bruised wrist and pulled him toward the door.

Vincent grabbed the edge of the doorframe in the hope of delaying it long enough for the police to arrive—they'd be here any minute—but it yanked him forward, and a terrible wet popping sound filled his ears. He fell to the ground; then the pain erupted in his wrist. It was so sharp that the world disappeared around him. He forgot about Sam and the monster and everything except the pain that had to be the worst sensation a human could physically experience before their nerves just shut down and they accepted death.

Vomit shot from his mouth, flooding the carpet with yellow bile flecked with bits of mushy food. The monster let his arm drop to the ground, and he vomited once more

BLOOD & DIRT - 435 -

before a spell of dry heaving.

"Look what you've done now." Its large hands encircled his waist. He was hauled into the air and thrown over its shoulder in a fireman's lift. He needed to kick and punch and get this thing to put him down, but he could barely breathe. The pain wasn't dying away. It remained just as intense as when it happened.

The monster started through the doorway, and Vincent hit against its back. The room came in and out of focus. He squinted his eyes and managed to see Sam, lying on her side and clutching her head, before it carried him into the hall. She was in pain, but she was alive, and the police would be there before long to help her.

The creature hurried down the hall, and every time Vincent collided with its back, the pain was so intense he thought he'd pass out at any minute. But unconsciousness refused to take him out of his misery. When the creature stopped for a minute, he looked up to find the office door of a professor whose name he didn't recognize.

Why'd it stop here?

Then, a *ding* rang out, and he realized it'd just been waiting for the elevator. Once the doors closed them in, he saw his pale face in the metal.

A pitiful sight to behold.

"You have to walk out of here," it said. Not a question. An order.

The monster set him down. His legs shook. He clung to the railing along the back of the wall with his good hand and leaned against the wall for support. He was determined to keep himself upright because the alternative was going back into that monster's hands. The hands that had caused purple and black patches to appear up his arm and who knew how much damage below the surface. It must have dislocated his arm or torn a tendon. And it didn't seem to care about whether he was okay as long as he was at its side.

The elevator doors opened.

It grabbed his uninjured forearm and led him into the empty lobby. "I'm parked just up the road."

It could crush this arm, too, and there was nothing he could do about it. And he was following along with it. Following it with no idea of what it intended to do to him. It'd told him it hadn't killed everyone yet. Was it saving the finale for him? Kill him and end this once and for all?

No, it wouldn't kill me.

But it was furious, and it did all sorts of things when it went into a fit of rage.

There had to be some way to stop it. This creature couldn't just take him without anyone interfering. He felt like he was back on the trail in Panther Hollow, praying for some heroic figure to save him yet knowing no one would. He was the only one left who could stop this monster, and beyond taking out his pocketknife and sawing off his good arm, he found no way to free himself before they got to the exit.

Shards of glass littered the ground just outside the building. They crunched under their shoes as the creature pulled him forward into the chaos that had erupted in the wake of Dr. Cowart's fall.

Somehow, Dr. Cowart had survived the three-story drop. From an initial pool of dark liquid, smears and handprints of blood led out toward the sidewalk where nearly a dozen people had crowded around his body with their phone flashlights on to get a good look at him in the dark.

A woman shouted to give him space. Others warned not to touch him until an ambulance got there. A man who'd stopped on the sidewalk asked about what'd happened, and another woman was on the phone with 9-1-1, shushing people to hear what the operator said. Through their legs, Vincent caught glimpses of red blood and white bone.

They were all so consumed with the man dying on the ground that no one gave Vincent or the monster more than a passing glance. They probably couldn't even see the blood staining its face in the darkness outside their circle of light.

Vincent could call out to them for help. Create a scene until the police got there. But even the brief glimpses of Dr. Cowart's body kept him quiet. There was no doubt in his mind that the monster would tear every single one of these poor bastards apart if they got in its way, so he went with it back to his car. He must have passed right by it on his way inside. He'd been so afraid the detectives had set a trap he'd completely missed it.

The creature opened the passenger's side door and pushed him into the seat. His bruised arm hung useless outside the door. He didn't dare try to use the muscles in his arm to lift it for fear it might put too much strain on whatever was broken or torn. He instead pulled it into the car with his good arm, and he screamed involuntarily as the pain flared.

The creature didn't seem to care. They'd gotten far enough away from the crowd that being noticed no longer seemed like a major concern. At least not with the revolver in its pocket. It snapped off the plastic car door handle and shut his door. As if he could make a run for it in his current condition. But he'd be lying if he didn't think about revisiting his plan of opening the door once they got going and letting the pavement put him out of his misery before the monster had the chance.

It got in the car and slammed the door shut behind it.

Vincent jumped at the sound. Pain shot through his arm. Cradling it, he pressed himself against the door to put as much space as he could between himself and that thing. The illusion of safety did little to comfort him. He was trapped in here with it.

"You don't have to do this," he said, trying to hide the fear that drenched every single one of his words.

It didn't answer. It turned the key in the ignition and pulled onto the street. The silence sat heavy in the car like fog on a summer morning. Vincent tried to wade through the pain and fear for something to fill it with, but he came up empty.

The sirens were what filled the silence. First, an ambulance that came up behind them and pulled to a halt in front of Posvar Hall. Then, two cop cars that came barreling down the road toward them, lights flashing. They passed by without even looking their way. Too focused on the scene ahead to acknowledge a random passing car.

The monster continued down the street. The sirens had barely faded away when muffled screams and pounding sounds filled the car. Vincent looked behind him, but the back seat was empty. The trunk. It had someone in the trunk. "What the fuck is going on?"

"I got him for you."

Vincent almost asked who, immediately fearing it had gotten to Henry, but the pieces fell together when, through the trunk and whatever it had gagged him with, he recognized the gravelly voice. The monster had been spotted leaving the scene of a shooting with another man. It hadn't killed the tall man. It'd captured him. Of all the people who'd been senselessly murdered at the hands of this monster, the one it decided to spare was the man who had caused all this pain and death in the first place.

"Why?"

"Because you will end this where it all started, and we can be happy again," it said simply, as if the plan was so obvious that any further explanation would be an insult to his intelligence.

"You..." He tried to process the monster's words. It wanted him to kill this man where it had all started. Panther Hollow. It wanted him to kill the tall man at Panther Hollow to end everything so that they could be happy? "You aren't making any sense."

"You let him get away at his apartment. You distracted me. He's yours to kill."

The monster didn't want to make Vincent its next victim; it wanted to make him a predator.

"I can't kill him. I just can't," he said.

"You will. What if someone like that professor of yours tries to hurt me again? You have to be able to protect yourself."

"He wasn't trying to kill you, I—"

"Enough!" It hit the dashboard with its first so hard Vincent expected the airbag to deploy. Veins were bulging in its forehead, but it had no veins. No blood beyond what had mixed with the dirt. An imitation of a human. Of James. A wolf wrapped in the skin of his lover.

They were close to Panther Hollow, and it was going to make him kill the tall man. He needed to think. The next few minutes could decide the trajectory of the rest of his life or, indeed, whether he had a life when this was all said and done. He used his good arm to run his fingers over the jagged edge of the door handle, but there wasn't enough of it left for him to get the door open.

He had to do something, but no ideas came to mind. Dr. Cowart was his only hope of stopping this creature, and he was as good as dead if he hadn't already died. Vincent thought back to his words on the phone. The police hadn't been feeding the professor lines or monitoring what he'd said. The monster had been doing it, and Vincent couldn't think of any other reason why Dr. Cowart would emphasize the "circular narratives" of these tales except to provide his student with a clue about how to defeat this monster.

They'd discussed the story structures of myths, legends, and folktales at the beginning of the semester. Like most of Dr. Cowart's classes, Vincent hadn't been paying much attention. Dr. Cowart didn't permit any of his students to take notes using their laptops because of how easily they could become distracted, so Vincent had spent the class doodling in his notebook. He remembered drawing a caricature of Dr. Cowart that day because of how much it had made his classmate, Jen, laugh.

However, he also remembered incorporating some of the story structure figures into his drawing. The linear one was just a straight arrow he'd drawn sticking out of Dr. Cowart's ass. That told a story straight through from beginning to end. He'd made one of Dr. Cowart's eyes the spiral structure, which was a story that progressed inward to the center. He didn't remember drawing the circular one though. He wanted to say that, given the name, it was just a big circle, but he couldn't remember anything about it or what a circle had to do with killing a monster.

Shit.

In any other situation, he'd just take out his phone and google it, but there was no way he was going to be able to maneuver around a half-working screen with the monster beside him. It'd probably think he was trying to call the cops, and there'd surely be consequences for such a betrayal.

He returned to what he'd researched about golems in the car with Sam in the hope of finding a solution. The story that had most closely matched what'd happened with him and James was the one where the creator had brought the golem to life by carving a word into its forehead. The way that golem had been defeated was by removing a letter from the word, which changed the meaning of it. But Vincent hadn't written any words on James's forehead. He'd just kissed him. And the monster's forehead had no blemishes Vincent could alter or remove.

Back to the drawing board.

Vincent knew that pleading with the monster was useless, but with only minutes separating them from the Panther Hollow, he had to do something. "Why don't we leave him for the police? A lifetime in jail would be a far more deserving punishment than death. Let them handle him, and we can leave. Go wherever you want. Boston even."

Only after he spoke did he realize he'd never talked to the monster about Boston. James had often talked about moving there after they both graduated. The monster would have no way of knowing that though. Then again, it knew a lot of things it hadn't just been told.

"We both know he wouldn't get life in prison for what he did, and he'd come after us. This is the only way."

He wished he could say that the creature was wrong, but it wasn't. The tall man probably wouldn't get more than a slap on the wrist, and with his testimony, Vincent would be wanted for murder. But he couldn't kill the tall man. He couldn't cross that line. He was supposed to be the monster's creator, not the other way around. It should take orders from him. An idea came to him then. He might not know how to defeat this monster, but he should be able to control or at least persuade it.

"I don't want this," he said. It started to speak, but he talked over it. "I never did, so if you do this, know that it isn't for me. It's for you."

The creature laughed. James's laugh. "You can't lie to

me. You asked me to keep you safe, and you knew what that entailed from the beginning. You wanted them dead. You might be able to lie to yourself, but not to me. I know you better than you know yourself. I'm a part of you. You wanted them dead, so I killed them."

No. He—it was lying. "I just didn't want those bastards to hurt anyone else. I didn't want anyone else to end up like us or Damien Wright or…"

His name escaped him.

"Who?"

"Todd Caldwell," he answered, but the creature had already made its point and delivered it like a punch to the gut. If all of this really was for Damien and Todd, then he'd be able to remember their names.

He hadn't thought of asking their attackers where they'd dumped Todd's body at any point when facing them. That had been the last thing on his mind. He was too worried about surviving to care about someone else. He hated their attackers, and he didn't want to spend his whole life waiting for them to find him, but he didn't want to kill them. He just wanted them dead. There was a distinction between the two, but he was having trouble finding it.

Vincent felt the tears coming, but he held them back. The creature was just messing with his head. It might have a point, but that didn't mean it was capturing the whole truth of the matter. It was neglecting all the innocent people who it had senselessly scarred and killed in its pursuit of their attackers. "I never wanted you to kill Tyler. Or Dr. Cowart. You did that."

"Everything I've done is for you. All of it. Blame who-ever you need to, but I've done this for us. It's us against the world, babe." It smiled at him. Not a vicious smile. A softer one. Loving.

James had always called him babe. Hardly a unique term of endearment, but how did this thing know to call him it? It said it was a part of him. Had it somehow tapped into his memories, or did it also contain some of the person from whom it had been modeled?

Maybe he could somehow appeal to the part of it that'd come from James. He took the monster's hand in his. Forced himself to kiss it. "Let's just go. Leave all this behind. I know you did this for us. I appreciate it, and we can just go and move past this. No one else needs to die."

It leaned over and kissed him. He ordered himself to stay where he was. Kiss it back. Pretend he loved it. It was the only idea he had left.

The smell invaded his nostrils. Beneath James's co-cologne was a rotting smell. One of blood and dirt and death. It had always been there, beneath the surface. He'd at-tributed it to something else in the apartment, but it had always been James.

"It'll all be over soon," it said, stealing another kiss.

Vincent wiped his mouth with the cuff of his jacket. If a part of James was in there, then it had been overshadowed by the monster long before now. A monster that could do who knew what to his wrist and murder people without giv-ing it a second thought. There was no arguing with it or persuading it. He'd do what it said or face its wrath.

He had nothing left. No new plan or strategy. He'd tried everything he could think of, and yet they'd arrived at Panther Hollow. Not the trail leading down to the park, but the bridge they'd been attacked under almost two months ago. It parked on the side of the road just before the bridge.

The monster got out of the car and walked around to let him out. "Let's go."

He got out, cradling his arm, and followed it to the back of the car. It opened the trunk, and the muffled screams grew louder. Inside was the tall man. His mouth was wrapped in duct tape. His arms were taped together at his wrists and his legs at his ankles. His clothes were drenched with blood, and his eyes were wide with fear. The wind carried the sharp smell of piss and blood from the trunk. For a man who he'd feared for so long, Vincent was surprised by how pathetic he looked.

The monster pulled the tall man from the trunk, shut it, and ordered Vincent to walk in front of him as he dragged the tall man, kicking and screaming, down the sidewalk by his wrists. No cars drove down the street, and there were no bystanders in sight. They passed the two panther statues that were eternally frozen in a pouncing stance at either side of the entrance of the bridge. He wished they'd come alive. Leap on the monster and end this, but they merely watched them pass.

Before he'd taken more than a few steps onto the bridge, the monster said, "Stop. Here's good."

Over the waist-high stone railing, he could barely make out the trail below in the darkness. They were above the very tunnel where he and James had first come across the tall man and his cronies. They'd come back to return the favor. He was supposed to kill the man here and leave with the creature to go who knew where.

He should be afraid, but he just felt empty. He'd done everything in his power to prevent this, but here he was, standing on Panther Hollow Bridge with the monster and the tall man. He wondered if this had always been planned—like it was some Greek tragedy and his fate had been written in stone. All there was left to do was to play his part. Kill the tall man and accept he'd forever be this monster's prisoner. That his death would be slow at the heavy hands of this thing. It had already destroyed one of his arms, and it would move to something else. He was sure of it. It would keep breaking him down until he was in too many pieces to survive.

It handed him the revolver. He expected his hand to shake under its weight, but his grip was steady. The metal of the gun reflected the streetlights. So much power in such a small thing. He just needed to pull the trigger, and this would be over. He'd been through so much just to reach this point. To do what this monster wanted.

The creature brought the tall man over toward the ledge and held on to his forearm to keep him in place beside him. "Shoot him."

Vincent raised the gun.

The tall man's face was red. His eyes were narrow. He was screaming, but not in fear. He was angry. Muffled curses at Vincent and the monster. The man hated them. He'd hated Vincent and James from the second he detected they were different. As many lies as the monster told him, it was right about one thing. Vincent hated him back. This sorry excuse for a human being had ended James's life and ruined his beyond repair. And he could end him with one pull of a trigger.

"Do it. Now," the monster ordered.

He aimed the gun at the tall man.

The gunshot echoed past the perched panther statues and the trees below in Schenley Park.

But Vincent hadn't fired the gun, and the tall man hadn't been shot.

A dark circle expanded across the monster's white shirt from the hole in its stomach.

Sam walked out from around the panther statue on the other side of the road, her gun aimed at the monster. She had a large red welt on the side of her head, but she otherwise looked unharmed. She must have gotten up and followed them here. Her jaw was clenched, and her eyes were glaring at the monster.

"Why won't you just fucking die?" she said, firing another shot into its chest.

CHAPTER THIRTY-TWO

CIRCULAR NARRATIVES

HIS SAVIOR HAD arrived, and he didn't know what the hell she was thinking. Those bullets wouldn't kill the monster. They'd only make her its next target. "Sam, stop!"

"Get out of here," she told him. Her eyes were illuminated in the streetlights, and even from where he stood, he could see they were filled with rage. She wasn't just here to save him; she was here to avenge Tyler's murder.

No words he could say would stop her from doing her best to kill this thing, but he tried anyway. "The bullets won't kill it!"

"Just go!" She buried another shot in the monster's

stomach.

The monster didn't even flinch. It looked down at the thick red mud pouring from its wounds and let out a growl of frustration. It tossed the tall man to the ground and started across the street toward her, ready to pull her apart limb from limb.

"Please, just let her go," Vincent pleaded, but if the monster heard him, then it made no indication.

He wasn't going to desert her now, but he didn't know what he could do to stop it. Bullets were useless, and he was too weak to get between them before the monster reached her. Dr. Cowart's clue was lost on him—he had no idea how to defeat, or even delay, the creature. He felt like he was staring at his mother in her hospice bed, hoping beyond any reason that a cure would magically appear in his lap so he could save her, but knowing all he could do was watch her die.

Sam fired into the monster's calf, and mud blasted onto the pavement behind it. The creature faltered, stumbling to keep itself upright, before it caught itself and continued forward. She kept pulling the trigger—another in its arm and one through its cheek—until she was out of bullets.

The monster didn't slow down. Mud poured from every bullet hole, covering much of the creature in blood-red clay from the neck down. Globs of mud fell in puddles on the road in its wake. It'd lost so much that Vincent expected it to fall over, but that only seemed to make it more determined to kill her. It ran forward, closing the last few feet between them.

Sam threw her gun at its face, and as it raised its hands to block it, she charged forward. She pulled a stun gun from her pocket and jammed it into one of the holes in its stomach. The clicking of electricity filled his ears, and the smell of baked clay permeated the air. Black smoke poured from the spot. The monster stood there, shaking as the electricity shot through its body, creating cracked dry lines in the mud.

A glimmer of hope.

Is this the key to defeating it? Bake the mud until it can't move?

"Die, you motherfucker!" She stuck the stun gun under its chin.

The monster's head shook like it was seizing, and black cracks expanded across its face. But then it grabbed her arm and pulled it back with such force that she dropped the stun gun on the ground. It wrapped its other muddy hand around her throat and lifted her into the air.

It had her.

Sam turned to Vincent, her eyes wet with tears. "Run! You need to—"

The monster cut off her airway before she could finish. She punched and kicked the monster like she had trained in a ring for years, but it barely noticed her struggles. And as it started back over to where the tall man squirmed on the ground below the ledge, there was little doubt what it intended to do with her.

It's going to kill Sam. Murder her like it did Tyler and Dr. Cowart unless someone does something.

But no one else was coming.

He was the only one left.

Run.

He heard the word in his mind, but he didn't see Sam scream it. He saw James mouth it to him. Just below the bridge, he'd stood by and watched James die, and here he was again with Sam, incapable of saving one of the only people left in the world who he loved. He was the same helpless coward who'd entered that tunnel almost two months ago.

Only now, he had better excuses. Physical injuries. Ones masking the reality that, even if he were in perfect health, he wouldn't interfere with what the monster did. He was too afraid.

"Run."

The cry was so hoarse and quiet he would have been convinced he'd imagined it if Sam wasn't looking at him. The monster neared the railing. Any second now, it would drop her, and she would die. And here he stood, too afraid to do more than watch it murder her.

Run.

He listened to her.

He listened to James.

Run.

He dropped the gun and ran. Not away from the monster, but toward it.

He was afraid—fucking terrified. His heart was pounding so hard he thought it'd break what was left of his ribs. His legs were shaking so much he expected to fall over at any moment. But this wasn't the first time he'd felt this way. He'd been afraid when he'd tried to stop the monster from killing the kid. And when he'd stepped between it and Sam. What he feared more than the monster, however, was that this thing was going to kill someone who was as much of a victim as he and James had been in that tunnel. This wasn't the same as watching his mother die. He could prevent this death.

Run.

His legs carried him forward. The pain was too terrible in his chest and arm to ignore it. So, he felt it. He felt the pain in his body. The pain of his mother's death. The pain of James's loss at the hands of terrible men. The pain of the deaths of all the innocent people who'd been murdered because he'd created this bloodthirsty monster to protect himself. He felt all of it. Used it as fuel.

He opened his arms wide to tackle it, and a moment before he collided with the monster, it turned to him. Shock and something else flooded its face at his betrayal. Fear. Yes, it was afraid of him.

He slammed into it. The monster stumbled backward and dropped Sam to the ground. She coughed as air reentered her lungs, and the monster fell over the railing. Its eyes locked on him. Anger extinguished any shock or fear. Reaching out a muddy hand, it grabbed the collar of Vincent's shirt and pulled him down with it.

There was no time for screams or anything beyond scrambling to find a way to prevent the beast from dragging him into the darkness below. In the mere seconds before he plummeted to the ground, Vincent managed to hook his good arm around the railing at his elbow. Any relief was overpowered by the pain that flooded his senses when the weight of the monster pulled down on him.

"Ahhhh!" His arm shook. The collar of his shirt cut into the back of his neck, and he had to pull his head back in order to keep it upright. He couldn't carry the weight of them both for long.

"What the hell are you doing?" it barked, and the rotten smell of death filled his nostrils.

Vincent tried to turn away, but he couldn't with the monster pulling down on his neck. "I won't let you kill anyone else!"

"You think this would stop me?" It laughed.

He knew it wouldn't, but it'd give him and Sam enough time to get away from the creature. "Then let go."

"You need me!"

Threads snapped as the collar of his old shirt ripped. The monster let go of the fabric, and just when he thought he was free of the beast, it wrapped its hands around his leg. The pain was so intense his arm slipped, and he grabbed hold of the top of the cold stone railing with his aching fingers.

"Fuck!" His grip was sliding. His fingers pulled away from the railing like snapped piano wires. He was going to fall and die in the very place where he and James were first attacked. Where he'd covered James in mud and told him he had to survive because Vincent couldn't make it without him. Where he'd created this thing. And where it would kill him.

They'd come full circle.

Circular narratives.

It was just a big circle. He'd drawn it around his caricature of Dr. Cowart—he remembered that now. A narrative that returned to where it started. All the different tales about golems had that in common. To kill the monster, you had to reverse whatever you did to create it in the first place. It was so obvious, so clear what he had to do now that he couldn't believe it'd taken him so long to realize it. And of course, he was too late.

He lost his grip, and he shut his eyes. He didn't want to watch his own descent. But there was no wind rushing through his hair. No strange sensation in the pit of his stomach as he fell. Just someone's sweating hands grabbing his arm and holding on to him for dear life.

He opened his eyes to find Sam's red sweating face looking down on him.

"You have to kick that thing off!" she told him, her grip loosening as she coughed.

Before Vincent could do more than look down at it, the creature was climbing him. Pulling itself up his body like he was a ladder until it was holding on to his shoulders and staring at him face-to-face. "You need me! You'll die without me!"

Vincent stared into the face of the beast. James's face. He knew the monster believed what it said because he'd believed it. He might not have known he was creating a monster off the trail in the darkness below them, but he had slathered James with mud because he didn't think he could survive without him.

"You're right," he said.

A smile spread across the monster's face.

"You're slipping. Get rid of it!" Sam urged.

"But you're not James." James had been dead for almost two months, and Vincent was still alive. He'd survived without him, and he'd continue to survive when this creature returned to the earth below them. He kissed its forehead in the same place as he'd kissed James's when he unknowingly created the beast, and he spoke the words to reverse its creation. "I don't need you."

"No! Take it back! Take it back!" The monster shook him, but it was too late. Pieces of it were falling off, dropping to the ground below in globs of mud. The weight of it was lessening, but it was still clinging to him for dear life, its eyes burning through him with pure loathing. If it was going to die, then it was going to take him with it.

His arm was sliding through Sam's grip. She couldn't hold on for much longer.

Vincent reached into his pocket with his throbbing, damaged arm and pulled out the pocketknife he'd carried with him since the attack. He flipped it open and jammed the blade into the middle of James's forehead where he had planted his kiss, and the monster released its grip, disappearing into the darkness below and letting out a garbled cry of fear before it hit the ground.

"You gotta help me!" Sam ordered.

Vincent grabbed hold of the railing with his other hand

and pulled. Sam lifted him over the railing, and together, they collapsed to the ground, Sam coughing and Vincent trying to breathe through the pain.

"It's gone," she said, hugging him.

Vincent had to be certain. He forced himself to his knees and asked for Sam's phone. Turning on the flashlight, he could make out a dark patch of red mud on the ground that was slowly sinking back into the earth. It was actually gone. They'd defeated it. "It's over."

Only in that momentary relief did Vincent realize there was still one person left, and over Sam's laughs of relief, he heard him. The tall man. He'd somehow managed to break through his arm restraints. He was crawling on the ground, leaving a blood-smeared path on the road to where Vincent had dropped his gun.

CHAPTER THIRTY-THREE

THE STORY

ANGER BURNED THROUGH his body like a flash fire, leaving only scorched hatred at the thought that this fucker was going to kill them after everything they had been through. He dropped Sam's phone and ran toward him. Just as the tall man was about to wrap his hand around the handle of the revolver, Vincent grabbed him by his bound ankles and pulled him back.

Pain rippled through his muscles, but that was the least of his concerns. Before the tall man even realized what'd happened, Vincent stepped past him, grabbed the gun, and aimed it at his head. He wanted nothing more than to put a bullet through the man's skull. "Give me one reason why I shouldn't blow your brains out."

The tall man got to his knees and pulled the duct tape down from his mouth. He didn't look afraid. Just disgusted. "Do it. Pull the trigger. Finish it."

"Vincent, don't. I'm calling the police," Sam said, punching the number into her phone.

"Shoot me, you pitiful fucking faggot!"

Vincent flinched at the word. That fucking word. He pulled back the hammer of the gun.

"He knows jail will be worse. Vincent, just wait." She focused on her phone. "Hello, there is something happening on Panther Hollow Bridge. I heard gunshots. Please, send help!"

"I knew you'd be too fucking weak," the tall man said.

You're not a killer, he told himself. *That's what separates you from the piece of garbage in front of you. You're not a killer.*

But this man had killed James. Slaughtered him and would've killed Vincent, too, if he had his way. He'd taken the lives of Damien Wright and Todd Caldwell. He would have killed every person at Cruze Bar and Blue Moon if he had the chance, and he wouldn't have batted an eye because to him they were just a bunch of disgusting freaks.

The tall man would never change his mind. For the rest of his pathetic life, he'd want to kill Vincent and anyone else like him for being different. And he'd brainwash others into believing it, like that kid.

Why should he get to live while James was dead?

Vincent's tears distorted the image of the man on the ground. This man had ruined his life, and he could end him with the pull of a trigger.

"You're better than this," Sam said.

"He killed James!"

"Just do it," screamed the tall man.

"It won't bring him back." Her words were muffled, choked. He didn't need to look away from the tall man to know she was crying.

A bullet through this man's skull wouldn't bring anyone back. It'd only wet his hands with more blood, but at this point, did that really matter? "I don't care. It'll save the next unlucky asshole who might come across him."

"Vincent, that thing wanted you to kill him, and you are playing right into its plan. It's gone. You don't have to follow its orders anymore."

"Maybe it was right about this," he said, but he knew the words were a lie before he spoke them into existence. He'd created the monster to protect himself, but anger and fear had blinded the beast until it became the very thing it was trying to fight against.

Sam was right, and he hated her for it. As much as Vincent wanted this man to die for the terrible things he'd done, he wasn't the one to make that choice. He lowered the gun. "Fuck!"

He couldn't kill the tall man. But soon, the police would swoop in, and he'd never have another chance to talk to this revolting thing on the ground. He asked him the question he should've asked when they'd first tracked down these fuckers. "Where's Todd Caldwell's body?"

"Who?"

"Todd Caldwell. Freckles. CMU student. You murdered him."

"Oh, that one?" He smirked. "You should have heard him crying. Such a little pussy."

Vincent raised the gun. "Where. Is. He?"

The tall man shrugged. "Swimming in the river with the other faggots. Where you'd be if that gun hadn't jammed." He snorted and spat thick yellow mucus on Vincent's ripped shirt.

"Vincent, don't." Sam grabbed his arm to pull the gun away from its target, but he shook her off.

"I'm not going to kill him."

But he'd be damned if he'd ever let this motherfucker hurt someone else. He aimed the gun and fired. A bullet ripped through his thigh.

The tall man screamed, doubling over. "Fucking faggot!"

Vincent raised the gun in the air and hit the tall man's head so hard he hoped this piece of shit never forgot what this faggot did to him. The tall man fell still.

The sirens started in the distance.

They'd be there soon.

Sam knelt and pressed two fingers into his wrist. "Was

that necessary?"

"I really think it was."

"He's out cold, but thankfully, he's alive."

"What a fucking asshole." Vincent spat on him.

Sam undid the tape around his neck. "Help me get this shit off of him."

Vincent laughed. "Why?"

"Because the police are going to be here any minute, and how can this guy be tied up when he kidnapped you and brought you here to murder you?" She raised her eyebrows like she had just explained the sky was blue and prayed he'd understood such a simplistic concept.

Vincent understood. With the monster gone, they needed some way to explain what had happened. He started to work on the duct tape wrapped around his ankles. "But what about everything else that happened?"

"Well," Sam said, crumpling the tape into a ball in her hand, "we have about a minute to figure that out."

By the time the police cars arrived, sirens blaring and headlights blinding, the duct tape was gone, their empty hands were raised over their heads, and they had their story.

"LET'S RUN THROUGH this just one more time," Ralbovsky said, walking back into the interrogation room with a Styrofoam cup in either hand.

Vincent took the cup and stared down at the gray liquid within that was supposed to be coffee and cream. He downed it in one gulp. They'd been at it for hours. After Ral-bovsky left for another coffee run, where he surely went to confer with Tillman, who had to have Sam held up in a similar room somewhere else in the police station, grilling her about their story, Vincent had started to doze off.

"You still with me?" Ralbovsky took a seat across from him.

"Yeah." Vincent looked down at his bruised and swollen arm. The medics told him they thought it was a torn tendon, but they said he needed to go to the hospital to get it examined. He'd decided to talk to the detectives first. He didn't want to wait any longer to face Ralbovsky and Tillman. Now, after hours of questioning, he was regretting the decision. He had a feeling Sam probably felt the same way by this point.

Ralbovsky took a long sip of his coffee, which didn't seem to have any effect on him either. "So, he follows you to your professor's office?"

Vincent stifled a yawn. "Yep. Like I said, I ran away after they mistakenly killed Tyler outside our apartment building, thinking it was me. He finally tracked me down to Dr. Cowart's office. I don't know where his other two accomplices went."

"And you went to your professor's office because...?"

Vincent sat up in his chair and took a breath before diving back into the spiel. "I was looking for someone to hide us. I was afraid they'd track us down to my father's house where I was staying before then. When Dr. Cowart got in his way, he threw him through the window. Then, he knocked

Sam unconscious and abducted me. He said he wanted to kill me where he should have in Panther Hollow. If Sam hadn't showed up, I'd be dead. She tackled him, and in the struggle between us and him, I shot him. He planned on killing me and dumping me in the river where he said he dumped Damien Wright and Todd Caldwell."

Ralbovsky nodded, but it was clear that similar to the last half a dozen times Vincent had told him the story, there was no way in hell he believed a single word Vincent had said. They both knew it was bullshit, but here they were. "Mathew Baker is awake. He has a different story."

The tall man.

Vincent's stomach turned. If there was anything left in it besides coffee, then he'd probably vomit. Apparently, Ralbovsky's coffee trip was far more productive than he could've imagined. He forced his face to relax, opening his mouth slightly to feign curiosity. "Oh?"

"He says a monster killed his friends and kidnapped him. A monster that looked like your boyfriend, James. Has some marks on his ankles and wrists that he claims are from being tied up and thrown in the trunk. Funny story, huh?" He smiled, but his eyes were dead, trained on Vincent to see his reaction.

"Yeah," Vincent said, hoping he sounded a little more convincing to Ralbovsky than he did to himself.

"Who'd believe a crazy story like that, right? Guy's probably trying to get the insanity plea. I wouldn't blame him with the number of charges he has coming his way if you're telling the truth."

Vincent knew better than to move an inch. He just stared at Ralbovsky, waiting. He could hear his pulse beating in his ears.

"Anyone who believed him would sound like a crazy person. I mean, even if I saw that thing with my own eyes, I'd sound insane if I told anyone. James has been dead for two months. We have the autopsy photos to prove it. If we dug him up, I'm sure we'd find his body."

"I'm sure you would." He didn't know what else to say. He felt like Ralbovsky was trying to lure him into a trap, and when he least expected it, it would be set, and he'd be thrown in jail for the rest of his life while the tall man walked away scot-free. He'd probably be better off locked in jail if the tall man was freed.

Ralbovsky cleared his throat. "Well, we'll certainly be looking into these claims."

He went over to the video camera and turned it off—or it looked like he did. Vincent couldn't be sure. Ralbovsky sat back down at the table. "But criminals turn on one another every day. Wouldn't be a stretch of the imagination if they did it in this case. Makes far more sense than a man returning from the grave as a monster, right?"

"Right." Vincent wasn't sure what was happening. Was he letting him go? Accepting their bullshit story to put a worse man behind bars?

"Leave a number at the front desk that you'll actually answer on your way out. We'll be in touch soon, especially after we talk to your professor. If he survives the night, of course. Or should I say morning?" He finished off his cup of coffee.

"So, I'm free to go?" Vincent wished he had kept his mouth shut. An innocent man wouldn't be so surprised by the fact, but both of them knew he wasn't innocent. He'd learned better than to underestimate Ralbovsky and Tillman.

Ralbovsky got to his feet. "You can wait here. We'll have an officer escort you and your friend to the hospital for medical attention." At the door, Ralbovsky stopped. "You know, it's a shame what happened to you."

It was the first genuine thing either of them had said in hours.

Vincent didn't know if Ralbovsky was referring to the attack, everything he'd done since then, or a combination of the two, but at this point, he didn't really care. Whatever way he meant it, it was true.

When the officer, who introduced himself as Charles, came to collect Vincent, he had Sam with him. She looked even worse than Vincent felt. Frizzy hair. Blotchy skin. Bruises around her throat that weren't half as dark as the purple bags under her eyes.

"Wow, you look like shit," he told her.

"And you're a fucking asshole," she said, hugging him. "You okay?"

"Yeah. You?"

"Yeah."

On their way out, they passed the detectives. Tillman looked like she wanted to kill him. He could be wrong, but he thought Ralbovsky looked almost impressed. They all knew what'd actually happened, but he and Sam weren't being arrested. They were leaving. Their story had worked.

WHEN THEY BOTH got out of the hospital, they sat beside one another on the curb, waiting for Henry to get there to pick them up. Vincent watched the sun rise between the buildings of the city. She rested her head on his shoulder, and he rested his on top of hers. Somehow, they had both made it through this never-ending night. He didn't know if he felt relieved. There had been too much death, too much destruction to feel something like that so soon after what he'd been through.

But, for the first time in a long time, as the morning sun warmed his cold bruised skin, he knew he would probably survive the day.

CHAPTER THIRTY-FOUR

SIX MONTHS LATER

VINCENT SET THE cardboard box on the pile in his back seat and shut the door. Wiping sweat from his forehead, he said, "I think that's about it."

"I'll go double-check," Sam said. She and Henry had taken down most of the heavier boxes themselves, but she'd barely broken a sweat.

Before he could protest, she bounded up the stairs back into the apartment building.

"Here." Henry handed him a bottle of water.

"Thanks." It was warm, but he couldn't care less at this

point. He chugged it and looked at his packed car. He wasn't sure how they'd fit everything in there, but somehow, they had. Most of the furniture was James's anyway, and his family had collected it and his other belongings months ago.

Henry stared at the car. "You know, you're always welcome to come back home. I mean, I'm glad you're going out on your own, but if you ever need a place, I'll be there."

His father was looking better than he had in years. His face was less bloated and red, and he was starting to act like he had before his wife got sick. Vincent patted his shoulder. "Thanks."

Henry took something from his pocket and handed it to him. A plastic emerald-green chip that read, *3 Recovery Months*.

"I tried quitting cold turkey a while back, but this time, it's been working. Didn't want to say anything before I thought I could go through with it."

Vincent thought back to his visit six months ago. Henry's hands had been shaking the whole time. He hadn't thought much of it, but that must have been the first time Henry had tried quitting. He handed the chip back to him. "Good for you.'"

Henry pocketed it. "Try to be happy, will ya?"

"Okay."

Henry pulled him into a bear hug. Vincent cringed, waiting for the pain to start in his ribs, but they'd long since stopped hurting. The worst they got now was sore on a damp day.

"No, it's fine, I got it." Sam walked past them, carrying a large box that obscured her face.

Henry went to help her.

"What the hell's that?" Vincent didn't even remember packing that box.

"Trash. Just an old sweeper box." She dropped the empty box on the ground.

"That reminds me, something came in the mail for you." Henry started across the street to his car.

Sam moseyed over to him. "How many hours is it going to be?"

"A little over nine." He had a long day ahead of him.

"Well, my classes don't start until September, so maybe I can make a trip up before then?"

Sam was going straight into med school at Pitt. Last week, Vincent and Henry had helped her move into a new apartment she'd be sharing with two other med students in the fall.

"That'd be great," Vincent said.

"As we both know, I'm an ugly crier, so all I'm going to say is I'll miss you." She hugged him.

"I'll miss you too." He felt the tears coming, but he held them back. They'd been practically inseparable since the incident on the bridge, and it'd be strange not seeing her every day.

"Here we are." Henry handed him an envelope from the University of Pittsburgh.

They must already want his first loan payment. They'd probably mentioned it in one of the many unread emails he had from them. He tossed it in the window of the passenger's seat where he had two boxes buckled into the seat. "Thanks."

"Drive safe," Henry said.

"I will." He got into the car.

"Call me when you get there. I want pictures of the new apartment," ordered Sam.

"I will. Thanks, guys. Love you both, and I'll talk to you soon." He'd miss them, but he knew he was making the right choice. After the trial, he needed a fresh start. He started the engine and drove away. They disappeared in the rearview mirror. He just had one more stop.

"STRANGE, BEING HERE during the day."

He sat in front of James's grave, running his hands over the patchy layer of grass that had grown up through the dirt. He hadn't been back since the night he and Sam had dug James up. Even now, flashes of his lover's cold lifeless face came back to him.

He made an effort to ignore them. He'd come here for a reason.

"I've been meaning to come here to tell you the news, but between moving Sam and then packing everything up and...well...being here reminds me of everything. I guess that doesn't matter now."

He resisted the urge to pluck a blade of grass to give him something to do with his hands. "Mathew Baker got life in prison. He'll never serve it though. He was in a fight in the jail yard within his first week. Unknowingly had a concussion from it and when he went to bed that night, he never woke up. I know, not exactly the miserable end I was hoping for him, but it's over."

But that wasn't the only news he came to tell him.

"I'm moving. To Boston. I know what you're probably thinking. I'm running away again. But I don't feel like I'm running from anything this time. I think I just need a do-over in a place that doesn't remind me so much of you and what happened. I have no idea what I'm going to do there. I guess that'd scare me before, but now it's kind of exciting.

"I won't be back to visit for a while, but we both know that doesn't mean I won't be thinking about you and wishing you were there with me. Sometimes I wake up so mad at the thought you're gone that I can't even think straight. And I just hate everything in this damn world. But other days, I almost get through the day without running through everything that's happened in my mind."

Tears blurred the sunlit cemetery. "But I can't lie down and die with you—as much as I want to sometimes. So, I'm moving to Boston. These last eight months, I've just been stuck here. Sam finished school, Henry even quit drinking, and I've done nothing but wait around for this damn trial and everything else to be over.

"I'm tired of waiting." He dried his eyes and looked around at the rows of gravestones surrounding him.

"I'm sorry I couldn't save you. I don't know if we would've lived happily ever after, but I think we could have made each other happy. I know it's pointless to think about that now. I will never know. And I can't spend the rest of my life wondering."

He hugged the gravestone, and he imagined that he had his arms wrapped around James's broad chest. "I love you. I always will. But I have to go."

He pressed his lips to the warm stone, and for a moment, he thought he felt James's lips. He knew he was just imagining it, but he let himself embrace the feeling. "Goodbye."

THE WALK BACK to his car was easier than it had been in the past. Vincent's body had healed, and while he was far from being in good enough shape to run a marathon, he'd started jogging again. He walked around to his driver's side door, and a car whizzed past him. He pressed himself against the car and froze. He took a few deep breaths and got into the car. He was all right, but he needed a minute before he started his long drive.

He took the envelope off the boxes on the passenger's seat and opened it. Surprisingly, it wasn't a letter informing him that he would need to start paying back his loans soon. It was a diploma in general studies for Vincent Vicar.

There had to have been some mistake. He grabbed his new cell phone and opened his email that he'd been ignoring. He had one from Dr. Cowart:

Vincent,

While you will be receiving the lowest possible passing grade, you will, in fact, be passing my class. You seem to have developed an understanding of myths and legends that few students in my class ever obtain.

Dr. Charles Cowart

Vincent laughed. He was shocked that, after breaking both legs, one arm, cracking most of his ribs, and sustaining a concussion, Dr. Cowart was feeling so generous. His professor had told the authorities he had no memory of the events surrounding his accident, which clearly wasn't the case. Vincent didn't know if Dr. Cowart was protecting him or if, like Ralbovsky, the professor knew no one could really admit the truth without looking as insane as the tall man. Either way, Vincent was grateful.

He pocketed his phone and sct his diploma on the passenger's seat. He couldn't believe how much had happened between when he'd gone to Dr. Cowart's office to complain about the grade on his final and now, but here he was, car packed, ready for a nine-hour, one-way trip to Boston. He started the car. Alive.

ACKNOWLEDGEMENTS

Thank you to my partner in crime, Caitlin Hensel, who took this journey with me and inspired me through her work, our midnight writing sprints, and her sage advice that shaped this book in so many ways.

Thank you to Timons Esais, Rebecca Drake, Nicole Peeler, Michael Arnzen, and many other faculty members of Seton Hill University's Writing Popular Fiction Program for working with me to take this idea and develop it into story that is not only comprehensible, but one that I couldn't have told without them.

Thank you to the many writers, friends, and family members for their guidance, support, and inspiration along the way, including, but not limited to, Sara Tantlinger, George Galuschak, Jesse Byrnes, Marisa Balatico, and Joe Lewis.

Thank you to Elizabeth Coldwell and NineStar Press for taking a chance on this story and sharing it with their readers.

About Corey Niles

Corey Niles was born and raised in the Rust Belt, where he garnered his love of horror. When he isn't advising college students, he enjoys binge-watching horror movies and traveling to hoard American history in his cheeks like a chipmunk. He hasn't met a creepy, isolated hiking trail he hasn't liked.

After studying creative writing and gender and women's studies as an undergraduate student, he went on to graduate from Seton Hill University with an MFA in Writing Popular Fiction.

In his spare time, he nurses his caffeine addiction and tends to his graveyard of houseplants. He is also a single father of a very fluffy cat named Alexander, who quickly forgot about his humble beginnings.

Email
coreylniles@gmail.com

Facebook
www.facebook.com/CoreyLNiles

Twitter
@CoreyLNiles

Website
www.coreyniles.com

CONNECT WITH NINESTAR PRESS

WWW.NINESTARPRESS.COM

WWW.FACEBOOK.COM/NINESTARPRESS

WWW.FACEBOOK.COM/GROUPS/NINESTARNICHE

WWW.TWITTER.COM/NINESTARPRESS

WWW.INSTAGRAM.COM/NINESTARPRESS

www.ingramcontent.com/pod-product-compliance
Lightning Source LLC
Chambersburg PA
CBHW050609110726
47899CB00001B/42